To Frank,

With all good wishes

Tony "A.R." Homer

August 2013

WHEN ROME FALLS

A Novel of World War II

A. R. HOMER

ISBN: 1483904881
ISBN-13: 9781483904887

Library of Congress Control Number: 2013905414
CreateSpace Independent Publishing Platform
North Charleston, South Carolina

For Carol, again

PRISONER-OF-WAR TRAIN NORTH OF ROME.

"You two ready?" Major John MacPherson stood back as Nolan and the Englishman took turns smashing open the lock on the outer door of their compartment with pieces of metal from the luggage rack.

The train had begun to lose speed, the clatter of steel wheels calling out a slower beat as it fought its way up an incline. It was still dark, but MacPherson could see a glimmer of light in the eastern sky.

"It's now or never, guys – if we don't get off this train, we'll be in the Fatherland this afternoon. And if you didn't much care for Campo Settantotto, wait till you get a load of the Kraut camp." As the black greens and grays of the predawn Italian countryside slid by, MacPherson made a rough approximation of the miles they had covered. About fifty, he guessed, since the train left Rome at four-thirty that morning.

"Now!"

Lawrence, the Englishman, flung the door open and the blast of air caught them all unawares. He hesitated, his body framed in the open doorway, the slipstream tugging at his jacket. Then in an instant he was gone, followed a few moments later by Nolan. MacPherson rushed to the open doorway. For a few seconds he hovered, trying to find a landing spot before launching himself from the train.

The shock of the landing blasted the wind from his lungs. The roar of the train sounded like thunder as he curled up and rolled through the sharp stones of the track bed, feeling an avalanche of pain as he thumped against the stump of a tree. An eternity passed as he tried to regain his breath.

As he pulled himself to his feet the caboose passed, and he was sure that even in the dim light he could see the guard in the turret at the top watching him. He turned to run back down the track towards the point where he hoped Nolan and the Englishman would be. Surely the German could see him as he ran, half stumbling on the rough ground and awaiting the crack of a rifle.

No shot came. His luck had held.

His heart thumped and his lungs heaved as he rushed away from the train, his feet pounding on the railroad ties. The noise of the train faded behind him, but still he ran. Again he marveled at his luck that not one guard had taken even a pot shot at him; now all he had to do was meet up with Nolan and Lawrence.

His legs began to tire. Dawn was still half an hour away but a half moon still shone through a gap in the thickening clouds. He stopped, listening. Surely there was no danger now. Nothing. The sound of the train had long since retreated from earshot. He crouched down on the track, catching his breath, blessing his luck. He still had to find the others, but at least he had escaped.

He fell forward onto the track bed when the rock cracked against the back of his skull.

ROME. JEWISH GHETTO.

Tap. Tap. Tap.

Lorenzo Rossi pulled the coarse blanket tighter around him, trying to shut out the noise and the pencil line of early morning light shining between the shutters.

Tap. Tap. Tap.

Please, God, just five minutes more. I'll go to temple next Saturday.

Tap. Tap. Tap.

Renzo cursed, threw the tobacco-colored blanket aside, sat up, and rubbed his eyes. God had not listened to him. Again.

Tap. Tap. Tap.

He opened the window, pushed the shutters aside, and looked down into the narrow street, the cobbles still glistening with the overnight rain. The old man tapped his way along the street, a blind man searching for God and the synagogue.

Tap. Tap. Tap.

Renzo watched as the old man reached the end of the street. Every day, not only the Sabbath, brought him out through the streets of the Roman ghetto, whatever the weather. Renzo closed the window as the old man turned into the Via del Tempio, the tapping fading. He wondered how a blind man could maintain such devotion. Perhaps he saw what Renzo could not.

He chuckled sourly at the irony. Many years had passed since he had been called up to read the Torah, a long time since he had donned a yarmulke and stepped into a synagogue.

He poured a small measure of cold water from the ewer into the basin; his rented room was hardly the lap of luxury. His reflection in the cracked mirror above the basin caught him unawares. An unruly mop of black hair hanging over deep brown eyes set in an unsmiling face heavily-lined for its twenty-six years. His mother had often said how like his father he looked; she always seemed so far away when she spoke of him. His father...his death at the hands of the fascists had created a Renzo who frightened him at times.

He looked down at the creased photograph of his parents on the table by the bed.

A Renzo who wanted revenge.

A CHURCH IN THE OLD SECTION OF ROME.

Via del Boschetto, 6. Father Francesco's soft shoes glided noiselessly across the marble floor of the nave of Santa Maria della Gloria. His eyes seemed fixed upon the altar cross, but his mind was elsewhere. *Via di Monserrato, 27.* Another silent mental tick.

He crossed himself, turned, and walked quickly to the confessional. *Piazza Mattei, 7.* He kissed his stole before draping it around his neck, drew the curtain, and entered. *Via del Governo Vecchio, 124.* The partition that covered the grille made a scraping sound as he drew it back. *Piazza Mignanelli, 12. Ristorante da Matteo.* He racked his brain. There were four more addresses. Lives of escaped prisoners of war depended on the list.

"Forgive me, Father, for I have sinned." The voice coming through the grille interrupted his thinking. Despite twenty years of hearing others' sins, he wasn't ready for this confession. *The crypt at the Protestant church on the Via Sistina.* The contrite words coming through the grille annoyed him; he concentrated harder on the list. *Via Barberini, 51.* Two more. He had to remember. *Via Parigi, 142.* His breath began to quicken. Just one place left on the list of addresses given him by his contact in the Vatican. Places where people could be hidden safely, away from the iniquitous eyes of the fascists and the Gestapo. Safe from betrayal.

One more, just one more. He'd read the list twenty times. Over and over. He could barely pay attention to the sounds droning into his right ear. He had destroyed the list after memorizing the addresses. If the list ever fell into the hands of the Gestapo....he closed his eyes and tried to read the last address on a list conjured up in his mind.

"Father?"

He almost had it, but the voice calling to him through the confessional grille blotted it out. "Say two Hail Marys and one Our Father."

He had it! *Via del Plebiscito, 12.* Near the church of the Gesu.

"That's all, Father?"

Perhaps the sin required more penance, but Father Francesco's smile refused to fade. He knew the list by heart!

"Ego te absolvo in nomine Patris, et Filii, et Spiritus Sancti. Amen. Go in peace."

But as he stepped out of the confessional fear squeezed his heart. What if the Gestapo captured and tortured him? Would he have the strength not to tell?

He came before the altar of the Rosselli Chapel and crossed himself. On the chapel's back wall was Pinturicchio's fresco of the Annunciation; although sandbags now hid the centuries-old masterpiece, Father Francesco could still feel its luminous presence, restoring in him some measure of peace. He crossed himself and knelt in prayer. Surely the Lord would help him.

NORTH OF ROME.

Major John MacPherson tried to lift his head, but let it fall back again on the straw as pain shot through his skull. Where in hell was he? His befuddled mind struggled to piece together fragments of memory. What had happened to him?

Nolan. Where was Buck Nolan? And the other one, what was the Englishman's name? Lawrence, that was it – David Lawrence. The last thing MacPherson remembered was jumping out of a train. A prisoner-of-war train. He thought he had made it, but then everything went black.

Had the other two got away? Nolan. Boston Irish. Nice guy, good sense of humor. And Lawrence, the Brit. Not a bad fellow, but rather cold and aloof. Never says much about himself. Both lieutenants – Lawrence was an RAF Flight Lieutenant – and for some reason there was bad blood between the two of them. MacPherson's eyes struggled to focus in the darkness as he tried to make out shapes.

How did they all wind up together, he and Nolan and the Brit? Campo Settantotto – he and Nolan were at the Italian prisoner-of-war camp at Sulmona, a hundred miles east of Rome. Then Italy signed the armistice with the Allies – was it only a month ago? – and all the guards just walked away and went home. Just walked away – for them, the war was over. One had even given him the name and address of a contact in Rome. MacPherson stifled a groan as the pain returned. Reaching for the back of his head, he was surprised to find a towel serving as a bandage.

Soon after he and Nolan walked out of Campo Settantotto, they ran across the Brit, who was also an escaped prisoner of war. They were trying to find a secure hiding place when their luck ran out and they ran into a German patrol. From there they went to a transit camp, then to the train to take them to Germany. But at least as officers they had been allotted a compartment in the train to themselves. All the other prisoners of war were crammed into closed boxcars.

And then they'd escaped. But where the hell was he now? He couldn't see much and trying to unravel what had happened was making his head hurt. He closed his eyes and fell back into a deep sleep.

ROME. NEAR THE PIAZZA COLONNA.

She knew she would be too late. Vittoria's lungs heaved as she ran through the Piazza San Silvestro toward the Largo Chigi. Why was her brother such a fool? She tried to fight the stitch tugging at her ribs. Ever since the armistice, when Italy pulled out of the war a month before, Fabio had been involved with the hotheads pestering the fascist police and the German occupiers. What did he think he was doing? Her legs began to feel heavy, refusing to answer her urgings. He was barely seventeen, but he wanted to assert Italy's independence – and his manhood.

The sound of the German trucks startled her. Everyone had expected the Germans to move north after the armistice, but they hadn't. They'd occupied the city. She stopped running and slipped into a shop doorway. The sight of the German soldiers brought fear, like a stab in her chest. How could Fabio think he could scare so many Germans? As the trucks passed by, Vittoria was sure that some of the soldiers were looking at her, but her concern for her brother overcame her fear. She emerged from the doorway and began to run again.

The truck sped off, turning down the Corso toward the Piazza Colonna – that was where Fabio said he was going. Her shoes clattered on the cobbles, still wet after the previous night's rain. Perhaps she could get there in time to stop Fabio.

"Merda!" she cursed as her feet slipped from under her. Her arm reached out, but she fell awkwardly. Gasping for breath, she sat up on the cobbles, her hands rubbing her grazed knee. Worse than her knee were her stockings – they were ruined. And she'd bought them only the previous week on the black market.

As she struggled to her feet, she wondered why such thoughts came into her head when Fabio was in danger. She limped to the corner of the Corso, her eyes casting over the Piazza Colonna to find her brother.

And then she saw him. A fascist policeman was pushing him into the back of a police truck.

ROME. VIA TASSO. HEADQUARTERS OF THE GESTAPO.

Dummheit. Stupidity. Only three weeks in the job as Gestapo chief of Rome and already a major distraction.

Obersturmbannführer Herbert Kappler let the order slip from his fingers to his desk top. His hand searched the pocket of his uniform and emerged with an almost-empty cigarette pack. Damn it, he had more pressing work to do. He lit the last cigarette and drew deeply. His main task was the Resistance. When Field Marshal Kesselring entered Rome a month ago, his troops had been met by armed partisans at the Porta San Paolo, and Kappler had no doubt they were regrouping. He exhaled and watched the smoke engulf the light bulb.

In addition, there were escaped enemy prisoners swarming the city, out of sight like cockroaches. Americans, British, Australians – they had all walked out of their cells when the Italian guards deserted their posts after their idiot king surrendered. He tapped his cigarette, watching the ash drop into the tray, then took a final long draw. Already he'd placed a spy in the escaped POW network. That spy was sure to bring returns.

Kappler stubbed out the cigarette. He didn't regret his promotion to Gestapo chief. He knew he could do the job. After all, hadn't he tracked down the place where Mussolini was being held prisoner? Hadn't he masterminded the Duce's rescue? The Duce – he shook his head and smiled as he wondered what use that blowhard would be in winning the war.

His smile suddenly fading, he crumpled the empty cigarette packet and hurled it against the wall. With what he had achieved and what he had yet to do, why did they now want to squander his time with a bunch of shopkeepers and rag peddlers?

He picked up the black-bordered order and focused on the source: *Reichsführer Himmler.* His eyes drifted to the underlined topic: *Order for the Roundup of the Jews of Rome.* He reread the line below: *Concerning their transfer to the north for liquidation.*

NORTH OF ROME.

"I thought you were a goner, Jay Mack. How the hell are you?"

MacPherson could just discern the smear of reddish brown that was Buckley Nolan's hair as he struggled through the painful fog that still enveloped him. "What happened, Buck? Where are we?" He tried to focus on the shadows cast by the feeble light of a kerosene lamp.

"We're in some kind of shed on the edge of a farm." Buck laid his hand on the major's shoulders as the officer tried to get to his feet. "Take it easy, Jay Mack." Nolan used the nickname he had given him at Campo Settantotto. "Everything's hunky-dory. The farmer's on our side. Far as I can make out, he's saying we can stay here for as long as we like." He reached for the lamp and turned up the wick. "As to what happened, I was hoping you'd tell me."

"Something – or somebody – hit me." MacPherson shook his head and blinked his eyes, trying to clear his mind enough to think straight.

"That I worked out a long time ago, Jay," Nolan said softly. "I was walking back along the track, trying to find you and the Limey. Nearly fell over you in the dark – you were out cold." He chuckled. "I have to tell you, Jay, you ain't a lightweight."

"Where's Lawrence?" MacPherson, still trying to focus his eyes, was at least beginning to feel his memory return.

"Search me." Nolan shrugged his shoulders. "Maybe he had more important business to attend to. Maybe he got lost on purpose. Maybe—"

"Lay off it, Nolan. If Lawrence hasn't been picked up by a German patrol, he's trying to find us right now."

"Sure, Jay." Nolan grinned. "But you know it's true what they say about absence making the heart grow fonder – the Limey's a lot easier to take now that he's not around."

"That's enough, Buck! My head hurts too much for your wisecracks about the Brit. Besides, we need to start thinking about getting out of here sometime after daybreak."

"Okay, chief. What time is it anyway?"

MacPherson propped himself up on his elbow and dug into the pocket of his jacket. He suddenly sat up straight – his watch wasn't there. Neither was the piece of paper on which was written the name and address in Rome.

NORTH OF ROME.

Even in the light of day and with a clear head, MacPherson still hadn't been able to work it out. Someone stealing the watch he could understand. An opportunistic thief, perhaps. Even so, who would be on a railway track in the middle of nowhere before daybreak? But with the slip of paper with the name and address missing, MacPherson was forced to accept any logic.

He gave a careful look before stepping outside the shed to take deep breaths of the sharp morning air. The air cleared his brain, but his head was still sore, despite the bandage and homemade ointment supplied by the farmer's wife. He peered around the farmyard; they had to take care in case of any sudden raids. During his previous escape, he'd learned that German troops often raided farms to commandeer livestock and provisions. If they were caught, he and Nolan would be put back on a north-bound train, but for the farmer and his wife the penalty for harboring escaped prisoners would be death. Taking care was vital.

Taking care was vital. Too late. MacPherson was angry with himself for having put the address in his pocket. He had thought nothing of it at the time of their first escape a month earlier. One of the defecting guards at Campo Settantotto had handed him the paper. "Escape Rome," was all he had said. He'd looked at the name and address but could barely read it. Father so-and-so. At Santa Maria something-or-other on the Via such-and-such. He had simply stuffed it in his pocket, hoping to decipher it when he got to Rome.

"All clear, Nolan." MacPherson nodded toward the farmhouse. "Let's try to negotiate some grub. This should be fun." They both chuckled because they knew the charade to come. As their Italian vocabulary was limited to the few words they'd learned from the guards at the camp, most of their exchange would have to be in mime.

Rome. German Embassy.

Anton von Breitland tried to gather his thoughts as he strolled in the walled gardens of the Villa Wolkonsky, which served as the German embassy. He had to catch Kappler during one of the intermissions of the opera that evening, and the conversation would be a difficult one.

As a military attaché, Anton knew most of the embassy's affairs, including the issue that troubled him most. The proposed roundup of Rome's Jews. He'd seen the decoded communication from Himmler's office.

Breitland sat on a garden bench and lit a cigarette. He knew what would follow the roundup. He'd read previous reports. Shipment to a camp. And liquidation. His eyes rested on a small fountain that splashed in the sunlight.

Liquidation. He had first heard the word the previous year, when he had been based at the Foreign Office on the Wilhelmstrasse. Sometimes he wished he hadn't joined the Diplomatic Corps, but his father had been proud when, like others before him in his Junker family, he had followed a career in the military.

But things hadn't turned out as he had hoped. He had persevered after what his father called 'the Austrian corporal' took power, despite the terrible things that were happening. He crushed the cigarette beneath his heel.

Liquidation. He was angry at his failure to oppose Hitler, but he knew he could do little. Surely there were others like him. But, like those others, he was unwilling to chance death and dishonor. But maybe this time he could do something.

He rose and began to walk back to the villa, his shoes crunching on the gravel path. He'd heard that Kappler was balking at organizing the roundup. Of course the Gestapo chief wasn't opposed on moral grounds; everyone knew Kappler supported the Führer with ruthless determination. But he also knew that Kappler had his hands full dealing with the Roman Resistance.

Perhaps he might find common ground with Kappler to oppose a roundup. Perhaps, if he played his cards right, he might gain an improbable ally by helping Kappler take the roundup off the Gestapo's agenda.

He looked at his watch. He had to dress for that evening's performance of *Siegfried* at the Opera House. And prepare to speak to Kappler. Broaching the subject of the roundup would be tricky, as the embassy had intercepted Himmler's confidential correspondence to the Gestapo chief and theoretically did not know about the contents.

There was another delicate issue. He wondered whether Kappler knew about his friendship with Adriana as he pulled on his gloves. One wrong word in front of Kappler and the Gestapo chief would have something to use against him.

ROME. VILLA NORTH OF THE PIAZZA DEL POPOLO.

"Mamma, don't you think that what you're about to do is dangerous?" Vittoria's voice was shrill with anxiety. "Not to mention the abomination of appealing to a fascist for help."

"Have you any other suggestion?" Adriana Corvo peered at her daughter from over her reading glasses. So like her when she was twenty-one, too many years ago. "The simple fact of the matter is that we have to get Fabio out of jail." She put down her newspaper and reached for her coffee cup. "I'm afraid we just have to set principles on one side in this instance."

Vittoria rose from her chair and began pacing the floor. "But talking to the wife of the chief of fascist police – it could backfire." She stopped and turned sharply, her dark hair swirling around her face, her brown eyes flashing. "Suppose she—"

"Actually, Vittoria, I think the wife of the questore only pretends to be a fascist because of her husband's position." She took a sip of her coffee. "Underneath her formality, she's really quite a reasonable person." She tilted her head pensively. "Like Fabio, she's in prison. But in her case, she doesn't know it."

She finished her coffee, put the cup down, and reached into her purse for her address book.

"Mamma, what do you think Signor Bartoli will think if he learns you're talking to the wife of the questore?"

"Cara, I really don't care what our great leader of the Resistance thinks. I think I've already made my contribution to his cause." She thumbed through the pages of the address book. "Last week, I carried four grenades in a potato sack through a German checkpoint for the man." She found the number and reached for the telephone. "But when it comes to getting Fabio out of jail, I don't give a damn what Bartoli thinks."

"I guess I understand, Mamma. You do what you have to. As for me, I'd rather not listen to you currying favor with a fascist." As she strode out, she collided with Giorgio, her ten-year-old brother, who was tearing in at top speed. "But you're in luck – the current man of the family has arrived to keep you company."

Rome Opera House.

"So tell me, Herr Obersturmbannführer, how's your work progressing?" Von Breitland was relieved to have succeeded in cornering the Gestapo chief at a small table in the Opera House bar.

"Better than the opera." Kappler sipped at his mineral water. "I could hardly wait for the intermission. Italians sing Wagner as though it were Verdi."

Von Breitland forced a laugh before savoring his glass of Orvieto. "But at least they know how to make a decent wine." He contemplated the contents of his wineglass, then leaned across the table. "May I ask what you intend to do regarding the roundup of the Jews?"

Anger flashed for a split second in Kappler's eyes. "That order was top secret. For my attention only."

"We had no choice but to read it – the embassy has to be aware of all matters that could affect Germany's relationship to the Holy See. How do you think the pope, as Bishop of Rome, is going to react to a roundup of Jews in his holy city?"

Kappler ignored the question as he looked around the bar area, nodding at an elderly marchesa, who wafted by in a cloud of silk and scent.

Von Breitland persevered. "Would it not, for example, serve the Reich better simply to enlist the Jews in the labor service?"

Kappler turned to face von Breitland. "What would serve the Reich better would be to leave me and my men to go about the real work. Breaking up Resistance cells is my work. Not providing transport out of Rome for all the rag merchants who scuttle in the ghetto but do no real harm. It all just goes to show how far Berlin has become removed from reality."

"How so?" Von Breitland knew he had to approach the situation cautiously.

"Because I have only forty-three officers and men under my command." Kappler gave a short laugh. "To carry out a roundup, I'd need a battalion."

"So what do you propose to do? Complain to Berlin?" Von Breitland was gaining hope, beginning to feel that a roundup could be averted.

"Complain to Berlin? Why waste my breath? But if the roundup has to take place—"

The bell announcing the end of intermission cut him short.

"Since you seem to feel so strongly, von Breitland, why don't you join me in a meeting with Kesselring? If it's got to be done, he's the only one who can provide the additional men." Kappler rose. "Now let's go see if the Italian tenor can manage to save Brünnhilde from the ring of fire."

October 12, 1943

VILLA AVORIO. FIFTEEN MILES SOUTHEAST OF ROME.

"Gentlemen, to what do I owe the pleasure of your visit?" Field Marshal Albert Kesselring joined Kappler and von Breitland on the terrace of the Villa Avorio on the lower slopes of the Alban Hills.

"I'm afraid business brings us here, sir," Kappler said. Von Breitland inclined his head in salute.

"A pity." Kesselring moved to the balcony overlooking the villa's grounds. "What do you think of my new headquarters, Kappler? Beautiful, isn't it? Unfortunately, it's only temporary; they're building me a bunker in Monte Soratte, north of Rome."

"It's magnificent, Field Marshal. But then I find Rome and all of Italy wonderful." The Gestapo chief held himself stiffly, somewhat in awe of the man who controlled the entire German military machine in Italy. "It's a magical place – I sometimes think there's no place on earth I'd rather be than Italy."

"I must confess that, while I admire Italy's beauty, at the moment I don't share your sentiments, Kappler. Indeed, right now I feel I'm making war in one vast museum."

"Yes, of course, mein Herr," Kappler replied quickly, embarrassed by his gaffe. "Battle plans must always consider the historical treasures."

Kesselring nodded. "Unfortunately, the enemy doesn't share Germany's fine scruples." A brief image of the lovely town of Frascati darted through Kesselring's mind. The site of his last headquarters had been reduced to rubble in a bombing raid a few weeks before. He smiled wanly for a moment, then sighed. "But the demands of war press on our time."

Kesselring took a seat at the terrace table and invited the others to join him. "So tell me, what is this business that's so important?" He took off his cap and placed it on the table.

"I've received this order from Berlin, sir." Kappler reached into his pocket, unfolded the paper, and passed it to Kesselring.

The field marshal put on his glasses and read quickly. "Whatever is Himmler thinking about? We're running a full-blooded war here and he wants to stop and round up the Jews of Rome?" He shook his head in bemusement, leaned back, and lit a cigarette. "But an order *is* an order, Kappler."

"Sir, my main task is to infiltrate and destroy the Italian partisan groups."

"Indeed." Kesselring thumped the table. "They're becoming an infernal nuisance. Sabotage is everywhere."

"If the Jews are allowed to remain in Rome, they might be useful. I could use them to gain information on the partisans."

Kesselring nodded, exhaling smoke. "Good point."

"Besides, I have only forty-three men, sir. There are at least two thousand Jews in Rome. I'd need an additional force of one motorized battalion to round up these Jews."

"Impossible." Kesselring sighed. "I can't spare any men."

Von Breitland had waited carefully for his moment to arrive. "Perhaps I could suggest an alternative, mein Herr?"

"Which is?" Kesselring looked at him sharply.

"Ask the Jews to work on building fortifications. Spell out the alternatives. Remember, we used that tactic in Tunisia. Platoons of Jews were deployed to work with the army."

"Yes, and a very sensible plan it was. Got good results." Kesselring squashed out his cigarette. "Right. I'll get a telegram off to Berlin at once. Perhaps, von Breitland, you can send your views from the embassy?"

"And I'll send my opinion, too." Kappler picked up the order, folded it, and placed it in the pocket of his tunic.

Von Breitland rejoiced inside. He didn't want to trust to his luck, but perhaps he would achieve his aim.

"But first, gentlemen," Kesselring beamed a smile, "perhaps we can enjoy a glass of the finest cognac. Specially shipped in from France."

ROME. JEWISH GHETTO.

"Ciao, Massimo, ciao, Emma!" On his way down the street to buy groceries, Renzo waved to his neighbors sitting on a bench. "What's the news, Massimo? Is the war over yet?"

Massimo looked up from his newspaper and grinned. "No, but I think we're making progress. It says here that Mussolini has just come up with a new name for us. We're now the Italian Social Republic."

"Hah!" Renzo guffawed. "A fancy name for a Nazi puppet state. Why didn't he just call us the Pinocchio Republic?"

Massimo laughed heartily while Emma looked nervously around to make sure they weren't being overheard. In her lap, made smaller by her huge abdomen – she was due to give birth soon – was a basket filled with socks that she was darning.

"How's business, Massimo?" Renzo asked. Massimo had a small stall in the Campo dei Fiori from which he sold used goods – clothing, small furnishings, kitchen utensils – during the morning markets.

"Good and bad, Renzo. Good because demand is strong. Bad because supply is short. No one can buy new things – they just hang onto the old. But we can't complain, can we, Emma?" He put his arm around his wife, kissing her on the cheek as she giggled.

Their young daughter, Luisa, who had been skipping, saw Renzo and ran over to join them. *Buon giorno*, Signor Rossi. Would you like to come to my birthday party?"

"Now, just when is your birthday, Luisa?"

"It's on Wednesday, the day after tomorrow. Two days before the Sabbath. I'm going to be ten!"

"Oh, yes, Renzo," added Emma, "please do come. I've been saving up a bit of flour and sugar to make a cake."

Renzo looked at the family of three – soon to become four – and smiled. His parents were gone, and although religion had long been out of his life, he felt a real kinship with these people.

He crouched down to address Luisa at eye level. "Your birthday party? Wouldn't miss it!"

ON THE ROAD TO ROME.

"Uh, Jay, don't you think it's about time we took a rest?" Nolan asked, brushing his brow with the back of his hand. "I'm just about whacked."

"Another mile, Buck, just another mile." MacPherson kept pounding along the dirt road, keeping his ears peeled for Germans and his eyes open for places to dive in case he heard them. "We're making pretty good time." His legs felt like lead, but he wanted to push on toward Rome.

They had made the decision to walk there before they left the farm the previous day; they had no other option. Although the farmer and his wife had been kind and might have been willing to accommodate them, Jay knew he and Nolan would be stretching their resources, besides endangering their lives.

"Whatever you say, boss." Nolan had been uncomplaining since they had set out. He had carried the knapsack the farmer's wife had provided and doled out the ration. The farmer had drawn a map of the surrounding area for them, indicating where they might find other friendly Italians, but once they'd passed the road to Vitorchiano, they were on their own. Despite the barely-believable disguise of the ill-fitting clothing the farmer had provided, there was always the risk of a German spot-check. With no papers and just the halting Italian Jay could muster, their chance of passing themselves off as local farm workers was laughable.

"We'll need to start looking for another farm this afternoon, Jay," Nolan said breathlessly. "We sucked on our last olive pit at breakfast." Every so often he had to break into a short jog to catch up with MacPherson's loping pace. "If we wait until dark to knock on a door, we'll scare the bejesus out of them."

"We'll scare the bejesus out of them anyway once they get a load of us in these getups." MacPherson winced. "These pants fit me like the skin on a baloney." He looked up at the sky and took note of the sun's position. Not quite noon.

"Hey, look – maybe we should stop early and try that one over there." Nolan pointed to a rutted path that led away from the road. At the end of the path stood a stone farmhouse. "I don't see any Kraut vehicles around."

MacPherson stopped to study the farmhouse and the surrounding yard. "Okay, let's give it a try." As they walked down the path, he thought about how much they were trusting to luck. Most of the farmers were sympathetic, but some didn't want to take the risk and there were still a fair number of Italian fascists around. But he and Nolan had no choice: they had to take chances if they wanted to get to Rome.

They approached the farmhouse, Nolan frequently looking back, checking that no one was coming down the long path behind them. As he reached the door of the farmhouse, MacPherson decided the direct approach was his best option. His knuckles knocked boldly on the door.

At first there was nothing, no sound. Nolan made a move toward a window about six feet from the door, but MacPherson motioned for him to stay still. He knocked again, more insistently, and he heard the subdued rapid chatter of whispered Italian, of which he could understand not one word. The curtain at a window was drawn aside for an instant and he thought he saw a woman's face, but the drape was released immediately and the incomprehensible chattering resumed.

"Maybe we should move on, Jay." Nolan tilted his head back toward the path.

MacPherson was about to take Nolan's advice when the door opened a crack, revealing a brown eye set in a sliver of a woman's face.

"*Sono americano,*" MacPherson stuttered. "*Mangiare.*" As he moved his fingers to his lips, trying to recall the Italian word for "drink," the door slammed in his face.

"Son of a bitch!" Nolan spat out the words. "Okay, time to go, Jay?"

MacPherson reluctantly nodded his assent, but as he turned to leave the door swung open wide.

The farmer was small and compact, with wide shoulders. A tattered cap sat on his head and a smoldering cigarette drooped from his lips. And a twelve-gauge shotgun nestled in his arms.

GESTAPO HEADQUARTERS, VIA TASSO.

Kappler resented the intrusion of the telephone's insistent ring. He had been studying the brief message from the spy he had planted and was feeling the warmth of anticipated success in his plans. He put down the message and reluctantly reached for the telephone. *"Ja?"* His voice was laconic, tired.

His body stiffened when he heard the voice on the line. Involuntarily, he leapt to his feet and stood at attention. *"Jawohl, mein Reichsführer!"* Kappler's lassitude vanished in an instant. His ear was attuned to every word that came from the telephone in Berlin.

"Of course, Herr Reichsführer. What is the name of your officer?" He shifted the telephone to his left ear as he reached for a pen on his desk. "Ganz. Hauptsturmführer Bruno Ganz. Mein Herr, he can be assured of my utmost cooperation." He put down the pen. "Herr Reichsführer, have you consulted Generalfeldmarschall Kesselring?" Kappler's face reddened as he listened to the Reichsführer's rant. "Very well, sir, it shall be done."

Kappler eased the telephone into the cradle with a sigh of relief. He sat down, undid the top button of his tunic, and kneaded the back of his neck. After a moment, he grabbed the receiver again. "Get me von Breitland." He drummed his fingers on the desk as he waited.

"Ah, von Breitland. I wonder if you could join me tomorrow morning. There's someone I'd like you to meet....Yes, tomorrow. His name is Bruno Ganz. He's a Hauptsturmführer with the SS....Yes, that's what I said, and he's to receive three companies from the field marshal....You assume correctly. Ganz will be taking over the roundup of the Jews.... He's acting on the full authority of the Reichsführer....Yes, von Brietland – Himmler."

On the Road to Rome.

MacPherson's hands shot into the air at the sight of the shotgun. *"Io sono americano."* He struggled to remember the little Italian he had learned in the camp. "Friend. *Amico.* Please help me. *Aiutami, per favore. "*

The man's surly face remained impassive, but from behind him came a woman's voice and a rapid babble of Italian that neither MacPherson nor Nolan could hope to grasp.

"What we gonna do, Jay?" A bead of sweat trickled down Nolan's temple. "Make a run for it?"

As MacPherson rapidly weighed his options, a woman appeared from behind the man. Her face didn't look old, Jay noticed, but her hair, done up in a bun coming undone at the temples, was mostly gray. He repeated his plea. *"Americano. Amico. "*He sought to fix her eyes as he begged. *"Mangiare. "*He slowly lowered one hand and brought it to his mouth. "Water. *Acqua, per favore. "* A similar action, with an imaginary glass in his hand.

She looked at him for a moment, then turned and spoke to the man with the gun, who shrugged his shoulders and turned back into the room.

"Prego, signori. " Her hand waved admittance into her home.

The room was large but sparely furnished. A long wooden table with benches on either side dominated the center. Two young boys, about twelve and thirteen, sat at the far end, their eyes wide with curiosity.

"*Prego.*" The woman motioned for them to sit at the table.

"*Grazie.*" MacPherson, wishing he had an Italian phrase book handy, took a seat. "We are hungry. *Noi abbiamo fame.*"

"*Si, si. Ho capito.*" A faint smile appeared on her face as she directed a torrent of rapid-fire Italian at him and, as she moved to a large cupboard, MacPherson silently rejoiced that a response appeared not to be required. She pulled down plates and glasses and placed them on the table. A larder opened, revealing a ham, cheeses, decorated earthenware jars, and large loaves. She made a selection and cut thick slices of bread.

As she arranged rustic delicacies on a plate, the boys stared open-mouthed at the Americans, occasionally nudging each other. The father spoke to them – sharply, Jay felt – and they jumped down from the chairs and made for the door.

Through the window the Americans could see the boys hop on their bicycles and ride off at high speed. Nolan shot an anxious look at MacPherson. "You don't suppose they're going to get the police, do you?"

MacPherson sighed. "We've got to trust somebody, Buck." He returned the woman's smile as she placed the plate on the table.

"*Non è molto, ma spero che sia buono.*" She waved her hand over the platter, inviting them to partake. They heard the pleasant 'plunk' of a cork being pulled, and the man came to the table with glasses and poured red wine liberally. "*Salute!*" he shouted, raising his glass.

"*Salute!*" the Americans replied.

"*I ragazzi sono andati a trovare il padre, perche...*" The man began to say more, but realized he couldn't be understood and stopped.

"What'd he say, Jay?"

"Not sure, but I think he said the boys have gone to find their father."

Nolan scowled but MacPherson shrugged and broke off a piece of crusty bread as he prepared to attack the salami and cheese.

ADRIANA'S VILLA.

"So you spoke with the wife of the questore after all, Mamma?" Although she knew her mother had been successful, there was still a hint of resentment in her voice.

"I can assure you, my dear, that she is a perfectly charming woman." Adriana spoke without turning from the mirror of her dresser as she adjusted her hat. "Her politics may be a bit confused, but her manners are impeccable." She moved her head one way and then the other as she sought to position the hat pin perfectly. "Besides, my little chat with her worked. It's taken a few days, but your foolish brother has been released from police custody." Pushing the pin home, she spun around on the tufted bench to face her daughter with a smile. "Aren't you pleased?"

"Of course." Vittoria wore a faint smile but looked sullen, pleased with the end but still resenting the means. "I was just uneasy about the principle of dealing with a fascist, you know that."

"The principle?" Adriana gave a half laugh. "For someone who buys her stockings on the black market, perhaps 'principle' is not quite the right word." She turned back toward the mirror, selecting a deep shade of red from the lipsticks lined up on a silver tray. "Principles are all well and good, Vittoria," she applied the lipstick, "but you and your brother need to know when to employ them. I'm not asking you and Fabio to keep out of trouble, because there's always that risk when you're involved in Resistance work. But," her eyes beseeched, "do be careful." A rarely-shown tenderness washed over her.

She blotted her lips and stood up. "And now I must be off," she said as she hurried for the door.

"You're going to see that German officer again, aren't you?" Vittoria shouted after her.

"What if I am?" Adriana turned to smile at her daughter before closing the door behind her.

FARMHOUSE NORTH OF ROME.

"Grazie, grazie, signora!" Jay patted his stomach and smiled at the farmer's wife as she carried the plates to a sink with a hand pump in the far corner of the room.

"Boy, that grub sure filled the hole!" Nolan whistled softly as he slid his chair back from the table.

The farmer squatted at the fireplace and poked at the recently-laid fire, provoking sparks to fly up the chimney. The old clock on the mantelpiece said almost one, but Jay suddenly felt a nip in the air. He had been in Italy for about three months, having been captured soon after the landing in Sicily. God, how he longed to go home, and the only way to get there was through Rome.

The single tinny chime of one o'clock cut across his thoughts like a dark cloud scudding across the sun.

"We need to get moving soon, Buck." MacPherson got up and went over to the man by the fire. *"Scusi, signore. Dov'è Roma?"*

The farmer put down the poker, pushed back his cap, and scratched his forehead. *"Roma?"* A bewildered look came to his eyes. *"È molto lontano. Forse tre o quattro giorni a piedi."*

"What's he say, Jay?" Nolan called.

"I think he said it's a three or four day walk to Rome." Jay picked up his jacket. "Time to wish our hosts good afternoon and hit the road, Buck."

The man and woman became agitated. *"No, no! Aspetti!"* The woman tugged at the coat in Jay's hand.

"What's going on, Jay?"

Nolan's question was answered by the sound of bicycle bells on the path. The man beckoned MacPherson to the window and pulled aside the curtain; the two boys were pushing at their pedals, ringing their bells. And behind them, peddling furiously with one hand clutching the biretta to his head, came a priest.

MacPherson could barely believe the cherubic face of the clergyman. Without doubt, the partially-knotted knuckles betrayed his true age, but his face still beamed with a youth his years disproved.

The priest brought his bicycle to a halt, mopped his brow, and dismounted. *"Buona sera, signori,"* he said, addressing the Americans. "I speaka da English."

ROME. GERMAN EMBASSY.

Anton von Breitland reluctantly let the telephone receiver slip from his fingers back onto the cradle.

After the call from Kappler, he had telephoned Kesselring in a desperate last-ditch effort that had failed. His fingers massaged his temples as Kesselring's words continued to ring in his ears. *My dear von Breitland, I tried my best, but how can I oppose Reichsführer Himmler's wishes? What would you do?*

Breitland realized the field marshal was right. Nothing could be done. The troops would be released to Himmler's henchman, Ganz, who would proceed to engineer the roundup of Rome's Jews.

What would Adriana think? Only yesterday afternoon he had boasted to her that the Jews would be safe. Now he could do nothing to prevent the roundup. He toyed with the idea of appealing to Kappler again, but soon dismissed the thought. Although Kappler had tried to wriggle out of organizing the roundup, the Gestapo chief would not raise his voice with Himmler if he thought it would threaten his career. If Himmler said jump, Kappler would clear a six-foot bar.

Von Breitland cast about for other hopes. What about Baron von Weizsäcker, ambassador to the Holy See? No, not him – he was a close friend of Hitler. All avenues had been closed.

Except one. Von Breitland stubbed out his cigarette and went into his bedroom. He removed his uniform and put on his civilian clothes. He could have phoned Adriana, but one never knew who was listening. Anyway, he preferred to tell her face to face, and they were meeting for lunch that day.

Adriana was his last hope. Perhaps she could get word to the Jewish ghetto.

NORTH OF ROME.

MacPherson and Nolan soon discovered the priest's English was rudimentary, at best, but nonetheless communication was improved. Names were exchanged and relations with the farmer's family were markedly warmer, with the two boys firing questions for the priest to translate.

The priest, escorted to the best chair of the house by the woman, seemed to relish his role of intermediary. "Pietro, he aska do you know – how you say? – Baytee Grahble?"

"Baytee who? Oh, you must mean Betty Grable." Jay humored the boys for awhile, but kept looking anxiously at the clock. If he and Nolan were going to make progress that afternoon, they would have to leave soon.

"Padre, can you ask the signore if he has a map of this area? A map showing how we get to Rome?"

The priest struggled with the words, but the angelic smile never left his face, and MacPherson wondered how a man so old could look so innocent and happy.

"Come on, Jay, let's just beat it." Nolan's patience with the friendly exchange between cultures was wearing thin. "We'll be here all night."

"Give him a chance, Buck."

"Mappa, mappa. *Si, si, una carta.*" The priest turned to the farmer and began a gesticulation-filled discussion that seemed long enough to encompass the geography of the entire region. At length, the priest turned back to MacPherson, his smile faded. "No, no mappa." Then he brightened. "But you wanna go Roma? *È facile* – how you say? – is easy. You need go—"

All eyes turned as the door banged open and a man, gasping for breath, shot in. "*Tedeschi!*" he shouted before unleashing a torrent of Italian.

As the priest's hand flew up to his chest in terror, MacPherson leapt up. "That's one word I do understand – Germans! Come on, Buck, we gotta get outa here. It's a farm raid."

The farmer spoke rapidly to the priest, who turned to Jay. "He say hide! Hide in barn!"

ROME. L'ORSO RESTAURANT.

The restaurant was well off the beaten path, nestled at the end of a tiny street in the Campo Marzio section of Rome, the heart of the old city. Adriana had spotted it in the early days of the war. At first, she'd used the place to get away and enjoy lunch on her own, to plan for the future.

"*Ciao, Signora Corvo.*" Signora Martucci greeted her as she opened the door. "*Come va?*"

She'd made friends with the owner long ago, and now she was a welcome, privileged customer. "*Bene, grazie.*" Adriana followed her to her favorite table in the corner by the window. Apart from another couple sitting at the far end of the room, the restaurant was empty. Adriana wondered how Signora Martucci made ends meet, particularly since everything was on ration. No doubt, like herself, she had excellent contacts in the black market. If you had the money, you could get most things.

"Will the signore be joining you?" The question was hushed.

Adriana nodded without speaking. She viewed herself a woman of the world, a woman who could defend herself in a world of men, but this time she wasn't sure what she'd let herself in for. She'd met him almost a month before – shortly after the Germans began their occupation of the city – at a performance of *Tosca* at the Rome Opera House. She knew he was German, despite his near-faultless Italian. He seemed different, unlike the other strutting Nazi bureaucrats who were full of themselves in their grotesquely impeccable uniforms.

Of course, she'd held herself aloof at the start. There'd been a few men since Alessandro had died nearly eight years before. She had a woman's needs, she knew, but she really didn't want commitment. The children, Fabio, Vittoria, and little Giorgio, were commitment enough.

Yet with Anton she'd felt different. After their encounter at the opera, he'd invited her to dinner. And she'd accepted. At first, she saw him because she thought that, with all his contacts in the embassy, he'd be useful, but she soon learned that his kindness needed no manipulation. There were times she wondered if he really were a German.

Perhaps he, too, like her, was smitten – engaged in a *folie à deux* that could explode at any moment. She remembered again the opera at which they had met. Perhaps, like Tosca and her lover, they were heedless of a disaster that could at any moment engulf them both.

She pushed such thoughts aside as she heard the door open, looked up, and saw him.

FARM NORTH OF ROME.

"You know, this whole thing could be a setup, Jay Mack." Nolan peered through the gap between the planks in the loft of the barn.

"Shut up, Buck, before the Krauts hear you," MacPherson whispered, squatting behind the wall of straw he had quickly shuffled together.

"Lots of noise and shouting over there, Jay. Holy smokes, get a load of that." Nolan nodded to the farmhouse and MacPherson took his turn peering through the gap in the boards. The German truck was parked in front of the farmhouse, the tailgate down. Three soldiers went back and forth into and out of the house, emerging with huge cheeses, hams, and other provisions. The priest by his side, the farmer stood on the doorstep shouting at a junior officer and pummeling the air to vent his rage.

"Hey," MacPherson nudged Nolan, "one of the Krauts is coming this way!" They burrowed into the straw as best they could.

They heard the thud of boots on the barn floor. The thudding came to a halt and all was silent as the German looked around. MacPherson was sure the soldier could hear the pounding of his heart.

There was a shout in German from outside and the boots moved away, the barn door creaking as the soldier left. The truck's doors slammed, the engine roared, and the tires crunched on the gravel as the raiding party made off with their booty.

"Bastardi! Figli di puttane! Cornuti!" Arms thrashing, the farmer stood at the door and continued to direct a string of curses Jay could never hope to understand in the direction of the now long-gone German truck.

"He no happy," the priest offered by way of translation, bringing a smile to MacPherson's lips. "But Germans no find wine. Hide."

They went into the house and the farmer's wife came forward with a bottle and glasses, setting them on the table.

"Jay, we gotta get going." Nolan nodded toward the door. "Rome? Remember? The place we're supposed to be heading?"

"Ah, Roma!" The priest spoke before Jay could react. "You say before you want go Roma, *si?*"

Jay nodded.

"No good travel at night. You stay here, no?" He spoke to the farmer's wife, who nodded.

"But we still don't know how to get to Rome."

"*Domani,* the boys they take you to the *caverne* near Vitorchiano."

"Take us to the what near where?" Nolan asked.

"I think he said caves."

"*Si, si,* caves," the priest nodded. "Many American soldiers in caves. And also English. *Infatti, vi è un soldato inglese molto importante lì.* How you say? Officer. English. He wanna go Roma, too!"

Nolan looked at Jay. "Maybe we've found the Limey."

ROME. L'ORSO RESTAURANT.

Anton immediately spotted Adriana sitting at a corner table. Looking up, she beamed a radiant smile at him, raising her hand and rippling her fingers in a little wave. How happy she seems, he thought as he made his way toward her, and how hard it will be to spoil her good mood with talk of the roundup.

Sitting down, he put his hand over hers and squeezed it. "You're looking especially lovely this afternoon."

"Anton, I feel really good today! Fabio's finally out of jail; isn't that wonderful? It's such a load off my mind! And now that I'm with you, what more could I want?"

"Adriana, there's something—"

Signora Martucci arrived with a bottle and two long-stemmed glasses, which she set before them. "Some Prosecco, compliments of the house. I thought you'd like to know that our special today is extra special – we've been able to get some veal, which the chef is now preparing."

"Did you hear that, Anton – veal!"

Signora Martucci smiled. "I take it that's a yes for both of you," she said, heading for the kitchen.

"I haven't had veal in ages," Adriana said with a sigh. "Now, what was it you were about to say, Anton?"

"Adriana, there's a very serious matter I must—"

She reached over and laid her fingers gently on his lips. "Please, Anton, no serious talk right now. Let's not let anything spoil our special lunch together. Besides," she added with a grin, "don't you know that discussing serious matters while dining is bad for the digestion?"

As she began to pull her hand away, he kissed her fingertips. "You're right, darling." He reached for his glass of Prosecco. "Here's to us."

She lifted her glass. "Here's to us," she repeated. "To hell with the war."

The veal was somewhat stringy but was served with a delicious butter-sage sauce, and Adriana declared it the tastiest dish she'd ever had. Throughout the meal, her laughter and sparkling eyes raised his spirits, but also made it harder for him to broach the subject of the roundup.

By the time they left the restaurant, the day had turned gray and a chill wind was sweeping off the Tiber, reminding him of the brutal realities of war. They were both quiet as they made their way down the deserted streets.

When they arrived at her tram stop, she pulled her coat around her. "My goodness, it's suddenly rather nasty for October, don't you think, Anton?"

Her question went unanswered as his eyes followed a piece of refuse skidding erratically down the street in the wind. Suddenly, he turned to her and said, "Adriana, I need your help. I need it desperately on a very urgent matter."

FARM NORTH OF ROME. A BARN LOFT.

By the light of a lantern, MacPherson smoothed out the straw that would be his bed for the night. "Lawrence turning up in those caves – it sure seems like a long shot."

"No skin off my nose if he's not there." Nolan adjusted his knapsack to provide a pillow and laid back. "Personally, all I want is to get to Rome and then find my way back home."

"We might get you to Rome, Buck," Jay said, shifting from his knees to squat against the wall of the loft, "but I think your trip home may take more time. Sure wouldn't mind joining you on that boat, though." He pulled a battered cigarette from his pocket. "Say, where exactly is home, Buck? Boston, I think you said?"

"Just south of Boston. Little town called Milton." Nolan folded his arms across his chest and gazed up at the rafters. "But I wasn't actually born there."

"Yeah? So where were you born?"

"County Cork. In the beautiful Emerald Isle."

"No kidding, Buck – you were born in Ireland? I didn't know that." MacPherson brushed some stray pieces of straw from his sleeve. "When did you move to the States?"

"Right after the Black and Tans killed my dad."

"Killed your dad? Black and Tans?"

"You probably never heard of them – most Americans haven't. 'Black and Tans' was what they called the Limey cops sent in to murder Irish patriots – good guys like my dad, guys who were fighting for their freedom. The cops got their name from their black and tan uniforms, see. Cruelest bastards you'd ever want to come across – once they even rode tanks out into the middle of a soccer match and fired into the crowd."

"Jesus, that's terrible." MacPherson fell silent. "Buck, is that why you don't like Lawrence? Because he's English?"

Nolan slowly turned his head away. "Maybe," he said quietly.

35

Jay regretted the question and changed the subject. "How old were you when you and your mom moved to the States?"

"About three. I was a little kid when my dad died, but, boy, I can still remember my ma weeping and wailing. Scared the shit out of me. She never spoke much about him, but when she did, she'd always add, 'Never forget him, son, never forget your da.'"

Jay contemplated his unlit cigarette. "Well, you seem to have done okay for yourself, Buck."

"Oh, yeah. I was lucky. I got a football scholarship to Notre Dame, then landed a job at an insurance agency. Life was looking pretty good, but it sure came to a grinding halt when the war broke out."

"Know what you mean, Buck. I was about to take over my dad's business – he owns a small construction company outside of Gaithersburg, Maryland – when I got the call from Uncle Sam." He looked at his unlit cigarette and pushed it back into his pocket. "Save it for tomorrow. Now let's get some shuteye – we'll need an early start to hoof it over to the caves."

They both settled down as Jay lifted the lantern glass and blew out the flame.

October 14, 1943

On the Way to the Caves near Vitorchiano.

The hike took about an hour.

The boys, who were leading them to the caves, seemed to treat the journey as a great adventure, sharing an occasional laugh with each other, but mainly keeping a serious eye on the surrounding countryside. They took the Americans across hills, through glades, over stepping stones fording a stream. Occasionally they stopped to let the less sure-footed Americans catch up, chattering at a speed which precluded MacPherson's understanding a single word.

"What do you think the chances are they actually know where they're going, Jay?" Nolan, breathless, cursed as he almost lost his footing on a slippery rock.

"Give 'em a break, Buck." Jay grabbed the branch of a tree to steady himself as the path descended. "They're smart kids. They've kept us off the roads – no chance of meeting up with a Kraut patrol – smart move!"

The boys turned around and faced the Americans with broad smiles. *"Eccole!"* shouted the older of the two, raising his hand to point to the hill ahead.

"Christ, at last!" Nolan moved forward. "The famous caves, number one tourist sight in Vitorchiano." The boys tried to stop him as he leapt over the brook.

"Fermatevi!" a deep voice shouted.

The boys stood stock still, their hands raised in the air.

Gestapo Headquarters, Via Tasso.

Within five minutes of meeting Hauptsturmführer Bruno Ganz in Kappler's office, von Breitland confirmed his view that he himself would be unable to prevent the roundup of the Jews.

As he watched the man annotating the list of names and addresses given him by Kappler with cool detachment, he wondered how Germany could have produced such a being. Six-foot-four and thin almost to the point of emaciation, he had a scar running upward from the left corner of his lips that seemed to give him a perpetual sneer.

"I'm dividing the list into four sections." Ganz looked up at Kappler. "I'll be splitting up the men from Field Marshal Kesselring into four companies. Each will approach the ghetto from different parts of the compass."

Von Breitland quickly saw that Ganz was meticulous and well-trained as an agent of death. It was as if the author of *Mein Kampf*, Dr. Frankenstein, and the SS Academy had all collaborated to produce this monster before his eyes. And the man came with the full authority of Himmler. Von Breitland could barely contain a shudder of disgust at being in the same room with him.

"My plan should succeed in all respects. I doubt that a single Jew will be able to escape." Ganz collected his lists and turned to Kappler. "What do you expect the reaction of the Romans will be, Herr Obersturmbannführer?"

"I'm not sure," Kappler replied. "Our reports don't give much evidence of anti-Semitism in Rome. On the other hand, my agents don't report any plans by the Resistance."

"And the Holy See?"

Kappler paused and took a deep breath. "The pope won't like it, but I doubt that he'll make too many waves. He doesn't much care for us, but as long as we're here, we keep his real enemy, the godless communists, at bay. Communists, after all, make up a large part of the Resistance."

"Excellent." Ganz pulled on his gloves and stood up. "But should there be any problems from non-Jews, we'll just throw them into the trucks, as well."

Kappler scowled. "But the order gives no authority—"

"We'll have to sort that out later. Of course, only the jews will be shipped north." He turned to leave.

38

"Herr Hauptsturmführer." Von Breitland's words caused Ganz to pause. "When do you propose to conduct this operation?"

Ganz turned, a crooked smile coming to his lips. "In two days. At six in the morning, just before dawn." His eyes became glassy with excitement and his lips expanded into a broad smile that accentuated his scar. "Don't you get the irony? It will be Saturday. The Sabbath!" He laughed and headed for the door.

Kappler and von Breitland waited for the door to click shut.

"Well, I'm glad he's on our side," Kappler said evenly.

Von Breitland, his mind casting about desperately for a solution, did not reply. Could Adriana get a warning to the ghetto in time?

THE CAVES.

"So sorry about all that bother." The white-haired English officer in charge of the prisoner-of-war operation spoke from behind his makeshift desk deep in the cave. "I'm sure you realize I have to take stringent security precautions."

"Sure scared the shit out of me." Nolan, still angry, loosened his collar as he sat on a crate.

"No problem – we understand," MacPherson added quickly. "What exactly are you running here?"

"A safe zone for escaped POWs. High in the hills, deep in the caves."

"How many men are you hiding?"

"God only knows." He pulled a pack of cigarettes from his pocket and offered it to MacPherson and Nolan. "Last count maybe seventy – mostly Yanks like you." He lit his cigarette and tossed the lighter to Nolan. "Some of us have been here since September – we arrived soon after the Italians threw in their hand."

"But why haven't you all headed to Rome?" MacPherson drew on his cigarette. "Get to Rome, head for the neutral Vatican zone, and – bingo! You'd be home free."

The Englishman chuckled. "I guess you haven't heard. The pope let a few of our chaps inside, but then, in his infallible wisdom, he decided to put the kibosh on taking any more."

"What sort of a crack is that? You got something against the Holy Father?" Nolan rose from his crate, his fists beginning to clench.

The Englishman remained cool to the outburst. "It wasn't any sort of a crack. I was merely trying to point out that the pope has stopped all POWs from entering and seeking sanctuary in Vatican City." He drew on his cigarette and exhaled a long stream of smoke in Nolan's direction. "Maybe he's afraid of being swamped. Maybe he doesn't want to antagonize the Jerries any further. Who knows?"

MacPherson stepped between the Englishman and Nolan, who retreated to the crate. "But isn't going to Rome, somehow getting inside neutral Vatican territory, pretty much the only way there is to escape?"

"Not anymore. As a matter of fact, we're actually paid to stay out of Rome."

"Paid?"

"There's an organization that looks after all the POWs in Rome outside the Vatican, but they've got their hands full. There are hundreds of POWs there, all in hiding. Most of them probably chaps who found out about the pope's ban only after they knocked on the door to St. Peter's."

"And got the bum's rush. I see. But you just said you get paid?"

"Yes, that's right. To stay here, to keep out of Rome, to save headaches all round." The Englishman tossed his cigarette on the floor of the cave and ground it out.

Nolan sat up, the conversation having piqued his interest. "Who the hell bankrolls this cozy little boondoggle?"

The Englishman shrugged. "Who knows? Rumor says the pope's gold."

MacPherson heard the two boys running and laughing outside the cave. "Do you suppose you could spare a little of that gold from the pope?"

"You need money?"

"Just a little. Maybe a few lire. For the boys who brought us here."

"How much?"

"Twenty-five lire?"

"Make it fifty." The Englishman stood, pulled several bills out of his pocket, and thrust them into MacPherson's hand.

"Thanks. And thanks for all the dope about Rome." MacPherson shook the Englishman's hand and turned to Nolan. "Okay, Buck, time to lift your butt off that crate and hit the road again."

The Englishman looked perplexed. "You're going to Rome after what I just told you?"

"Yep, we're going to take our chances in the Eternal City. We're not completely stupid – it's going to start to get cold in these caves in a few weeks!"

Nolan rose and picked up his bundle. He began to follow MacPherson out of the cave, then turned sharply to the Englishman. "Say, you wouldn't happen to have a guy by the name of Lawrence here? He's another Lime—another Englishman, like you."

"Do you mean David Lawrence? Why, yes. He arrived two days ago. Royal Air Force Flight Lieutenant. Rather quiet – never pipes up when the other RAF chaps trade stories about their missions. Useful chappie, though. Has just started doing our dealings with the local farmers. Speaks Italian like a native. He's making the rounds of the farms right now. Should be back tomorrow if you'd care to wait."

As MacPherson spun around, Nolan raised his eyebrows and shrugged.

"And before you do leave, I advise you to stop by our Thos. Cook & Son office and pick up some travel documents." The Englishman pointed to a corner where another officer was working with pen and paper atop stacked crates. "Henry over there, he'll fix you up with some identity papers. False ones, obviously. Might not get you out of Gestapo headquarters, but could help."

ROME. JEWISH GHETTO.

A dozen neighbors and relatives squeezed into Massimo and Emma's tiny apartment to celebrate Luisa's birthday and share the small but elaborately-decorated cake Emma had baked. Renzo had bought, second-hand, a doll for the girl. Although the doll's hair was painted on, the eyes opened and closed perfectly, and to cover its nude and discolored cloth torso, he purchased some baby clothes from Massimo's stall in the Campo dei Fiori.

Luisa was thrilled. "I'm going to call her Sara," she told Renzo as she hugged the doll. "That was my grandmother's name. If our new baby is a girl, I hope my mamma and papa will name her Sara, too."

"And what if your new baby is a boy?" Renzo asked, squatting to address the child.

She thought hard. "Maybe they'll name him Renzo."

He smiled and gave her a hug. "Happy birthday, Luisa."

"Thank you for Sara. I shall love her forever." Luisa smiled shyly back at him and, on a sudden impulse, shot up and gave him a peck on the cheek, then blushed and ran away.

MOUTH OF THE CAVE.

"Delighted to see you on this side of the grass, gentlemen." David Lawrence reached out a hand to MacPherson, who stood with Nolan at the mouth of the cave enjoying the warm rays of the sun after a chilly night inside.

"The feeling is mutual," MacPherson said as he gave a broad grin to the tall, lanky Englishman with sandy-colored hair.

"So what the hell happened to you?" Nolan kept his hands in his pockets as Lawrence's extended hand swung around to him.

Lawrence brought his hand back and crossed his arms. "I was about to ask you the very same question."

Damn it all to hell, thought MacPherson. Nolan's still wearing the chip on his shoulder.

"Actually," Lawrence continued, "I walked up and down the track for over an hour. Eventually found a barn. Friendly *contadini*. Eventually got here, as you did."

"Yeah, but we did it the hard way – without your grasp of the lingo." Nolan's voice was surly.

Lawrence refused to rise to the bait. "Yes, as usual you're correct. A grasp of the lingo does have its advantages. For one thing, it's made me very popular here at the cave camp."

MacPherson sought to change the subject. "So where did you learn Italian, David?"

"At school, then at Oxford." Lawrence sighed as his mind briefly recalled a long-past time. "Before this bloody war spoilt everything, I was Language Master at Rugby School. But that was long ago, and now I've got a different job. Provisioning the camp." He pulled a list from his pocket. "Let's see. Milk, meat, onions, potatoes—I say, would you chaps like to join me? It's quite safe, really. We know there's a small German army post about five miles away, so we just keep clear of that. And we have to be careful when we go into villages, just in case there's a German patrol. Or a raid."

MacPherson nodded. "You don't have to tell us – we're experts on Kraut raids. But yeah, sure, we'll come along. Say, what do you use for moolah on these junkets? "

"I pay the farmers with this." Lawrence pulled out a wad of bills.

Nolan's eyes grew large. "Wow, get a load of that!"

"Apparently, it comes from the Rome POW organization on a regular basis. I sometimes wonder if they've got a printing press down there." Lawrence stuffed the money back in his pocket.

"Speaking of Rome," MacPherson sat down on a log, "me and Nolan are taking off for there later this morning. Pope or no pope. Wanna come? We sure could use your gift of the gab with the natives."

Lawrence thought for a while. "I'm not sure, Jay. The chaps are relying on me to do a job for them."

"Soon be winter, Lawrence." MacPherson pressed his argument. "You really want to hang out with the stalactites when it's freezing?"

"Let me think about it, Jay." Lawrence moved to the mouth of the cave. "In the meantime, I'd better go in and tell the boss you two are joining me today."

When Lawrence was out of earshot, Nolan turned to MacPherson with raised eyebrows. "Language Master, huh, Jay? I'm willing to bet our Limey speaks German, too."

ROME. JEWISH SYNAGOGUE.

She would be arriving soon.

Ugo Foa lifted his yarmulke and scratched the thinning white hair beneath it. What was her name? He picked up the hand-written note on the cream-colored vellum stationery that lay on the desk in his office behind the synagogue. *Signora Adriana Corvo* was embossed at the top. *A matter of great urgency* was scribbled in blue ink.

He'd heard of Signora Corvo. As president of the Jewish community in Rome for the past twelve years, he made it his business to know who the most important people in Roman society were. She was a rich socialite, a noted art collector. And a Gentile. What business did she have with Roman Jews?

He looked up quickly as the door flew open and Adriana strode into the room, her expensive scent preceding her and the clicking of her heels on the tile floor announcing her resolve. Scurrying behind her in frustration was his secretary. "I'm sorry, Signor Foa, but she wouldn't wait, she…" Foa waved his secretary away, stood up, and offered his guest a chair with a flourish of his hand.

After sitting back down and engaging in some perfunctory pleasantries, he picked up her note. "So tell me, signora, what is this matter of great urgency?"

"The Nazis are about to round up all the Jews of Rome and ship them out of Italy. To the death camps. Tomorrow. On the Sabbath."

ON THE ROAD TO ROME.

"Hitler…he's only got one ball
Goering…has two but very small
Himmler…has two very similar
But poor old Goebbels has no balls at all."

The voices of the three officers rang out to the tune of the Colonel Bogey March as they made their way along the dirt road heading south.

"I've gotta admit, English," Nolan said, in an apparent change of heart, "it might be a pretty good thing having you along."

"I'll second that, David," MacPherson said. "You knowing the lingo should help no end. Christ, you should have seen the two of us back at the last place."

"Oh, yeah, Lawrence, you would have died laughing," Nolan added. "This Italian version of Jimmy Cagney comes storming out of his front door, waving a shotgun and rattling off something that sounds like the Eytie version of '*you dirty rats!*'"

MacPherson chuckled. "Yeah, and the next thing we know we're sitting down to a feast prepared by his smiling wife. Say, I think it's starting to rain."

"You two were indeed fortunate. That farmer might very well have been a fascist." Lawrence pointed to the turnoff in the road. "This way, chaps. Incidentally, I have to admit I'd already made up my mind about going to Rome. You're right – I didn't fancy spending winter in those dank caves. Gets cold, even in Italy. And our leader back in the caves was good enough to entrust me with the address of a contact in the POW organization in Rome who should be able to arrange a place for us to stay."

"Swell! Can't wait to lie back and order room service in our four-star hotel." Nolan couldn't resist a note of sarcasm.

Lawrence smiled. "Perhaps our accommodations won't be quite that grand, but I expect they'll be a bit better than the caves."

"So what exactly will the drill be when we get to Rome?" Nolan raised an eyebrow as he turned toward Lawrence.

"I'm not at liberty to say right now." Lawrence's smile was gone.

"Yeah? Why not?"

MacPherson put a hand on Nolan's shoulder. "Maybe we shouldn't ask questions until we get there, Buck."

"You're right, Major. Careless talk costs lives." Lawrence repeated the old adage.

"Oh, yeah? Are you implying—"

MacPherson pushed his way between them. "Cut it out, Nolan. All Lawrence is saying is that's the way the POW organization is run – on a 'need to know basis.'"

Faced down by his superior, Nolan backed off. "So is he saying I'm a blabbermouth, Jay Mack?"

"No, I'm not." Lawrence answered the question directly. "I'm just saying everyone needs to be careful. What you don't know, you can't accidentally let slip out."

"Say, this rain is getting heavy," said MacPherson, anxious to dispel the tension. "Maybe we should start looking for a place to sleep. Okay, Lawrence, here's where your lingo skills are gonna save the day."

ROME. JEWISH SYNAGOGUE.

"You have been misinformed, Signora Corvo." Ugo Foa smiled politely. "As president of the Jewish community for many years, I can assure you there is no threat to the Jews of Rome."

Taken aback by his apathy, Adriana shifted in her chair and adjusted her fur stole. "And I can assure you, Signor Foa, that the Jewish ghetto will be the target of a Nazi roundup." She cleared her throat as she tried to control her growing anger. "On the Sabbath. Tomorrow."

Foa glanced away and, still smiling, shook his head, as though seeking to find a way to explain something to a simpleton. "Look, Signora Corvo, we hear many such rumors. If I had reacted to every one of them, I would have evacuated the Roman community at least twenty times."

Adriana uncrossed her legs, shifted to the edge of her chair, and leaned forward. "But surely, Signor Foa, as president of the Jewish community, you must be aware of the camps in Poland?"

Foa hesitated, the smile fading from his face. "Yes, I've heard such rumors. But even if they're true, here in Rome that sort of thing could never happen. The situation is entirely different. Jews have been in Rome since the time of the emperor Claudius. The Germans won't attack us. Besides, we have an understanding with Gestapo Chief Kappler."

Adriana and everyone else in Rome knew about the Jews' 'understanding' with Kappler. Two weeks earlier, the Gestapo chief had demanded fifty kilograms of gold from the Jews against the threat of their deportation. With the help of many outside the Jewish community, the bribe was paid in full within the two-day deadline Kappler had imposed. How could they trust a man who would stoop to such evil extortion?

"Signor Foa, I must tell you that I have this information from the most reliable source," Adriana said in a raised voice, astonished at the man's capacity for self-delusion.

"And what source might that be, Signora Corvo?"

Adriana lowered her eyes. "I'm afraid I can't reveal my source." How could she say she was privy to the secrets of the German embassy?

"Then I ask you to tell your source not to spread such dangerous rumors." The old man glowered in stern remonstrance.

"But, Signor Foa, I can assure you, it's true!" she shouted, thumping her fist on his desk in frustration. "The Germans will round up every Jew in this ghetto," her eyes flashed in anger, "tomorrow!"

"Signora Corvo," the old man stood up, "I'm afraid you have been seriously misled. I cannot let my people be panicked by such rumors. As president of the Jewish community, I will personally go into the ghetto this afternoon to allay any fears that may unfortunately have arisen because of this unfounded rumor." He walked over to the door and grasped the knob.

Adriana stood up and, looking into Foa's eyes, realized he was serious. The Jews of Rome would be defenseless, doomed. "But don't you see—"

Foa raised a finger to his lips and with the other hand opened the door. "I think you've said enough already, Signora Corvo. I bid you good day."

ON THE ROAD TO ROME. A FARMHOUSE.

"Well, Jay Mack, looks like the Limey really hit the jackpot for us this time." Nolan flopped down on the single couch.

"Before you start counting sheep, Buck, that's my bed." MacPherson smiled. "Privilege of rank."

"Aw, shucks. You mean I gotta sleep on the floor?"

"Yup. Along with Lawrence."

Nolan rose and began looking around for the best place to bunk. "Speaking of Lawrence, what did you make of what that other English guy, the leader of the POWs in the caves, said about him? About how Lawrence never joined in when the other RAF guys were shooting the bull about their missions. Think maybe our Lawrence didn't say anything because he's got something to hide?"

"Knock it off, Buck. I'm too tired to argue with you right now."

"Okay, chief." Nolan picked up his pillow and blanket and arranged himself on the floor. "Sure wish I had my photo of Rita Hayworth right now. The patriotic one of her on the car. The one where she's pointing to a sign on the back of the car that says, 'Drive carefully – my bumpers are on the scrap heap.'" He rolled over on his back and clasped his hands on his chest. "Say, where'd the Limey get to, anyway?"

"I think he's fixing up a meal for us with the farmer's—"

The door to the room opened with a bang and Lawrence burst in.

"What's up, Lawrence?" Nolan asked, propping himself up on an arm. "You're looking a bit down in the mouth. Did the farmer's wife run out of steak and kidney pie?"

"The farmer just told me—" Lawrence shook his head in disbelief. "He just told me that the Germans raided the caves."

Jay shot up from his chair. "The POW hideout? When?"

"Sometime after we left. The farmer says no one escaped."

ROME. JEWISH GHETTO.

Something was wrong. Renzo Rossi turned in his bed and rubbed his eyes. There was barely a glimmer of light in the sky, surely too early to get out of bed. But something was wrong.

Something was different, but he couldn't quite place what it was. He heaved himself from the lumpy bed and shuffled past the chair to the window to look down the Via del Portico. Nothing. A hint of light in the eastern sky. His eyes ran along the barely-lit street, the houses cheek by jowl. The old bench outside his apartment building sat empty. Renzo looked to the other end of the street. Nothing. And then he heard the noise.

He rushed back to the chair and grabbed his clothes, pulling on his pants. What had happened to the old blind man? No echo of his white stick tapping its way along the street. He shoved his feet into his shoes and pulled on his cap. Instead, there was another sound, a sound that grew louder as the light of the new day grew brighter. The sound of soldiers' boots beating against the cobbles.

The tramp of the soldiers' boots came to a sudden halt at the end of the Via del Portico d'Ottavia. The thin lips in the gaunt face of Hauptsturmführer Ganz called his four company officers to one side.

"Give one of these to whoever opens the door." He pulled out a card from his pocket and held it up. "This message from the Third Reich tells them they have twenty minutes to pack a small suitcase, personal effects, money, jewelry, some food.

"You must not miss a single Jew!" He spat out the words. "Not one. The smallest child, the oldest hag. Take them all down to the trucks waiting for them by the Portico d'Ottavia. Is that understood?"

The officers' arms stretched out in salute as their heels clicked. They turned and strode back to their companies.

Renzo looked down into the street and heard the shouts of the soldiers. The light was growing very slowly, as if the sun, like himself, was frightened of what the day would bring. The sound of a rifle butt smashing against a door at the far end of the street pushed the thought aside. He had to move, and he had to move quickly. He already knew the general path of escape out of the ghetto. Across the tiled rooftops. The men of the ghetto had warned him of the occasional roundups – men all over Rome were rounded up and shipped to Germany as slave labor. Renzo looked down and saw soldiers pushing old women along the street. This was no roundup of slave labor.

He had to find an escape across the rooftops. There was no path to the roof from his apartment building, but he knew there was a route through the attic of the house next door.

He shoved the photograph of his parents in his pocket and flung open the door, his feet clattering on the steps as he ran down. "The Germans are coming! Get out of here!" he shouted as he passed the door of the landlord's ground floor apartment, but he heard only disgruntled noises coming from inside. He knew he should stop and give his landlord full warning, but there was no time.

His hand rattled the latch as he opened the front door. A German soldier stood across the street.

The antiquarian from the SS had come down from Berlin for this extraordinary opportunity. He turned away from the window of the synagogue, away from the jarring noise of the troops outside. He knew what was going on – he had been at the briefing. But, as a captain in the ERR – the Einsatzstab Reichsleiter Rosenberg, a commando unit specializing in the plunder of precious art and historical objects – he had more important matters at hand.

The captain moved along the corridor to the library of the temple. Two weeks before, he had spent several days sorting through the magnificent treasures of the written word housed in the Biblioteca Communale, the library of the Jews. The papyri, the codices, the palimpsests, the fourteenth century manuscripts – all were to be shipped to Munich. He entered the library and marveled at the documents stacked on tables around the room. A tingle of excitement shot through him as he reached out and stroked a rare edition.

As the German soldier crossed the street, Renzo slammed the door shut and turned the key. He dashed down the ground floor corridor toward the back, realizing he was running out of time when he heard the German's rifle butt already crashing against the front door. He lifted the latch, ran across the small terrace, and vaulted the dividing wall. As he approached the back door to Massimo and Emma's apartment building, he paused. The door was open. Something was wrong.

"Get them into the trucks! The line's too long!" Ganz shouted to his soldiers. "Into the trucks!" He paced back and forth in agitation as his men ushered the Jews into the area in front of the ancient Roman portico. "Faster! Stop treating them like fine china – they're Jews!" His face reddened as he screamed his exhortations. "Throw them into the trucks!"

Renzo gently pushed open the back door of the apartment building where his friends lived. He could hear a hubbub of noise and cries from the street, but from their building, nothing. Looking through the hall he could see that the front door was hanging from the hinges, and suddenly he felt sick to his stomach. The Nazis had already called.

He moved quietly down the hall, passing a ransacked ground floor apartment. Arriving at the foot of the stairs, he stopped: what if there were still Germans upstairs? He listened for a few moments. Nothing. He had no option. He charged up the stairs.

From Massimo's apartment on the second floor, there was a room with a window leading to a small balcony. From there, perhaps he could jump to the next building and make his escape across the rooftops. Breathless, he reached the top floor and opened the door. Furniture was overturned, dishes smashed.

Suddenly, he stopped. There was someone else in the room.

"Be careful with those books!" the antiquarian shouted at a soldier who had been detailed to load the trucks standing outside the synagogue. He, himself, wore gloves as he handled an incunabulum which had been in the library's possession since shortly after its printing in fifteenth-century Siena.

Renzo was relieved to see the little girl in the corner of the room: the sound he heard had come from Luisa, tears flowing down her cheeks from brown eyes that were magnified by those tears. He leaned forward to embrace the child and was alarmed when she leapt back from his touch. "Luisa, where are your mother and father?" he whispered.

She struggled to answer, her sobs breaking up her speech. "Gone." Her small hands covered her eyes and her body shook with sobs.

"Luisa, please come over here." Renzo gently guided the child to a chair in the corner. "Please tell me what happened to your mamma and papa, Luisa."

She stared at the floor. "The soldiers came and took them away."

He pulled her to him and felt her small frame convulse again with sobs. As he gently rocked her, her eyes, grudgingly becoming trustful, rose to look at him.

Renzo's gaze fastened on the girl. "But they didn't take you, Luisa?"

As the clamor in the street intensified, her eyes darted toward the window with alarm. When the noise subsided, she turned back to him and pointed at a small armoire in the corner. "They put me in there. They said if I loved them, I had to be very quiet." Her shoulders convulsed as she began sobbing again.

Holding her, Renzo cried silently into the child's hair. His dear friends, Massimo and Emma – what was happening to them now? What would happen to them later?

"I want to be with Mamma and Papa." The child's small body continued to shake.

"And so you shall, Luisa." He was surprised at how easily the lie came, his thoughts preoccupied with escape. For both of them.

"Come, Luisa. Come with me." He led the child by the hand to the door that opened onto the balcony.

❖ ❖ ❖

A soldier moved toward an old Jew who was shuffling slowly and glancing behind him. "Get a move on, you senile idiot, you're holding up the line!" He thrust the butt of his rifle into the old man's ribs, sending him flying to the cobbles.

The man struggled to get up, spittle dribbling down from his white beard. "My wife – I need to help her – she's back there." He pointed toward the end of the line, where four young Jews were carrying a paralyzed woman strapped to a kitchen chair.

The soldier motioned the chair bearers to the front of the line. They loaded the old woman, chair and all, into the truck, her husband falling again as he tried to follow her.

Renzo didn't know what to do. He looked down over the edge of the terrace at the alley thirty feet below. On his own he could jump the five-foot gap to the terrace opposite. But with the child? Perhaps he should leave her, tell her to go back into hiding in the closet. Surely she'd be safe; the Germans had already searched the house – surely they wouldn't return. And even if he made it to the other balcony, she wouldn't be able to accompany him across the steep roofs to get away.

"Perhaps, Luisa, you could..." His voice faded away as he looked down at the tear-stained face. He picked up the child, had her sit piggyback, took a deep breath to steady himself, and jumped.

Renzo gasped with pain and relief as he landed, collapsing on his knees on the opposite terrace. Luisa clambered down from his back. Rain had begun to fall; it would make the way across the clay-tiled roofs with the child even more difficult.

"You'd better come inside. Now!" The voice startled him.

Ganz's rage was palpable as he arrived on the scene. "What's the delay? Why the holdup in the line?"

"Some of the old Jews can't climb into the trucks," a soldier answered.

Ganz looked with disgust on the old man lying on the ground. "Then throw them in!"

The soldiers bent over the fallen Jew, grabbed him by his coat and pants, and flung him into the back of the truck.

"Perhaps the child would like a drink of milk, Bellina," the man said softly to his wife. Luisa nodded weakly.

"I don't understand." There was still a racket in the street outside, punctuated by angry shouts in German, and Renzo's strong impulse was to continue his flight across the roofs. "Haven't the Nazis searched your house yet?"

"No, of course not."

"Why not?"

"Because we're not Jewish."

Some of the trucks carrying the Jews away were uncovered, and by eight in the morning the rain began.

In one of the open trucks, the paralyzed woman in the kitchen chair sat stoically, her hair drenched and matted, water dripping off her nose. Her husband crouched on the floor where he had landed, his knees drawn up, his face buried in his hands. Behind him, a mother tried to shelter her cold and hungry baby, its face red with crying and fists pummeling the air in futile protest. Next to her, a father wrapped his arms around a child who clutched a sodden teddy bear. And behind them, Massimo clasped his sobbing wife, Emma, to his bosom and prayed for a miracle for their little girl, Luisa.

Renzo felt a brief relief. Signora Benedetti came in with a glass of milk and set it on the table, then sat down next to the girl and put a comforting arm around her.

"The Germans were working from lists of names and addresses." Signora Benedetti rose and walked over to the window. "We could see them from here. Anyone on the list got a knock on the door."

Renzo shuddered at the thought of meticulous German efficiency in the service of cold-blooded brutality. His own name must have been on one of their lists. Perhaps at that moment some German officer was checking his list, wondering why his name hadn't been checked off. He was anxious to get away, to escape across the rooftops. But he couldn't take the child.

"There's no need to ask." Signora Benedetti had read his thoughts. "Of course we'll look after Luisa."

Renzo stood up and began to move toward the balcony door. "But what if the Germans come back to check?"

"Well, we'll just say Luisa is my niece; we're looking after her while my sister is away." Signora Benedetti smiled and gave the girl a wink. "Now, you'd better get going before the Germans start checking the rooftops." Accompanying Renzo to the balcony door, she added, *sotto voce,* "Of course, we'll have to share our rations with the child, so we won't be able to keep her forever, much as we'd like to. I'm sure you understand."

"I understand. You've been most kind." Opening the door, he turned to look at the girl. "I'll come back for you, Luisa."

Although there was a semblance of a smile on her lips, the child's eyes were heavy with sorrow.

As the trucks full of Jews wound slowly through the ancient cobbled streets, other Romans came out to watch. Most gazed in disbelief and horror. Others shook their fists at the hated Germans. One dropped to her knees and prayed.

He'd escaped. Renzo shimmied his way down the drainpipe and jumped the last few feet to the ground. A hasty look up and down the street confirmed that the German soldiers who had driven the Jews of the ghetto into the waiting trucks were all gone. The images lingered in his mind: the screams of the women, the children's sobs. If there were a God, he thought, He was without mercy.

He looked carefully around as he walked along the street. No Germans. No fascists. The seeking brown eyes of Luisa, the little girl, had burned an image in his mind. He hoped she'd be all right. Surely the Gentile couple would look after her for a while, but one never knew nowadays.

"Fermati!" He heard the shout. An Italian command from a German mouth.

The antiquarian from the SS sighed as he collected the last item to be taken. A treasure not to be trusted to any soldier – a manuscript dating from before the time of Christ, before the emperor Augustus erected the portico that now stood across the street from the synagogue. His gloved hands caressed the carefully-wrapped treasure, which would travel with him on its journey to Munich with the rest of the library.

Renzo felt sure the German boots behind him were getting nearer, but he did not turn to look. His arms pumping, his lungs gasping, his legs screaming in agony for rest, he ran for his life. If they caught him, they'd soon find out he was a Jew.

As he swung sharply around a corner, he bumped into an old lady, sending her sprawling, but he did not stop as he fought to regain his balance. "I'm sorry," he shouted without turning his head. Fear gripped him; he twisted and turned down alleys, but the thumping of German boots seemed to get louder.

Suddenly, he stopped. About fifty yards up the street were three other German soldiers. Within moments they heard the shouts of their colleagues and started to run towards him.

Renzo cast his eyes about desperately. An old church on the piazza. He had no option. He bounded up the steps, pulled open the door, and rushed in.

The darkness of the interior caused him to hesitate as his eyes struggled to adjust and he winced as his shin caught the edge of a wooden pew. In the candlelight, the path of the aisle came into focus and his shoes clattered on the marble floor as he ran towards the altar. He stopped in the apse, looking frantically for an escape route. The Germans would be through the door at any moment.

"Are you in trouble, my son?" The voice startled him. He turned to see a priest looking down at him from the altar steps.

"German soldiers—"

The priest raised his hand. "Have no fear, my son. The Germans have no authority here in the precincts of this church. This church belongs to the Holy See – this church is therefore in a neutral country." The priest turned and began to walk to the vestry entrance. "Still, we should take no chances. Some of the Germans are godless people. Come, let us go to the church's monastery." He opened the door. "My name is Father Francesco. Come quickly, my son."

Approaching Rome.

"Frankly, I don't think I'll be asking you to take my confession." Nolan's eyes rolled at Lawrence's disguise as a priest, a moth-eaten cassock and a frayed biretta conveying little spirituality.

"As long as it gets us past the German checkpoint I'll be happy." Lawrence spoke from the seat of the uncovered wagon, squeezed between the farmer and his daughter, a pretty young woman who drove the wagon, gently slapping the reins on the horse's withers.

"Another thing, Father Lawrence – try to remember you're a priest and behave yourself," Nolan smirked. "Don't dirty your mind with unholy thoughts about the frisky little hussy sitting next to you."

"Your attempt at humor falls flat, Nolan." Lawrence struggled with his temper. "This young woman and her father are risking their lives to smuggle us into Rome."

"Will you two pipe down?" MacPherson hissed.

"Excellent idea, Jay," said Lawrence. "The farmer says the German checkpoint is coming up a couple of hundred yards down the road." He spoke rapidly to the farmer and his daughter before turning back to the Americans in the back of the wagon. "Here's the plan. The farmer and his daughter are headed for the Campo dei Fiori to sell their wagon-load of cabbages – that much is true. My story is that he's giving me a lift because I've been recalled to the Holy See. You two just stay buried as deeply as you can beneath the cabbages – and don't move!"

Lawrence turned forward to see a young German soldier fifty yards down the road, his arm raised. The farmer's daughter tugged gently on the reins.

Rome. A Working-Class Neighborhood.

They sat unsmiling around the table in the cellar of Dante Bartoli's small house. Bartoli, as leader of the Resistance group, sat at the head. To his right sat Vittoria and her brother, Fabio, together with Bernardo, Cesare, Ludovico, and his wife, Sofia. The six represented the newly-formed unit for the central district; opposite them were five partisans of the eastern district.

"I feel so ashamed." Vittoria stared at her clasped hands and shook her head. "We did nothing, absolutely nothing, to stop the roundup. All those poor people sent north. I can't begin to imagine their fate."

"I, too, feel ashamed." Fabio's voice was heavy with frustration. "If only we'd known."

"We did know," Bartoli said tersely. "Or, at least, I knew."

Vittoria, looking up, slapped the table with the flat of her hands and leapt to her feet. "You knew?" Her face was flushed with anger. "You let the roundup—all those people—?"

"It was a matter of—"

"You could at least have told us!" Vittoria shouted. "We could have—"

"We could have done nothing!" Bartoli shot up, his chair clattering loudly to the floor.

All eyes in the room were fixed on him. Vittoria, who had never seen their leader angry before, began to realize he was right. Chastened, she sat down, sullen and embarrassed by the reprimand.

Bartoli righted his chair and sat down. "There was nothing we could have done. Nothing." His voice had returned to its normal soft register. "I regret our helplessness as much as you do." His eyes circled the table, locking eyes with each one of them in turn. "But we are still a small organization. Throughout Rome, we number a hundred, maybe a few more. We have little in the way of arms and our organization is ad hoc, at best. We have merely our zeal."

Only a slow drip of water somewhere in the cellar could be heard as he once again scanned the partisans around the table.

"All of you, at this moment, are worth your weight in gold. You are the backbone, the very foundation of this Resistance."

When his eyes came to Vittoria's they stopped. "I'm sure you realize that, had I ordered any action yesterday, many of us would now be in the Regina Coeli prison or in a cell at Via Tasso Gestapo headquarters. Or, worse, in the morgue."

The leader waited a few moments for his words to sink into the minds of the young partisans. "Don't think for a moment that I'm not as anxious as you are to strike a blow against the Nazis and the fascists as soon as possible." He leaned forward on his chair. "I've waited over twenty years for this chance. Ever since Mussolini came to power I've been forced to live in the shadows. Fascist spies everywhere." His voice pulsed with passion. "Friends disappearing, found floating in the Tiber or dead in some ditch. Always living in fear."

Bartoli rose again from his chair, fire in his eyes. "But now, now more than ever, the need to strike back has come. For Matteo, for Gianfranco, for the many friends I wish could be here with us for this time." His voice began to falter. "But we must wait until we're ready."

There was a hush in the room for a long while after he sat back down.

Fabio broke the silence. "We understand, Dante."

Bartoli's head snapped in Fabio's direction. "Do you?" he said sharply. "Do you really?"

He paused for a moment, then turned to Fabio's sister. "Now, let's begin. Vittoria, please tell us about the bomb-making workshop you are going to set up."

GERMAN CHECKPOINT ON THE OUTSKIRTS OF ROME.

From the first exchange, Lawrence could see that the German soldier at the checkpoint viewed his task as a chore.

His Italian covered only a few basic words, and he seemed more interested in the farmer's daughter than in his job.

"Dobbiamo vendere i cavoli." As the farmer slowly explained his need to sell his produce in the Rome market, the German scowled, and Lawrence was tempted to translate into German for him but thought better of it. The soldier leaned over the side of the wagon to pick up a cabbage, and Lawrence prayed he would not uncover an American foot. The soldier reached for another cabbage.

Lawrence was frantically considering his options if the soldier discovered the Americans when the farmer's daughter suddenly jumped down from the wagon and crashed into the back of the soldier, falling into the road. *"Mi dispiace, mi dispiace,"* she said by way of apology to the soldier, but Lawrence knew what had happened was no accident. She tugged at her skirt to untangle it from beneath her knees and reached out a hand to the soldier, who needed no further invitation.

With one arm he gently clasped her hand, while his other arm shoved his rifle against a tree before encircling her waist and hauling her to her feet. *"Va bene?"* he asked, his hand lingering in hers.

"Si, si. Grazie," she said, looking into his eager eyes, then lowering hers before raising her lashes again to fix him with an irresistible smile. *"Mi scusi, ma forse...?"* she said pointing to the wagon's seat. The German needed no second bidding, placing both hands around her waist and hoisting her up. She smiled again, pointing to the horse and raising an eyebrow.

"Si, si, signorina." The German waved them on and she flicked the reins against the horse.

Just as Lawrence was beginning to breathe more easily, he heard the German's voice.

"Alt! Alt!" The soldier had recovered his rifle and was running after the cart. Lawrence could see the farmer twist his handkerchief nervously as his daughter brought the cart to a halt.

The German's hand dug deeply into his breast pocket. *"Per Lei, signorina."* He reached up and pressed a bar of chocolate into her hand.

"What a smooth operator!" Nolan cried out after Lawrence had recounted what had happened. "Hey, Jay Mack, whaddya think? Did she play him for a sucker, or what?"

"Sure does sound like it," MacPherson said, freeing a leg from a pile of cabbages. "Hey, David, please thank her and tell her she did a swell job working on that Kraut's vanity."

Lawrence spoke softly to the young woman, who smiled sweetly before replying.

"So what's the word from the signorina, English?" Nolan asked, tapping Lawrence on the elbow.

He turned to face him, a faint smile on his lips. "She said that all men are vain, Nolan, all men are vain."

ROME. PIAZZA NAVONA.

Renzo stood at the edge of the scaffolding that protected the Fountain of the Four Rivers, the red scarf Father Francesco had told him to wear for identification around his neck. When he had spoken of his desire to join the Resistance, the priest had listened to him intently and, after a few days and many questions, had sent him to the piazza.

He looked around the square. Before the war, the Piazza Navona had been a lively center of Roman life, fountains playing, cafés buzzing, vendors hawking, children laughing. Now it was gray and lifeless. Life went on, but the Romans in the piazza now were merely passing through on their way to somewhere else, their heads hung low and their eyes cast down.

Guttural voices cut jaggedly across his thoughts and reminded him of the source of the people's despair: two German officers stood arrogantly in front of the Borromini church of Sant'Agnese in Agone, their expensive cameras in hand.

He turned his head away and remembered the piazza in a happier time, a time when being Jewish was no more important to anyone else in Rome than eye color. As a young boy, he used to walk with his mother and father to the piazza, his small body dwarfed between them and his hands reaching up to grasp theirs. They lived in a run-down section of Trastevere, and every Sunday they would cross the ancient Fabricio bridge from the Tiber Island and make their way up through the Jewish ghetto to the splendid piazza a half mile away. And his father would somehow always find a few lire for ice cream. His father...

He looked across at the gelateria, now shuttered. His father had taught him everything he was passionate about – the need to fight the fascists, the need for socialism, how the working-class had to rise up, how they had to take power. Dangerous views to hold in Mussolini's Italy.

A father who had been taken from him so suddenly two years ago. No one knew what had happened. His father had been a member of the Communist Party and, like so many in the illegal organization in fascist Italy, he had been snatched from the street. Vanished. His mother's desperate pleas to the authorities had met with no response. Three days later, his body was found in a roadside ditch on the outskirts of the city. His mother's sobs and piteous keening still rang in his ears.

Her grief put her in an early grave. Pneumonia, the doctor had said, but Renzo was certain she had died of a broken heart. He felt a pang of anguish beginning to grip his chest—

The hand dropping on his shoulder made him start. "Lorenzo Rossi?"

Renzo turned, surprised by the small, squat man. Somehow he'd expected someone taller and more rugged-looking to be the leader of the partisans. "*Sì, sì!* And you?"

"That doesn't matter." His face was unsmiling as it turned towards the Germans. "Let's get away from this scum."

Historic Center of Rome.

"Somehow, I don't think we're in Kansas anymore, Toto," Nolan quipped. The trio, walking in the old Campo Marzio section of the city to an address known only to Lawrence, passed a church with an ornate Baroque façade and marble angels playing long-necked trumpets on its roof.

After they had walked several blocks and passed a second and then a third church, each as elaborate as the first, Nolan called out, "So where the hell's our hotel?"

"Pipe down, Buck," MacPherson whispered sharply to Nolan. "This place is crawling with Krauts."

"As for our digs, you'll need to be patient." The Englishman looked around, checking for police. "I need to meet a contact."

"Yeah? Who? So where do we go to meet him?"

"There's no need for you to know." Lawrence turned to MacPherson. "Jay, perhaps you two could wait for me in that little park over there." He looked at Nolan. "And perhaps you can keep quiet for five minutes while I'm away." He slipped down a narrow side street and was gone.

"Well! What do you make of that, Jay? I ask a simple question and the Limey bites my head off."

MacPherson sighed. "Take it easy, Buck. As I explained to you before, the POW operation is run on a need-to-know basis. You've gotta learn to direct your feet to the sunny side of the street a bit more – sometimes you're just too sensitive."

"Maybe. But how can you be sure he isn't going to get the Gestapo?"

"Cut it out, Buck."

"Okay, okay, Jay Mack. It's just that I always like to know where I'm going, what's going to happen to me."

MacPherson, tired from the journey and out of patience with his buddy, stopped short and faced Nolan. "You want to know where you're going?"

"Yeah."

"You want to know what's going to happen to you?"

"Yeah, I do, Jay Mack."

"See that park? That's where you're going. And what's going to happen to you is you're going to sit on that bench with me. With your mouth shut. Do you read me, Lieutenant?"

ROME, VIA VENETO. EXCELSIOR HOTEL.

Kappler sipped on his schnapps and looked over the large polished bar of the Excelsior Hotel, which served as a standby officers' club in the evenings.

"May I join you, Herr Obersturmbannführer?" There was a formal click of heels.

Kappler looked up to see Ganz, who had led the roundup of the Jews the day before. Ganz was not one of his favorite people, but Kappler was grateful that he and his men had been relieved of having to carry out the roundup.

"Please, take a seat, Herr Hauptsturmführer." Kappler gestured to the plush armchair opposite him. "May I congratulate you on the efficiency of your operation yesterday? It enabled me and my men to concentrate on seeking out Resistance members." Kappler gestured to a waiter. "Schnapps, Ganz?"

"Yes, thank you." Ganz settled into his chair. "Is the Resistance really a serious problem for you? I would not have thought so – they weren't at all in evidence yesterday. Just some fools shouting at the trucks."

"Perhaps the Resistance wasn't interested in the fate of the Jews." Kappler paused as the waiter set down the drinks. "My information is not clear on that point, but I do know that they are not yet ready to make a move. *Prost.*" He raised his glass. "But perhaps they will be soon."

"*Prost,*" Ganz replied. "And then? How will you deal with them then?" He set down his glass. "I've always wondered how the Gestapo worked. Cloak and dagger, I expect?"

"Cunning and persuasion would be my choice of words." Kappler still found the suggestion of a smile caused by Ganz's facial scar an annoying distraction. "Cunning in placing my agents in strategic locations, penetrating secrets, sowing distrust to throw the blame elsewhere, capturing the swine." He opened his cigarette case and held it out to Ganz.

"And the persuasion?" Ganz took a cigarette.

"That's done at our headquarters in Via Tasso." Kappler extended the lighter. "Not very pleasant work, I'm afraid, but it gets results."

"I understand, completely. Persuasion!" Ganz sniggered as he brought a fist down on the table. "Such a refined and delicate choice of terminology – persuasion!"

Kappler did not smile. He did not like torture, but it was an unfortunate necessity of Gestapo work.

"And where do you place your spies?" Ganz took a long drag on his cigarette.

Kappler, on a whim, decided to intrigue his guest. "I have an agent among the prisoners of war."

ROME. A MODEST APARTMENT.

"*Signora Silvestri, le presento Major MacPherson.*" Lawrence's smile was forced as he introduced the woman who owned the billet the three of them would be sharing.

MacPherson hesitated as his mind groped through his inadequate Italian vocabulary. "*Piacere.*" He smiled with relief as he found the word.

Her warm smile was captivating. Somehow, MacPherson didn't think she was Italian; her eyes were gray with flecks of green, set wide in a young face.

"*Ah, Lei parla italiano!*"

Her words caught him unawares. "*No, no, signorina, non parlo italiano.*"

Lawrence quickly corrected him. "It's *signora*, Jay. She's a married woman."

Nolan looked around and shrugged. "So where's the man about the house?"

There was a rapid exchange between Lawrence and the woman before he turned back to the Americans. "Thanks to Mussolini's wish to help the Führer, her husband is on the eastern front fighting the Russians. She hasn't heard from him in over three months."

"Oh." MacPherson felt a pang of guilt. He thought he'd been handed a bad break having to hide out from the Germans in the Italian countryside; but this woman's husband would be feeling the first blasts of approaching winter, with Stalin's army throwing everything they had at him. "Tell her I'm sorry, David."

"Thank you," the woman said with downcast eyes. "I appreciate your concern."

"Well, whaddayaknow – the signora speakah da Eengleesh!" exclaimed Nolan.

There was another exchange between Lawrence and the woman. "She says she studied English in university," Lawrence said, "but she doesn't want to embarrass herself by speaking incorrectly to people she's just met. She says she's sure it'll come back to her, though. We three are her first POW guests, and she says she's a bit nervous."

"She'll get over it. Now can I ask a practical question?" Nolan's voice interrupted the moment. "Where do we sleep? And what do we do for grub?"

"There's a room set up in the back of her apartment. We sleep there, lie low, if necessary." Lawrence exchanged words with the woman. "She says she'll prepare our meals, but remember – there's rationing and shortages. It won't be like it was in the country, where the farmers grow their own food and barter with each other for whatever else they need, so don't expect meat and potatoes. Well, maybe potatoes, but don't count on the meat. And if you happen to fancy spaghetti dishes, you're in luck."

"We've done worse," MacPherson said. "The food in the POW camp wasn't exactly five-star cuisine."

"But who pays her, English?" Nolan asked. "It sure as hell can't be us – we're broke."

"I'm not sure, Buck. Rumor has it that the British and Americans fund the kitty. They have embassies marooned inside the Vatican for the duration of the war, making contact with the outside world through the Swiss Legation." Lawrence shoved his hand in his pocket. "Apparently we're not the only ones here – there're several hundred of us, hiding all over Rome." His hand emerged with a wad of Italian bills. "And here's some money for us!" He doled out notes to the Americans.

Nolan looked at the bills. "Gee, thanks. Say, what're the chances there's a friendly bar nearby?"

"Um, maybe we should be careful, Buck."

"Perhaps we can make an exception for a quiet celebration on our safe arrival." Jay took his share of the money. "And perhaps the signora would like to join us?"

Lawrence's Italian exchange with the woman was brief. "She says it would be unwise for her to come, but she thanks you for the thought."

"What's your first name, Signora Silvestri?" asked MacPherson, as slowly and distinctly as he could.

"Maria," she replied, smiling shyly.

"Maria's a wonderful name – especially for us Catholics," Nolan said. "Okay, now that we've got the pleasantries out of the way, let's go try the vino. Hope it's better here than that sour stuff they gave us in the country." He began to head out. "You coming, Jay?"

MacPherson, smiling, continued to look at his hostess. "Ciao, Maria," he said, waving as he turned to leave.

As they made their way to the door, Maria called after them, "Please watch out for the neighbor in the ground floor apartment – she makes it her business to know everyone else's!"

ROME. EXCELSIOR HOTEL.

"Prisoners of war? Here in Rome? What prisoners of war?" Hauptsturmführer Ganz signaled to the waiter.

"None for me, Ganz." Kappler waved away the offer of another drink. "You mean to say you haven't yet seen the American and British prisoners who have escaped from the Italian camps and are now making themselves at home in Rome?"

"Not really." Ganz examined his fingernails, trying to make light of his ignorance.

"Then let me have my driver take you on a tour of the city tomorrow." Kappler's lips began to form a mocking smile. "We'll find them everywhere, walking the streets, speaking in English, lounging in bars, all fed by money from the American and British embassies in the Vatican. Hundreds of the scoundrels."

"I'm sorry, I don't understand." Ganz furrowed his brow. "If you know of these men – and you have a spy among them – why don't you just round them up and throw them into camps?"

"And pay for their keep with good German money?" Kappler's smile widened. "Of course, every so often we do get the Italian police to round up a few to ship back to Germany. But, in truth, they are no real threat to us now. You can be sure they're not keen to return to active service." Kappler allowed himself a half laugh. "Return to active service and face German bullets? Or drink in the bars of Rome? What sort of choice is that?"

Ganz laughed and then fell silent. "But if the escaped prisoners pose no threat, why do you have an agent planted in their midst?"

"Because, while they are of no importance now, one day they might be very important."

"And that day would be…?"

"If we ever have to leave Rome."

"Leave Rome?" Ganz snorted. "That won't happen. Kesselring is going to smash the Allies."

"Your patriotism is laudable, Ganz," Kappler crushed his cigarette in the ashtray, "but, as head of the Gestapo in Rome, I have to be prepared for the worst possible outcome – that we may be forced to leave Rome."

Ganz became agitated. "But surely we would defend it, street by street. Like at Stalingrad."

"Unthinkable." Kappler raised his eyebrows and affected a shudder. "Rome is a city like no other in the world, a treasure, Ganz. We Germans are not barbarians. How can you not appreciate the art and architecture, the ambience of ancient history in every street?"

Ganz's vacant stare soon discouraged Kappler from trying further to stimulate enthusiasm in a philistine.

"But if we don't defend Rome," Kappler offered up a silent prayer, "then the escaped prisoners must be rounded up and taken north with us – I have made a firm commitment to Kesselring that they would not be left behind to swell the ranks of the enemy's army. To fulfill this commitment, my agent has been charged with determining the places where they're hiding out."

"And that's your plan?"

"Only part of it, Ganz. Because when we round them up we'll have them march at the head of our retreating troops or put them in leading trucks. And we'll let the head of the US Fifth Army, General Clark, know."

The puzzled look on Ganz's face convinced Kappler that, while Ganz could be relied upon for blind obedience, the subject of military tactics was not one of his strong points.

"You see, Ganz, then the American bombers and fighters – who, as you're well aware, have recently started their barbaric attacks on Rome – would not dare strafe our columns."

Ganz's eyes narrowed as the idea penetrated. "I see. Yes, an excellent idea. And, should a retreat be necessary, I presume your agent would then continue to remain in Rome."

"Yes, of course. He'd stay behind enemy lines to spy for me." Kappler drained his schnapps and stood up. "And now, Ganz, you must excuse me. Work at the Via Tasso goes on at all hours."

"Ah, yes, the *persuasion.*" Ganz pronounced the word with considerable relish. "If you ever need help with persuasion, please don't hesitate to call on me. I have some expertise of my own in persuasion."

"I'm sure you have, Ganz, I'm sure you have." Kappler clicked his heels. "Good night."

ROME. TRASTEVERE.

At last Renzo had been given his first task as a member of an action group.

After a great many questions, Bartoli had told him to move out of the monastery, find himself a safe house, and wait. And wait Renzo had, in a tiny apartment owned by his aunt, who had moved north. Until this assignment. Not that the job struck him as one to knock the Nazis and fascists back on their heels.

He pushed open a shutter and looked through the small window onto the somber, dull sky that greeted the morning. Below him, crumbling buildings with grimy orange-red façades flanked a narrow street. The area was a dump, a slum. But, yet, it had a degree of comfort for him: he felt safe here in the district where he had grown up. This part of Trastevere was a solid working-class neighborhood and, even after so many years, the fascists were still reluctant to venture into it. The chances of a planted spy were rare: Trastevere had its own way of dealing with spies.

Still, Renzo knew he had to take care. It was Signor Bartoli's cardinal rule: always watch your back.

He looked down at the package of fliers Bartoli had asked him to deliver to a place on the other side of the city. How printed pamphlets were going to send the Germans packing, he wasn't quite sure, and Renzo wondered whether the underground leader was testing him before moving him onto other, more challenging assignments.

The address given him was committed to memory. Nothing was to be written down: another of Signor Bartoli's rules. *Via Panzani, 12.* A posh part of the city where they still walked with their noses in the air. Even after the Germans had ground Rome into the earth. How unlike the dingy labyrinth of cobbled streets and run-down buildings he could see from his window. What did the elite class know about revolution, about fighting for the freedom of the working class?

'United Front' work it was called, the upper class joining forces with the working class to overthrow the fascists and the Nazis. Renzo didn't like it, but the work had to be done.

He rubbed the day-old stubble on his face. He wouldn't shave; the la-di-dahs would have to take him as he came.

ROME. CHURCH OF SANTA MARIA DELLA GLORIA.

Even MacPherson's jaded eye was overwhelmed by the splendor of the church's interior. He stood just inside the door and looked down the nave: tall columns were reflected in the floor of polished marble like trunks of trees reflected in a pond. Along both sides of the nave were small chapels, some separated from the nave by decorative grillwork, others by marble balustrades. Each of the chapels was different, and he could see places where paintings and other objects had been removed for safekeeping. In one chapel, the entire wall was sandbagged to protect whatever was behind. He walked to the center of the church and craned his neck to look up into the cupola. Small windows along the cupola's base lit up the luminous fresco painted on its concave interior in shades of blue, violet, yellow, and magenta; his lower jaw dropped as he gazed in wonder at angels and saints ascending through pink-tinged clouds into heaven.

But he was not there to sightsee, he reminded himself as he resumed his walk toward the apse. He'd received an urgent request from a Colonel James to meet him at this church. The colonel was top dog over the organization of all escaped prisoners of war hiding out in Rome. Top dog of the down and out; he wondered again how a full colonel could be a prisoner of war. Perhaps he'd ask him. Then again, maybe not.

He continued walking toward the altar, which looked down on the rows of pews. Fifth row on the left. He saw the colonel. Balding, slight of frame. Seated away from the aisle. MacPherson entered the row and sat, his head lowered, about five feet from the man.

"MacPherson?" came the whisper.

"Yes."

The colonel kept his head bowed as he moved toward him. "As of next week, you're to take over my responsibilities here. Namely, your responsibility will be to organize all Allied prisoner-of-war accommodations in Rome."

ROME. STREET ABOVE THE PIAZZA DEL POPOLO.

Perhaps he'd not found the right address. The building that stood before him seemed too grand to be a place where anti-fascist business was conducted. The massive door, over-hung with a balcony, was surrounded by faceted blocks, and the pedimented windows had large sills braced by stone scrolls. Renzo walked back to the corner to check the street name and returned to check the number on the building; everything tallied with the address Bartoli had given him. Then a discrete ceramic rectangle embedded in the wall above the house number caught his eye: "Villa Ranieri." Good God, the place even had a name. He shrugged his shoulders and, with the package of fliers tucked under his arm, rapped on the door with the elegant knocker.

As he waited for an answer, Renzo looked up at the second floor windows. The drapery of the corner window was parted briefly, a face appeared, then disappeared as the drape was closed. He shuffled from foot to foot, his eyes anxiously casting up and down the street, checking for any police. He was about to knock again when the door inched open, revealing the small body and unruly mop of black hair of a young boy about ten.

"Password?" the boy asked.

Renzo hesitated before getting out the password given him by Bartoli. Were young children part of the Resistance? "*Specchio.*"

"Come in." The boy opened the door, ushering him into a large hall hung with tapestries. "Wait here, please." The boy's heels clicked on the marble staircase as he ran up.

Renzo tried to organize his thoughts. Was he really in an anti-fascist headquarters? He looked at his image in a gilded mirror that hung over a Baroque table. Damn, the hall was bigger than his aunt's apartment. The people who lived here were opposed to fascism? He was thinking of leaving when a voice rang out from the top of the stairs.

"Are you Signor Rossi?" The upper class voice came from the lips of a woman about his age leaning over the marble balustrade, her long dark hair cascading around her face. He could not deny her attractiveness, but her posh accent stuck in his craw.

"Yes," he answered sharply. "You know, you shouldn't leave the security of the organization in the hands of a young boy. For all he knew, I could have been a fascist policeman."

"Giorgio's not stupid – fascist policemen wouldn't know the password." He tried not to be distracted by her large brown eyes. "Actually, for a minute my brother said he thought you might be a hobo."

Her barely-suppressed giggle infuriated him. His unshaven face, an act of defiance to class distinction, had instead branded him as a penniless outcast.

"Please bring the fliers up here, Signor Rossi. If you'd like to use the elevator, it's at the back of the hall."

Yes, Miss La-di-dah. Anything you say, Miss La-di-dah. You even have an elevator in your house, Miss La-di-dah. His feet stomped angrily on each step of the staircase.

Rome. Church of Santa Maria della Gloria.

MacPherson was stunned by the order, but before he could say anything, the colonel continued.

"I've been told to go north to Florence. Special undercover assignment. No need to say more." He placed his forefinger across his sealed lips. "When I'm gone, you'll be the ranking officer in Rome. So you got the job of looking after the POWs."

The colonel paused, and MacPherson felt obliged to fill the void. "To be honest, sir, I welcome the opportunity to do something useful. What do I have to do?"

"There's nothing to the job, MacPherson. Just get organized, know the safe houses, and maintain security." He turned to look directly at MacPherson. "Security. That's the critical thing. Always security. Keep the goddamned noses of the fascist and Nazi bastards out of your business."

"Yes, sir. How does the operation work?"

The colonel turned back and bowed his head. "Well, as you're probably aware, most POWs that make it to Rome head for the Vatican." He sighed. "Easy mistake to make, I guess. They all know Vatican City is a neutral country, so if they can just set foot on it they'll be in friendly territory."

"My buddies and I were tipped off about that, sir. We were told that's not an option any longer."

"Good. Saved us some trouble. As for the others who weren't tipped off, the pope took a few in at first, but then it seems he got fed up with having every American, Brit, Canadian, and Aussie turn up on his doorstep to try to live on his nickel."

"So he throws them all out."

"Not quite as heartless as that. The pope does, after all, have a conscience." The colonel gave a wry smile. "So he sends them to this church. Vatican property, even though it's outside the walls of Vatican City. There's a monastery attached where our men can hole up for a day or two. But, with so many POWs making their way to Rome, they can't all stay here so they have to be moved out to safe houses." He turned and tapped MacPherson's arm. "That's where you come in."

"How many safe houses are there?"

"Fifty. Maybe sixty at the moment."

"So you'll give me a list of all the addresses?"

The colonel shook his head. "No lists. Lists are too risky. Lists can fall into the wrong hands."

"So where do I get the addresses?"

"From the padre over there. Name's Father Francesco."

MacPherson looked at the priest, a middle-aged man with a full head of hair and, behind wire-framed glasses, large eyes darkened by a scowl that seemed more contemplative than stern. With the grace of a dancer he moved about the altar, his head bowed and his cassock swirling around his ankles.

Father Francesco of Santa Maria della Gloria. The name of the priest and his church sounded familiar, very familiar, and suddenly MacPherson remembered the slip of paper the Italian guard at the prisoner-of-war camp had handed him when he had said, 'Escape Rome.' The slip of paper that was stolen along with his watch after he had jumped from the train. He was almost certain the scrawled writing on it had said 'Father Francesco, Santa Maria della Gloria.'

The colonel's raspy whisper brought him back to the present. "You'll like the padre – he's a real sweetheart. He'll feed you the addresses as you need them."

"As I need them?"

"When new POWs arrive. When new space becomes available. He'll feed you maybe four or five addresses at a time."

"That's a relief. It's a bit easier than trying to memorize fifty or sixty addresses all at one time."

"Yup. Of course, you'll have to check back with him often. Things change."

"Change, sir?"

"Raids. New landlords come on board. Existing landlords decide they don't want to take the risk anymore. That sort of thing. So your guys sometimes have to be moved."

"It's beginning to sound a bit complicated, sir."

"You'll get the hang of it. When you meet with Father Francesco, take a pad and write it all down while you commit the addresses to memory. But whatever you do, destroy the piece of paper before you leave his study." The colonel began to inch his way to the end of the pew by the side aisle. "Anyway, go talk to Father Francesco now. He'll give you all the dope on the padrones." He stood up and started to head for the door.

"Padrones, sir?"

"The Italian landlords, the ones who provide the safe houses." The colonel looked at him sharply. "Your Italian not so hot?"

"Practically nonexistent."

"Bit of a problem." The colonel scratched his head. "Maybe I can get you some help. May take a few days."

"I've got someone billeted with me who speaks the lingo like a native."

"What's his name? Rank? Unit?" The colonel sat back down at the end of the pew.

"Actually, he's a Brit – Royal Air Force Flight Lieutenant."

"How long you know him? Can you trust him?"

"We were captured together. Then he helped me and a buddy escape from a train."

The colonel thought for a few moments. "Okay. But make him subject to the same rules. No permanent lists. Secrecy. Remember, MacPherson, security, security, security. The lives of hundreds of Allied soldiers will be in your hands. Not to mention the lives of their Italian hosts who are hiding them."

"I will, sir. I've got another buddy hiding out with me who could help as well. An American lieutenant."

"He speak Italian, too?"

"No. He's Irish-American."

"Then don't involve him. The fewer who know the details of the operation, the better for everyone."
"I understand. Sir, may I ask you a question?"
"Sure. Fire."
"How did you become a prisoner of war?"
The colonel stiffened for a moment, then smiled. "Probably the same way you did. By being careless." He rose from his seat and began to walk down the aisle.

MacPherson smiled and made his way toward the altar to get the first list of addresses from Father Francesco.

VILLA RANIERI.

"Come in, please." The patrician voice of the young woman continued to irritate Renzo, but the 'please' came as an unexpected surprise. As, indeed, did her smile – so warm and friendly, he found it difficult to associate with her voice.

As she led him into the drawing room of the *piano nobile*, his eyes darted quickly around, taking in the high ceiling, the silk Tabriz carpet, and paintings that looked as though they belonged on the walls of the Borghese Gallery. He glanced up at the high ceiling, upon which was painted a fresco with what looked like mythological figures; in the corner by the large windows stood a grand piano bearing framed family photographs. Two young men were sitting before the carved marble mantel of an enormous fireplace.

"What's your first name, Signor Rossi?"
"Lorenzo." Her smile was so warm he could not help returning it. "But everyone calls me Renzo."
"Well, Renzo, I'm Vittoria." He was surprised to find the clasp of her hand so firm. "And those gentlemen there are Ludovico – you can call him Ludo – and my brother, Fabio. "

Renzo nodded his acknowledgement toward the two men, then returned his gaze to Vittoria. There was something about her eyes....

"Well?"

"Yes?"

"Are you going to show us the fliers?"

"Oh, yes, of course." Renzo, dropping the package of fliers on an inlaid table, had almost forgotten his reason for being there. "Are these really all that important?"

"Every little bit helps." Fabio said, coming over to open the package. Picking up one of the fliers, he began to read it aloud. "Defend Rome! Down with fascism! Organize to throw out the Germans!"

"Is that stuff really going to help?" Renzo asked.

"We'll soon find out," Fabio said. "We'll be handing them out in the Piazza Venezia tomorrow."

"Are you mad?" he asked.

"Perhaps you need a touch of madness to be a partisan."

Church of Santa Maria della Gloria.

MacPherson liked Father Francesco. The priest was a soft-spoken man with a warm smile who broke the ice at their first meeting with conversation over a glass of sherry in his private study. Father Francesco had spent several years at a seminary in the United States, and his English was excellent.

When MacPherson inquired about how he had become involved in hiding Allied prisoners of war, the priest merely said, "The church has always been a place of refuge for those looking for asylum. If the situation had been reversed – if German soldiers were seeking sanctuary from Allied assailants – I would probably have done the same."

MacPherson was taken aback by his honesty. "Does that mean you're not taking sides in the war, Father?"

The priest smiled. "The Vatican is neutral, you know. Officially, my superiors don't take sides. And neither did I at first."

"At first? Have you changed your mind, Father?"

The priest set his glass down and began to finger his prayer beads. "When I saw what the Germans had done to the Jews of Rome, I did two things. First, I prayed for the Jews and asked for forgiveness of the Germans who took part in the roundup. And then I decided there could be no question about which side's cause is just."

They finished their sherry and began their work, Father Francesco guiding MacPherson through the complexities of the prisoner of war organization with a small map that helped him begin to understand the labyrinthine geography of the streets of Rome.

"Today's list of addresses is small," Father Francesco continued. "We'll start you off slowly, with only a few addresses for you to memorize."

MacPherson agreed to follow a fairly simple modus operandi. He would call at the church every Monday and Thursday. Once he had committed the addresses of the safe houses to memory, he would make the rounds between visits to see if the padrones needed anything and to ensure the 'guests' were not causing any trouble. When new escaped POWs arrived at the church, Father Francesco would put them up temporarily in the adjacent monastery until MacPherson made a regular visit. They would then be distributed among the safe houses.

They then began what would be their twice-weekly ritual. As Father Francesco repeated the names of the padrones and the addresses of the safe houses, MacPherson wrote them down on his notepad with a pencil. He then recited the information to himself until he felt he had committed it all to memory. Then, with the paper turned over, Father Francesco quizzed him mercilessly.

When the priest was convinced that the names of the padrones and their addresses had all been mastered, the flimsy sheet was torn from the pad and burned in a censer that hung on the wall, the perfumed smoke wafting through the air until the priest was satisfied that the piece of paper had been completely destroyed.

"One final request, Signor Jay. It would be best not to mention my name to any of your friends or acquaintances."

"I understand, Father."

"And now, may God go with you."

VILLA RANIERI.

"Some of you have already met Renzo," Dante Bartoli spoke from the head of the gleaming mahogany table in Signora Corvo's dining room, "but I want to introduce him to the full unit."

Renzo, glancing around the table, wasn't too happy with what he saw. Most of them seemed younger than his twenty-six years, and not one of them looked as if he'd done a hard day's work in his life.

"I'm Cesare." The voice came from a tall, gawky young man with an unkempt bush of black hair. Cesare looked Renzo over with seeking, cold blue eyes.

Sitting next to Cesare was Vittoria's brother, Fabio, who seemed as though he'd barely started shaving.

Ludovico, next to Fabio, was older. "Ciao, Renzo. I'm Ludovico – we met here when you were delivering the fliers."

"I'm Sofia," said the intense young woman with pulled-back hair and glasses. "Pleased to meet you. You should know that Ludovico's my husband." She turned to smile at her man.

Bernardo was short and wiry – the kind of guy no one especially notices, which Renzo thought could be useful in Resistance work.

"And you know me!" Vittoria waved from the other end of the table, beaming the beautiful smile that Renzo found so disturbing.

"And I'm Renzo. I live in Trastevere." He was sure he saw Fabio wince, as if the thought of someone from the working class penetrating their group alarmed him. He thought of telling them that he was also a Jew, but decided one shock at a time was enough. He tried not to jump to conclusions, but the idea that the people around the table could strike fear in the hearts of the occupying German army struck him as far-fetched.

"Before we get down to business, I want each of you to take one of these." Dante reached into his pocket and pulled out a number of what looked like business cards; he checked each card before handing it out.

"Hey, this is a membership card for 'Blood and Honor.'" Ludovico looked at the card in his hand with disgust.

"I'm not sure I want to even pretend to be a member of a fascist organization." Vittoria frowned at the card. "I suppose this is a forgery?"

"Actually, no." Dante could not suppress a smile. "You are all fully paid-up members. You will keep these cards on you at all times."

Renzo grasped the point quickly. "So if we're picked up by the police, we produce this card."

"Precisely. Probably a long shot, but if you can make a convincing story, the ruse may work. Don't lose it, whatever you do. Now, down to business. First of all, it's important to remember we're just a small unit in an ever-growing organization." To Renzo, this news was somewhat heartening. "And we ourselves are not quite ready for operations." Taking off his glasses, he pulled a handkerchief from his pocket and began to wipe the lenses. "Bernardo, give us a progress report on the bomb factory."

"We're almost ready with it. It's located in a cellar on the Via della Scrofa. We got the explosives from the army officer you said—"

"No names, please!" Bartoli said sternly. "And you shouldn't have given its location."

Bernardo leaned back in his chair. "Sorry. Anyway, to cut it short, Vittoria's already made two bombs."

Renzo glanced over at Vittoria and detected a hint of smugness in her smile.

"In that case, I think we can start operations next week. The German fuel tanks parked overnight in the Piazza Gigli by the Opera House – my information is that they're not too difficult a target." He looked around the table. "But first we need to designate teams. Small teams are safest. Two people can hide better than four."

Renzo respected this guy, even if the rest of the group didn't exactly inspire confidence.

"Ludovico and Sofia – you're a natural team. You two understand each other." He turned to Fabio. "You and Cesare will be responsible for communications among ourselves – as well as with the central committee. It's an important role."

Bartoli nodded at Renzo. "You will team up with Vittoria," he said turning to her. "And as you've made the bombs, Vittoria, you will lead the first attack. Next Friday. At the piazza in front of the Opera House."

A Hotel on the Janiculum Hill.

"I'm worried for you, Anton." Adriana rolled over on the bed and looked out the window of the room they used when time allowed. The day was warm, with a gentle breeze rustling the curtains; outside, the crowns of stone pines looked like great green clouds hovering over the gardens below.

"You're so tender-hearted, carissima." From the sound of his voice she could tell he was beaming the smile that made her forget the war and her forty-something years. "It's one of the things I love most about you. But please don't worry."

"Not worry?" She got up from the bed and slipped on a yellow silk robe. "With all the risks you take?" There was a hint of anger in her voice, anger mixed with fear that any tiny slip on his part could take him from her.

"I assure you, dearest Adriana, that I know what I'm doing." He rose and placed the flat of his hands on her cheeks, begging for a kiss, but he dropped his arms as she took a step backward.

"I realize you're no fool. But neither are those you work with. Haven't you considered that one day you might be caught? I mean, all those German passes for partisans? Ration cards for the Jews in hiding?" She reached out and grabbed his arm. "You know better than I what the Gestapo would do to you if they caught you."

He gently removed her hand from his arm and brought it to his lips to kiss. "I understand perfectly well what I'm doing. A life without taking some risk for others in desperate need is hardly worth living. But I could put the same question to you. What about the risks you take? You help the partisans, you find hiding places for Jews, and now you say you're about to get involved with hiding prisoners of war. You don't think I worry about you, as well?"

She looked away and sighed. "Perhaps you're right, Anton," she said, turning back to him and stroking his cheek, "but Rome is my beloved home and I know that I can never stop fighting for its freedom. I have to do what I can to save Rome, even though my head struggles to control what my heart feels so passionately."

He pulled her to him and embraced her tightly. "When you're around, my head finds it impossible to control what my heart feels passionately."

They sought each other's lips with the hunger of a long-past youth.

A BUILDING ON THE VIA DELLA SCROFA.

"Is it true you've really made two bombs?" Renzo whispered as he walked along the Via della Scrofa with Vittoria.

"Well, of course." Her barely-suppressed laugh annoyed him. "How do you think we're supposed to blow up the fuel tanks? For a proletarian warrior, you seem a bit naïve." Again the laugh. As their pace slowed, she looked up and down the street. A safe house was kept safe only by care she thought as she turned the key in the lock. Renzo made a final check before following her into the house.

"No, what I meant was that you, personally, haven't made two bombs."

"Why would you think that?" She led the way down into the cellar, her nose wrinkling at the stale, damp air. "After all, I do have a degree in chemistry from the University of Rome."

"Oh, of course. I'd forgotten about your education." There was a hint of rancor in his voice. "If all the beggars in Trastevere had your education, we could blow the whole German army to hell."

Vittoria ignored him as she switched on a bare light bulb suspended from the ceiling, her eyes running over a workbench in the corner. She picked up a piece of black cast iron pipe, about four inches in diameter and a foot long; Renzo could see that a wad of plaster covered one end, but that the pipe was empty. "From this, I can make a bomb." She caressed the pipe provocatively, causing Renzo to blush.

Reaching into one of several cartons pushed against the wall she pulled out a candle-sized cylinder wrapped in blue waxy paper. "TNT." She tossed the cylinder from hand to hand, then suddenly threw the package toward Renzo.

He was sure his heart stopped as his fingers desperately sought to catch the bundle, which landed with a thud on the floor. "In the name of God, Vittoria, don't ever try that with me again!"

She smiled. "Didn't anyone ever tell you that TNT won't blow without a detonator?" Her smile bubbled up into a giggle.

"And didn't anyone ever tell you, Vittoria, that you're a bitch?"

Maria's Apartment.

"Gin!" Jay Mack spread his hand on the table. "Lucky again, eh, David?"

Lawrence tossed down his cards. "Too rich for my blood, Jay."

"The meal will be on the table in five minutes," Maria called from the kitchen.

"I can hardly wait," Nolan called back.

MacPherson gathered up the cards. "Any more thoughts on helping out with the POW organization, David?"

Lawrence looked down at the table and sighed. "Not sure, Jay. Maybe I could help out if you've got real translation problems with padrones who speak only Italian." He shrugged his shoulders. "Otherwise, I'd rather steer clear of it. And your Italian is improving no end – you'll be fine on your own." He offered a lame smile. "Fact of the matter is I've got other things I need to do."

"Hah!" Nolan laughed derisively. "So a Brit POW who's holed up in a safe place with a comfortable bed and a terrific cook can't be bothered to help other escaped POWs who aren't so lucky. Because," his voice became sarcastic, "it doesn't fit into his busy schedule. Can you beat that? So what keeps you so busy, English – you giving guided tours to the sights of Rome?"

"I don't have to put up with this!" Lawrence leapt up and stormed into the kitchen.

"My, my. Rather touchy, isn't he?" Nolan leaned back and twiddled his thumbs.

"Take it easy on him, Buck. We're all under pressure."

"Granted. We're lying low, and that's got its drawbacks. But if he's under so much pressure, why does he pussyfoot in and out of here every day, huh?" Nolan rose from the sofa. "All I'm saying is that maybe he's up to something fishy. Myself, I think maybe we ought to keep an eye on the Limey."

"Aw, loosen up on him, Buck."

"Okay, okay. But let me tell you again my offer's still good – I'm willing to help you out with the POWs. I'm willing to do anything, even the grunt work."

"We talked about this before, Buck. You can't speak any Italian. You can't help."

"Okay, have it your way. But don't say I never asked. Anyway, let's get into the kitchen – it wouldn't do to let Maria's swell grub get cold."

A Building on the Via della Scrofa.

Renzo looked down at the TNT package on the floor. "Enough of your silly tricks." He spoke firmly, but without anger, although his eyes flashed. "Enough." He breathed emphasis into the word.

The smile faded from Vittoria's lips. What she had intended as a joke had hit a raw nerve. She had wounded more than his masculinity, although there was a hint of that. His next words confirmed her thoughts.

"Perhaps I'm not as clever as you are. Perhaps I can't make bombs." For a moment his eyes broke away from hers, then returned. "But I'm one of the guys who's going to place those bombs."

"I know that." Vittoria sought to make amends. "Would you like me to show you how to make one?"

"Sure." He picked up the package of TNT from the floor and placed it in her hands.

She broke open the package and began to stuff the contents into the hollow cast-iron pipe. "The important thing to remember is to leave a slot that can take the detonator." She pushed a pencil into the soft explosive, creating a channel into which she threaded a small detonator. Her hands worked a plaster cast to close the open end of the pipe and she crimped the fuse at the other end of the tube. *"Eccolo!* One *spezzone!"*

"Spezzone?"

"That's what we call these bombs. So all we need to do is apply a lit cigarette here, and thirty seconds later, Boom! *Requiescat in pace,* German invaders."

Renzo looked at the metal pipe in Vittoria's hands. "So that's it? That's all there is to making a bomb?" He shook his head when Vittoria smiled and nodded. "You don't need a university degree in chemistry to make that!"

"And you don't need to be a logistics expert to plant a bomb among the Germans." Her smile vanished as she sensed his hostility. "You heard the order from Dante. You and I have been designated as a team. We've got to place this bomb among the German convoy that parks in front of the Opera House every night. Next Friday. At five-thirty."

October 29, 1943

NEAR THE PIAZZA DEL POPOLO.

MacPherson strolled along the Via di Monserrato cloaked in his disguise of a brown suit and a Borsolino hat. The day was warm, and the rays of the late afternoon sun were imparting a honey-colored glow to the travertine walls and columns of the old buildings he passed. In the Piazza del Popolo a number of couples were enjoying the last vestiges of Indian summer, and he looked around and sighed at all the beautiful women of Rome he knew he would never meet.

He'd just come out of one of his scheduled meetings with Father Francesco and was going to check out the padrone at the address at the top of the list he had just memorized. Having almost mastered the organization of POW safe houses made him feel pride and a sense of accomplishment.

Number twelve on the Via Panzani. The padrone was a new one, a Signora Adriana Corvo. Looking up and down the street to check for police, he side-stepped into a doorway, ostensibly to light a cigarette, but also to check the old creased map Father Francesco had given him. MacPherson was quite pleased with his increasing knowledge of the streets of Rome; he'd always had a good sense of direction and now more than ever he needed it.

Via Panzani, 12. The place must be ritzy because 'Villa Ranieri' had been written after the address on the sheet Father Francesco had given him to memorize. Somewhere above the Palazzo del Popolo, the priest had told him. He located the street on the map. Exit the northern gate of the piazza, four blacks ahead, turn left. Perhaps he should have asked Lawrence to come with him, but his own Italian was becoming more proficient every day, thanks to his daily chats with Maria.

Maria. He left the piazza, whistling happily as he ambled along. He loved his chats with Maria and wished his Italian could hurry up and advance beyond household objects and observations about the weather. Perhaps he might invite her out for dinner at—

"*Alt! Alt!*" The German command startled him and the whistle died on his lips. With a start he realized he had been whistling *In the Mood,* the theme song of the Glenn Miller Orchestra.

Piazza by the Opera House.

Vittoria felt nervous – she was well aware of the risks involved in their mission. Her hand shook as she passed the bomb to Renzo. "Here, put this in the deep pocket inside your overcoat." Parked in the Piazza Gigli in front of the Teatro dell' Opera were the German trucks which were to be the target of their bomb.

It would be their first attack on the Germans. Previously, the group had sought out only Italian fascists, but Bartoli had decided the time was ripe to attack the Nazi occupier. Vittoria recalled his words: 'You will strike the first blow for the freedom of Rome. The Nazis must be made to realize that they cannot walk the streets of Rome unscathed; they will then begin to fear every turn of every corner in the city.'

"You okay?" Renzo checked the fuse on the bomb before concealing the steel tube in his pocket. "What's on your mind, Vittoria?"

"Nothing really. I was just thinking about what Bartoli said."

"He's a leader." Renzo shrugged. "Leaders have to spout a lot of pompous words. Makes them feel important."

"But he's right, Renzo!" Her eyes flashed. "We have to attack the Germans – we have no choice."

Renzo heard her words but saw the tremor in her hands and knew she was trying to talk herself into doing something that, deep down, she didn't want to do. For him, attacking the Germans was an easy choice. The sounds of German soldiers dragging away the Jews of the ghetto still rang in his ears; the memory of Luisa sobbing for her lost parents would remain fresh until his dying day. "Come on. Let's go do as the leader asked."

Her forced smile was almost a grimace and the shaking of her hands became more pronounced. Renzo raised an eyebrow. Perhaps she wasn't Miss High-and-Mighty after all.

NEAR THE PIAZZA DEL POPOLO.

MacPherson heard the bullet zing off the pavement as he willed his legs to their limit to escape. The Borsolino hat flew from his head as he ran, bobbing and weaving through the crowd. A second bullet made every bystander fall to the pavement, but his only thought was to make it to the safe house at number 12, Via Panzani.

He chanced a look behind him. The German soldiers were a block away, having lost some time by stopping to take shots at him. He turned and ran for his life, realizing that, as an American in civilian clothes, capture would mean he'd be shot as a spy. Fear sent an impulse to his legs and they sped up, jumping nimbly over people who had flattened themselves on the ground.

One more block to the left. He turned onto Via Panzani, his eyes searching the numbers. 20, 18, 16... In thirty seconds, the German soldiers would get to the turning. Number 12 – he had found it. Twenty seconds. He hammered on the door. Nothing. Ten seconds. He hammered louder. Open, damn you, open!

PIAZZA BY THE OPERA HOUSE.

As the sun began to dip below the buildings on the western side of the Piazza Gigli, Vittoria and Renzo sat on a wall opposite the Opera House pretending to be lovers, embracing to divert the curiosity of any passers-by. Renzo had anticipated playing this role with considerable pleasure, but at that moment his mind was elsewhere.

The edges of the piazza were jammed with German trucks which, Vittoria and Renzo knew, were packed with supplies and ammunition for the German forces in the south around Cassino. The Nazis used the Opera House piazza and other such places to avoid American bombing: they knew the Allies would never drop bombs on the center of Rome.

"That's the one," Renzo whispered in Vittoria's ear as he tilted his head toward a large gas tanker. "When that one blows, the rest will go up with it."

Vittoria nodded her agreement and cast her eyes around the piazza. No one. She rejoiced that they had found the square deserted.

"I think we should do it now," she whispered back. "I'm amazed there's no German guard."

"They've never been attacked before. Perhaps they're overconfident."

He felt the tight squeeze of Vittoria's hand on his arm and his breathing quickened as he swiftly lit a cigarette. One last look around. He could not stop his hand from shaking as he opened his overcoat and applied the lit cigarette to the bomb fuse in his deep pocket. Vittoria gasped as the fuse spluttered into life. They had fifteen seconds to place the bomb and then get to safety.

Renzo ran toward the gas tanker and reached for the bomb in his pocket.

Vittoria gasped in horror as he struggled to free the bomb from his coat pocket: it was snagged. Her instinct was to run, to get away as fast as possible.

Villa Ranieri.

After an eternity, the door at 12 Via Panzani opened to reveal a woman who was clearly startled to see such an apparition in her doorway. Jay struggled for words. "Tedeschi!" He pointed down the street. "Soldati!"

She pulled him inside and slammed the door. "Please speak in English – I'll understand you better. Are the Germans chasing you?"

"Yes." MacPherson struggled to recover his breath.

"So that's what the shooting was about."

"I was given your address as a safe house. I'm pretty sure they saw me come in here."

"It wasn't very smart of you to lead them to a safe house." She scowled and shook her head as she thought. "Now you've put us *all* in danger. Either we find you a hiding place here or you'll have to get out of here. What's your name?"

"Jay."

"Well, Mr. Jay, I suggest we go up to the top floor – maybe you can get away over the roofs. But it's a big jump to the roof of the house next door."

Jay began to rush to the staircase.

"No, come this way. It'll be faster if we take the elevator."

"Elevator?"

"Giorgio! Vieni qui!" she shouted.

A young boy appeared at the top of the stairs. *"Si, Mamma."*

She spoke rapidly to the boy as she led MacPherson down the hall, pushing him into the small elevator and squeezing in behind. She slammed the collapsible grille door and set the contraption in motion. The cage shuddered before beginning a slow, rattling ascent.

"What did you say to the boy?"

"I told him to delay the Germans as long as he can. But it won't buy us much time." She scowled and shook her head. "They'll soon push their way in and, to be honest, I'm sure the gap between the two roofs is too far for you to jump." He was dismayed by the look of desperation in her eyes. "I'm afraid it doesn't matter where I hide you. If the Germans do a thorough search, they're sure to find you."

Piazza by the Opera House.

With a desperate heave, Renzo managed to wrench the bomb from his coat and quickly wedge it under the rounded side of the tanker. "Run, Vittoria, run!"

Renzo sped after her, catching up to her just as they rounded a corner. He grabbed her in desperation and pulled her down to the sidewalk; he could feel her body tense against his.

The explosion partially deafened them. The first blast of the bomb was quickly followed by the conflagration of the gas tanker. Vittoria heard the crashing of glass as every window of the Opera House imploded. Then came the blast of hot air, pulling at their clothes, driving the breath from their lungs.

Renzo struggled to his feet, fighting for his breath. The square was brighter than in daylight. Of the gas tanker, little remained. All the other trucks, coated with the exploded gasoline, were burning fiercely.

He bent down and helped Vittoria to her feet. As an after-effect of the extreme tension, he felt a burst of euphoria and began to laugh. "Perhaps we should do this more often!" He watched in awe as a truck full of ammunition began to explode.

"Come on, let's get out of here." Vittoria, still holding his hand, began to tug at him. "Only next time, I'll use a thirty-second fuse!"

Villa Ranieri.

"I'll take your word about the jump to the next-door roof." Jay wondered why he was whispering to the woman as the elevator rattled its way up to the top floor.

"But if you're not going to jump, where are you going to hide?" Adriana tapped her foot impatiently as she waited for the elevator doors to open on the top floor.

100

Jay followed her out of the elevator into the hall. "There must be somewhere where there's access to the elevator motors." He looked around the floor, anxious at the sound of sirens he could hear through the windows.

Adriana leaned over the banister and looked down into the ground floor hall where the boy stood looking up at her, wide-eyed, by the door. "If anyone knocks, Giorgio, keep them waiting," she shouted to him.

She turned back to Jay. "Whenever the man comes to service the elevator, he goes through there," she said, pointing to a small door set in an alcove.

The sudden and emphatic knocking on the front door caused them both to start. Jay ran to the alcove and pulled on the door. "It's locked. Quick, where's the key?"

"How would I know?" she cried out with outstretched arms. "I live here – I don't repair elevators."

The knocking became louder, and Jay could hear the guttural shouts of German soldiers through the door. "It's a Yale lock. Quick, get me a knife!"

She rushed into a nearby bedroom and emerged with an implement from a manicure set. "Will this do? Giorgio, don't let them in, whatever you do!"

"But Mamma, they're beginning to break down the door!"

"I'd better go down and help my son fend them off."

"Don't take the elevator!" he shouted after her. As he thrust the small knife into the gap between the jamb and the door, he could hear the rapid-fire clicks of her shoes descending on the marble steps. Sweat broke out on his brow as he heard her voice echo up from the downstairs hall in words he could not understand but which clearly were said in anger. The blade moved again, and at last the lock sprang open. Heavy boots were pounding up the stairs as he ducked into the alcove and pulled the door shut behind him, the lock clicking home.

Inside, he could see nothing at first in the darkness, and he cursed as his head hit a beam in the low ceiling. He dropped to his haunches, listening silently, but all he could hear was a hubbub of chatter.

"I demand to know why you're here," Adriana shouted at the policeman. "I'll have you know I'm a friend of the questore."

"Quite so, signora," the policeman replied as he continued up the stairs with barely a glance in her direction. "But these two German soldiers said they were chasing a possible escaped American prisoner, and they saw him enter this house."

"Do I seem like the sort of woman who would harbor criminals, Inspector?"

"Of course not, signora," the policeman forced a smile, "and the soldiers will not have to impose upon you once they've searched the house. They'll start at the top. One of my men is down below in case the escaped prisoner entered without your knowledge and tries to flee out the door."

At last MacPherson's eyes began to adjust, aided by a sliver of light that came through under the door he had entered. The attic was low-ceilinged, heavy with dust, full of storage boxes and bric-a-brac. Crawling past the boxes, he found the small opening that led to the elevator's motor and apparatus. He shuffled his way toward it, still squatting to avoid the beams. Dust rose up and caught his nose. He sneezed.

"Gentlemen, please search anywhere you like. Why don't you start over here." She led the policeman and the German soldiers to a balcony. "Perhaps your criminal jumped to the next roof."

The men assessed the twelve-foot gap, looked at each other, and shook their heads.

"We're wasting time, signora. We'll decide where to conduct our search," the Italian policeman said, making his way toward a door.

"Oh, by all means, why don't you start there," she cried after them. "That's my bedroom – who knows what you may find there?"

Jay's eyes could just make out what lay beyond the opening at the back of the small room: the roof of the elevator, the pulley, the wires. Still crouching, he made his way to the small opening. As he reached it, he looked down the gap between the elevator and the walls of the shaft. Instinctively, his eyes pulled away from the forty-foot drop to the ground floor below. He dragged himself onto the roof of the elevator, carefully keeping his hands away from the pulley and the wires. His movements disturbed the dust and he fought a strong urge to sneeze again.

"Are you satisfied, gentlemen?" Adriana's assumed smug smile hid her tension as the officers returned from searching all her rooms. "Did you find anything of interest?" She turned to confront them. "I trust you'll be leaving now."

"Just as soon as we've finished our search, signora," the policeman answered coolly. He opened the door to a bathroom and checked the linen closet, then returned. "Well, I think that's—wait a moment," he said, pointing to the alcove door, "what's that?"

"It's a service door. The elevator repairman uses it."

The officer walked to the door and tugged on it. "It's locked."

"Of course it's locked – the serviceman has the key." She struggled to keep her voice from betraying her anxiety. "If you wait a moment, I can get you his address and you can—"

"No need," said the officer briskly as he turned to the soldiers. "Break it down," he ordered.

Jay froze as he heard the splintering of the lock. Motionless, he clung noiselessly to the roof of the elevator, trying to keep his breathing as shallow as possible.

"How dare you do that?" The woman's voice came through the dark. "That's private property!"

The inspector said nothing as he crouched in the small alcove door. Jay could see only the dim light behind the storage boxes which hid him from view. He heard a cry and a muffled curse and guessed the Italian had hit his head on the overhead beam. The light dimmed as the officer backed out of the space and pulled the door closed behind him.

"I've never known such disrespect for the private property of a Roman citizen!" Adriana shouted. "You may rest assured that my complaint will be on the desk of the questore first thing in the morning. I expect the police department to pay every lira for the repair."

"But of course, signora," mumbled the inspector, gently rubbing his left temple. "For now, we will go." He stepped into the elevator and pressed the button.

Jay tensed as he heard the grille gates of the elevator rattle open and bang shut. He braced himself for the shudder

104

of the car as the machinery began to whirr into action, and he prayed his hands were clear of the wires and pulleys. His stomach lurched as the gears sprang into motion and the elevator began its descent. The hum of the wires buzzed in his ears, and it seemed an eternity before the old car rocked to a halt. The grille door creaked open and closed, then he heard footsteps and voices, and finally the sound of the front door being slammed shut. After a few moments, the elevator door opened and he heard the woman's heels click inside.

"They've gone. You can come out now."

"That's swell, but I can only get out on the top floor. Please send the elevator back up," he said, allowing himself a sigh and bracing himself for the rocky ride back.

"Well, we had a stroke of luck there, mister," Adriana said crossly as the American emerged from the alcove door.

Jay wiped his palms on his trousers and pulled himself erect. "Name's Jay, ma'am. Sure sorry about all the trouble. Perhaps I should explain why I came." He cleared his throat. "It's about the POW organization—"

"I think this is not an opportune moment, Mr. Jay. Later, perhaps."

"Then I guess I'll be on my way."

"You'll do no such thing." She walked to the window and looked both ways down the street. "The Italian police may be fascists, Mr. Jay, but they're not stupid. I can't see anything, but I'm sure there'll be a policeman down the block watching the door. They saw you come in here after all."

"Back door?"

"They'll be watching that, too." She reached for the telephone. "We have to try a little subterfuge." Her conversation on the telephone was too fast for Jay to understand.

After twenty minutes, a carpenter arrived and started to fix the lock and alcove door while Giorgio, mouth agape, sat quietly as his mother directed a steady flow of Italian at him.

Jay, anxious to leave, could contain himself no longer. "Could you please let me know what's happening, signora?"

"Oh, forgive me, Mr. Jay. I should have explained it to you. Please," she said, motioning to him to sit down. "When the carpenter is finished with his repair, you will take his coat, cap, and toolkit and leave here with Giorgio."

"But won't the police know something is wrong?"

"Why should they? They saw an Italian carpenter enter – and then he leaves."

"But how does your son Giorgio fit in?"

"He'll leave with you and will speak non-stop Italian to you. And the way Giorgio speaks, the policemen will hear every word."

"But I won't understand what he says."

"No need. Just say '*si, si*' every so often, and if you can manage an occasional '*va bene,*' that would help as well."

Jay thought for a moment. "I don't like it. I'll be putting your boy at considerable risk."

Adriana rose to her feet and placed her hands on her hips. "And you'll be putting him – and me – at even greater risk if you don't get out of here!"

"I understand. But what about the carpenter? If they search the house, they'll find him. "

"With his thick Sicilian accent, he's not a likely candidate for an escaped American prisoner of war. Besides, his papers are in order and he can confirm who he is with a call to his employer. By that time, you'll be far away. " She looked at her watch. "I suggest you leave in twenty minutes. Why don't you practice with Giorgio?"

She spoke to her son, who shot up with enthusiasm, grabbing Jay's hand and taking him into the front hall. As he walked

Jay up and down the corridor, he babbled away in non-stop Italian. Finally, an inflection indicated a question.

Jay, stepping into his role on cue, said, *"Si, si. "*

Adriana began to titter, then Giorgio, then the two of them were howling with laughter.

Jay scowled. "I don't get it. What did I do wrong?"

"Giorgio asked," Adriana clapped her hand over her mouth as she tried to stop laughing, "Giorgio asked you if you thought the Duce would look even more handsome sporting Hitler's mustache."

Jay looked crestfallen. "I don't think I can carry this off."

Adriana stifled her laughter. "It was a joke, Mr. Jay! A joke!"

MARIA'S APARTMENT.

Maria hummed softly as she worked. The cleaning of her apartment complete, she could now devote her full attention to preparing dinner for her guests. Slicing the onions stung her eyes, and she quickly tossed the rings into the hot oil, let them sizzle for a few seconds, then stirred them with a wooden spoon.

Over the past weeks, she had become comfortable with the three men. They were well-behaved – quiet and discrete, although they occasionally went out for a drink at a local bar. She liked the Englishman, always so courteous and proper, and his fluency in Italian made her work so much easier. Buck, the scrappy American with reddish hair and broad shoulders, had put her off at first, but she had learned to overlook the remarks he made that were apparently jokes she didn't understand, and he never failed to compliment her on her cooking. Most of all she liked the tall, good-looking major, who helped her with small chores and always tried to speak to her in the few words of Italian he knew.

Her knife quickly diced the beef heart. Even offal was difficult to come by at the black market. She had to shop there since the men had no ration cards, and she couldn't remember when she had last seen a chop or a steak. She added the pieces of heart to the onions, savoring the aroma. It wasn't much to give her guests, but a glass or two of red wine would round out the meal.

Two cubed potatoes left over from the previous night's meal were added to the mix. Like everyone else in the neighborhood, she desperately hoped the Allies would arrive soon. She knew the risk she took hiding the prisoners of war, but she took those risks gladly. She despised the fascists – they had sent Marco to fight on the Russian front. She hadn't seen her husband in four hundred and twelve days, and his last letter arrived almost three months ago.

The door to the kitchen opened. "Wow! That sure smells delicious! *Delizioso!*" MacPherson's tongue stumbled over the new Italian word he had just learned. "Can I do anything to help?"

"Thank you, Jay." She handed him the wooden spoon. "You can stir this while I cut up some garlic." Now relaxed in the presence of her guests, she had become more confident in speaking English. They worked in silence for some moments.

"Tell me, Jay. Are you married?" She glanced over at him shyly as she peeled a garlic clove.

"Me? Nah," he said, pushing the spoon around the pan mechanically.

"Do you have a girl in America?"

A smile came to Jay's lips. "Nope. Still waiting for some lucky lady to snap me up. Had a girl I was almost engaged to. Met her in college and dated her for several years after we graduated, but we broke up a few months before I shipped off. Guess our backgrounds were too different – she was high class, my folks are more blue collar." He looked up from the frying pan he was stirring. "Of course, sometimes having different backgrounds can add spice to a special friendship, don't you think?"

"I'm not sure—" Her words were cut short by the ringing of the telephone. "Excuse me, Jay."

She put down the knife and rubbed her hands on her apron as she walked into the hall to answer the call. "*Pronto,*" she said into the receiver.

"*La tua zia è ammalata,*" came the voice from the other end of the line. *Your aunt is sick.*

Maria slammed the receiver into the cradle and ran out of the hall.

OUTSIDE THE EXCELSIOR HOTEL.

Sofia's right hand clutched tightly at the pistol in her pocket as she walked along the Via Veneto with Ludovico at her side. The gun felt both reassuring and frightening.

This mission was different from any they had done. Bartoli's orders were clear. A German captain left the office of a high-ranking officer in the Excelsior Hotel every weekday at three. He was a courier, taking messages and documents to German army headquarters.

Sofia recalled Bartoli's words. "You are to shoot him and get Cesare to bring his briefcase to the statue of Pasquino behind the Piazza Navona. I'll meet him there at four."

Shoot him. Her hand tightened nervously on the pistol. She'd been on several missions, but she'd never killed anyone. Sofia forced herself to think of their friend, Bernardo, who had been taken to Gestapo headquarters on the Via Tasso. He hadn't been seen since.

"You okay?" Ludovico's voice brought her back to the present. "Look, if you want, I can—"

"No!" Sofia spat out the word. "I'll do it!"

Ludovico said nothing but nodded in the direction of the hotel across the street. The officer had emerged from the revolving door and was making his way down the staircase. Sofia's eyes were drawn to the face of the man she had to kill: sharply drawn jaws, narrow-set eyes beneath his peaked cap. She forced her eyes to fix on the briefcase: German secrets, secrets that would help the Resistance.

"We'll follow him for three blocks." They began to trail the officer at a safe distance. "Then we'll check to make sure there are no police around before..." She let the sentence die.

MARIA'S APARTMENT.

"Maria, quando—" MacPherson forgot the rest of the sentence he had carefully constructed in Italian when Maria flew in and turned off the gas under the skillet.

"What's up, Maria? *Che succede?"*

"Dov'è l'inglese?" She reverted to her native language, wringing her hands nervously. "Where's the Englishman?"

She turned and threw open the door to the small living room. Lawrence looked up from his book and put it aside when he saw the anxiety on her face. They spoke rapidly.

"Say, what's going on?" Nolan put his cards down on the small table where he was playing solitaire and stood up.

Lawrence leapt up from the sofa. "We have to get out of here!"

"What, and leave that wonderful dinner I can smell cooking?"

"It's serious, Buck." Lawrence began to pick up his things. "Collect your stuff. The fascist police are on their way over here."

"How does she know?" MacPherson spoke from the doorway.

"Yeah, how does she know?" Nolan chimed in.

"Because she received a coded message by telephone." He stuffed his reading glasses into his rucksack. "There's a mole at the front desk of the San Stefano Police Station. Come on – we've got to move fast." Maria grabbed Lawrence's arm and spoke rapidly. "She says they'll be here in fifteen minutes. Hurry – let's get the cots put away."

They rushed into the small room at the back where they slept and folded up the bivouac cots.

"Bring them in here!" Maria ran into her room, pressed a catch, and motioned for them to stow the cots in a compartment that opened in the wall.

"Well, would you get a load of that," said Nolan. "A secret hidey-hole."

Jay pushed past him and shoved the cots into the space and Maria closed the door so it was flush with the wall.

"So now what do we do?" said Nolan, picking up his cards and adding them to his bag.

"We can maybe go for a drink – there's still two hours to curfew. Whose is that?" MacPherson pointed to a copy of *The*

Oxford Book of Selected English Verse lying on the arm of the sofa.

"Mine," Lawrence said. "Has anyone seen my cigarettes?"

"Hey, shouldn't we be sticking around to protect Maria?" Nolan asked.

"No! You must go!" Maria stamped her foot. *"Andate via! Get out of here!"*

"Well, I sure got my answer there." Nolan followed Lawrence and MacPherson to the door.

Maria watched from the hall as the three men trundled down the stairs and slammed the front door behind them. She was about to turn to go back into her apartment but stopped. The door to her neighbor's ground floor apartment was ajar and Maria was sure she had just seen an eye in the gap before the door was gently closed.

NEAR PIAZZA BARBERINI.

The German officer walked briskly and Sofia had almost to run to keep pace. He had turned off the Via Veneto onto a side street and was now on the Via di San Basilio.

"Come on, Sofia, we've got to catch up with him!" Ludovico whispered, tugging on her arm as he quickened his step. He knew they couldn't draw attention to themselves by running, but Sofia was clearly having difficulty keeping up. "Perhaps you should give the pistol to me."

She answered with a brief glare at her husband as she forced her legs to move faster.

"We have to do it before we reach the Piazza Barberini, Sofia. Too many people there."

She said nothing, but his use of the word 'we' annoyed her. She was the one who would be pulling the trigger.

"Wait!" Ludovico grabbed her arm. The officer had stopped halfway along the deserted street. The German shook his head, as if he had forgotten something. Suddenly he turned and began walking back towards them.

Maria's Apartment.

The slow, deliberate knock on the front door surprised Maria, even though she knew it would come. She breathed deeply for a few moments, checked her hair in the mirror in the hall, and fixed a smile on her face before opening the door.

"Buona sera, signori," she said, using all the warmth she could muster.

"Polizie, signora." The man at the door raised his hat as he produced his badge.

"What can I do for you, *Ispettore?*" She recognized the inspector; she'd seen him in the bar she used to tend on Friday and Saturday nights. The man standing behind the inspector she didn't know.

"You are Maria Silvestri?"

"Yes."

"We have come to search your apartment, Signora Silvestri." The inspector took a step forward.

Maria held her ground. "Whatever for?"

"There have been reports, signora."

"Reports? Of what?"

"Of men frequently coming to this apartment." His hand reached inside his coat. "Naturally, I have a search warrant with me."

"There's no need for such formalities. Please come in, gentlemen."

As she closed the door behind them she managed a playful laugh. "Of course men come here often. My father-in-law and his two sons come all the time to help out. You see, my husband, Marco, is fighting on the Russian front. Putting his life on the line for the Duce." Unlike the two of you, she thought. "Times are hard, and it seems something is always broken in this place. Marco's father and his two brothers are kind enough to help me." She fixed the inspector with an earnest gaze and had the satisfaction of seeing him avert his eyes.

"I am truly sorry, signora, but if I may—"

"Yes, please, look around wherever you want." She waved her hand in acquiescence and led the two men into the living room. As soon as she entered, she saw it: *The Oxford Book of Selected English Verse* still lay on the arm of the sofa.

NEAR PIAZZA BARBERINI.

"Now, Sofia," Ludovico hissed in her ear.

The officer was almost upon them. Sofia hadn't expected him to be so close when she pulled the trigger, hadn't expected to look into his eyes. She had imagined a shot in the back from a distance, a rush to pick up the briefcase, a run to escape. But now she saw his face, his thin lips, his puzzled gaze.

"Now, Sofia, for Christ's sake, now!"

Her hand shook as she pulled the pistol from her pocket and aimed. The bullets barely made a sound as they entered the man. She could see two holes in his uniform, then a slow trickle of blood, then a dark stain expanding beneath the fabric. His eyes looked at her in blank surprise for a few moments before he slowly collapsed on the cobbles.

"Quick, Ludo, get the briefcase!"

He reached the fallen man quickly and picked up the briefcase. Turning to go, he felt the case tug at his hand. "Hell, the damned thing's on a security chain!" There was panic in his voice as the officer began to struggle. "I've got to get his belt off."

As Ludovico's fingers reached for the buckle, now slick with blood, there was a grunt as the officer tried to resist. *"Nein! Nein!"*

"Give him another one, Sofia – now!"

Somehow, the German found the strength to turn to look at her as she leveled the pistol at his head. She began to squeeze the trigger.

"Got it!" Ludovico shouted. "Let's get out of here!"

The German's head fell lifeless to the pavement, his open eyes staring blankly at the sky.

MARIA'S APARTMENT.

Trying to avoid any show of panic, Maria ambled across the room and sat on the sofa, draping her hand over the slim volume of poetry.

"As you can see, gentlemen, I have a collection of keepsakes here in the living room. They have sentimental value to me, so please don't break any of them." Her request seemed to whet their appetite to examine the curio shelves immediately, and as they checked inside vases and looked under figurines, she slipped the book of poems into the pocket of her apron. The Englishman had been foolishly careless.

When they had searched all the other rooms thoroughly, the inspector asked, "Is there no children's room, signora?"

"No." She tried to keep anger out of her voice. "Marco and I were married only two weeks before he had to ship off."

"I'm sorry, signora. Of course, we all have to make sacrifices."

She would have liked to have asked him what sacrifices he had made, but she bit her tongue.

He sniffed the air and made his way to the kitchen. "You've been cooking, signora?"

"My brothers-in-law are visiting. It's a special treat for them."

"Indeed!" He made a show of writing in his small notebook and then snapped it shut. "Well, signora, I apologize for disturbing you. It appears there's been a mistake." He nodded to his subordinate and they made for the door.

"No apology is necessary. I realize that, in your line of work, each lead must be investigated." She afforded him a wide smile as she closed the door and reached for the phone.

The two policemen were at the end of the street when she replaced the receiver. She hoped the fascist spies who eavesdropped on everyone's telephone calls weren't paying too close attention to her conversation. Her brothers-in-law would stop by to back up her story.

Peeking through the curtain, she could see the inspector looking back at her apartment and she knew he'd be back. The mole would be able to keep her informed, she hoped; in the meantime, she had to make sure, every minute of every day, that she was on her guard.

RENZO'S APARTMENT IN TRASTEVERE.

Renzo's first reaction to the knock on the door to his apartment was to look at the clock. It was nine – only half an hour until curfew. Who would come knocking at such an hour? The fascist police? The Gestapo?

The knock was repeated, a little more insistent. Renzo opened the door a crack and knew at once that, while he was not in danger, the bearer did not bring good news. It was the man in whose apartment little Luisa was staying. From time to time Renzo sent a few lire to help with her upkeep, but he had never gone back for the child.

"Good evening, Signor Benedetti. Please come in." Renzo looked up and down the hall for prying eyes before he closed the door. "I imagine you've come about Luisa. Please have a seat."

"No, thank you. I'll only be a minute." Signor Benedetti shuffled uneasily.

"How is Luisa?"

"She's as well as can be expected, but I'm afraid I must be honest with you, Signor Rossi." He paused, searching for the right words. "The situation is not good."

"Is Luisa ill?" Renzo asked with growing concern.

"No, no – nothing like that." Signor Benedetti hesitated. "It's difficult for me to say this…" He paused and took a deep breath. "To be honest, we can no longer afford to keep the child." His voice became distant. "Because she's a Jew, we can't apply for a ration card for her…I'm sure you understand. I'm a carpenter. There's no work anymore."

"I'll give you some more money for her food." Renzo reached into his pocket.

"It's not just a question of money for her food." Signor Benedetti shook his head. "The child is miserable, disconsolate. She cries all the time, she asks for her mother and father. We don't know what to tell her." He looked down at the floor, ashamed of his failure. "We can't let her out on the street to play – the Germans still patrol the area for Jews."

"But I can't bring her here." Renzo looked around his cramped apartment.

Signor Benedetti looked imploringly at Renzo. "You must understand that my wife can take no more. She's a woman of delicate sensibilities, and it breaks her heart to see the child so distraught. My wife can do nothing for little Luisa, nothing to make her happy. My wife, she weeps all night."

"I understand." Renzo's mind raced. "I need three days – maybe four – to make some arrangements. Then I'll come to take Luisa off your hands."

Signor Benedetti's face relaxed in profound relief as he grabbed Renzo's hand to shake it. "Thank you, thank you Signor Rossi. Now I must be off – it's nearly curfew. And I must get home and tell my wife."

When the door clicked shut, Renzo slumped into his threadbare armchair and thought about the little girl. Skipping rope, cutting her birthday cake – a happy child whose life had been ripped apart. He had only a few days to sort out a solution, to somehow rescue the child.

And he had not the slightest idea of what to do.

PIAZZA DI SANT'AGOSTINO.

Kappler hung back in the shadows of the Via dei Pianellari. He had ditched the uniform of an Obersturmbannführer for the disguise of an ordinary merchant's clerk: pin-striped suit, trilby hat, and highly polished black shoes. In the failing light of the evening, he cast his eyes over the small piazza, looking for the signal he awaited. With the approach of curfew, the rest of the square had been abandoned as people hurried for the safety of their homes.

Kappler circled the small piazza, holding to the growing gloom at the edges. Then he saw it. One, two, three flicks of a lighter before the flame was applied to a cigarette. After carefully looking around, the Gestapo chief walked casually to the man who sat alone at the far end of the third tier of steps leading up to the church.

The man descended the stairs, scanning the square anxiously. "Why did you want to see me?" He took a long drag on his cigarette. "Meeting face to face could be dangerous."

"So could a written communication carelessly handled." Kappler spoke quietly but assuredly. "And in our situation, a middleman cannot even be contemplated." He lit his own cigarette, the flame reflecting off his silver lighter and briefly illuminating the planes of his face. "I need to know what progress you've made."

"I've made good progress. I've identified the leader of the POW operation."

Kappler raised an eyebrow. "And I suppose there are excellent reasons why you've not already reported this to me?"

"Yes, several. The arrest of this man would be a mistake. It could possibly blow my own cover, and, more importantly, if we let him run long enough he'll lead me to the whole network of padrones of the Rome POW organization." The man drew on his cigarette and smiled. "Give me time. What I'll be able to deliver eventually will be worth waiting for."

Kappler looked up at the early Renaissance basilica, its moonlit façade silhouetted against the night sky. "I appreciate your cunning, but you must understand that I'm under a good deal of pressure from Field Marshal Kesselring. He thinks the number of escaped prisoners of war wandering freely around the streets of Rome is a disgrace – it makes us look as though we've lost control. I have to take some action."

"The solution to that problem seems obvious – just arrest a few dozen POWs on the street."

"I could easily do that, but it would only be cosmetic. I need to strike fear into the heart of this POW leader you seem to have identified. I want to paralyze the organization."

The other man paced a few steps, then suddenly turned. "There is a way. A way that would put the leader on notice without implicating me. Do you have something to write with?"

Kappler pulled a small ringed notepad from his coat and a fountain pen from his lapel pocket and handed them over.

"Here's an address for your police to raid," the man in the shadows wrote carefully in block letters, "together with special instructions for them to follow. You should also investigate the front desk of the San Stefano Police Station." He handed the notepad and pen back to the Gestapo chief. "One of the police officers there is a mole for the partisans."

Kappler glanced at the sheet. "It's a start, but you've got to work harder and faster, my friend, if you're going to earn the money I'm paying you." There was an undisguised harshness in his voice. "I need the names and addresses of all the padrones in the network, and I need to be able to get them when I call for them. I have to be in a position to shut down the whole POW operation at a moment's notice. "

Kappler flipped the notepad to a new page and scratched hastily with his pen. "In the meantime, let the benefactors of the operation continue to pay for the POWs' upkeep. I just want them out of sight, but available when I need them." He tore off the sheet and handed it to the man. "Here's where you can reach me – preferably between five and six on Friday afternoons."

The paper disappeared into the man's pocket. "Can I be sure this is a safe number?"

"My dear friend, the telephone is located on the desk of my office at Via Tasso, Gestapo Headquarters. It doesn't get any safer than that." He ground out his cigarette with his heel. "And don't fail me. I need to know that you have all the details of the POW network." He walked away, his heels echoing on the cobbles of the deserted square.

PIAZZA MATTEI.

"I took the briefcase to Bartoli," Cesare said softly as he approached Sofia and Ludovico. He had found the couple sitting on the wrought iron railing that surrounded the Fountain of the Tortoises in the small, deserted piazza. "Seems like you two hit the jackpot." He looked around the piazza to see if there was anyone who might overhear, then leaned over toward them and spoke softly. "He showed the contents to his interpreter who said they were plans of the entire German anti-aircraft emplacements in the area." He grinned from beneath his untidy bush of black hair. "Quite a feather in your caps, I'd say!"

His grin faded when their solemn faces failed to brighten. "Hey, what's the matter, Sofia?" His eyes turned to her husband. "What's going on, Ludo?" He shook his head. "You two pulled off a huge, huge coup and now you're sitting here looking like you've been invited by Herr Kappler to his headquarters at Via Tasso."

"Have you ever killed anyone, Cesare?" Sofia asked bluntly.

"Well, yes, sure," Cesare answered. "I was at a bombing raid at the German barracks some time ago." He smiled. "Killed over a dozen *tedeschi.*"

"Wasn't that with a timed bomb, Cesare?" Sofia looked at him icily. "You were two hundred meters away at the time of the explosion."

"Sure, but I got to see the body parts fly through the air. Say, what is this?"

"What she's saying, Cesare," Ludovico cut in, "is that it's somehow different when you shoot a pistol at someone who's looking you in the face and you get to watch the life drain from his eyes."

Cesare ruffled his hair and thought for a moment. "Yes, perhaps it is." He shrugged. "But whatever, it's just another dead German. You shouldn't be so sensitive, comrades."

"It's not a question of being sensitive, Cesare." There was a small tremble in Sofia's voice. "It's when you see the humanity of, well…" She hesitated and shrugged her shoulders, unable to explain herself and feeling on the verge of tears.

Cesare was unmoved. "The Germans have lots of barbarity left, and there's a lot of them left to kill. Anyway, Bartoli wants to see you. Maybe he wants to congratulate you, so cheer up." He stood up and made to leave. "I've got to get copies of your prize maps into other hands."

He took a few paces, stopped, and turned to them. "It was a lousy job, I know. You did well. And just remember that those maps will save lives. Roman lives."

VILLA RANIERI.

"You all right?" Renzo looked at Vittoria over the edge of her mother's fine crystal wineglass as he sipped his Lambrusco. "You're rather quiet this evening."

"I was just thinking about Sofia." Vittoria looked down into her glass, which she had hardly touched. "She's having a really tough time coming to grips with having shot that German."

Renzo drained the glass and set it down. "She needs to snap out of it if she wants to continue to be useful to the Resistance."

"I agree, but I keep wondering how I would have felt if I had to shoot someone at point-black range." Vittoria put down her glass and walked across the room to stare out of a window. "I told her to remember that the German was the enemy, a part of the evil machine that's killing Romans every day."

"She has to make herself think that way, Vittoria. Remember Bernardo, who disappeared into Gestapo headquarters at the

Via Tasso? No one's heard from him since. Sofia acted for him, if for nothing else."

Renzo's jaw stiffened as anger seized him. "Me, I'd have no compunction in wiping out the lot of them." He brought his fist down on the arm of his chair. "Together with the fascists, they've taken just about everything I have. First my father. Then my mother. Then my people, my community. They've even taken away my identity – I have to go around with false papers, pretend to be someone else." He reflected for a moment. "And now they're even threatening Luisa."

Vittoria arched an eyebrow. "Luisa?"

"She's only a child."

Vittoria was silent for several moments, her eyes darting nervously about the room. "I didn't know you had a child," she said with a catch in her throat.

A brief smile crossed Renzo's lips. "You've got it all wrong, Vittoria. Luisa is a little girl. I rescued her when the Germans raided the ghetto." The smile vanished as the memories returned. "Her mother and father, Emma and Massimo, they were such good people. Friends of mine, but they're gone now. Probably dead."

"But how did the girl survive? Is she still in danger?"

"At the moment, she's with a nice Gentile couple who live on the Via Paganica, just inside the ghetto." He poured a little more of the red wine into his glass. "But they can't keep her any longer." He sighed. "I guess it's hard enough to deal with an unhappy child when she's your own, but when she's some-one's else's, it's really tough. And they haven't the money to feed her. She obviously can't get a ration card, and they can't afford the food on the black market."

"So what are you going to do?"

"Not sure. I've given the couple some cash to keep Luisa fed for awhile, but for them it's not just a question of money. The wife can't deal with Luisa's constant sulking. They can't even let her go outside to play because the Germans are still patrolling that area." He shook his head. "To be honest, I'm not sure what to do. She can't stay at my place in Trastevere. I'm hardly ever there, between meetings of the Resistance and doing odd jobs wherever I can get them for a few lire. Not to mention the fact that I have no experience raising a small child."

"Bring her here, Renzo."

"What?"

"Bring her here." Vittoria began working out the practical details in her mind. "We've got plenty of room. And she'd be quite safe."

"But your mother – the cost—"

"Mamma? She'd love it – she's always up for a new challenge. She'll find a way to make Luisa happy, or die trying. And as for money, well," she looked around at the ornate décor and priceless artwork, "I don't think it'll be a problem. Besides, my mother seems to be able to conjure ration cards out of thin air."

"But the risk to your mother—"

"With all the partisans she puts up with around this place, do you think one little Jewish girl is going to make any difference? But it's the risk to…"

"Luisa."

"…to Luisa that's of more concern." Renzo could almost see the wheels turning in Vittoria's head as the arrangements in her plan began to take shape. "I'll talk with my mother tonight and you and I can go pick up the girl tomorrow. How old is Luisa?"

"She's ten, I think."

"Perfect! She'll make a great playmate for Giorgio." She laughed. "If she can put up with the little monster."

A great warmth washed over Lorenzo. In just a few moments, this wonderful woman had unburdened him of a problem that had kept him awake the entire night. Better still, Vittoria was smiling again.

"You know something, Vittoria?"

She shook her head. "What?"

"You're wonderful."

MARIA'S APARTMENT.

Nolan sighed with contentment as he pushed back his chair from the dinner table, the aroma of garlic sautéed in olive oil still hanging in the air. "Maria, I know you struggle with rationing and shortages and all that, but somehow you always manage to dish up the most wonderful food."

"I'll drink to that." Lawrence gently dabbed his lips with his napkin and held up his almost-empty glass toward his hostess. "I've never had better *spaghetti aglio e olio.*"

"Thank you. You're very kind." Maria stood up and began collecting the plates.

"Hey, where's that big smile we always look forward to, Maria?" MacPherson asked. "You seem a bit down in the dumps."

"I've got a lot on my mind, Jay." She put the dishes in the sink and turned to look at him. There was an awkward silence.

"Well, I guess I can take a hint." Nolan got up from his chair. "Say, English, how about a game of gin rummy? Or are you afraid of getting whupped by a Yank?"

"That's a challenge I couldn't possibly refuse. You'll excuse us, Maria?" Lawrence followed Nolan into the living room.

"Why are Englishmen always so polite, Jay?" Maria gave a sad smile.

"Ouch! So much for American manners, I guess." He winked and smiled at her, but she didn't smile back. "Hey, Maria, something is wrong, isn't it?"

She closed the kitchen door. "Jay, about the raid yesterday…"

"Sure was a close call. Thank God, we all escaped."

"Not all of us."

"Maria, what are you saying?"

"Giancarlo didn't escape."

"Giancarlo?"

"The mole who works at the San Stefano Police Station. He called and warned me about the raid."

"What happened?"

"He was arrested this morning. He's now at Via Tasso."

"Via Tasso?"

"Gestapo headquarters. Jay, I have to ask you and your friends to leave. Tomorrow. For your own safety."

Villa Ranieri.

With Renzo's hand urging her forward, Luisa shuffled in, her eyes downcast, looking at the floor. Renzo had gone with Vittoria that morning to collect the child from the apartment of Signora Benedetti who, though grateful to be relieved of the responsibility of caring for the girl, had cried as she left.

As Renzo and the child walked in, Adriana rose from the sofa, smiled, and clapped her hands. "Oh, Luisa – thank you for coming and welcome." She grasped the child's two hands in hers. "I'm so very happy to meet you!"

Luisa did not reply, her eyes never leaving her shoes.

"Please say hello to Signora Corvo, Luisa," Renzo prompted.

The child responded with little more than a sigh.

"My, what beautiful dark hair you have," Adriana said as she took in the girl's scuffed shoes and frayed dress. "Come, please sit down here beside me on the sofa. Would you like something? A glass of milk maybe?"

Luisa took a seat at the far end of the sofa and shook her head.

Vittoria came in carrying several small dresses on hangers. "Look, Luisa, see what I found in my closet. I used to wear these, but I really think they might look good on you." She held up a blue dress with short, puffy sleeves, an eyelet bib, and a fixed sash that tied in the back. "This one was always my favorite. Isn't it pretty? And now it's yours."

Renzo whispered in Luisa's ear, "What do you say, Luisa?"

"*Grazie,*" came the soft reply.

The child fell silent, her eyes fixed on the carpet. Vittoria was horrified to think the child's mood was her fault, remembering how humiliated she had once felt when someone offered her a hand-me-down. Renzo sighed, understanding full well the great burden that he had laid on Signora Benedetti. Adriana wrapped an arm around Luisa. How futile, even foolhardy, it had been, she thought, to pretend she could bring happiness to the girl just by offering her smiles and a comfortable home; the blow the child had been dealt was one from which she might take years to recover.

The ticking of a clock dominated the room, and Adriana sought to break the awkward silence. "Well, I think I'll just go see about—"

A small but forceful presence bounded in.

"Giorgio!"

"Sorry, Mamma. I didn't know you had company."

"Come over here, Giorgio – there's someone I'd like you to meet."

The boy strode over to Luisa. "Ciao. I'm Giorgio. What's your name?" He thrust out his hand.

"Luisa," came the soft reply as she gave his hand a limp shake.

"Luisa – that's a pretty name. Say, Luisa, I have something you might like to see. Have you ever taken a look at one of these?"

Scowling, she lifted her eyes to a small booklet he held up.

"Watch this, Luisa." As he fanned the pages of the booklet with his thumb, she watched in wonder as the pages came alive.

A man in a tuxedo bows to a woman in a beautiful gown who is seated next to a potted palm. He takes her hand and she rises, and off they go to dance. As they look into each others' eyes, they sway and turn, sway and turn, until the dance ends with a kiss.

"Would you like to try it, Luisa? All you have to do is this." He demonstrated how to fan the pages before handing the little book to Luisa, who was anxious to recapture the magical world of the dancing couple. She flipped through the pages once, twice, three times, and a tiny smile began to appear on her lips before she finally handed the booklet back to the boy.

"I have another book like this, Luisa," Giorgio said. "It's a funny one – a waiter carries a tray in a restaurant and slips on a banana peel. Mamma, may I show my waiter book to Luisa?"

Adriana looked at Luisa, whose smile was broadening in her eagerness, and nodded.

"Come on, Luisa, you've got to see this!" Giorgio led the girl down the hall. "Oh, and I also have some hand puppets you'll love – I could be Pulcinella and you could work Arlecchino. Or maybe you'd rather have a look at the model I made of ancient Rome. And then there's...."

As his voice trailed off, Adriana smiled. "Never again will I doubt the superior wisdom of my ten-year-old son."

VILLA RANIERI. LATER THAT DAY.

A half smile came to Adriana's lips as she answered the knock on the door. "Surely not you again."

"Name's Jay, ma'am, if you remember."

"Oh, I remember you very well – you were the one who brought the fascist police to my house." She quickly looked beyond the two men standing on either side of MacPherson and checked the street.

"You can rest assured, ma'am, that we've been very careful to make sure that no one was following us." Jay offered a shy smile. "And that nobody was watching your house."

With barely a moment's hesitation she bid the three enter and closed the door behind them. "Well, I presume you haven't come to ride the elevator again?" She smiled archly.

"No, ma'am. Let me introduce my fellow officers, RAF Flight Lieutenant David Lawrence and Lieutenant Buck Nolan."

"Officers?" Adriana's eyes ran quickly over the ragtag civilian clothing that served as their disguise. "You all look like beggars to me."

"We're escaped prisoners of war, ma'am," Jay explained.

"Well, what can I do for you, gentlemen?"

Jay cleared his throat. "As you know, when I visited last month I was establishing liaison with you as a padrone of a safe house. What I did not explain was that I am the officer responsible for billeting all prisoners of war in Rome. I am informed that you have three vacancies."

"So, you and your friends want to move in here," Adriana said, nodding her understanding. "As organizing officer I guess you had your choice of the best billet available."

"It may seem that way, ma'am," Jay sought to deny his embarrassment, "but we had to leave our present billet for security reasons. The lady padrone has been visited by the police."

"You seem to have the police following you everywhere you go. I do hope you can break the habit while you're in my house. But now that you're here, let me get you all a drink, if it's not too early in the day for that, so we can get to know each other. Come, let's go up to the drawing room. And please call me Adriana." She smiled, easing the tension.

As she led them up the marble staircase, Lawrence craned his neck and squinted at the tapestries while Nolan, taking in the overall grandeur of the décor, simply emitted a low whistle.

They entered her salon. "Of course you are welcome to stay in my house. Please, have a seat and we'll discuss the rules." She motioned to a group of chairs that faced the fireplace and they all sat down.

"You'll have to be restricted to the cellar and you'll also have to keep quiet. When you must go out, please use the back way. And please stay away from all the others in the house – it'll be better that way. My cleaning staff comes here once a week, and on certain days a woman comes in to prepare food at eleven but leaves before one. They're all trustworthy, but it would be better if they did not know you're here."

"And your butler, signora?" asked Lawrence.

"Killed in North Africa two years ago. I've never replaced him. Good servants are impossible to find nowadays."

She poured scotch into four glasses. "You'll find that it's somewhat damp down in the cellar, but there's a stove and a small kitchen so you'll have heat and also be able to cook for yourselves. And please don't trip over the remnants of the ancient Roman foundations that protrude from the floor on the northern end."

Adriana handed the glasses around and raised hers in the air. "To the liberation of Rome!"

"To an Allied victory in Europe!" Lawrence added.

"To the Krauts getting the bum's rush!" Buck shouted.

"And, most of all, to our gracious new hostess, Adriana!" said Jay, raising his glass.

The three men drained their glasses quickly and with pleasure.

Adriana took a few polite sips and set her glass down. "And now I must go search through my late husband's wardrobe for some better clothes for you. Three down-and-outs entering this place could well arouse suspicion. Besides, whatever would the neighbors think?" A barely-suppressed laugh came from her lips before she stood and headed upstairs.

CHURCH OF SANTA MARIA DELLA GLORIA.

"I don't like that. It's scary," said Luisa, pointing at the sculpture of a grinning skeleton holding an hourglass above the marble sepulcher of a church prelate.

For Giorgio, who had a young boy's taste for the macabre, the funeral monument was one of the highlights of the church, but he did not press his case. "Come on, Luisa, I'll show you something you might like better."

But the mosaic labyrinth on the church floor, its marble tesserae worn down by centuries of pilgrims' feet, also failed to enchant her. While Giorgio, who apparently had mastered the maze on previous visits, began to make his way via a circuitous route toward the image of the dove in the maze's center, Luisa became frustrated with the blind alleys and gave up.

She wandered over to a small marble sarcophagus against a nearby wall and ran her fingers over the low relief of cherubs bearing baskets laden with grapes. The cherubs were climbing enormous vines to pick the fruit, but among the vines were giant birds, twice the size of the cherubs, who thrust their beaks forward to steal the cherubs' harvest.

"It's beautiful, isn't it?"

The deep voice startled her and she looked up to see a priest. "Yes, it is, sir, but, please, can you tell me what it is?"

"It's the casket of a small child who died many years ago. The child must have been greatly loved to have been given such a splendid resting place, don't you think?"

Luisa studied the priest. "Who are you, sir? Are you the rabbi of this temple?"

He smiled warmly. "Yes, in a manner of speaking, I am. And my name is Father Francesco."

Giorgio, having reached the dove in the center of the maze, came over and greeted Father Francesco while Luisa's eyes returned to the small casket. "Why are the birds so big, and why are they stealing the fruit of the little angels?" she asked the priest.

"Perhaps the carving is a metaphor."

"A metaphor?"

"A metaphor is something that appears to be one thing but stands for something else," the priest replied.

"Just like the lamb stands for Our Lord, Jesus Christ? Or the dove in the center of the maze stands for the Holy Spirit?" asked Giorgio.

"That's right, Giorgio. Perhaps the artist who carved these cherubs in the vineyard was trying to tell us that God has provided a bounty of wonderful things, like the grapes the cherubs are picking, but as we help ourselves to this bounty we need always to keep a careful eye out for the evils – the giant birds – that lurk in our midst."

Giorgio narrowed his eyes in thought. "So the birds are like the Nazis and the fascists?"

"Something like that," Father Francesco replied with a faint smile, sensing it was not the right moment for a discussion of personal sin. "Would you children like to have a copy of this carving?"

Luisa nodded enthusiastically, but Giorgio pointed out that they did not have a camera.

"There's another way to get a copy. Wait here," said the priest as he walked off.

As Luisa studied the child-sized sepulcher, she began to frown. "My mamma and papa loved me, too, but they didn't put me in a beautiful box – they put me in a closet."

Giorgio could see Luisa's eyes beginning to brim with tears as she thought of her parents, but, while seldom at a loss for words, he could think of nothing to say. Studying his shoes in silence, he was relieved to hear Father Francesco returning. He had something in his hands.

"Look here, children – if you hold the sheet of paper up to the carving, then run the pencil back and forth – see, like this

– you can make a copy of the image on the tomb. Here, you try it. Giorgio, you hold the paper up and let Luisa move the pencil across the image."

Father Francesco walked back toward the vestry, leaving the children to ply their newly-learned skill. Despite a few mishaps, cherubs and birds and vines soon began to emerge on their sheet of paper. Halfway through their project, Giorgio glanced over at Luisa; she was smiling again.

VIALE GIULIO CESARE. MILITARY BARRACKS.

Vittoria could feel the anger in the seething mass of women that pushed and shoved at the police line before the yellow buildings of the barracks.

"Release our men! Release our men!" The united chant came from the throats of nearly three hundred women, many of whom raised their fists at the police line. Vittoria spotted Sofia handing out leaflets in the midst of the crowd.

The Resistance cell had learned of the demonstration earlier in the day. About a hundred men had been rounded up at random from the streets of Rome for forced labor service. The fascist police, at the behest of their German masters, had raided bars and emptied buses to arrest any able-bodied men they could find.

"Release our men!" The chant grew louder. The men rounded up were now held in the military barracks behind the police line on the Viale Giulio Cesare. Like many other innocent men before them, unless a miracle occurred, they would be transported to Germany to work in munitions factories, virtual slaves to the Nazi war machine.

"Germans out!" Vittoria sought to invoke a new chanted slogan. Only she and Sofia had been told to join the demonstration; the men in the organization were ordered to keep away.

"Germans out! Germans out!" Her cry was picked up by the women around her and then echoed by the rest of the crowd. Vittoria pushed her way through the throng to the front, where a line of fascist police, strengthened by several German soldiers, their rifles at the ready, stood between the shouting women and the barracks.

"There he is!" A woman near Vittoria pointed to a third floor barred window. Vittoria saw a face appear briefly at the window. "That's my husband!"

Vittoria looked at the woman. She was tall, the top of her dark hair standing well above everyone else.

"Arturo, it's Gisella!" the tall woman shouted.

Suddenly, there were men's faces at all the windows of the barracks, and they began shouting her name. *"Gi-sel-la! Gi-sel-la! Gi-sel-la!"*

Vittoria was swept up in the press of the crowd as they pushed against the line of police and German soldiers. The women shoving at her back made her feel uneasy, and she reached into her pocket and groped nervously at the handle of the pistol she was carrying.

The cries from the barracks continued. *"Gi-sel-la! Gi-sel-la! Gi-sel-la!"*

"Ar-tu-ro! Ar-tu-ro!" the women shouted back as they forced their way through the line, making way for Gisella in the front.

Vittoria saw a German soldier raise his rifle; she pulled the pistol from her pocket.

Crack!

Three hundred voices died in their throats as the sound of the rifle shot echoed around the square. All watched as Gisella lurched forward, toppled to her knees, and fell to the ground, the life ebbing from her body.

Rage seized Vittoria, and she leveled her pistol at the German, some ten yards away, but the moving throng of women prevented her from taking close aim. Some women tried to escape down the street, but the majority pressed forward and

Vittoria was jostled, willy-nilly, her hands and the gun pressed to her sides.

Suddenly, the arm of a policeman was looped around her neck, trying to pull her from the pack. Some women around her tugged at him, refusing to let him drag her off, but the policeman locked his other arm around her waist, determined to win the tug-of-war.

Vittoria knew what she had to do. She dropped the pistol to the pavement.

Other policemen fired into the air, frightening the women into retreat as the policeman dragged Vittoria behind the police line.

"Here, Luigi," he said, dropping her heavily in front of a colleague, "cuff this one and throw her in a cell. She's a trouble-maker. Maybe the inspector would like a word with her."

MARIA'S APARTMENT.

Maria felt despondent as she looked around her empty apartment, listening to the silence. After Marco had left for the eastern front, she had become used to the hollowness of the empty rooms, but the recent stay of Buck and the Englishman, and especially of Jay, had brought life back into the place. Indeed, Jay had brought life back into her.

Yet she was relieved they had moved on. Ever since the arrest of Giancarlo, the mole for the Resistance at the police station who had tipped her off about the raid, she had felt danger lurking. How did it happen? How had they found out about Giancarlo? She sighed and adjusted a vase to center it on a table.

She had been so careful, speaking to no one, minding her own business. The police must surely have learned about Giancarlo from some other source; she was certain they had found nothing incriminating during their search. She shook her head as she moved into the kitchen. Her worst fear had been that they would discover the compartment in her room where cots and people could be hidden, but they had not. And she had been able to conceal the book of poems the Englishman had carelessly left behind. It was not a crime for an Italian to own a book in English, but David's had his name and English address inscribed inside.

Still, she would miss hearing the Englishman's perfect high Italian. She ran her hand over the tablecloth to smooth out a fold. And she would miss Buck's compliments on her food, even when the ingredients, the best she could get, were still of poor quality. Most of all, she would miss Jay's wide grin, their Italian lessons, the way he made her laugh.

But they were gone, and it was for the best. Perhaps there would be no further danger now that they had moved on. If the police called, they would find no one.

She returned to her small living room and sat down, but the loneliness of her apartment gnawed at her and she felt the need for company. Perhaps she would drop in on her father-in-law, take him some of the apples she had bought that afternoon. She rose and headed for her hat and coat in the hall.

The sharp knock on the door startled her.

MILITARY BARRACKS.

The clip of bullets in her pocket felt like a hot coal in her hand; she had to get rid of it.

Vittoria looked around the dingy room where she was being held. Not a prison cell as such; there were no bars. Windowless, it had dirty pale green walls and a grey cement floor. An unlit stove occupied a corner and a small table took up half of the remaining space in the room. She sat facing the table and the empty chair on the other side.

They hadn't searched her yet, and her mouth had gone dry with anxiety. She'd got rid of the pistol in the street, but she'd forgotten about the clip of bullets. Her eyes darted around the room while her ears listened for the turn of a key in the lock. There was no cranny, no recess where she could hide the clip. The stove. Her eyes fell on the stove. She acted quickly, jumping up and removing the plate at the top through which wood was fed into the stove.

She hesitated, her heart racing as she heard noises in the corridor outside. She turned, fixing her eyes on the doorknob, expecting it to turn at any moment. Nothing. She exhaled slowly with relief as she turned to peer into the cold stove. Ashes. She pushed the clip down deep, as deep into the ashes as her arm could reach.

Please, please don't come yet, she prayed. She retreated to the table, staring at the door as if she could control it. She sat down and realized her arm was covered with soot. Frantically, she brushed at the tell-tale signs, licking her fingers to remove a particularly stubborn spot. Her hands were still dirty when she heard footsteps stop at the door and a key being shoved into the lock; she heard the key turn. She thrust her hands into her coat pockets, cleaning the rest of the soot off her hands on the pockets' linings.

As the policeman entered, she tried to hide her fears behind the warmest smile her lips could muster.

A STREET IN ROME.

Jay ran his hand over the camel hair topcoat that Signora Adriana had found in her late husband's wardrobe and, as the cold wind came biting down the street, he pulled it tighter around him. He thought of the POWs still out in the countryside, how they would soon be clamoring to move to the city to escape the rigors of winter. Soon there would be new demands on the POW organization, and his visits to Father Francesco had a new urgency.

He checked the crossroad for police presence and decided on a little detour from the quickest route to Santa Maria della Gloria. He usually took a different way to get there – routine, he knew, often played into the hands of the police. Shading his eyes against the December sun, low in the afternoon sky, he turned the corner.

He had another reason for the diversion: he wanted to see Maria. Regret filled his heart as he thought about all the problems caused by the raid, and he had been sorry to leave her apartment. Truly sorry – he missed Maria's radiant smile, her gentle voice with its musical lilt when she spoke her native language, the way she batted her lashes when she blushed.

Sometimes he thought he had become too fond of her. He remembered the time he had helped her fold sheets when, laughing, she had remarked that the process was like dancing together. But for him it was more than that: each time their hands touched when they stepped forward to join corners, he had come close to kissing her. Nothing had ever happened between them, but at times he had felt guilty just sitting near her and enjoying her warm companionship while her husband was fighting on the eastern front.

The roar of a German troop carrier brought his thoughts back to the present and he waited for a few moments before crossing the avenue and turning into the street where Maria lived. Maria, he knew, was barely scraping by; as paymaster of the POW organization, he planned to give her some back rent to help her make ends meet.

Checking for police, he was about to approach her apartment building when he felt a gentle tug on his sleeve. He turned to see the plump red face of the woman who lived in the ground floor apartment of Maria's building. She pulled on his sleeve and gestured toward him. Deducing what it was she wanted, he lowered his head so she could whisper in his ear.

His basic conversational Italian couldn't handle her rapid-fire communication and he cut her off. "*Signora, parla piu lentamente, per favore,"* he said with some annoyance at the interruption. After several repetitions, he grasped the horrendous news: the police had stormed Maria's apartment two hours before. The woman said she saw them lead her out, throw her in the back of a car, and speed off.

MILITARY BARRACKS.

Vittoria was surprised at the young face of the policeman. He couldn't have been much older than she was.

"I'm Inspector Tartaglia," he said tersely. "Please stand up and raise your hands above your head."

"But—"

"I have to search you – it's routine procedure."

Vittoria did as he asked and felt revulsion as his hands coursed over her body, grimacing as they lingered on her breasts.

He felt her body tense. "You'd be surprised what women hide in their bras." His hands moved on.

After what seemed an eternity to Vittoria, his hands left her body. "Okay, you're clean. Sit down."

"Why am I being held? I demand to be released!"

"You were arrested because you were involved in a violent demonstration." The inspector barely looked up from the report he was writing. "Please empty your pockets and put the contents on the table."

She pulled out her lipstick, her cigarette pack, and a handkerchief. As her fingers reached for her lighter, she felt the card Bartoli had given them at one of their first meetings. She plucked it from her pocket and, without any show of emotion, placed it on the table before him. "That's why I was at the demonstration today."

The inspector glanced at the card and gave her a look of surprise. "You're a member of Blood and Honor?"

"Of course. For several years now."

"Then whatever were you doing with that mob of scream-ing women?"

"We were told to intervene, move the women along, coun-ter the communist propaganda, calm them down." She heaved a disgruntled sigh. "Fat chance of calming them down after that German soldier shot the woman. What an idiot!"

"The Germans are stupid and arrogant, it's true." He sighed with resignation. "But they are also strong, and we have to live with them."

"Yes, of course." Vittoria flashed him her warmest smile. "So, are we finished here? May I go now?"

"I really should formally check out this membership card." He picked it up and flapped it against his hand for a few moments, the muscles in his jaw tensing as he thought. Then he put it down and smiled at her. "But I'm sure there's a way we can speed things up," he said, using a tone of voice and look in his eyes Vittoria had encountered before.

She hesitated, playing coy and smiling as sweetly as she could, although she raged inside.

"I know a restaurant – special guests only, you know." He gave her a wink.

Of course she knew. Half of Rome was on the breadline, but policemen lived high on the hog. "Why not?" She gave him a coquettish look. "A good meal is hard to come by nowadays."

He handed her Blood and Honor membership card back to her. "Shall we say seven o'clock on Tuesday? Do you know the little place at the end of the Vicola Valdina?"

Vittoria nodded and he hurried to open the door for her.

"What's that noise?" With the door open, she could hear the sound of wailing echoing down the corridor.

The inspector looked through the door. "It's the husband of the woman who was shot. He has to identify her body. Routine, you know."

Vittoria nodded and forced a last smile at him before hurrying for the outer door. She might just turn up for that date, she thought. And shoot his balls off. Routine, you know.

Villa Ranieri Cellar Quarters.

"Maria arrested? Jesus, that's awful news, Jay!" Nolan rose from the sofa in the sparsely-furnished cellar. "Anything we can do to help her?"

"I'm not sure, Buck." Jay couldn't conceal the emotion in his voice. "I thought of mentioning it to Adriana – she probably has all sorts of high-level contacts – but I ditched that idea. If Maria was arrested because she was hiding us, it would be natural for Adriana to think of her own situation. Hiding us, that is."

"Yeah, Jay, you're right. And I also get the idea Adriana's got you pegged as the Typhoid Mary of the American army. But if you think of something we can do to help Maria, count me in. I'm always here for you, Jay. Which is more than you can say for our good pal who's once again missing in action."

"Lawrence is not my main problem, Buck." Jay sank onto the sofa. "I suppose I could've used him today, but I managed to decipher the lingo myself." He pulled off his shoes and tossed them aside. "My feet are killing me in these fancy Oxfords!" His hands reached down to rub his toes. "You say Lawrence is out again?"

"Yup. He's becoming a regular gadabout." Nolan walked over to the cast-iron stove and used the tool to open the round lid. "When I ask him where he's going, he mutters something about visiting the historic sites of Rome." He picked up a log from the bucket by the side of the stove and tossed it into the flames, replacing the lid. "Regular historical scholar, our Lawrence. When I politely ask him more about what, specifically, he goes to see, I get the brush-off. It's fishy, Jay – sure as hell something's not right."

145

"I don't know, Buck. I'm not sure," Jay said, massaging his eyes with the palms of his hands. "Right now I can't stop to worry about Lawrence. I need to think about what to do about Maria."

"Sure thing, Jay," Nolan said, "but I think you also need to think about what to do about Lawrence." He fixed MacPherson with a stare. "Soon."

December 3, 1943

Santa Maria della Gloria.

"What is it, my son?" Father Francesco came down from the altar to greet Jay at the end of the aisle. "You seem weighed down by some great burden of worry."

Jay cast a glance around the nave. Two nuns, a few old women, their faces framed by scarves. "I need to talk with you, Father." He drew the priest aside to a far chapel in one of the transepts. "You remember the padrone at Via dei Barbieri, 4, the apartment where I was first billeted?"

The priest's eyes looked up toward the dome as he sought the name. "Yes, of course. Signora Maria Silvestri. You and your companions left her place shortly after Signora Silvestri received news that her contact in the police station, the one who warned her about a raid, had been arrested."

"Now Maria Silvestri has been arrested, Father."

The priest pinched his eyes closed and shook his head slowly. "That is indeed terrible news. May God be merciful to her and bring her solace. I will pray for her."

"I was hoping we could do a bit more, Father. Perhaps you could find out where she's being held and take this to her?" He held up the basket he was carrying. "I obviously can't go, but I've heard the authorities allow priests to make visits to prisons to take confession and provide spiritual comfort. Perhaps you could visit her and bring her this small offering of food and toiletries?"

"I'll try, Signor Jay, but I'm not always allowed access to these places." The priest took the basket. "I'm sure she would welcome this gift. Perhaps we could also help her find some comfort in the grace of God's abiding love."

"Yes, of course, Father." As he thought about Maria's perilous situation, Jay wondered if there was anything that could bring her comfort.

Villa Ranieri Cellar Quarters.

The feet pattering down the old stone steps were too fast to be Lawrence's and not heavy enough to be Jay's. Nolan, alone in the POW's cellar apartment, turned and saw that the feet belonged to Giorgio.

"Put 'er there, pal," he said, extending his hand and giving Giorgio's a single emphatic shake.

"What's buzzin', cousin?" replied the boy. Giorgio, tutored in English from an early age, spoke it well; Nolan had been helping the boy to perfect his English by teaching him American slang.

"So whatcha got for me today, kid?" asked Nolan.

"Take a look, Signor Nolan." Giorgio smiled and held up a sack.

Giorgio was helping Nolan make a doll's house as a surprise for Luisa, to be presented to her on the day of Epiphany, twelve days after Christmas, the night the Wise Men gave gifts to the baby Jesus and the night the witch, La Beffana, brought presents to good Italian children.

Everyone knew La Beffana would be hampered in her work that year by severe shortages, and most of the witch's gifts to Roman children would be meager, at best. But tucked away in a corner of the cellar, Nolan had found a small woodworking shop with tools and some materials and was determined to help La Beffana carry out her duties – at least, as they pertained to Luisa. Of course, the girl, raised in a Jewish household, would never have missed La Beffana's largesse since up to that time she had never celebrated Epiphany. At Giorgio's request, Nolan had set about making this gift, a doll's house, for the girl. Giorgio's task was to forage upstairs for all the extras needed to finish off the house.

Giorgio turned the sack over and gently emptied its contents on the table.

"Looks like you really hit the jackpot, kid," Nolan said, examining the contents. "Cellophane. Great for the windows. And

148

we can use these toothpicks to make the individual window-panes." He picked up some wrapping paper. "I like this. Nice small print on it – good for wallpaper for one of the rooms. And this fabric is nice and plush – we can use it for rugs."

He reached for a large rolled-up sheet of paper. "What the heck is this?" he asked, unrolling it and holding it up as he squinted. "Looks like big bad birds terrorizing small boys."

"Luisa and I made that at the church. We held a piece of paper against a carving and ran pencils against it, and the picture on the carving came out on the paper."

Nolan studied the tracing for a moment. "It's swell, kid, but I don't think we can use it. Pattern's too big for the house." He rolled it up and returned it to the sack. "Hey, would you like to see how the house is coming?" Giorgio nodded enthusiastically.

Nolan made a great show of looking around to make certain they were still alone before leading the boy to a table with an amorphous shape covered by a sheet. Whisking off the sheet, he uncovered the bare bones of a doll's house resting on its façade and revealing, through its open back, each of its rooms. "So how am I doing so far?" he asked.

"Benissimo!" exclaimed Giorgio. *Well done.* In his enthusiasm, he had lapsed into his native language.

"Benito?" Nolan wore a puzzled frown. "Hey, kid, let's keep Mussolini out of this."

OLD QUARTER OF ROME NEAR THE TIBER.

Renzo pulled his short red scarf tight around his neck and blew on his fingers, his breath cloudy in the frigid air. Everyone said Rome had never been so cold in December. He sat on his bicycle trying to beat out the bitter chill that seemed to claw through his overcoat. He would have put on gloves, but he needed his fingers for the mission that was at hand: to prime the large bomb buried in his deep overcoat pocket.

He blew on his fingers again as he looked down the incline from his bicycle. At the bottom, some thirty yards away, an old movie theater fronted the street. Once the hang-out of many young lovers, it had been requisitioned by the Germans in October for their soldiers, and the Roman populace shunned it.

Which suited Renzo and the partisans to a tee. Every Tuesday and Thursday, the Germans trucked in about fifty soldiers for a matinee. And every Tuesday and Thursday, precisely at five in the afternoon – Renzo wondered if the Germans realized that their unerring punctuality was a great help to the partisans – the soldiers would leave the theater and board an open truck to return to their base. There was no need for a group attack, Renzo had argued: he alone could reap a rich harvest.

Renzo looked up as a truck lumbered down the street and screeched to a halt outside the cinema. His fingers reached inside his overcoat and checked the bomb and its thirty-second fuse. He lit a cigarette as the Germans filed out of the building and began to board the truck. He applied the cigarette end to the fuse, tossed the cigarette aside, and began to pedal down the incline towards the truck.

Twelve, eleven, ten...Renzo ran through the countdown in his head, bracing with both hands against the pull of the cobbles as long as he dared. "This one's for you, Papa," Renzo whispered, suddenly yanking the bomb from his overcoat pocket and lobbing it into the back of the truck as the last of the soldiers climbed in.

As his feet pedaled furiously, he heard shouts of consternation. Four, three...the roar of the explosion was premature. He felt the blast of air against his back, threatening his balance. He fought with the handlebars, increasing the pressure of his feet on the pedals.

Behind him came the screams of agony from those mangled by the bomb. He did not stop to look back, but pedaled furiously as another sound came to his ears: the crack of firearms. He was about a hundred yards from the truck when he heard the bullets zinging off the cobbles, the whistle of one close to his ears. He crouched down over the handlebars as his eyes picked out the footbridge ahead, the Ponte Sisto. His plan was simple: once over the bridge, he would lose himself in the maze of the streets of Trastevere. Still the bullets came, forcing him to extra effort.

He was twenty yards away when he saw them: a patrol of fascist militia was standing guard at the far side of the bridge.

REGINA COELI PRISON.

The prison guard closed the large outer door, selected a key from his ring, and locked it. "Please follow me, Father." The guard's boots echoed on the tiled floor of the cavernous antechamber of Regina Coeli, the largest prison of Rome located just a stone's throw from the Vatican. Father Francesco mused on the name as he followed the guard: "Queen of Heaven" was a strange name to have given the place. To the priest, the name hinted at blasphemy; the Queen of Heaven held within her walls the followers of the Prince of Darkness.

"Name?" The voice of the head of the guardhouse cut across the priest's thoughts.

Father Francesco looked up into the window of the guardhouse, situated by the side of the inner door that led to the prison wings. "Francesco, from the Church of Santa Maria della Gloria. I come as an emissary of the Holy Father."

"Father, I know *your* name." The officer smiled. "I certainly remember you from your many previous visits. But who are you here to see?"

"Oh! Maria Silvestri."

The officer ran his finger down his order paper. "Yes, the permission is here." He leaned over and whispered to another guard before turning his attention back to the priest.

"Come through, Father, and—" He paused. "Wait, what are you holding in your hand?"

"It's a small parcel for Signora Silvestri."

"Father Francesco, you ought to know the rules by now. No parcels."

"But it's merely a gift of Christian charity, Sergeant."

The officer shook his head. "What's in the parcel, Father?"

"Food and—," the priest lowered his eyes, "and other things a woman would need."

"Father, I would like to take your word, but I'm obliged to follow the rules." The officer motioned to the guard, who reached out and took the parcel from the priest's hand. "If there's nothing suspicious in there, she'll get it, I promise. Now, one of my men will admit you through the inner door and take you to her cell."

Father Francesco heard the rattle of the key in the lock and the creak of the door.

"I do hope she appreciates your visit, Father." The chief of the guard waved Father Francesco through. "She's charged with harboring escaped prisoners of war. Last month, the German Gestapo raised the severity of the offence. She's under penalty of death."

Ponte Sisto to Trastevere.

They had spotted him. The explosion had alerted the fascists and Renzo saw their patrol move to block the center of the road leading from the bridge. Renzo briefly wished he had brought his pistol, but realized it would have been of little use against so many. He saw one of the patrol reach into his holster.

From behind him, another blast erupted as the truck's gas tank caught fire, followed by a hail of bullets aimed at him. Renzo zigzagged his bike in the hope of escaping a hit when he saw that the fascist patrol was also seeking to avoid the fusillade of fire, rushing out of the road and hiding behind walls at the far end of the bridge.

Renzo seized his chance, speeding across the bridge, urging the bike between the crouching fascist patrol, and pedaling onto the street beyond. He risked a quick look behind him. Two of the patrol had collected bikes from the side of the road and had mounted in pursuit of him.

Regina Coeli Prison.

Father Francesco felt the fierce cold of the damp cell. Maria was shivering, but he was not sure whether the cause was the freezing weather or fear of the peril in which she found herself. She looked exhausted. Her eyes were ringed with dark circles and her clasped hands trembled over the bare table that stood in the corner of the cell, lit dimly by the small window set high in the wall.

"May the Lord be with you." Father Francesco moved toward the battered wooden chair opposite Maria.

"Forgive me, Father, but I almost don't care where the Lord is." She rubbed at her tired eyes.

"My dear child, you must not despair of the Lord."

"Then please ask the Lord why the evildoers are rewarded while misery is brought down upon those trying to do good."

Father Francesco hesitated. He had heard this grievance many times before: why has the Lord deserted me? A mere mortal could not answer for God, and the argument that He works in mysterious ways had become trite through repetition.

"The Bible tells us that whom the Lord loves, he chastens," is all he could offer. "But can I be of help? Perhaps you have messages for friends I can pass on?"

A glimmer of hope seemed to brighten her eyes. "Please let my father-in-law know what's happened to me. Or perhaps he already knows and has sent you?"

"No, my child."

There was a prolonged rattle of a key in the lock, and the door slowly squeaked open. Maria glanced over anxiously as the guard entered, placing the opened parcel on the table. "The chief says it's all right for the prisoner to have these things," he said to the priest. "Must be getting soft-hearted in his old age." He winked and left, locking the door behind him.

"What's this?" Maria's fingers delved into the small box, plucking out a small sausage, some bread, cheese, and a half bottle of wine.

"It's a gift." The priest saw the glint of delight in her eyes, as if each item were a treasure found on the shore.

Her fingers delved deeper, and a small sigh of pleasure greeted a toothbrush, comb, and tube of lipstick. "A gift? From your church, Father?"

"No, no, my child, it's from Signor Jay. He's very worried about you." He watched as her eyes returned to their glassy appearance. Her hands dropped the items back into the box. "What is it, my child? What's the matter?"

"Jay was one of the three prisoners I was hiding." Her voice fell to little more than a whisper. "When the police arrived and arrested me, they went directly to the hidden closet in my room where the cots were stowed. They also found a crumpled-up cigarette package inside; they said it had words printed in English on it. The three prisoners I was hiding were the only people, apart from my husband, who knew the secret compartment existed. Is it possible one of them could have betrayed me?"

Father Francesco shook his head. "How could that be so, my child? Men you were keeping safe from the enemy would have no reason to betray you." He paused, then added, "I assume you were on good terms with them all?

"Oh, yes, Father. I got along very well with all of them. They all seemed to like me."

He smiled. "I would expect nothing less. But might any of your neighbors have known the men were staying with you?"

"The men sometimes went out – they liked to go to bars occasionally for a drink – and someone could have seen them. Possibly the woman downstairs, the one in the ground floor apartment, she may have seen them on occasion. She's rather nosy."

The priest remained silent for several moments. "I need to think seriously about what you have said. There are still fascists in Rome; I must warn Signor Jay to exert tighter control over the prisoners so as not to put in peril the kind Romans who are giving them shelter." He looked at his watch. "And now I must go. But, with your permission, I will call again."

She nodded and tried to smile. "It was kind of you to come, Father."

The priest moved to the door and called for the guard, then paused and turned. "I hope you will get some enjoyment from the items in your package. That was Signor Jay's hope."

The door opened. Father Francesco made the sign of the cross and left.

TRASTEVERE.

The tires of Renzo's bike hummed over the small cobbles. A rapid glance behind showed that the fascist pursuers were

156

still fifty meters back. He had a decent lead, but he had to shake them: he was well aware of what his fate would be if they caught him and turned him over to the Germans who were collecting their dead at the theater at that moment.

The thought drove him to a frenzy of effort as his mind struggled to find a way out. His original plan had been to lose them in the warren of alleys behind Santa Maria in Trastevere, but that was unlikely now. He needed to make two or three quick maneuvers to get out of their line of sight, then quietly disappear.

He made a mental note that the Via del Gatto would soon appear on the left. He recalled that forty meters along that street was another street to the right that ran for thirty meters before turning right again. He had little choice: straight ahead lay the broad avenue of Viale di Trastevere, where he would have little chance of escape.

He began to turn sharply into the Via del Gatto but saw, when it was too late to change course, a fascist up ahead gesticulating to the ones behind him, indicating that his maneuver had been seen. Renzo redoubled his effort and turned right before his pursuers entered the Via del Gatto; soon they would pass by. But his relief soon turned to dismay: he had turned too soon into a dead end no more than ten meters long.

He cursed his misjudgment as he dismounted and wheeled the bike back to the entrance. Going back out would be fatal as the fascists would have realized their mistake and turned around. He found a small alcove in the dead-end alley and pressed himself into it.

As soon as he had, he saw the man at the alley's entrance watching him. From his inadequate hiding place, Renzo could see the man move out into the Via del Gatto, waving his arms and shouting *'Attenzione! Attenzione!'* The man was trying to draw the attention of the fascists! Renzo looked for a way to escape – a wall to scale, a window to break and climb through – but there was none.

"*Attenzione!* Are you looking for a man wearing a red scarf on a bicycle?"

"*Si, si!*"

"Well, he turned right, down that road there!" He pointed down the street.

"*Grazie! Grazie!*" The fascists mounted their bicycles and made off.

After they had made the turn, the man bent his right arm at the elbow and made a fist, slapping the upper part with his left hand in an obscene gesture. Then he turned toward Renzo and gave him a wink and a grin.

December 5, 1943

SANTA MARIA DELLA GLORIA.

"How's Maria?" Jay's voice was anxious but quiet as they sat at the back of the deserted church. "Is she all right?"

"She's frightened, my son." Father Francesco peered over his glasses. "As can well be understood. She fears the death penalty. And she refuses to accept succor from the Lord."

"Is there nothing that can be done?" Jay asked, trying to hide the helplessness in his voice.

The priest sighed. "I have a contact in the Vatican who has access to fellow Catholics in the German embassy," he said, casting his eyes downward, "but I cannot hold out much hope."

"You've got to pursue your contact, Father. We've got to do all we can." Jay paused. "Did she like my little gift?"

"She did, Signor Jay," his fingers played nervously with the rosary beads that hung from his waist, "she did, indeed. But she also told me things that give me great concern for the security of our organization."

"Such as?" Jay spoke too loudly, then looked around the church, knowing that his raised voice would carry down the transept. "What did she say?" he whispered.

"She believes the woman in the ground floor apartment might be a fascist informer."

Jay remembered the plump red face of the woman who had accosted him the day of Maria's arrest. Hadn't there been a glimpse of malice, perhaps of triumph in her eyes? But why had she pulled him, of all people, over to tell him about it? "You think that…?"

"Yes—perhaps she saw you, and the other men—"

"David and Buck?"

"Maybe the woman in the downstairs apartment saw you all when you went out."

Jay's mind reeled. "Of course she did. She used to peer out of her front door at us as we went by. But she always smiled and seemed so friendly…"

"The devil has many guises, Signor Jay." Father Francesco let his rosary beads drop from his hands as he stood up. "And can be found where we least expect him."

BRIDGE OF ANGELS.

Jay looked down at the Tiber from the Ponte Sant'Angelo, trying to control his anger with himself. Maria was in jail because of his stupidity. The three of them—Buck, David, and he—had treated Rome as a playground, drinking in bars, talking loudly in the streets, riding the trams. And they hadn't been alone – Rome was crawling with escaped POWs who were doing much the same.

The POW community was housed and fed by money provided by the Allied embassies – British and American – in Vatican City, although Jay had no contact with them and worked only through Father Francesco. Each POW was given an allowance of one hundred lire per man per day. With few living expenses and an allowance to spend, many of the POWs seemed to regard their stay in Rome as a paid vacation. Some of the men even liked to pay social calls on their buddies in other billets.

Jay was sure Maria wasn't the only one who had been put at risk. No doubt many other padrones were in danger, as well, risking their lives because of the indiscretions of former prisoners of war to whom they had offered the meager but welcome comfort of their own homes. The organization had to be brought back into control or other padrones would be arrested. And if other padrones were arrested, the POW operation itself would be jeopardized as it became harder to find replacement padrones willing to take the added risk.

Disgusted, Jay flicked his cigarette at his own reflection in the river and watched the light die. The organization needed to be tightened. Changes were necessary. But for Maria, it was too late.

VILLA RANIERI.

MacPherson saw Nolan sprawled on the sofa as he opened the door to their cellar apartment in Adriana's house.

"Where's Lawrence?" he asked, slamming down his pad of paper on top of the chest of drawers.

"He's out back in the kitchen, rustling up our grub. Can't you smell something burning?" Nolan turned over the book he was reading, stood up, and stretched. "Don't you just long for the chow we used to get from Maria?"

"Maria's still in jail, Buck. And it's not looking good for her right now."

"What do you—"

"Go get David in here, Buck." Jay lit a cigarette and drew deeply. "We've got to discuss another matter." As Nolan disappeared to summon the Englishman, Jay's mind conjured up an image of Maria in her prison cell and his guilt compounded.

Lawrence appeared in the doorway. "Buck just told me that Maria's still in jail. That's really bad luck."

"Bad luck, eh?" MacPherson was surprised at the vehemence of his own voice. "Think about it, guys—we used to wander in and out of her place as though it was Grand Central Station, and now we wonder why her apartment was raided?"

"What's the problem, Jay?" Nolan fell back onto the sofa.

"*We're* the problem!" MacPherson shouted. "*We* put Maria in jail. And we'll do the same to Adriana unless we shape up."

Nolan scowled and stood up. "What are you talking about, Jay?"

"We've got to stop acting like we were on vacation in Rome. Someone apparently spotted us coming out of and going into Maria's apartment, and that's why she was arrested."

"So are you saying we gotta stay inside all day long, Jay?" Nolan did not sound happy. "With no one but ourselves for company?"

"Yep. That's exactly what I'm saying," Jay replied with vehemence. "We've got to establish better security – even if Adriana herself is lax in that respect. And I'll be issuing a stay-put order to the POW billets all over Rome."

"Okay, I'll buy it, Jay." Nolan flopped back down on the battered sofa. "Sure sounds boring, but I've seen all the Rome I ever need to see. Give me Boston any day. Besides, I have my little projects – like the doll house I'm building with Giorgio. I'll try to hang out down here until our guys march in and bail us out. Which I'm hoping will be before I finish all the books in English in Adriana's library."

Lawrence stepped forward and looked Jay in the eye. "I'm afraid I can't go along with such a regime."

MacPherson glowered back at the Brit during a long silence. "You're not prepared to safeguard Signora Corvo's safety?" he said, pronouncing each word slowly.

"Signora Corvo's safety will not be at issue," Lawrence replied. "I speak Italian well. In fact, everyone outside these walls thinks I'm Italian."

"With your blonde hair?"

"They think I'm from the north of Italy. Besides, Signora Corvo doesn't do herself any great favors. You know that she's having an affair with—"

"Hey, have I been missing something?" Nolan sat up and leaned forward. "Is there some juicy scandal going on?"

"Nothing you need to know, Yank." Lawrence uttered the last word with venon.

Nolan rose from the sofa. "So, Flight Lieutenant High-and-Mighty Limey is not prepared to protect the safety of a lady whose generosity he enjoys?" He squared up to Lawrence. "Why don't you just make it an order, Jay?"

"I'm an English officer," Lawrence said before MacPherson could speak. "I don't have to take orders from an American, regardless of rank." He turned on his heel and stormed up the steps, slamming the door behind him as he left.

Nolan waited a few moments as the Englishman's footsteps faded. "Jay, that guy's always been big trouble. If you want him to move on, that's okay by me."

"Maybe you're right, Buck." MacPherson stubbed out his cigarette in an ashtray. "But I think before he leaves I'd like to check him out a little more."

A TRAM.

Father Francesco stared out the rain-streaked window as the tram passed another group of beggars on the Corso Vittorio Emanuele. Thousands of families had flooded into Rome, some even bringing their livestock, which they hid from the Germans in garages, private gardens, and caves beneath the Janiculum Hill. The priest looked at the emaciated frames of the beggars standing in the rain: the Romans had been generous to the refugees, but they couldn't give what they did not have.

The day before, Christmas Day, Father Francesco had opened the church hall to refugee families who had been camping out beneath the colonnade that encircled the piazza in front of St. Peter's. While the meat of the scrawny chicken diced into small cubes was hard to find in the soup he served them, which consisted mainly of potatoes, onions, cabbage, dried peas, and macaroni, the wine he had brought up from the monastery cellars had done much to add to the cheer of the day. As had the small toys the brothers of the monastery had made for the children.

Renzo Rossi, a Jew who had never before celebrated Christmas, had come to help with his friend, Vittoria Corvo, whose kind mother had sent a quantity of old curtains and drapery fabric that could be fashioned into clothing for the refugees. And sandals had been made by the brothers to replace the refugees' worn-out shoes, although the sandals had to be made of wood as there was no leather in Rome.

The tram made a stop and the priest got off; the rain had turned into sleet. He turned up his collar and began the long walk to Regina Coeli Prison.

L'Orso Restaurant.

The sight of beggars on her way to the restaurant cast a pall on the joyful anticipation of her holiday celebration with Anton. Adriana had pressed a few hundred-lire notes into the hand of a girl with a dirty face, but the child had shown little emotion. Most of Rome was starving.

She looked up as Signora Martucci, the restaurant's owner, appeared at their table. "Good afternoon, signora, signore. I'm afraid I haven't much to offer you today, what with the shortages and the Germans keeping the best quality of—" Signora Martucci's eyes darted over to Anton as she realized her gaffe. "Beg your pardon, sir."

"Not at all," he said, inclining his head graciously. "What you say is true."

"I'll just have a glass of your excellent Frascati," said Adriana, quickly changing the subject. "I'm really not very hungry today."

"And the same for me, please, signora." Anton watched the hostess disappear into the kitchen. "I'm sorry she was so embarrassed," he said. "It is we Germans who should be ashamed. We grab the lion's share of the food and what's left over gets into the black market where only the rich can afford it. Meanwhile, the poor of Rome starve."

Adriana found it difficult to put aside her own guilt as she thought about her lifestyle, lavish by comparison. "Well, we won't solve the problem this afternoon, so let's try to enjoy our time together."

"Why don't you start by telling me about your Christmas day?"

"It was lovely," Adriana said with a wistful smile. "I invited the Englishman and the two Americans up from the cellar for a hand-puppet show the children have been rehearsing for weeks, supposedly in secret. Giorgio made up the story, so it had lots of puppet chases, puppet arms thrown up in indignation, puppet knockings of head. Then the Englishman played the piano and we all sang Christmas carols, making up whatever words and tunes we didn't know. There was lots of laughter, and it was good to forget about the war for an afternoon."

When the hostess had served them their wine, Anton reached beneath the table and brought up a box wrapped in gold foil and trimmed with a wide red silk ribbon. "A small Christmas gift for you, darling."

She opened it, saving the ribbon and smoothing the paper. Inside was a boxed set of records. "Oh, Anton, Brahms's *Liebeslieder-Walzer.* His love-song waltzes. I heard them performed once – they're wonderful!"

"Composed by a German and sung by Germans. To show you that we Germans do have our redeeming qualities. The words are quite lovely. There's a line in one that always makes me think of you. *"Wenn so lind dein Auge mir/Und so lieblich schauet—/Jede letzte Trübe fliehet,/Welche mich umgrauet.* 'Whenever your beautiful eyes rest on me so lovingly, every care I have instantly flies away.'"

"You already fill my life with beauty, but I will treasure this gift." She squeezed his hand, then drew out a wrapped package from her handbag and gave it to him.

When he tore off the paper and ribbon, he gasped. "It's stunning, Adriana." In the silver-framed portrait photograph, she was wearing a black evening gown and leaning back on a bench, propping herself up on her arms. Her eyes were turned toward the camera and the three-quarter perspective of her face showed her features to advantage in dramatic planes of light and shadow.

"A friend of mine is a portrait photographer," she said, "and I wanted to throw some business his way. There's not much call for formal photography these days, it seems."

He placed his hand on hers. "A more splendid gift I cannot imagine. Thank you." He raised her hand to his lips and kissed it.

Afterward, they sipped their wine in silence, each of them lost in thought.

Adriana broke the silence. "Anton, what's to become of the two of us?"

"What's to become of any of us?" he answered. "Everyone in Rome, all of us, can do no better than to live from day to day."

"And be grateful when we wake up the next morning in our beds unscathed," she added, thinking of the continuing threat of roundups, raids, and random arrests.

He paid the check and they left the restaurant, each wondering what the new year would bring. Surely the arrival of Allied forces and liberation. But would the arrival of the Allies mean the destruction of Rome as the Germans left? And when the Germans left, what would happen to the two of them?

Regina Coeli Prison.

His first glimpse of Maria as the guard opened the heavy door to her cell startled him: she was almost skeletal. Her face was chalk-white and her lips were cracked, the only color in her countenance the reddish-brown of the hollows surrounding her eyes. Her hair was limp and stringy, and she sat with her arms wrapped around herself, rocking from side to side. When he entered she looked up but did not greet him.

"How are you, my child?" he asked, sitting down at her small table.

"*Così-così*," she replied. So-so.

"Signor Jay has sent you another gift." He gently pushed the small basket toward her on the table. He did not tell her that the guard who had checked the package had helped himself to a small bar of soap – a rare commodity in occupied Rome.

Maria pawed through the basket perfunctorily, then shoved it aside, saying nothing.

"Have you had any news?" Father Francesco asked.

With a glassy stare she fixed him with her eyes. "Yes, I have as a matter of fact. My father-in-law came to visit yesterday. He's received word that Marco, my husband, has been reported missing in action." She looked away. "That can only mean that he's dead."

Father Francesco held up his palm, as if trying to ward off evil. "No, no, my child, don't say that, don't give up hope! We must pray for your husband's safety."

She looked up at him and a smile began to form on her lips. "What good would that do, if he's already dead?"

"But he may not be dead – he may be injured, or maybe he's in hiding."

Maria's half-smile faded. "I fervently hope you are right, Father." Maria shook her head slowly. "If not, I have little left to live for."

VILLA RANIERI.

"It was good of you to make time to see me, Adriana." Small, overweight, a red plumpish face sitting atop a neck that hung over a frayed collar, Dante Bartoli looked like anything but a partisan, Adriana thought, as he moved into the well-appointed room.

"It's unusual to see you so late, Dante." Her extended hand offered him a leather-upholstered club chair, upon which he sat carefully, almost deferentially. "I'm sure you realize it's less than an hour till curfew." She glanced over at the gilt clock.

"I come on a serious matter." His corduroy pant legs shuffled uneasily on the chair. Although he dressed like a worker, everyone knew he was a messenger for a small law firm. He looked around the room. "I take it we are alone?"

"Of course." She poured from the teapot she had prepared. "Giorgio and Luisa are playing with her doll's house, the three POWs are in the cellar, and I have no idea where Vittoria and Fabio are. No doubt working on one of your harebrained schemes."

"They are neither my schemes nor are they harebrained." He spoke softly but his manner was cold. "We're trying to expunge the fascist and Nazi tyranny that now shackles Rome. You know that, Adriana."

"Of course, Dante. I'm sorry. I just don't want anything to happen to my children. They're fervent about what they do, but they think themselves immortal – and leave me to do the worrying." She sipped at her tea. "And they're so very young." She gave him a look meant to elicit his sympathy, but he remained impassive.

"Anyway," she put down her cup and saucer, "what is this serious matter? I hope you've not come about money, Dante – I'm still waiting for an art deal to come through. Times are tough, even for us 'bourgeois,' you know." She arched an eyebrow and gave a wry grin.

"Your generosity has always been appreciated, Adriana." He was well aware that she gave readily to the movement's funds, even selling some of her art treasures. Moreover, as a doyenne of Roman society, her contacts sometimes gave her valuable information which she passed on. But it was a dangerous game, and one that could threaten the partisans.

"I haven't come about money." He hesitated, studying the black marble cherubs that adorned the sides of the clock as he sought the right words.

She spoke before he gathered his thoughts. "You're not still miffed about my having used the wife of the Chief of Police to get Fabio released from Regina Coeli?" She gave a low chuckle. "You really are worrying about nothing, Dante. The wife of the questore has a brain the size of a fava bean – and her husband's is not much larger."

"Adriana," Dante spoke softly, "it's about the German."

"So that's it." She breathed quickly, trying to control her anger. "You've come here to lecture me about my love life. Silly me – I always thought you communists poured scorn on – what do you call it? – petty bourgeois morality."

"Personally, I don't give a fig about your personal life," his voice remained calm, unruffled, "but I do care about the safety of my organization."

"So you think I'm engaged in pillow talk, is that it?" She tried to remain composed but could feel her cheeks reddening. "Then let me tell you something, Dante. Where do you think I get the ration cards for the escaped prisoners of war? And do you think the identity cards for the Jews in hiding grow on trees?" She took a cigarette in an attempt to regain her composure, but her hands trembled with rage as she lit it. "Anton has no truck with the Nazis. He hates them. Did you know that he tried to work out a deal to save the Jews?"

"But he's still a German, Adriana." Dante met her glower with a measured stare. "As such, he could put you in danger." He got up and moved toward the door. "Perhaps you think I'm in full control of my organization. Not so. In any partisan unit there are hotheads – young people who see everything in black and white. They see a German and…" He let his voice trail off. "You could be in danger."

"Danger? My helping your organization has put me in danger, but I've never complained about it!"

"I know, Adriana, and it's much to your credit." He stood up and headed for the door. "But your friendship with this man could result in carelessness," he said facing her, "and this time it's not just you who are in danger. Perhaps the German…" Palms raised, he shrugged by way of finishing the sentence, then left the room and descended the marble stairs.

He hadn't liked doing what he had done, but the needs of the movement were far more important than the feelings of any individual. He opened the street door a crack and peered up and down the road. Everyone had to be careful. He pulled up the collar of his overcoat and surveyed the neighborhood once again before he stepped out. Everyone had to be careful.

EXCELSIOR HOTEL.

Kappler sat at his usual table in the bar of the Excelsior Hotel trying to control his anxiety, an anxiety that had spread throughout the bar.

His mind was churning over the decisions and plans he would have to make soon when he saw Bruno Ganz approaching from across the room. He reached for his pen and began scribbling a few notes, hoping to be left in peace, but sighed and looked up when he realized there was no escape.

Ganz eased himself into the chair opposite. "Herr Obersturmbannführer, have you heard the rumor?"

"But of course, Ganz." Kappler waved his hand toward the bustle and noise that rose up from the room. "And, as you can see and hear, so has the rest of the officer corps." He took a sip of his schnapps. "And, Ganz, it is no longer a rumor. The enemy has indeed landed at Anzio."

Ganz scowled. "I don't know why our intelligence was so off. I read reports that said there would be no enemy invasion before March." He raised his hand and looked around for the waiter.

Kappler closed his notebook and pocketed his pen. "And now, Ganz, it seems the road to Rome is wide open. Unfortunately, we have only a couple of SS police battalions between here and Anzio – hardly enough to stave off an onslaught from the enemy." He gazed off into the distance sullenly.

"So what do we do now, Herr Obersturmbannführer?"

"Do now? Do we have a choice? It's obvious what we must do. We must make immediate plans to withdraw from Rome."

"Retreat, Herr Obersturmbannführer? Is that our only option?"

"Can you suggest another?"

Ganz was silent for a few moments as he considered the question. "Well, if we must leave, then we must leave Rome in ruins." Ganz thumped the table with his fist. "As we did in Naples. By God, we must mine the historic district, set the city ablaze, wreck—"

"No, Ganz, that's not an option." A vision of his beloved Rome in ruins left Kappler feeling uneasy.

The waiter put down Ganz's drink and retreated. "But, Herr Obersturmbannführer, the Romans might follow the example of the Neapolitans. You remember – every man, woman, and child was armed with something, from shotguns to roof tiles." He took a sip of his drink. "They dug trenches in the rubble—"

"I am well aware of what happened in Naples, Ganz. You needn't repeat it all."

Ganz was not easily dissuaded. "If they tried anything like that, I would order my men to turn their guns on the crowd." The contents of his glass sloshed over as he slapped it back on the table.

Kappler leaned back in his chair and sighed. "There will be no need for any of that, Ganz. Do you remember what I told you Kesselring asked me to do? You and I spoke about it right here, in the bar of the Excelsior, a couple of months ago."

Ganz screwed up his eyes as he thought. "Something about rounding up escaped enemy prisoners who are now hiding in the homes of Italian swine."

"Very good, Ganz. Well, my agent now knows most of their hiding places. So not only are they not draining our resources in prison camps, but they will become useful when we leave." A vague smile began to appear on Kappler's face. "Picture it, Ganz. A column of escaped enemy soldiers and their Italian landlords. All of them moving out of Rome with us under heavy guard." His smile grew wider. "I think that should give pause to any Roman militants who might be planning to threaten us."

176

Villa Ranieri Cellar Quarters.

Jay sat on the tattered sofa, gazing absently at the wood stove. After Father Francesco's last visit to the Regina Coeli prison, the news about Maria had not been encouraging. Perhaps he—his thoughts were interrupted by the sound of shoes thudding down the stone steps. Lawrence's exuberance shook him out of his reverie.

"What's up?" he asked.

"Haven't you heard the news?" Lawrence could scarcely contain his excitement. "Our lads have landed at Anzio!"

"Anzio? Where's that?" Jay asked, rising from the sofa.

"It's a town on the coast, about twenty-five miles south of here," Lawrence said breathlessly. "Two divisions – British and American – are now ashore! Do you realize what this means?"

If the Allied troops arrived in Rome soon, Jay thought, Maria could be released from prison.

"Yeah, I know what it means." Nolan's gruff voice cut into Jay's thoughts; he spoke without looking up from the shoe he was shining. "It means more POWs will be flooding into Rome. More work for you, Jay Mack."

Lawrence's face flushed with rage. "Is that all you can say, Nolan?"

"Yeah, Buck, that's pretty lousy, even coming from you," Jay added.

"Okay, okay, I'm sorry." Nolan put down the shoe and raised his hands in mock surrender. "But I've heard it all before. Either of you remember Salerno? Five months ago we landed, and we're still growing moss down here in this crummy cellar."

"But this landing's different," Lawrence said. "Two divisions, with artillery. Heavy bombardment from our warships."

Nolan narrowed his eyes. "How come you're up on all the details?"

"I, um…" Lawrence cleared his throat. "It's the talk of the city right now. Everyone knows."

Nolan persisted. "How do you know it's not all German propaganda? I can see it now: suddenly all the POWs come out dancing in the streets and the Germans gather them all up, saying 'Gee, thank you very much.'"

"It's not propaganda – it's been on BBC Radio," Lawrence exclaimed with exasperation. "And if you'd care to take the trouble to climb to the top of the Janiculum Hill, you could see for yourself – smoke and flashes from the artillery." He turned and steamed up the stone steps, slamming the door at the top.

MacPherson sighed and flopped back down on the sofa.

"Touchy, isn't he?" Nolan broke the edgy silence.

"Why do you do it, Buck? Why do you always have to try to get his goat?"

"But where'd he get all that information? Number of divisions, 'heavy bombardment from our warships' – how does he know all that stuff?"

"He told us, Buck – from the BBC, he said. Adriana's always listening upstairs."

Nolan picked up the other shoe. "So the Limeys broadcast all the details on the radio." He rubbed the shoe furiously with his rag. "If they're such blabbermouths, maybe we should've chosen a different ally."

"Cut it out, Buck. I know you don't like the guy, but don't drag me into it."

"I'm telling you, Jay, there's something about Mr. Lawrence that doesn't quite feel right."

MacPherson, once again locked in his thoughts about Maria, gave no answer.

PINCIAN HILL.

Bartoli pulled up his collar against the piercing wind that coursed through the stone pines at the overlook on the Pincian Hill. He peered over his flapping newspaper, his eyes flitting from side to side, scanning the deserted Piazza del Popolo below. Not a sign of him. He'd received a message from Gappisti headquarters – by personal messenger, nobody trusted the phones anymore – that he had to meet an Allied agent. Something to do with the Anzio landing. The agent would be wearing a green scarf. Bartoli's eyes scanned the piazza again. Nothing.

He shivered despite his heavy overcoat – the worst winter for decades was now blowing through Rome. Everyone was struggling with the freezing weather and the reduced rations, which produced a gnawing hunger that exacerbated the cold. And there was no fuel for the fire. He could feel his own stomach growl but he knew there were many, many more worse off than he.

He stood up and stamped his feet as he cursed the Germans into the bowels of hell, although he knew his curses would just drift away on the cold wind. How long did the Allies need to get from Anzio to Rome?

He checked his watch as he sat back down: twenty past four. As a distraction he began counting all the domes he could see among the rooftops of Rome – St. Peter's, the twin churches at the entrance to the Corso, the Pantheon—where was he? Where was the damned agent? Another ten minutes and Bartoli would go home. His wife didn't know where he was and she'd be angry with him at first. But then they'd have the comfort of a hot bowl of soup followed by the warmth of clutching bodies beneath the blankets. The temptation of such comforts overwhelmed him and forced a decision to cut short his waiting. He got up from his seat and took one final look around. He should have been happy when he saw the man with the green scarf, but he was not.

"You're late," Bartoli snapped at the young man after the customary exchange of passwords.

"I'm sorry. I had to dodge a round-up by the Germans – they were stopping all the trams and arresting the males for the forced labor service."

"You're damned lucky to escape," Bartoli grunted, ushering his contact into the Villa Borghese gardens. They sat down on a marble bench next to a fountain shaped like a fish, bereft of the shimmering stream of water that arced from its gaping mouth in summer. "Thousands of Romans have been rounded up and sent to Germany."

"Yes, I know." The man gave a nervous cough. "But soon the nightmare will be over. When the Allies arrive in Rome." He turned away from the wind and cupped his hand to light a cigarette. "My job is to be liaison between the partisans in Rome and the Allied Command at Anzio. At the moment, the plan is for the Rome Resistance to prepare the way for the arriving troops by blocking retreat roads, cutting communication lines – general sabotage, that sort of thing. I'll provide more details later, but your job will be to give me detailed information on German positions in Rome."

Bartoli sighed. "And, my friend, if I told you the position of every German tank in Rome, can you tell me when the Allies will arrive from Anzio?"

The man with the green scarf took a long drag on his cigarette before throwing it down on the gravel and crushing it out. "Soon," was all he said.

But Bartoli could sense the lack of conviction in the man's voice.

PIAZZA VENEZIA.

Vittoria felt ill at ease as she walked into the Piazza Venezia with her brother, who was carrying a bundle of propaganda leaflets under each arm. She pulled her coat tighter around her against the piercing wind. "I'm not sure you should be doing this, Fabio." She spoke in little more than a whisper. "Don't you think you should have discussed it with Bartoli first?"

"That old fuddy-duddy?" Fabio gave a derisive laugh. "He wouldn't know a revolution if one bit him on the backside." He plunked the bundles down on one of the steps leading up to the Victor Emmanuel monument.

Vittoria looked around nervously. "I still think it's too much of a risk." Over the past six months, Fabio had undergone something of a transformation. When they were growing up, he had been a shy boy, clinging to his mother's skirts and afraid of his own shadow. She had been the bold one, daring him to take chances while displaying her own courage. She recalled the time they were hiking in the Dolomites and came to a deep ravine that could be crossed only by a fallen tree; after she had scampered over the log, she looked back and saw her younger brother crying in fear on the other side. But after Fabio joined the Resistance, the sense of purpose he gained had given him a self-confidence that now seemed to border on bravado.

Fabio cut the strings and began removing the brown paper wrapping that protected the leaflets. Vittoria had come along with him mainly to keep an eye on him. He'd surprised her soon after breakfast, showing her the leaflets and announcing his intention to hand them out 'right in front of the Typewriter,' he had said, using the Roman term of derision for the massive monument that dominated the piazza.

"There's no time to lose." Fabio rifled his thumb through the stack. "The Americans and British will be here within the week, and we have to get the people ready for the uprising."

"But the Americans and British are not here yet, Fabio." Vittoria remembered the strange euphoria that had swept through the partisans when they had learned of the Anzio landings – she herself had not escaped the feeling that, at any moment, the Allies would appear at the gates of Rome. But none had appeared and news from the beachhead – such as there was – did not offer much encouragement.

"Fabio, I insist that you stop this and come home this instant!" Vittoria realized that people were now standing and staring at them. Fabio just laughed and plunged into the crowd, handing out the leaflets.

Vittoria looked at the faces in the crowd. Cold, gaunt with the lack of food, few with so much as a sparkle of hope in their eyes. She saw some of them read Fabio's leaflet with a sardonic smile before letting the tract slip from their fingers; others crumpled it in their hands and tossed it to the cobbles without even glancing at it. The Americans had not come. The Germans still ruled the streets of Rome and the people were in no mood for challenging them with an uprising.

She had lost sight of Fabio, but the noise from a scuffle in the park across from the monument caught her attention: Fabio was in the hands of a fascist policemen. A number of people had gathered around her brother and were pushing and jostling the policeman. "Let him alone! Leave him be! There's no need to arrest him – he wasn't harming anyone!" they shouted, not wishing one of their own to be yielded up to a police cell. But Vittoria realized that, despite their outcry, the policeman had little sympathy.

"It's all right, officer," Vittoria shouted, pushing her way through the last few people surrounding the fracas, "he's with me!" She pulled out her Blood and Honor fascist membership card and flashed it in front of the policeman. She knew it was a brazen bluff but she saw no alternative. "I'll take care of him now." She tapped her temple with a rigid index finger, a clear indication that her brother was not in full possession of his mental faculties.

"Come now, let's take you home." Vittoria shoved her brother through the crowd. The policeman hesitated for a moment, then sensed the mood of the people. He shrugged his shoulders and turned on his heels.

As she led him down the deserted Vicolo Doria, he wrenched himself free. "You had no right to treat me like an idiot! What I was doing has to be done by someone, regardless of the consequences!" Fabio's pride remained undaunted. "And frankly, I really don't care if you tell Bartoli!"

"Tell Bartoli? Oh, Fabio, I'm going to do something much worse than that." As he turned to her, she saw a flash of dread in his face. "I'm going to do something you'll really regret. I'm going to tell Mamma."

She watched as his pride deflated before her eyes.

January 28, 1944

Via Tasso Gestapo Headquarters.

The envelope from Kesselring's headquarters in his in-tray gave Kappler concern. His fingers tore at the paper and he smiled with relief when he saw the invitation to the Opera House the following week. Cocktails at seven. Formal dress uniform. *The Barber of Seville.* The choice of opera heightened his expectations – Italians at last singing in Italian.

The next report in his in-tray put a damper on his buoyant spirits. According to his chief of staff, a synthesis of all the reports from the agents placed all over Rome showed increased activity by partisan units. Kappler lit a cigarette and walked over to the window of his office that looked down on the Via Tasso. Ever since the Allied landing at Anzio, the Resistance had become emboldened, expecting the arrival of Americans in Rome any day. He himself had been anxious at first and had, in fact, made preparations for evacuation. But the situation at the beaches had been stabilized by Kesselring. Several Wehrmacht divisions had been transported quickly down from the north. The Allies were going nowhere fast. Yet still the Resistance acted openly, as if their liberation were at hand.

The scream from one of the interrogation rooms on the floor above interrupted his thoughts for a moment, but he quickly came to a decision. He needed to step up his attacks on the Roman Resistance; they needed to be taught a lesson. Their arrogance would be their downfall.

He returned to his desk, crushed out his cigarette, and pressed the intercom button. "Please come into my office, Berthold."

His chief of staff entered, saluted, and sat down opposite the desk at Kappler's beckoning.

"Berthold, we need to tighten up our operations." Another scream came from the floor above.

"How so, sir? Our interrogation rooms and detention cells are almost full."

"Almost full is not full enough, Berthold." Kappler's fingers drummed on his desk in frustration. "The Resistance think they have the run of the city. The attacks on our soldiers continue almost daily." His hand reached into a pile of papers on his desk. "Do you know how many of our men have been killed since January first, Berthold?"

"Seven, sir." He smiled as Kappler scanned the document in his hand. "That's the report I wrote yesterday, sir."

"We have to fight back." Kappler let the paper drop to the desk. "And now could not be a better time – the communist scum think the Americans will arrive next week." He smiled. "But we know they won't."

"How do you wish to proceed, sir?"

"Carefully. We mustn't rush things." Kappler looked at the ceiling as his mind formulated his plan. "We must gather all the news from our informants first." He offered his chief-of-staff a cigarette. His hand momentarily held back his lighter as a shriek of pain and the thud of a heavy boot came through the ceiling. "Including our present guests here at Via Tasso."

"Very well, sir."

"You know our undercover agents. Use them." Kappler stood up. "With the Resistance being brazenly open in the streets, it shouldn't be difficult to grab a few more of their number, Berthold." He took his cap from the coat hook. "And then they can discover all the comforts of Via Tasso and tell us of their friends. And then we can put a stop to their games."

Kappler turned to his chief of staff as he opened the door. "And please—," he frowned in irritation as he waited for another scream to die down, "and please inform Field Marshal Kesselring that I shall be delighted to accept his invitation to the opera next week."

A Modest Apartment.

"And where did you get this information about a plan for your son to escape from prison, Signora Balotelli?" Sofia asked across the table in the widow's meager but immaculate kitchen.

"I told your friend, here," the woman nodded towards Cesare, who sat at Sofia's side. "A man came to my door this morning and said he had been in the same cell as Gianni in the Regina Coeli." Signora Balotelli's hand wrung nervously at a dishtowel in her lap. "He said his name was Paolo and that he'd just been released."

"How did he know your address?" Sofia asked.

"Gianni had given it to him. He said," the woman began to sob, "he said that my son had been tortured mercilessly, over and over."

"Her son was arrested two weeks ago, Sofia," Cesare said softly in Sofia's ear as she stroked the woman's upper arm in an attempt to comfort her. "A member of the Bandiera Rossa in the northwest sector. Her son wasn't exactly a friend of mine, but I knew him from my communications work."

"Those German swine!" the woman shouted, dabbing at her eyes with her towel as she struggled to compose herself. "But this man who came to see me – this Paolo – said my Gianni had a plan. Gianni was going to tell the Gestapo that he could take no more torture and that he would lead them to the secret headquarters of his communist friends."

"Did this man tell you where these headquarters were supposed to be, Signora Balotelli?" asked Cesare?"

"*Si si.*" The woman's hand began to search in the pocket of her apron, her fingers emerging with a scrap of paper. "The man, this Paolo, he gave me this address."

She handed the paper to Cesare, whose eyes ran over the address, then lifted to look at Sofia. "It's not an address known to me," he said.

"No, no! That is not a Resistance address!" Signora Balotelli became excited. "My Gianni, he's clever, *si?* He will lead the Gestapo to that address – and you and all your friends will be waiting to shoot the Germans!"

"Sounds rather simple to me," Cesare said with a hint of sarcasm. "Did this Paolo fellow give you any time when Gianni would lead the Germans to this address?" He tapped the paper.

"Tomorrow. Or maybe the day after. He wasn't sure."

Cesare drew Sofia aside. "It's fishy. I don't like it."

Sofia thought for a moment. "But it could be a big opportunity for us. I think we should talk with Ludo and Bartoli."

"Okay, but I'm sure they'll agree with me."

"You're going to help Gianni, aren't you?" the woman tearfully beseeched them as they carefully surveyed the street through the window.

"We'll do the best that we can, Signora Balotelli." Sofia placed a reassuring hand on the woman's shoulder.

"If you don't mind, signora," Cesare said with embarrassment, "I think we'll leave by the back door."

EXCELSIOR HOTEL LOUNGE.

"Obersturmbannführer Kappler."

The Gestapo chief looked up at the tall, wiry figure of Ganz looming over his table in the corner of the Excelsior Lounge. "An unexpected pleasure, mein Herr!" Ganz said. "Would you accept my favor of a schnapps?"

Kappler occasionally had to get out of his Via Tasso office for breaks, but whenever he came to his favorite haunt he ran the risk of being taken hostage by Hauptsturmführer Bruno Ganz. Still, in the interest of maintaining cordiality with Himmler's hand-picked man in Rome, he smiled up at him, trying to hide his feelings that he would have preferred better company, or none at all. "But of course, Ganz."

The Hauptsturmführer snapped his fingers at a passing Italian waiter and placed his order. "I haven't seen you for some time, mein Herr – where have you been?" Ganz eased himself into the chair on the other side of Kappler's table.

"I'm sure you cannot have forgotten that the enemy has two divisions not thirty kilometers away from Rome?" There was more than a hint of sarcasm in his voice. "When they first arrived, I was busy making plans for our evacuation from Rome."

"Yes, of course." Ganz paused as the waiter placed the drinks on the table; he scribbled his signature on the tab. "You and I discussed this earlier. As I recall, you were preparing to round up enemy prisoners hidden in Rome to head our columns."

"Very good, Ganz. Well, in the end I did not have to put the plan in place at that time." Kappler sipped at his drink and offered his cigarette case to Ganz. "The Americans failed to follow through on their obvious advantage, giving Field Marshal Kesselring time to arrive and bottle up the beachhead."

Ganz leaned into Kappler's proferred lighter, then eased back, exhaling smoke. "Yes, I am well aware of all that. And I'll bet there are a number of people here," he turned around to look at the score or so of officers who sat in the lounge, "who are grateful to the Führer for releasing the divisions from up north."

Kappler nodded. "And it's given me the opportunity to round up more of the Resistance." Kappler smiled. "You have no idea how lax they've become, thinking the Americans were about to arrive."

"Unfortunately, the Jews hiding in Rome are not so foolish." Ganz ran his finger around the rim of his glass. "We know there are still a lot of them out there, hiding all over Rome, but they rarely show their faces."

"Not had much luck?" Kappler sipped again at his glass. He had half forgotten Ganz's special Himmler-directed mission. For Kappler, rounding up Jews was a waste of time and resources.

"In general, no, but every now and then we succeed." Ganz chuckled. "You would not believe our best weapon."

"And that is—?"

"A Jewish woman." Ganz leaned forward across the table and lowered his voice conspiratorially. "A Jewish woman," he repeated.

Kappler's brow creased in puzzlement. "Knowing your record, Ganz, I'm surprised you haven't transported her to the north by now."

"No, you misunderstand me." Ganz looked furtively from side to side, checking that no one else in the bar was listening. "She betrays her fellow Jews for a thousand lire each!" He slapped his thigh. "Can you believe it, mein Herr? She fingers her own people for the price of two pork chops on the black market!" He wheezed at his own macabre sense of humor, then fell silent at the sight of Kappler's impassive face. "Of course, after she's served her purpose, I'll ship her north. For resettlement."

"I wish you luck, Ganz, but you must excuse me now." He drained his glass, stood up, and clicked his heels to take his leave. His thoughts turned to his own mole.

RESISTANCE MEETING.

"I have never known such carelessness!" Bartoli was red-faced with anger. "Are you all fools?" He walked around the dimly-lit shed, his eyes fixing everybody in the Resistance cell, one at a time. Renzo sensed the raw power under the dumpy appearance; everyone looked at the floor, avoiding his eyes.

"All of you have been openly meeting in the streets, as if you were at a Ferragosto festival and all the Germans had gone back to Berlin. In so doing, you have put the whole group in danger." He shook his head, as though in disbelief.

"You, Fabio." Vittoria winced as she saw Bartoli's finger pointed at her brother's chest. "You decide to distribute unauthorized leaflets in the Piazza Venezia."

"But we had to do something to start organizing the people for the uprising. The Americans are coming, and I thought—"

"You are not in this organization to think!" Bartoli's acid voice made Fabio cringe. "Do you see any Americans on the streets of Rome? I see only Germans and Gestapo." He stared again at Fabio. "You put all of us at risk. All of us – Vittoria, Cesare," he pointed his finger at each one, "Sofia, Ludo, Renzo. If it hadn't been for your sister, you'd be in the Via Tasso now, telling who knows what to Kappler's henchmen."

"I would never say anything to the Gestapo!" Fabio shouted.

Bartoli sighed as he sat back down. "Ah, yes, we are all so brave. Until we see the knuckledusters, truncheons, and knives of the Gestapo! Then perhaps we sing a different song."

He turned to the others. "Sofia and Cesare, you took an unacceptable risk visiting that woman. It was such an obvious

191

Gestapo set-up. At least you had the sense to get out quickly or you, too, could have been guests at the Via Tasso."

"Why have you brought us to this new meeting place?" Ludovico asked.

"We must reestablish our security." Bartoli looked around at everyone. "From now on, all our meetings will be at different places. Cesare will be told two hours before, and he will inform everyone of the venue. All of us will observe stricter security."

He leaned back in his chair and lit a cigarette. "I know you all want to have the opportunity to deliver a blow against the Germans. That day will come, I promise. But we can't strike back if we're in prison!"

RESTAURANT AT THE EXCELSIOR HOTEL.

Kappler blotted his lips, put down his napkin, and pushed his chair back from his favorite table in the Excelsior's dining room. Things were better, and not just because of the excellent veal Milanese he had just savored. The waiter cleared away his plate and the Gestapo chief lit a postprandial cigarette.

As he looked through the window down the quiet after-curfew Via Veneto, he fought the temptation to be overly confident, but there was no doubt that the situation in Rome was better, much better. The Anglo-Americans seemed to have lost their nerve and had been unable to break out at Anzio, nearly a month after landing. He drew on his cigarette, recalling the panic in the days following the invasion – everyone, including himself, working on emergency evacuation plans. Now, Kesselring had told him, there was every chance he could destroy the Allied beachhead.

Kappler nodded to the waiter who delivered his digestif. Perhaps the war could still be won.

What gave him a special feeling of satisfaction was how quiet the Resistance had been of late. Just after the Anglo-Americans had landed, the partisans had been arrogant - and their security had become lax. His men had called it 'The Happy Time.' Via Tasso had never been so busy; there were daily executions at Fort Bravetta. But now all that had changed.

Kappler sipped his cognac. He knew he shouldn't get carried away, but perhaps the Resistance in Rome was broken.

Resistance Meeting.

The tension in the air at the Resistance cell meeting was palpable. Renzo could see that Bartoli was uneasy, despite his efforts to appear calm.

"With respect, Comrade Bartoli," Ludo spoke first, "it must be said that your orders to cease attacks on the German occupiers are, to put it mildly, very frustrating for all of us." He looked around the table and was pleased to see heads nodding in agreement. "We don't think sitting on our backsides for weeks is likely to upset the Germans."

"I told you the reason." Bartoli spoke brusquely. "Security became too lax after the Anzio landing and Kappler had a field day. Many cells were compromised. But fortunately *not this cell.*" Bartoli tapped his finger on the table to reinforce each word.

"Okay, so we were overconfident," Cesare said from the far end of the table. "But we thought the Americans would arrive within days. We all knew there weren't many German troops between Anzio and Rome. A troop of women pushing baby carriages could've done the job."

"Well, it didn't happen," Bartoli said acidly, "and it still hasn't happened."

"I don't think Cesare expressed our feelings fully," Vittoria said. "We have taken no action against the Germans for weeks. Not only are they controlling the Allies at Anzio," Renzo, sitting next to her, sensed the anger growing in her voice, "but they're controlling us. The bastards strut along the streets of Rome as though they owned our city. And yet we do nothing!"

"Vittoria's right." Renzo spoke before Bartoli could reply. "Perhaps your order made sense a month ago – when we were all a bit too eager, thinking the Americans would be marching in and joining us soon. You were right to order us to lie low back then." He paused. "But I believe that now is the right time to strike. By our own lack of action they – the Germans – have been lulled into a false sense of security. Now," his fist smashed down on the table, "now is the time to strike the Germans, to show them that, even without the Americans, we're still a force to be reckoned with!"

The other partisans cheered, beating on the table with the flats of their hands.

Bartoli waited some moments for the emotion to die down, then raised his hand to stifle the chatter. "You may be surprised to learn that I agree with you. Yes, we must take action. But it must be unlike any other action we have taken so far." He waited until there was complete silence in the room before speaking again. "I shall lay the general plan before you as soon as I can – there are still details to be finalized."

Bartoli stood up and looked around the table. "I am proud to be the leader of this cell."

PIAZZA DI SPAGNA.

"Giorgio, why—"

"Shhh," Giorgio said with his finger to his lips, "I think I can hear them." When Luisa cupped her hand to her ear and listened hard she detected a faint but regular sound coming from somewhere up the Via del Babuino.

"Why have we come here, Giorgio?" she asked.

"To see a parade, Luisa. Don't you like parades?" He shaded his eyes and looked down at the Fontana della Barcaccia, the Fountain of the Old Boat, at the bottom of the Spanish Steps on which they were standing. For centuries the unseaworthy little vessel had been spouting leaks from its holes in a perpetual act of sinking, and at that moment people were drawing water from its arcing streams to fill their jugs.

"I haven't seen many parades," mused Luisa. "Once, when my father and I were trying to cross Via Arenula, we saw a Catholic parade. There were men in robes carrying a statue—"

"Listen!" Giorgio said in a loud whisper. Luisa heard a noise that reminded her of her mother beating carpets in the courtyard: the sound of marching boots. The people with the jugs had heard, too, and they began to scatter away from the fountain. Before long they could hear voices singing; then came the column of SS police, preceded by men holding submachine guns across their chests.

Luisa shrank closer to the wall: the horrendous procession was a chilling reminder of the day the men came to take her parents away. Had these men come for her? But when Giorgio took her hand she began to feel safe again. "They're not interested in us, Luisa," he said. "They do this every day – they go to some barracks north of the Colosseum to practice."

"What do they practice?" she asked.

Giorgio thought for a moment. "I guess they practice how to be nasty to people," he answered.

The men were singing a strange song, *"Hupf, Mein Mädel,"* their voices ringing in step with their feet. After a few minutes, the procession had passed by the children's vantage point on the Spanish Steps, an armored truck with a mounted machine gun having brought up the rear.

As the column left the Piazza di Spagna and began to make its way down the Via Sistina, a man who had been trying to fill his water jug earlier wandered back into the middle of the piazza toward the fountain. On the way he stopped, waved his free arm angrily at the marchers, and spat in their direction.

"Please don't bring me to see any more parades, Giorgio," said Luisa. "Those men looked really mean, and I didn't like their singing very much."

"I'm sorry, Luisa. They weren't very nice, I know," Giorgio replied. "But they did march rather well, don't you think?"

An Apartment in Central Rome.

The tramp of soldiers' boots echoed up from the street below.

"The reason I've brought you here to my friend's apartment," Bartoli looked around at all the cell members gathered on the balcony high above the street, "is to show you these despicable newcomers to Rome."

"Arrogant bastards, aren't they?" Ludovico growled as he looked down on the three-hundred strong column of SS police marching by, lock-stepped, their submachine guns carried menacingly.

"Yes, they are," Bartoli agreed. "And they display their arrogance by marching at the same time every day, along the same streets, singing the same songs."

"They must be new to Rome," Sofia said. "Until two weeks ago I'd never seen or even heard of them."

"Who the hell are they?" Renzo's question was almost lost in the thunderous stomping of the soldiers' boots on the cobbles and the harsh chanting of their marching song.

"I think we'd better continue this discussion inside," Fabio shouted. Bartoli nodded and they all filed into the apartment and sat down at the large table.

"Comrades," Bartoli looked around the table, "you have just seen the Ninth Company of the Bozen SS Police Regiment, a company made up entirely of men from the South Tyrol in the Italian Alps."

"They're traitors!" shouted Fabio.

Bartoli held up his hand for order. "The South Tyrol, as you know, is now a part of the German Reich. The men in the Bozen SS Police Regiment, born Italian, not only opted for German citizenship, but also chose to be in the SS."

"I've heard of these guys," Cesare said. "They're German-speaking – and Nazis to a man."

"But what are they doing here?" Vittoria asked from the end of the table.

"They're basically SS police thugs," Bartoli answered. "They've been brought into Rome to beef up Kappler's Gestapo operations."

"Kappler, that son of a bitch!" Fabio slapped the table.

"And now I can tell you why I've called this meeting. The men you just saw marching below – they are to be our next target."

A brief moment of silence preceded the buzz of anticipation that ran around the table as the Resistance cell digested Bartoli's news.

"The central committee has approved my plan. The German column you just saw will be our target, and we have been honored with carrying out the task." There was passion in Bartoli's eyes as he spoke. "That they march down our streets every day is an insult to Rome and all Romans. We will attack them, blow them to hell, and show the Nazi bastards that they cannot walk with impunity on the streets of our city."

The cell remained silent as Bartoli struggled to control his breathing after his tirade. "I'm sorry, comrades, to burst out like that, but I have waited so many years, so many years…" His voice died away.

"We'll be using a bomb, I suppose?" Renzo asked after a silence.

"Yes, of course."

"It'll obviously have to be a large bomb – we've seen how big the police regiment is."

"I don't think we'll have any worries there, Renzo. Our army defectors have provided us with plenty of explosives, and," Bartoli looked down toward the end of the table and smiled, "we're very fortunate to have an expert bomb-maker in our cell."

Renzo looked over at Vittoria and saw she could not fight off a blush of pride.

Bartoli stood up. "Now that you know the basics of the operation, we need to work out the details. I want you all to give that some thought. We'll meet to discuss the plan on Monday; Cesare will tell you the meeting place by Sunday. Regarding the operation," Bartoli concluded, "the main questions we face are: where and when?"

A Bar in Central Rome.

As the bar door closed behind him, Jay knew he had made a mistake. The bar was quiet, unlike on his previous visits, and even the table in the corner where the old men played dominoes every day was unoccupied. The bartender caught Jay's eye, his head nodding toward a table at the far end of the room. An Italian fascist officer. The obvious plainclothes disguise – the hat, the overcoat – didn't fool Jay. He turned to leave and saw the armed guard barring his way.

"Signor John MacPherson," came the voice from the table at the back, "please don't leave. I wish to talk with you."

Jay was surprised by the Italian's clear English. He scanned the room anxiously for an escape route, but there was none.

"In fact, I insist," he said, rising from his seat. "You're under arrest."

Resistance Meeting.

"We ended our previous meeting by agreeing that the key questions regarding our bomb attack on the Bozen regiment were, simply, where and when." Bartoli cast his eyes around the room of partisans. "The technical details of the bomb should pose no problem—"

"May I make a suggestion as to when?" Vittoria interrupted Bartoli, who nodded for her to continue.

"In three days it'll be the twenty-third of March." She saw the others' eyes widen as they realized the importance of that date. "That will be the twenty-fifth anniversary of Mussolini's founding of the *Fasci di Combattimento*. It's a really big deal for them – I hear they're planning celebrations all over Rome, everything from a church service in the morning to a huge parade in the afternoon."

"I like your idea, Vittoria. Symbolic. It doesn't give us much time, but I like it." Bartoli smiled as the rest nodded in agreement. He unfolded a large map of Rome on the table. "Now to the question of where."

FASCIST POLICE HEADQUARTERS.

Jay had no idea what would happen to him. So far, there had been no threats, no physical intimidation. He looked around his cell: a table, two chairs, a small window high in the opposite wall that looked out on a March sky smudged with dark clouds clinging to winter's departure.

Jay cursed his ineptitude. There was no way he could get word to Father Francesco, and now the whole prisoner-of-war operation in Rome was jeopardized. They would torture him, he thought as he looked down at his hands, his fingers. How much pain waited for him in those digits? He tried to force his eyes and his thoughts away from his fingers, but his mind kept finding its way back to the thought of the pain.

Jay jumped at the sound of a key rattling in the lock. The door opened, revealing the fascist officer who had arrested him.

"Signor John MacPherson," the officer said with a tired voice, "I am Commissario Giovanni Lippi." Jay was surprised at the officer's smile. "We need to talk."

Somehow Jay found it difficult to see Lippi as a policeman. The uniform stretched desperately over a copious frame that spoke eloquently of many years of overindulgence.

"*Prego.* Help yourself." The commissioner tossed a pack of cigarettes onto the table, his keen eyes above a wide nose suggesting astuteness and cunning.

"Why have I been arrested?" Jay pulled out a cigarette and leaned forward into Lippi's proferred match. "I demand an explanation."

The commissioner sighed as he tossed his expended match into the ashtray. "Signor John MacPherson. American officer. Leader of the escaped prisoner-of-war operation in Rome." He reached into the drawer, pulled out a fairly thick dossier, and placed it on the table between them. "It's all in there," he said, tapping the file. "I doubt our friends in the Gestapo have such a file."

Jay sensed there was an implied threat. "But if you had all this information, why wasn't I arrested a long time ago?"

"I cannot speak for the Gestapo." Lippi drew on his cigarette. "We have little truck with them." He didn't try to hide the displeasure in his voice. "We do their bidding. But only when we have to."

"But I ask again: if you know all that," Jay pointed to the file, "why didn't you arrest me before?"

"That's simple." Lippi's eyes sparkled, his lips forcing a smile onto his round face. "I had to wait for the right opportunity."

RESISTANCE MEETING.

"Since the bomb will be large," all eyes turned to Renzo, "where we explode it poses a serious problem."

"What do you mean?" Fabio asked. "After all, the Germans take the same route day after day."

Renzo looked at Fabio in astonishment. "Haven't you thought about our fellow Italians along the route?" He stood up and leaned over the map. "Here, for example, the column marches by the entrance to a tunnel underneath the Quirinal Hill. Lots of bombed-out refugees live inside that tunnel."

"Good point, Renzo, and I've already taken it into consideration." Bartoli spoke quickly, trying to diffuse any ill-feeling between Renzo and Fabio. "I propose we explode it here." He tapped on the map. "No shops, no offices, and it's not a busy street. Right here, at the top end of Via Rasella."

"Yes!" Fabio brought his fist down on the table. "We'll be striking a blow for freedom! The people will rise up and throw out the Nazi occupiers!" Fabio's excited voice filled the room.

Renzo fell silent. He knew the psychology. The assassination of so many soldiers would provoke reprisals by the Germans. Romans would be shot. The infuriated population would rise up in response to the atrocity and throw the Germans out, as the Neapolitans had.

But what if they didn't?

"So now what?" Jay couldn't figure out what was happening. "Are you going to turn me over to the Gestapo?"

"*Gesù-Maria,* no." Lippi chuckled. "Why would I kill the goose who could lay the golden egg?"

"What do you mean?" An inkling began to sink into Jay's mind that the inspector had a hidden agenda. "What golden egg are you talking about?"

"The money." Lippi nonchalantly tossed out the seductive word.

MacPherson didn't like cat and mouse games but saw no alternative but to probe the inspector's thoughts. "What money?"

"Don't treat me as a fool, Signor MacPherson." Lippi scowled. "I know many of our police obediently jump at the orders of our Gestapo friends, but I have other aims."

"So, are you saying you no longer support the fascist party?"

"Of course I support the fascist party." A smile began to creep across Lippi's face. "But I support Lippi more."

"Yeah, and I'll bet the closer the American army gets to Rome, the more distance you'll want to put between you and the fascist party."

Lippi leaned back and smiled broadly. "You are very perceptive, my friend, but my politics are not at issue at the moment." He stood up, put his hands behind his back, and began to pace. "But money is. I need a good pension for when…"

"For when the Allies arrive and you're out of a job?" Jay asked sharply.

"For when, shall we say," Lippi raised his eyes, as if contemplating the cracks in the ceiling, "for when circumstances change and I retire. I wish to make you an offer."

"An offer?" Jay's intestines clenched as he felt the fear return. "What are you talking about?"

"Let me explain. It may save you a visit to Gestapo headquarters on the Via Tasso."

Renzo continued to worry as he thought about the logic behind the attack on the SS police regiment. What if the people were cowed and did nothing after the attack? Suddenly, he wasn't so sure it was a good idea.

"After we've made the bomb, how do we deliver it?" Vittoria's voice brought him back to the present.

A simple but vital question, Renzo thought as he looked across at Vittoria, delighted that his half-smile was warmly returned.

"I have an idea about that," Sofia said, her eyes focused on the far distance, as if her mind were elsewhere.

"Uh-oh. Danger. My wife's been thinking again," Ludovico said, snorting a chuckle.

Sofia ignored his comment. "How about a street cleaner's cart?" she suggested. "You know, those little wheeled buggies carrying a trash can and a broom."

Renzo revised his opinion about Sofia. She was sharp. Her suggestion was perfect. Street cleaners' carts were all over Rome. Nobody would suspect such a device.

"Great idea, Sofia!" Vittoria said with enthusiasm. "I can put a large bomb in the bottom of the trash bin. The metal will become shrapnel. Much more effective."

Bartoli began folding up the map to bring the meeting to an end. "It looks like we've got the major points of the operation worked out," he said. "We'll attack the Nazis with a fragmentation bomb. On March 23rd. In the Via Rasella." He picked up the map. "I'll submit the plan to the central committee."

"But I assume we can get started on the preparations," Vittoria said.

"Yes, of course, Vittoria." Bartoli stuffed the map into his inside pocket. "By all means, start preparing the bomb. Ludo and Sofia – you need to organize the back-up support – tommy guns and grenades for both of you. Cesare – you will attack the column from behind after the bomb explodes."

Bartoli turned to Renzo. "I'd like you to help Vittoria make and assemble the bomb." Renzo smiled at Vittoria, who was smiling back at him, but Bartoli's next words rankled him. "And I'd also like you to help Fabio steal the street cleaner's cart."

Renzo's smile disappeared. "Are you sure I can handle that? After all, it's dangerous – theft of city property carries harsh penalties." The others laughed, but Renzo hadn't meant it to be funny.

Bartoli ignored the comment. "And you, Fabio, you'll wheel the cart bomb into place and ignite it."

As he watched Fabio swell with pride, Renzo had difficulty in controlling his growing resentment. His role in the biggest attack on the Nazi occupiers had been reduced to an act of petty larceny – stealing a trash cart, no more. And the task of leading the mission had been given to a wet-behind-the-ears idealistic dreamer.

He waited for the meeting to end and skulked away.

Commissario Lippi's nicotine-stained fingers unfolded the single sheet of paper he had pulled from his pocket. As he sat back down, his palm tried to iron out the typewritten document on the table.

"There it is." The wide smile returned to his ample face as he looked across at Jay. "For you and your prisoner-of-war friends, a ticket to a safe life. For Lippi, a ticket to a richer life." His raucous chuckle echoed around the cell.

Jay pushed his hand forward and lifted the document, his eyes flitting over the words. "I'm afraid my Italian's not all that good. What is it?" he asked, raising his eyebrows questioningly.

Lippi drummed his fingers on the table, then rose slowly from his chair and walked to the door, listening for any noise in the corridor outside. Reassured, he turned back to Jay.

"That document is the Operational Order of the Day for the Squadra Mobile Romana."

"Which is?"

"Our unit whose sirens you hear and fear every day as they head out to round up criminals, communists, and—," he paused for effect, "escaped prisoners of war."

"And you are saying…?" Jay could scarcely believe the direction the conversation seemed to be taking.

"I'm saying how would you like to receive this," Lippi waved the document in front of Jay's eyes, "every day, twelve hours before it's given to the Squadra to implement?"

Jay was suspicious. "How do I know you're speaking the truth? And if you are, how can you possibly guarantee delivery of such classified information?"

"*I* don't guarantee delivery," he said with a smirk, "your five thousand lire a week guarantee delivery."

"Five thousand!" Jay gasped. "Five thousand lire is a lot of money!"

"Fifty dollars a week?" Lippi raised a chiding eyebrow. "Fifty dollars a week is too much to ensure safety for your fellow escaped prisoners?"

"But how do I know daily bulletins will contain accurate information?"

Shaking his head and sighing, as though his honor had been insulted, Lippi picked up the document. "These are the orders for tomorrow, March 21st." He pulled his pince-nez glasses from his pocket and perched them on the end of his nose. "At four o'clock," he read, "a unit will raid Via del Seminario, 16 and arrest all occupants."

Jay tried not to react. He knew the address as a safe house. Signora Carlotti was the padrone, hiding three escaped American prisoners and a Canadian.

"I need time," Jay said, wondering how far he could trust Lippi. "I have to talk to some people."

"Yes, of course. I understand." Lippi's smile had become a permanent fixture. "But I suggest you talk to the occupants of Via del Seminario, 16 immediately, as well." He collected the papers, got up, and began walking toward the door. "And remember, fifty dollars a week will also ensure your name and address don't appear on the list." He turned in the doorway. "In forty-eight hours."

A BAR IN TRASTEVERE.

Renzo was drunk and he knew he was drunk. He signaled to the bartender that he needed a refill, waving away the questioning arched eyebrow. And he knew why he was drunk. It wasn't just because Bartoli had chosen Fabio instead of him to lead the Via Rasella attack. He picked up his replenished glass and drank deeply. If the partisan leader wanted to jeopardize the operation by giving the bomb delivery to some snotty-nosed schoolboy, that was his business.

No, that wasn't the only reason he reached for his glass again after just having put it down. It was her. Little miss high-and-mighty. He felt the cheap grappa dance sourly on his tongue before he consigned the liquid to his gullet. All right, he tried to reason with himself, perhaps he had tried to go too far with Vittoria this evening. The liquor exploded in his stomach in concert with his anger. But they had been on raids together, had shared the fear, had practically lived in each other's pockets for months. He'd tried to resist his feelings, but he knew he'd become crazy for her. Yet when he'd made an advance, she refused him, turning her head and pushing him away.

He drained his glass and called for another. It wasn't the right time, she'd said. She was about to say more, but he'd stormed out. Was there ever a right time? He fumbled for a cigarette from his pack.

"Do you have a spare?" The voice startled him. He turned, forcing his eyes to focus through the smoke of a hundred cigarettes that hung in the air. She was young and pretty, with ebony hair and dark brown eyes. "Do you have a spare cigarette?" she repeated, her voice betraying her working-class origins.

"Sure." His shaking hand waved the packet in front of her. Her fingers clutched his wrist, steadying his hand as she plucked a cigarette from the pack, and he was surprised at the firmness of her grip. On her wrist, he saw a bracelet with a pendant icon. He was suddenly alert when he saw that it was a tiny 'chai,' the Hebrew letters for 'life,' a Jewish symbol.

"Are you going to give me a light?" She put the cigarette in her mouth and leaned toward him provocatively, with a warm but knowing smile.

"Sure." He pulled his lighter from his pocket but couldn't trust his hand, so he put it on the bar. She gave a half laugh and picked it up to light her cigarette, the pendant dancing before his eyes.

"Isn't it dangerous wearing that thing?"

"What?"

"The bracelet. The 'chai' symbol. Is it wise to advertise you're a Jew in Nazi-occupied Rome?

She leaned forward, looked around, and whispered. "Would you believe you're the first person ever to notice? Most people think it's just a decorative bangle." Her fingers toyed with the bracelet. "You're obviously a Jew yourself to recognize something like this."

He offered no reply, his hand grabbing awkwardly for the lighter which he stuffed in his pocket.

"Maybe we should go somewhere. What do you say?" Her voice was soft, her eyes were wide.

"Got any ideas?" Why not? his befuddled mind thought.

"I know a place where we can go." She lowered her eyes and slipped off her barstool with a flash of thighs. "Wait here while I go to the Ladies' Room."

Perhaps he shouldn't, Renzo thought, but his conscience soon lost the battle. He pushed a fifty lire note toward the bartender.

He finished his drink, his mind trying to grasp the possibilities of the night ahead and the seductive promise of those dark brown eyes and white thighs. He drummed his fingers on the bar. She was a long time in the Ladies' Room, he thought. Maybe he shouldn't. Maybe he should just go home and sleep it off.

His eyes caught a movement at the door. A silence suddenly gripped the bar. The man at the door wasn't wearing a uniform, but everyone knew he was Gestapo. Renzo turned to escape by the back door, but his legs struggled with the instructions from his drunken mind and he fell to the floor. He looked up and saw the Gestapo man looming over him.

"Well, Jewboy, you can sleep it off in a cell at the Regina Coeli."

A picture of the hated jail flitted across his mind. There was one more thought before his conscious mind drowned in the sea of grappa. Where was the woman?

A CELLAR WORKROOM.

The unshaded bulb cast a harsh light around the cellar, illuminating the old but sturdy wooden table at which Vittoria worked. She was excited by the technical challenge of making such a large fragmentation bomb and, since the planned attack was only three days away, she was anxious to get started. After the meeting, she had tried to convey this urgency to Renzo, but he had other things on his mind, grabbing at her and pulling her toward him. Normally she would have welcomed his embraces. But how could he possibly have romance on his mind at such a time?

As she got up to get another packet of nitroglycerine, she wondered again where he was. He was supposed to help her – that was the assignment he had been given by Bartoli.

She tamped the explosive into the large metal box that sat inside a five-gallon gas can, taking care space was left for the detonator fuse. The bomb would be the largest she had ever made, and she was feeling tired. She needed Renzo's help, but there was no sign of him.

She had filled the space between the box and the can with bolts, rusty nails, and old scraps of metal, every piece of which would become a deadly bit of shrapnel when the bomb exploded. After Fabio lit the fuse, this bomb was going to cause real havoc.

She pushed back in her chair and blew a wisp of hair out of her eyes. Her work was going well, but she needed a cigarette break. Where the hell was Renzo?

March 21, 1944

REGINA COELI PRISON.

"Get up! Slop out time!"

The voice in the distance, accompanied by metal banging on metal, forced its way into Renzo's dulled consciousness. He tried to resist, but the insistent voice would not be denied. He turned once on a mattress so hard he thought he was on the floor. Images began to seep back into his throbbing brain: Vittoria's pushing him away, the bar, the drinks, the Jewish woman...

He sat up with a start: he was in a prison cell. A tiny, high window, grey damp walls. And the insistent voice of a prison guard. *"Get up! Slop out time!"*

"Welcome to Regina Coeli Prison!" The cheerful voice coming from the other side of the cell startled him. "The Queen of Heaven – the prison of choice for discriminating Roman Jews. Name's Vito Del Pietro."

Renzo forced his eyes to focus on the man opposite him: dark, silky hair, deep brown eyes astride a broad nose, burly, he sat grinning on the edge of his cot. On the wall behind his cot was a crucifix. "How would you know if I'm Jewish?" Renzo asked.

"Last night, the guard drags you in and tosses you onto the straw. 'Well,' he says, 'looks like the Black Panther bagged another one.'" Vito picked up an empty pipe and began sucking on it.

"Black Panther?"

"The beautiful Jewish woman. She fingers other Jews to the Gestapo," Vito lifted his hand and rubbed his thumb and index finger together, "for a thousand lire each."

Renzo massaged his temples, trying to ease away the headache. "I can't believe that. A Jew betraying her own people for the cost of a bag of groceries?"

"When the alternative is the firing squad at Fort Bravetta, money to buy a bag of groceries is very acceptable."

"I could never do that!"

Vito laughed. "Then prepare yourself for a final cigarette at Fort Bravetta. Or, if you're lucky, deportation to a German slave labor camp. Myself, I wouldn't mind the labor camp – it would be an improvement over this hellhole."

Renzo's head kept pounding and he wished the man would stop talking, but Vito continued. "Me, I'm inside for another four years," he said. At least in a labor camp I'd be on the out-side – I'd have a chance to escape."

Renzo felt a sudden coldness pass through him. Black Panther, Fort Bravetta, last cigarette, slave labor camps—

"Get up! Slop out time!"

SANTA MARIA DELLA GLORIA.

"I didn't expect you so early, Signor Jay." Father Francesco moved quickly around the altar, lighting candles in preparation for Lauds. "I must be honest – the price Commissario Lippi is asking is not a cheap one." He genuflected as he passed before the cross to apply his taper to another candle.

"I know. I've got my own doubts about this deal, as well." Jay spoke softly from the front pew, although he recoiled as his whispers echoed around the cavernous church. "But we have this afternoon's police order to test him."

"Yes, I remember. You told me he said they're going to raid Signora Carlotti's apartment on Via del Seminario. Three escaped American soldiers and a Canadian."

"I think I'd like to err on the side of conservatism." Jay rose from the pew. "I'm going to evacuate the apartment – hide the padrone and the POWs somewhere else."

"Perhaps there are times one must trust a scoundrel." The priest lit the candles at the head of the aisle. "Lippi knows the

American army will arrive soon, so he has little to lose. And from the amount of money he's asking, he has much to gain." He blew out the candle in his hand and looked around anxiously at Jay. "But, truly, I'm not certain sufficient funds can be made available."

"In any event, Father, we have to find a way to get the money to pay Lippi. If Signora Carlotti's place is raided, we'll have to pay."

Father Francesco nodded. "Is there something else, my son?"

"Yes, Father. I have a favor to ask." Jay dug into his breast pocket and pulled out an envelope. "The next time you visit Maria, could you give her this?"

The priest slowly shook his head. "Prisoners' mail gets read. She must receive nothing that could further incriminate her."

"But I didn't even sign it! There's nothing—"

"I'll tell Maria you are thinking of her, Signor Jay." Father Francesco turned and resumed his task of lighting the candles. "And, I hope, praying for her, as well."

CAFFÈ GRECO.

Vittoria looked anxiously at the door of the café, willing Renzo to enter. She squirmed nervously in her chair. She had toiled in her workshop past curfew and had slept there overnight but Renzo had never shown up. She pushed her spoon rapidly around in her chamomile tea as she looked at her watch. What the hell had happened to him?

Much as she tried to thrust the idea from her mind, images from their meeting the evening before pressed in on her. He had been angry that Fabio had been given command of the Via Rasella operation. It was certainly true that Renzo had demonstrated more bravery and competence, and even she had to admit that her brother was a strange choice for the command role. But Bartoli's decisions were not to be questioned.

Vittoria knew about the importance of pride to men, but there had been even more to upset Renzo the previous evening. The images paraded across her mind. He had pressed forward, begging for a kiss, perhaps seeking some solace at his earlier rebuff. Had it been any other evening she would have returned his affection with pleasure, would have felt a familiar warmth wash over her, would have gladly nestled in his arms. But the previous evening had been different: she had been overwhelmed by Bartoli's announcement of their next action and was preoccupied with the technical details of designing a larger bomb. She hadn't meant to reject Renzo, but his timing had been all wrong.

She looked up eagerly as the café door opened and tried to hide her disappointment when she saw Sofia framed in the doorway.

Via del Seminario.

Jay looked at his watch. Four o'clock. The time Lippi's report said the raid would take place.

The shriek of the police wagon sirens did not evoke the usual fear in Jay. From the corner of the street, he looked over at the apartment building at Via del Seminario, 16, the address given in Lippi's report. The tires of the wagon screeched on the cobbles, the black-shirted police leapt out, poised for arrests Jay knew would never happen. Signora Carlotti's guests had been evacuated hours before.

He watched as the fascist policeman hammered on the door, were invited in by the signora, and came out half an hour later looking frustrated. Lippi's information was correct.

He thought about the next step: now Father Francesco had to persuade a donor to provide the funds.

CAFFÈ GRECO.

"Sofia, have you seen Renzo?" Vittoria asked urgently as her friend sat down at her table.

"Not since yesterday's meeting. Something wrong?" She turned to the waiter and placed her order.

"Renzo was supposed to meet me last night to help me make…" Vittoria let her words die away.

"I wouldn't worry if I were you." Sofia pulled out a compact from her handbag and checked her hair in the mirror. "The tram system has been completely screwed up by the American bombing. Maybe he couldn't make it to your workshop before curfew."

"But Renzo's never failed me." She looked down into her cup. "Perhaps this time there was a reason."

"Uh, oh – I smell man trouble." As the waiter placed a steaming cup before her, Sofia put the compact away and gave a half chuckle. "I remember," she raised the cup to her lips, "soon after I first met Ludo—"

"It was serious, Sofia."

"These things are always serious, Vittoria."

"I rejected him, Sofia." Vittoria's cup clattered in her saucer. "I pushed him away. My mind was on Barioli's announcement, making the bomb. I didn't want—"

"Relax, Vittoria, it happens to most of us one time or another." Sofia blew into her blackberry leaf tea. "My mother once told me men are driven by only one thing."

"Perhaps. But Renzo is different."

"Of course he is, Vittoria." Sofia took a sip. "All men are different – but exactly the same." She made a face. "Ugh! I just can't get used to these tea and coffee substitutes."

"Then what happened to Renzo?"

"Don't worry, Vittoria. A man will always turn up again. Whether you want him to or not."

"I guess you're right," Vittoria said with a sigh. "As an old married woman, I guess you've seen it all."

"You don't know the half of it." Sofia paused, biting her lip and setting her cup down. "But there's something else I wanted to talk to you about. Something important."

Santa Maria della Gloria.

Father Francesco made his way toward the transept as he hurried to a confessional nestled in the far corner, away from the nave. He crossed himself as he passed the Chapel of Saint Catherine, her compassionate martyred face looking down at him from above her wheel, as if sympathizing with his plight.

His thoughts turned to more worldly concerns. The English and American legations at the Vatican had refused his request to provide funds for Commissario Lippi's daily report, saying they were forbidden to have dealings with fascist blackmailers. Fools, he thought, as he kissed his stole and draped it around his neck, pushing the confessional curtain aside and entering the booth.

"Forgive me, Father, for I have sinned." The words came through the grille of the confessional box. The priest struggled to put aside the voice of his conscience. Wrong, the voice cried, what you are about to do is wrong. But he knew the man beyond the lattice of the confessional was now his only hope as a source of money to bribe Lippi.

Father Francesco silently prayed for forgiveness for what he was about to do. "What is the nature of your sin, my son?"

"I have too many sins to enumerate, Father. I pray only that the resources I provide to help your cause may reduce my time in purgatory."

"Perhaps sinners in the cause of God will receive forgiveness."

"But what is the new cost of forgiveness, Father?"

"Five thousand lire a week." The priest answered quickly, as if to avoid embarrassment. "You already know what the funds are for."

"The Roman fascist police's 'Daily Operational Order.' Even the office of the German embassy could not acquire such a gem."

"Then you will provide the funds?" Father Francesco's fingers toyed nervously with his rosary as he awaited an answer.

"Maybe. But couldn't you arrange for my forgiveness with a dozen 'Hail Marys' instead? It would be a lot cheaper." A soft chuckle came from the other side of the confessional.

Father Francesco peered through the wooden lattice, but the face on the other side had gone.

Caffè Greco.

Sofia looked around to see who was nearby; all the other tables were full, their occupants engaged in lively chatter. "Have you made it yet?" Sofia's whispered question was tentative, as if hoping for a negative answer.

Vittoria knew she was talking about the bomb for the attack on the German column. "Yes. When Renzo didn't show up, I just worked on it myself throughout the night. Fabio has only to wheel it into place in the trash bin, light the fuse, and," her voice dropped to a whisper, "boom!" She unclenched her hands, her fingers shooting out like petals on a flower. "It should take out several dozen Germans. Pretty good, huh?"

Vittoria felt deflated by Sofia's reaction; she sat quietly, without a smile, staring into her cup. "You're not happy about the plan, are you, Sofia?"

"The plan looks fine, Vittoria."

"But." Vittoria lit up a cigarette. "I can sense a 'but.'"

"Yes, I can't deny there's a problem." Sofia looked up, her eyes hardening as they fixed Vittoria. "So you blow a dozen or so Germans to Kingdom Come. Then what?"

"We will have delivered a powerful message, that those who oppress us are no longer safe to walk Rome's streets as if they owned them."

"But," Sofia toyed with her teacup, "and I make no apology for the word, but what if the Germans decide to make reprisals?"

"Oh, come on, Sofia, there won't be any reprisals. Eight Germans were killed when Renzo bombed the cinema and there were no reprisals. Italy isn't the same as one of the other countries the Germans occupy – less than a year ago, we were their allies."

"But suppose they do carry out reprisals? Suppose the Germans kill a lot of innocent Romans?"

"Then, as Fabio says, it still works to our advantage, because the people of Rome will rise up."

"I wish I shared your confidence." Sofia leaned back and pushed her half-drunk tea away, the cup clattering in its saucer. "But I still think it's a gigantic gamble."

RESISTANCE MEETING.

"The news is not good." Bartoli looked at the apprehensive faces of the group gathered around the table in the cellar. "I understand that our comrade, Renzo, was arrested two nights ago."

Vittoria's hand flew up to her mouth.

"But how?" Ludovico asked. "Renzo has always been so careful."

"Yes," Cesare agreed, "and being a Jew made him all the more careful. This is the guy who escaped the roundup in the ghetto over the roofs of Rome with a child on his back."

Bartoli shrugged. "Well, it would appear his carefulness deserted him. He's now locked up in a cell of the Regina Coeli jail."

"Hard to believe," Ludovico said frowning, "that anyone as shrewd as Renzo could suddenly become careless. Remember how he escaped on the bicycle with Nazis and fascists flying at him from all directions?"

"Do you know what happened, Dante?" Sofia spoke from the far end of the table.

"Apparently, he was arrested in a bar." Bartoli hesitated. "He was drunk. Totally drunk."

"Renzo drunk? Why should he be drunk?" Fabio asked.

Vittoria caught Sofia's sidelong glance and looked quickly away. She sought to deny to herself that she was the cause of Renzo's reckless behavior, but she could not suppress a stab of shame mixed with deep remorse. She was the reason Renzo had become careless in the bar.

"I suppose," Fabio sounded depressed, "this means we'll have to postpone the attack in Via Rasella tomorrow."

"Far from it." There was a coldness in Bartoli's voice. "We must proceed with the attack without delay."

"But don't you think Renzo might be tortured and talk?"

"I'm not sure, but I don't think so. My information is that he was arrested because he was a Jew, not as a Resistance fighter."

"There's a difference?" Vittoria asked hopefully.

"Resistance members are moved to Gestapo headquarters at Via Tasso and have blowtorches applied to the soles of their feet." Bartoli strove to control the emotion coming into his voice. "Jews are shipped to Fort Bravetta and shot."

Santa Maria della Gloria.

MacPherson entered the church and looked around for Father Francesco, but the church was empty except for an old lady in the back row, a pregnant woman lighting a candle in a side chapel, and a German soldier kneeling before the altar. Walking quietly down a side aisle, he headed for Father Francesco's study.

"Any news?" he asked, closing the study door softly behind him.

"Ah, Signor Jay, *buona mattina,* how good to see you." Father Francesco, not one to allow the exigencies of the moment to interfere with civilized life, looked up from his desk and smiled. "I hope you are well today. And yes, the copy of the fascist police order arrived this morning!" The priest was pleased to see the relief on the American's face as he dropped into a chair. "As promised by Lippi. At seven-thirty this morning." Father Francesco could not stifle a chuckle. "It was delivered by a policeman on a motorcycle." He shook his head in disbelief. "And he actually gave me a police salute!"

"But what does it say, Father?" Eyes wide, Jay shifted to the edge of his chair. "Is it the promised 'Daily Operational Order'? Does it say where the police will raid tomorrow?"

The priest laid the document on his desk and smiled. "Signor Jay, the answer to all your questions is yes." He pointed to the top of the paper. "Here's the official seal of the Roman police department." His eyes ran down the document. "At nine in the morning, Commissario Lippi is to be escorted by police outriders to a meeting with the questore. At noon," the priest blushed, "there is to be a raid on a house of ill repute in Trastevere." His finger ran quickly down the document. "Ah, here it is – here's what we're looking for."

"They're going to make a raid on one of our safe houses?"

"*Si*. At four-thirty. Via dei Coronari, 29. That's one of our houses. We must move quickly to get the prisoners hidden elsewhere."

"I'll get right on it, Father." Jay rose from his chair. "But I'm amazed at the efficiency of the fascist police. How on earth could they already know about Via dei Coronari, 29?"

Father Francesco frowned. "Yes, I'd forgotten. We moved their first guests there only two days ago. How could the police have found out so soon?"

A Trattoria.

"Here's your cut." Lippi put the envelope containing the money behind the menu and passed it across the corner table buried deep in the rear of the busy restaurant. The commissioner wore his civilian clothes; he rarely wore his uniform outside the police headquarters and knew that he would soon be forced to throw it away and flee from Rome with, he hoped, as much money as he could amass.

A hand reached from the shadows, seized the envelope and thrust it into a pocket. Lippi guessed his informer would also soon need to leave town. The policeman sighed. A pity. The racket had been simple, yet most profitable. For one thousand lire a week, the person across the table provided addresses – how his informer got these, Lippi neither knew nor cared – of prisoners of war in hiding in Rome. Lippi arranged for those addresses to be included in the police operational orders that he sold to MacPherson for five thousand lire a week. His profit of four thousand lire a week, along with other purloined valuables he had stashed away, would let him buy a comfortable anonymity in some northern village when the time came.

"I expect to have more addresses next week." There was an anxious edge to the voice speaking to Lippi from across the table. Lippi smiled and nodded, but didn't really care. In a month's time, more or less, Lippi expected that the American army would arrive and he, Lippi, would be gone with the cash and the loot.

The policeman finished his glass of wine and stood up, tossing a few coins on the table. He had nothing to fear from the pathetic creature opposite him. Indeed, he had enough information to expose the whole POW operation.

Lippi put on his hat, pulling the brim down over his eyes. But exposing the POW operation was the last thing on his mind. Involving Kappler would have the Gestapo trampling over everything with an absolutely disastrous impact on his own plans. Lippi doffed his hat to his informant and turned to go. Perhaps this person would find a safe haven, perhaps not. But one thing was certain: Commissario Lippi would.

VILLA RANIERI.

Jay Mack ran his fingers over the pebbly leather cover of the small book, the only tangible connection he had to Maria. Alone in the POWs' cellar apartment, he quietly indulged his feelings of sadness for her arrest and remorse for having been, in some degree, the cause of her arrest. At the same time he struggled to suppress other feelings he had for her.

He flipped through the thin onionskin pages of the book, a pocket-sized Italian-English dictionary. She had given it to him during one of their Italian lessons, sitting down next to him, close to him, to point out the various sections of the little volume. He could still remember the warmth and sweet scent of her body.

Oh, how he wished he could go to see her. He never failed to ask about her when he visited Father Francesco, but the priest always answered with a perfunctory reply accompanied by a dark scowl which spoke more eloquently than his words.

If he couldn't go to see Maria and he couldn't write to her, perhaps he could again send some things she might need – food, toiletries, whatever he could get his hands on, despite Father Francesco's warning that the guards opened all packages and stole all useful items.

But at least Maria was still alive. If she could just hold on long enough, the American army would arrive. And then she'd be free.

Jay patted the little book tenderly and carefully placed it back in his drawer. When would the army break out of Anzio? What was taking them so long? He desperately longed to see her again.

THE DAY OF THE VIA RASELLA ATTACK.

Even though there was a chill in the March air, Fabio felt hot as he pushed the refuse cart housing the bomb along the street. His hand brushed away the soot that had dropped on his face from the underside of the street sweeper's peaked cap. His eyes watched for any threat, his hands tightly clutching the handles of the cart as the wheels bounced along on the cobbles.

He knew the route he would take to reach the Via Rasella. He glanced at his watch: one thirty. At two, the German police column would march up the Via Rasella, he would set the fuse, and—

"Hey, watch where you're going!" The image of the planned attack fled from Fabio's mind as the policeman shouted.

"I'm sorry," Fabio shouted back as he pushed the cart toward the sidewalk, trying to stop his legs from trembling. He forced himself to concentrate on the task ahead. The Via Rasella, German troops. Ignite the bomb. He pulled his worker's cap down over his forehead. A little less than a mile and he would be there. On the Via Rasella.

"Hey, what have you got there?" The voice startled him. He looked up: two real street sweepers, dressed just like him, were pushing carts in his direction.

"I'm bored." Giorgio tossed aside his book and got up from his chair, his hands tugging at his belt to hitch up his short pants. "Come on, Luisa, let's go out."

The girl paused, her hand hovering over the jigsaw puzzle of the Sistine Chapel ceiling. "You always want to go out, Giorgio." Her fingers, holding the jigsaw piece of a man's outstretched arm, hung briefly over the puzzle before gently laying it aside. "Shall we go to the church and make some more tracings?"

"No. That's too boring." Giorgio yawned. "It would be nice to see Father Francesco, but he's sometimes boring, too."

"Well then, what would you like to do?" Luisa picked up another piece and found its location in the puzzle.

"If you were a boy, we could go play soccer in the park."

"But I'm not a boy, Giorgio," Luisa said, the large blue bow in her hair bobbing as she shook her head. "This afternoon, I was going to play with the doll's house Signor Nolan made for me."

"You think *I* want to play with a doll's house?" Giorgio replied scornfully.

"Well, what do you want to do?" Luisa raised her shoulders in a small shrug. "I suppose you want to go and see the marching soldiers again." She sighed as Giorgio nodded enthusiastically. "Why do boys always like marching soldiers?"

Her question went unanswered as Giorgio grabbed his cap and ran to the door.

Vittoria stood on the corner of Via Rasella looking down the street that fell steeply toward the Via di Due Macelli, along which the German column would soon march. She looked at her watch: in half an hour – the Germans were always methodically prompt – the Nazi platoon would leave the Due Macelli and come marching up the Via Rasella, where Fabio would detonate the bomb. Fabio should be arriving on the street at any moment; she frowned as she worried that he would look awkward and unauthentic pushing the unfamiliar trash cart holding the bomb as it rattled over the uneven square cobbles.

For a moment, her eyes lingered on the black cobbled pavement flanked by the walls of apartment buildings and courtyards that tightly enclosed the narrow street. In less than

230

half an hour, life on that street would be changed. The present quiet order, caressed by the homey aromas in the restaurant at the bottom of the hill some two hundred meters away, the ordinariness of everyday life – all would be reduced to chaos.

Draped over her arm was an overcoat; after the explosion she would give it to Fabio as a disguise to cover his escape. She looked at her watch again. In a little over twenty-five minutes, the German soldiers would come marching up the street.

Fabio, forced to bring his cart to a halt as the two street sweepers blocked his path, fought his fear. Sweat began to form on his brow.

"So, what have we here?" The cheeky smile on the face of the taller of the two workers seemed threatening.

"I'm just going to sweep up the streets of—"

"With a high-class accent like that, my guess is you've never even cleaned your own room, much less a street." The tall man chuckled. "You've got black market meat in that cart, don't you?"

The two street cleaners approached Fabio's cart. "Shall we just have a little look, Pasqualino?" He gave a wink to his colleague as he stretched out his arm to open the lid on Fabio's bin.

"Actually, it's a bomb. To blow up Germans." Fabio watched as the hand halted over the handle to the bin.

"What bullshit." The hand began to move again in the direction of the handle. "Now we know it's black market goods," the tall street cleaner sneered. "Cigarettes? Nylons?"

Fabio preempted the outstretched hand, flipping open the lid of the bin. "See for yourself."

The worker's eye widened as he saw the fuse and the tangle of wires that led to the bomb. "He's telling the truth!" he said, turning to his workmate. "It is a bomb! Let's get out of here!"

He grabbed the handle of his own cart and took off, his friend close behind him.

Fabio watched for a few moments as the street cleaners scurried away, their rubbish bins clacking on the cobbles, before he turned his pushcart toward the street where the Germans would march. The Via Rasella.

Vittoria fretted: the German column was late. She checked her watch again. Almost two thirty. They had observed and timed the Germans several times and they were always prompt, always singing their marching song. Now they were late. She looked at her watch again: over twenty minutes late.

Forty meters down the street she saw Fabio standing next to the wheeled garbage bin that contained the huge bomb she had made. At the right time, he had only to apply a lighted cigarette to the fuse and their mission would be accomplished. She could see that Fabio was nervous, swishing his broom across the same set of cobbles over and over again. Thank God the street was deserted; anyone could have seen he was a fraud.

The sounds alarmed her, but also came as a relief: the stamp of Nazi jackboots, the raucous singing. Arms swinging, the column was turning the corner and coming up the Via Rasella. She looked at Fabio: he had seen the signal from Ludovico at the bottom of the street and had drawn heavily on his cigarette, lifted the lid of the bin, and applied the cigarette tip to the fuse. He looked down at the approaching column and started to move up the street.

Vittoria sighed. Everything was going according to plan. She shifted the overcoat she was going to give Fabio to disguise his escape to her other arm and began to get ready for him. A glance at her watch: in forty-five seconds the bomb would blow as the Germans marched past. She smiled as she thought how proud she was of her brother.

Vittoria's smile fell from her face as she saw them walking on the cobbles beside the German column. Giorgio and Luisa.

Adriana's teacup clinked loudly in its saucer as she abruptly put it down and looked up from her newspaper at the clock. For some reason, she had felt a sudden chill run through her. Was she coming down with something?

She pulled her sweater tightly around her and focused on the black marble cherubs frolicking up the sides of the gilt clock, their chubby arms pointing to the time: two thirty-five. The cherubs. The children: Giorgio and Luisa. They had gone out earlier that afternoon. Were they safe? Had they remembered to dress warmly? She felt a strange sense of foreboding.

The children! Vittoria fought the paralysis seizing her mind. Giorgio and Luisa were walking up a narrow sidewalk alongside the column of German soldiers. Why on earth were they there?

"Fabio! Fabio!" She had no option but to call out, to alert her brother. He was hurrying up the Via Rasella, away from the primed bomb. The German soldiers continued to march, the stamp of their boots marking off the seconds left on the fuse of the bomb.

"Giorgio!" Vittoria waved her arms, pointing behind Fabio.

Her brother's pace slowed, and for a moment Vittoria thought she would have to run down the street toward the bomb. Her eyes turned toward the children, still walking alongside the soldiers, happy, smiling and keeping pace with their march. Then her eyes shifted to the trash cart, the bomb that would explode in less than a minute.

"Fabio!" she screamed, her voice echoing off the walls of the narrow street, its shrillness rising above the singing chant of the marching soldiers.

At last Fabio heard her and responded. While everything that followed flashed rapidly before Vittoria's eyes, to her it seemed as if it were in slow motion. Fabio turned and saw the children walking up the street towards the bomb. Vittoria's body stiffened. Less than twenty seconds to detonation. The leading elements of the German column had already passed the trash cart bomb.

She saw Fabio run down the street, grab his brother under the armpits, and throw him into the open door of a courtyard that lay behind a wall facing the street. Within seconds the small frame of Luisa followed. Fabio fell to his knees with the effort.

Vittoria watched as Fabio struggled to his feet. He looked up at her: there was a smile on his lips.

The bomb exploded.

Within five minutes of the explosion that had echoed all over Rome, Kappler's staff car swung into the Via Rasella. The Gestapo chief had seen many horrors during the course of the war, but none so horrendous as this vision of hell that assailed his eyes as he jumped down from his car.

Towards the top of the street, clearly the place of the explosion, was a baleful scene of unremitting carnage. At least two dozen soldiers lay dead on the cobbles. Some severed limbs littered the pavement – legs with boots polished earlier that morning, arms with hands clutching rifles they would never use. A severed head lay in the gutter, fixing Kappler with sightless eyes. And around the head a flow of blood, trickling down into gutter drains.

The gruesome sights had deadened Kappler's ears. He looked up, and suddenly the sounds came bursting into his consciousness. The chatter of the survivors' guns, still firing at the upper windows of the buildings that lined the street. "The bomb came from up there!" someone shouted. There were other cries, cries of pain, cries of fear, cries from men vainly trying to deny death's clasp.

The scene was chaos, and Kappler knew there had to be order. He turned to his chauffer. "Hans, go immediately to headquarters. Call for medics and ambulances to get here at once." The orderly saluted and was gone.

Kappler looked around, identified the officer in charge, and moved towards him, shouting. "Herr Kommandeur, order your men to cease firing." There was hesitation. "At once!"

The chatter of rifles and submachine guns fell away, leaving a street hushed of all noise save the groans and cries of the wounded.

The officer turned to Kappler, his face red with rage. "Herr Obersturmbannführer, what has happened here is an outrage, an atrocity. I demand retribution – revenge!"

"And I'm sure you'll get it, Herr Kommandeur," Kappler assured him as the wails of ambulances approached. "But for now, have your men arrest all males who live in the apartments on this street." He looked up to see the ambulances, sirens screaming, turn into the top of the street. Behind them came a truck loaded with his own men. "And have some of your men help clean up the dead – and those!" He pointed to the body parts that littered the street. "My men will take those arrested away for interrogation."

Kappler saluted the officer. "And now I'm sure you realize that I must make a full report of this attack to Field Marshal Kesselring." He strode away, knowing what the result of his report would be. Reprisals. And not of a pretty nature. He knew that the day ahead would bring him much work. Unpleasant work. Necessary work, no doubt, but nonetheless unpleasant.

Via Tasso Gestapo Headquarters.

Kappler looked down at the incomplete list and shook his head. Kesselring had told him the Führer had demanded ten Italians for every one of the thirty-three German troopers killed in the Via Rasella. Already he had almost three hundred names, most of them having posed no problems. First on the list were the names of all those sentenced to death by Italian courts. Then there were those who were obviously guilty of capital crimes, although not yet subjected to trial. And, of course, the Jews.

Kappler put down his pen and sighed. He needed thirty-six more names. Thirty-six more names to meet the quota for reprisal, a target of three hundred and thirty to be shot. The Gestapo chief hesitated, for a moment unsure of his actions, before he realized that his failure to achieve his task would not be looked upon favorably by the powers in Berlin.

He picked up his pen. All the communists held in the Via Tasso and the Regina Coeli jails. The names were added quickly to the list. Paolo Romagnoli. Angelo Passerella. The nib of his pen scratched the names on the list. The names came more easily as he neared the target number.

Still three names short. Kappler put down his pen. His fingers shuffled through the reports that lay on his desk, until his eyes lit on one that could resolve his problem: "Arrests Documented on March 22" – the day before the murderous assault.

His finger ran down the list – petty thieves, drunks, and pimps. Kappler would have liked to have added such useless specimens of humanity to the list, but he knew that there were political considerations. Two men arrested for distributing communist propaganda caught his attention and were added without hesitation.

Kappler's eyes returned to the names of those arrested. He was exhausted, but he needed one more name. Tomorrow morning he had to present the complete list of those to be executed to Kesselring. He saw the word 'Jew' and looked at the name opposite. Kappler picked up his pen and scrawled the name on the list. *Lorenzo Rossi.*

He screwed the cap tight on his fountain pen and returned it to his pocket. Within twenty-four hours, the Jew would be dead, alongside three hundred twenty-nine others, shot by Kesselring's troops.

His fingers pinched at the bridge of his nose. The clock showed four in the morning. Time for a few hours of sleep. He reached for the bottom drawer of his desk, where he knew a half-empty bottle of schnapps was hidden. The cork came away quickly in his fingers and he raised the neck of the bottle to his lips.

The liquor felt warm in his tired stomach. He had performed his task. The list was ready. After he had seen Kesselring, the reprisal would be conducted: three hundred and thirty Italians would die for the thirty-three German soldiers killed in the Via Rasella.

Kappler picked up his list and moved to his billet at the end of the corridor. For a brief moment, the name of the last person he had added to the list rattled in his brain. A man now locked in a cell of the Regina Coeli Prison who did not know that, by the morrow's end, he would be dead.

Kappler looked down at the list one final time, at the last name on his list. Lorenzo Rossi. He sleepily eased his head back onto his cot, the name drifting from his mind forever.

March 24, 1944

Santa Maria della Gloria.

Father Francesco waited for a quiet moment in the church before entering the Chapel of the Rosary. He looked up at the tranquil face of the Madonna and crossed himself. Prayer had always been important to Father Francesco, and so many times had he come to this chapel to seek help with a moral issue or guidance on his actions. But he could not remember when last he needed to pray so earnestly.

Late last evening, Sofia, a young woman in the Resistance, had come to him and asked him to hear her confession. Over the years he had heard many confessions, but none had ever chilled him as much as the words that came through the confessional grille that night.

He contemplated the statue of the Madonna. She was not one of the priceless works that warranted removal to the chambers deep beneath the Vatican for safekeeping, and he was glad of that for he prized her company. The Virgin stood with eyes cast down and arms outstretched in a gesture both welcoming and imploring. On her lips was a smile of simple serenity, the serenity of having yielded completely and eternally to God. At that moment, a shaft of morning sunlight was illuminating her smile; he took it as a sign.

He fell to his knees in prayer. At this desperate time, there was little he or anyone else could do but put his full faith and trust in God. He prayed for the dead and the families of the dead and he prayed for those who had carried out this terrible deed. But most of all he prayed that the German authorities would not continue the carnage by carrying out reprisals. Tears ran down his cheeks when the words came to his heart, words not so much of rational thought, but as a surge of pure devotion.

He crossed himself, rose from his knees, and gazed up again at the Madonna's face. The shaft of light was gone, and her smile was now in shadow.

MONTE SORATTE, NORTH OF ROME. FIELD MARSHAL KESSELRING'S BUNKER.

"I've managed to draw up the list of the required three hundred and thirty names, Field Marshal." Kappler pulled a bulky sheaf of papers from his breast pocket, unfolded it, and held it out to Kesselring.

"You have done well, Kappler." The field marshal hovered over his breakfast of eggs and sausages that shared his desk with assorted papers and glanced briefly at Kappler's list. "But spare me the details." Kesselring handed the list back and turned to the messages on his desk. "I'm sure you'll forgive me for the very important matters I must attend to." He reached over the papers and speared a sausage.

Very important? Kappler thought. What was more important than the execution of the three hundred and thirty persons on the list he had compiled through the evening and early morning hours? The list that had drawn on every ounce of his skill?

"Anzio, Kappler." Kesselring, still chewing, answered Kappler's unasked question.

Of course. Anzio. Kappler watched as the field marshal finished the sausage and dabbed his lips with a napkin. "We must waste no time," the field marshal continued, "in implementing our new strategy to retake the beachhead."

Kappler fought to keep awake. He had worked on the list until four in the morning, sleeping for only a few hours before driving the twenty miles to Kesselring's bunker. All he needed now was Kesselring's approval and he could sign off responsibility. And then get some sleep.

"So you approve the list, sir? According to the orders from Berlin, the reprisal shootings are to take place before sundown this afternoon." He refolded the list of names.

As the field marshal returned to his messages, Kappler waited for instructions as to who would be in charge of carrying out the executions. He cleared his throat as Kesselring scribbled notes on a pad. "Perhaps the list of names can now be forwarded to the Kommandeur in charge of the battalion attacked in the Via Rasella?"

"Absolutely not!" Kesselring looked up and slammed his pen down.

"But, mein Herr—"

"The Third Battalion wants nothing more to do with this tragedy."

Kappler's tired brain found difficulty understanding what was happening. "Field Marshal," Kappler's breath was labored, "I have set up the place of execution and I have arranged for the transfer of the prisoners to that site – the Ardeatine Caves, southeast of Rome."

"So?" Kesselring got up from his desk.

"Sir, I need soldiers to carry out the executions this afternoon."

"I hope you're not expecting me to provide them." Kesselring picked up his cap and made for the door.

"But, sir—"

"I'm afraid you'll have to deal with the whole business yourself." Kesselring rammed his hat on his head. "After all, that's what you Gestapo fellows are good at, eh?"

Villa Ranieri.

Vittoria rolled over, tangling again in the twisted sheets. She wondered if she would ever be able to fill the hole of helplessness that was now the center of her soul. It had been a long, sleepless night, but she had no more tears to shed. She knew it was daytime, knew she should get up and pretend to resume normal life, but she could not summon up the will to do so.

Throughout the long night the image kept returning, relentlessly, to her mind: her brother being obliterated, blown to bits. By the bomb she had made. She turned again in her bed, thumping the pillow, but was powerless to drive the images from her mind. For some reason, she could remember every stick of explosive she had pushed into the bomb in the trash cart. She had made a number of bombs, but never before could she recall such detail.

And there was the final detail, the one she would never forget. She saw Fabio's face in the instant after he had thrown the children to the safety of the courtyard. There was a brief look of hope in his eyes, just before the bomb had taken him away. The bomb she had made.

She rolled over again in her bed. They had, at least, attacked the Germans, she rationalized. Surely that was a bit of success against the Nazis? But she knew she was struggling to reach out for the tiniest vestige of hope to fight against the despair.

Her mother's sobs from the adjoining bedroom the night before had pierced her breast like pieces of shrapnel. For her, there would never be closure. There could be no burial; any ceremony for Fabio would tell the Nazis who the attackers were.

For the whole family, Fabio was a ghost they could never lay to rest. Vittoria clutched at her pillow, exhausted, but not sleepy. And then she thought of Renzo.

REGINA COELI PRISON.

The waft of stale sweat and urine assailed his nostrils as Renzo swung his legs from his cot. Even after two days he found it difficult to adjust to the all-pervading atmosphere of the prison, the aroma of oppression and privation.

"So lover-boy finally awakes from his beauty sleep." The grating voice of Vito Del Pietro, the man who shared his cell, brought the full hardship of the prison home to Renzo. Vito, Renzo had learned, was in for a long stretch for having cheated some high fascist officials on the black market.

Renzo sat on the edge of his cot and listened: there seemed to be a different atmosphere in the prison that morning. During the past two mornings there had been relative quiet, with few words spoken among the inmates and only the occasional clatter of buckets disrupting the drab silence of the prison. Today, Renzo sensed, was somehow different. The whole jail was abuzz, a cacophony of prisoners and guards speaking excitedly. From time to time he could hear names being called out.

He jumped down from his cot and moved to the cell door. "What's going on, Vito?"

"Probably another forced labor roundup." Vito peered into the bowl of his pipe, as if wondering what had happened to all the tobacco. "From time to time, they decide to round up several hundred of us and ship us to Germany." He shoved the pipe into his mouth and began to suck on the stem.

"Yeah, I know." Two months ago, from a safe distance, Renzo had watched as Rome buses were stopped by German soldiers and emptied of all able-bodied men on their way to work. "Fritz has so many soldiers fighting Ivan there's not enough men to keep the Führer's factories running. So Romans, who begin their day just trying to go to work, wind up heading for factories in the Fatherland, instead." Renzo moved instinctively away from the cell door as the sounds of prison guards' boots in the corridor became louder. "Sure hope they're not coming after me."

"You must learn to look on the bright side, my friend." Vito smiled. "At least on the train journey to the Fatherland, you'd get a chance to escape – to jump the train. In this place," he knocked on the wall to emphasize his point, "the only thing you can do is pray for an earthquake or a well-placed bomb to hit." Vito stood up and began to pace. "The way I look at it, you've got more chance of being elected pope than escaping from this hellhole. But if you get on a forced labor crew, the first thing they do is march you out the front door. And for me that's a step in the right direction."

He stopped short as the cover to the small grille window in the cell door rattled open.

"Which one of you is Lorenzo Rossi?" the prison guard's voice barked.

"I am." Renzo raised his finger.

"Prepare for transfer." The guard crossed Renzo's name from his list. "A German soldier will come for you in ten minutes." He slammed the grille window shut.

"Hey, what about me?" Vito shouted. "Vito Del Pietro. Isn't my name—" Vito's voice trailed away as he realized he would have to remain in the cell.

Renzo sighed. "I'm not too happy about it, but at least it looks like I'll get that chance to escape from the train you mentioned."

He turned to his cellmate. Vito's face was contorted in rage and envy.

VIA APPIA ANTICA.

Kappler looked at his watch as his staff car sped through the Porta San Sebastiano heading south. Four o'clock. He saw the sun glinting in the windshield. Another two hours and the job would be done.

He lit a cigarette. Despite the bombshell of Kesselring's refusal to provide an execution squad, the day had gone remarkably well. He'd briefed his subordinates, trying to keep their instructions simple. Each group to take five prisoners at a time inside the caves. Make them kneel. Apply the pistol to the nape of the neck. Return to the trucks for the next five prisoners.

Kappler sighed. He'd seen the look on some of his men. There'd be problems, he was sure. Some were used to doing 'interviews' where muscle was sometimes needed, but most of them were clerks, paper shufflers who had only elementary training in the use of firearms.

He drew on his cigarette, seeking an unprovided relief from the tension building inside him. Behind, he knew, was Ganz, shepherding the trucks carrying the prisoners to the execution site. Kappler had asked the fervent Nazi for assistance, which Ganz was only too glad to provide. The Hauptsturmführer had arranged the collection of the prisoners from Regina Coeli and the other jails and would now be heading with them to the place of execution.

Kappler tossed the cigarette butt through the open window of his staff car as it continued to speed south. The Ardeatine Caves. He'd chosen the place carefully. The caves were, in fact, disused mining quarries in an isolated rural spot. He'd vetted the place earlier, before Kesselring had thrust the executions upon him. There would be no prying eyes, and after the last prisoner had been shot the mines would be dynamited to block the entrance and prevent the discovery of the corpses. There would be nothing, in short, that might cause an outraged city to explode.

Kappler looked again at his watch. He had calculated that killing five prisoners at a time, each with a single bullet to the back of the head, would take a little over three hours. If nothing went wrong, the whole operation would be completed by sundown.

He saw several of his men waiting by the roadside as his car braked to a halt. Kappler hadn't liked giving them the messy job and he hoped they'd hold firm. And, if they didn't, perhaps the dozen bottles of cognac in the trunk would help.

VILLA RANIERI DRAWING ROOM.

As he sat in the drawing room looking into the fire, Giorgio tried not to cry. He had to be brave for his mother.

He got up and prodded a log with the poker to watch the sparks fly up. Firewood was scarce, but on that day they needed the comfort of the hearth. No one had much to eat or say that day, and Vittoria, after having been up for only an hour or two, had gone back into her room. His mother now sat on the sofa rocking Luisa, who had begun whimpering again. Giorgio looked over at his mother; she seemed to be trying to draw strength from the rocking and the humming as much as she was trying to comfort the little girl.

He knew it was his fault. If they had gone to the church yesterday afternoon to do the tracings, as Luisa had wanted, none of this would have happened and his brother would still be alive. It was all his fault.

Luisa fell asleep and his mother gently laid her down on the sofa and came over to sit beside him and gaze into the fire.

"You mustn't blame yourself for what happened, Giorgio," she said, as if having read his mind. "There was no way you could have known what was going to happen. Your brother acted with great courage, and we must always honor his memory for that." Then she turned toward him with a tender look. "And you must promise me that you will never tell anyone about what happened. Not even our friends, the soldiers who are staying in our cellar. It's as much for their sakes for ours."

"I promise. Mamma—" Giorgio felt the pinpricks of tears beginning to sting his eyes. "Mamma, I miss Fabio so much."

Adriana grabbed her son and pressed him tightly to her breast. He could feel his mother's body making little shuddering movements, and he knew she was crying into his hair.

ARDEATINE CAVES.

Not long now. The simultaneous volley of pistol fire echoed from the caves. Kappler looked over Ganz's shoulder as the Hauptsturmführer's pencil crossed another five names from the prepared list. By the Gestapo chief's calculations, only a few prisoners remained. Another ten minutes would complete the reprisal and he would be able to return to the city and catch up on long lost sleep.

"Name!" Ganz shouted at the next prisoner in line. The boy shuffled forward despondently, his wrists bound tight before him. "Name! Name!" Ganz repeated. Kappler had been amazed at the reaction of the prisoners: they had gone to their doom with hardly a murmur. Except for the one who tried to get away by giving a false name.

The prisoners had posed no problem, but his own men continued to worry him. A mass reprisal was not the usual work of clerks. But most of them had managed to struggle through, and Kappler felt that his provision of cognac had helped to steady their nerves.

"Last contingent ready, mein Herr!" Ganz, the one man who had not needed any spirits to bolster his own, looked up from his list. Kappler looked across to the table where his adjutant had prepared and reloaded the pistols all afternoon, surprised at, but proud of, the man's emotionless face.

Kappler nodded at the five members of his staff who were to perform the next and final shootings. Each man went to the table, collected a newly-loaded pistol, grabbed a prisoner, and walked toward the cave. Earlier, one man had baulked at the task, but Kappler had taken him aside, then accompanied him into the caves, helping him as he forced the prisoner to kneel, then pressed the pistol muzzle into the nape of the neck. A slight pressure on the trigger, and the man fell forward.

Kappler ached for the day to be over. In his long Gestapo years, he had never killed anyone, but that day killing had become a mechanical program. He had done his duty, he thought, as he headed for his car.

He sensed the smell of blood and death that was upon the air. The growing buzz of the gathering flies assailed his ears. He closed the window of his car as the engineers' explosives sealed the caves. He had not wished to give his men such a task. But he felt the job had been well done.

Villa Ranieri. Adriana's Room.

Adriana pulled the belt of her robe tight as she looked down at her dresser. Why she had moved Fabio's baby photo from there she did not know. For years the photo had sat there, a memento of happy times gone by and, once, a hope for promising years to come.

She looked back into the mirror. She averted her eyes, from which more tears sprang. The photo of Fabio was now in the bottom drawer of her dresser where she had hastily put it, hidden beneath her clothes. Her fingers could easily reach down and retrieve the photo, place it once more where it had always stood. But her hand moved only to wipe away a tear.

Adriana moved toward her bed, in part to escape the image in the mirror. She knew why she had hidden the photo. The past needed to be forgotten now: Fabio's smile of years gone by hurt too much. And the future of that smile was no more, snuffed out in an instant.

She dropped onto the bed. She tried to feel for the grief of her daughter, Vittoria, who had made the bomb that killed her brother. And for Giorgio, who blamed himself. And for Luisa, who had seen more violence in her ten years upon the earth than any human being should see in a lifetime. She fell back on her pillow, staring up at an unseen ceiling.

For them all there could be no closure. No body parts had been found, she had been told. Even if there had been, there could be no burial, no final rites for Fabio. She would forever be denied the cleansing ritual of a funeral.

The emptiness invaded her, twisted inside her painfully. She got up from her bed, seeking relief from the pain. Leaving her room, she shuffled down the corridor and quietly opened the door to Giorgio's bedroom. Despite the traumas of yesterday, despite his cuts and bruises, he slept soundly, his breathing deep and even.

She envied Giorgio's escape. She closed his door and retreated to her room and to another night of black thoughts. Damn the war. And damn all the Germans. All the Germans except one.

A Hotel on the Janiculum Hill.

Anton saw her on the bed before the hotel room door closed behind him. He didn't know what to say. Death had inhabited his war – indeed, it was a constant companion – but he had no words to offer this time. Adriana came to him quickly. The deep hurt was in her eyes, but he also saw there a hunger, a hunger to reaffirm life.

"Anton!" Her voice rang in his ear, her hands clutched at his back.

"I'm sorry, Adriana," he rested his hand on the back of her neck, "but there is nothing I can say – I cannot find any words."

"I don't need words." The hurt in her eyes sought to hide itself deep inside her. She reached for his body with an urgency that surprised him.

Afterwards, her tears flowed freely. "I'm so sorry, Anton. I hope you can understand that I'm trying to find an answer." She sat up, propping herself against the headboard. "Even though I know there is none."

His arm reached out to offer what comfort he could.

FASCIST HEADQUARTERS.

"I'm glad you could come, Major MacPherson." Commissario Lippi waved his hand, inviting Jay to sit down in the chair opposite his desk. "You see," his lighter hovered over the cigarette hanging from his lips, "we have a bit of a problem."

"Problem?" Jay stiffened in his chair. "What problem? Haven't you been getting the payments?"

"There is no problem with the payments. On the contrary, Major," ashes rained on his desk as the inspector flicked his cigarette in the direction of the ashtray, "payments are always made promptly." He looked up and forced a smile, alerting Jay to watch out for a sting. "Unfortunately, however, they are no longer enough."

"What are you talking about? We're paying you the five thousand lire a week you asked for. That's what the deal was. That's what you agreed to."

"So I did, so I did." Lippi chuckled, as if amused by the recollection. "But – you know how it is – the war has a way of changing things overnight."

"Okay, let's hear it, Lippi." MacPherson leaned forward angrily. "What do you have up your sleeve this time? What's your new trick?"

"*Gesù-Maria*, there is no trick, Major." Lippi threw back his head and laughed heartily. When his head came back down, the smile was gone and he fixed MacPherson with a cold stare. "Just a question of appearances."

"What do you mean – appearances?"

"Let's look at it this way." Lippi reached down to the bottom drawer of his desk and drew out a file. "Since our agreement," he shuffled through the papers, "you have been informed of a dozen or so raids on your safe houses."

"Eleven to be precise." MacPherson looked at him quizzically. "And we have made the requested payments for that information. Done deal – a successful operation for all concerned."

"Too successful, I'm afraid." Lippi gave another one of his fleeting smiles that warned Jay that trouble lay ahead. "You see, the questore doesn't like people to think his department is inefficient. Eleven raids, no arrests. How do you think that looks?" Lippi spread his arms wide and shrugged to emphasize his point. "What conclusion do you think the questore will come to? That his police are stupid? Inefficient? Or maybe both?" Lippi slapped his hand on the table to emphasize his point.

"So to pay for the questore's, uh, humiliation," Jay said, "the price is about to go up."

"Something like that." The police officer avoided Jay's angry stare. "I'm sure you understand that circumstances have changed."

"By how many lire have circumstances changed?" Jay asked dryly. Whatever it is, he thought, it will probably double next week.

"I will need ten thousand dollars."

"Ten thousand dollars? You've got to be crazy! And in American money?"

"Yes, I need United States dollars. The lira is declining in value. Soon it will be worthless."

"How the hell am I supposed to lay my hands on Uncle Sam's legal tender? There probably isn't that much in all of Rome!"

Lippi narrowed his eyes and pursed his lips. "With your people's access to the Vatican, I'm sure you can work something out. In any event, perhaps you can arrange to get the money within a week."

"That's impossible! How can I get such a huge sum so quickly?" McPherson's voice betrayed more than an edge of desperation.

"Let me offer you an inducement." Lippi's hand pulled a folded sheet from his pocket and slid it across his desk. "Here's one of the next addresses to be raided."

Jay picked up the paper. *Via Panzani, 12.* Adriana's address. Where he, Nolan, and Lawrence were currently hiding out. He saw the smug smile on Lippi's face and resisted the urge to swing his fist at the fat lips.

Lippi stood up, indicating that the meeting was over. "Of course, if you get me the money by this time next week, I'll ensure the raid will be called off."

VILLA RANIERI.

As he opened the door to the cellar hideaway, Jay was pleased that he had somehow managed to miss everyone in the Corvo family. At that moment, he didn't want to have to tell Adriana that her house could be in line for a fascist police raid.

Ten thousand dollars. In the States, you could buy a beautiful house for ten thousand dollars. He'd made a brief call on Father Francesco on his way back to Adriana's house, and the priest's face had said it all. There was no chance of raising that sum of money in American currency at short notice. The priest had shaken his head, like Jay bereft of any ideas on how to avoid a roundup of Rome's hidden prisoners of war. Jay pushed open the door at the bottom of the stairs.

Nolan lay sprawled on an old sofa reading. "Hey, look at what the cat dragged in!" An expression of concern came to his face as he watched Jay sink solemnly into an armchair. "Hey, buddy, what's up? You look like you just lost a dollar and found a dime."

Lawrence came in from the kitchen where he was peeling potatoes. "I've managed to get some—oh, hello, Jay. Is something wrong?"

MacPherson pondered for a moment before deciding to share the dilemma. There was no longer any need for tight security – Nolan and Lawrence both knew he headed the POW operation in Rome, and the Rome police already had all the details of that operation.

"Yeah, we've got a problem. A really big problem." He told them of his meetings with Lippi and of the latest development.

"Wow, Jay – I guess you didn't see that tackle coming." Nolan grimaced. "Looks like this fellow Lippi's got you in between the devil and the deep blue sea."

"What do you mean 'you'?" Lawrence gave the American a withering look. "Don't you think all of us are in the soup, Nolan? Not to mention all the hundreds of POWs in Rome?"

Nolan reacted angrily. "Godammit, Lawrence, who the hell are you to talk? You're hardly ever around. Chances are when the cops come by to round us all up, you won't even be here."

"Okay, you guys, knock it off!" Jay raised his voice, already regretting his decision to share his problem. A guilty silence followed. "Besides, it's not just the POWs who are threatened, it's the padrones – the hundreds of Italians, like Adriana – who are looking after the POWs all over Rome. If, God forbid, we and the other escaped POWs get arrested, we get shipped back to the camps. But if the padrones are picked up—"

"They'll have no hope if they're harboring escaped POWs." Lawrence spoke in a matter-of-fact voice, without emotion. "Torture at Via Tasso. Followed by the firing squad at Fort Bravetta."

"And one of those raids will happen in this house if I can't find the money. What the hell am I going to do?" Jay hunched over and ran his fingers through his hair. "I can't possibly move all of the POWs out of their safe houses – where would I put them all? And I can't send them outside of Rome, what with all the German reinforcements surrounding the city since the

Anzio landing." He sat up straight. "What I can't figure out is how does Lippi get all his information?"

"Well, it's a dead cert there's a leak somewhere," Nolan said. "Have you considered there may be a spy somewhere up the line, somewhere above your contact? Say, who is your contact anyway, Jay?"

"Not at liberty to say, Buck." As Father Francesco had directed, Jay had told neither Nolan nor Lawrence about him; it was information they had no need to know. "But I doubt seriously there's a spy up the line. Security's too tight. I've only told you guys because the problem could affect you directly."

"Well, thanks for the warning, Jay, but I'm clean out of ideas." Nolan reached for his coat. "So if you don't mind, I'm going out for a beer – a quiet beer, I hasten to add." He turned at the bottom of the stairs. "And remember, Jay, whatever you want me to do, just ask. You know you can always count on me." He gave a mock salute and was off.

MacPherson and Lawrence sat quietly, listening to Nolan's steps retreating up the steps.

Regina Coeli Prison.

When the guard opened the cell door, Father Francesco didn't see Maria for the darkness. But when she stood up and her face caught the thin afternoon light filtering through the small barred window high in the wall, he saw that she was beaming a smile that lit up the room.

"My child, God seems to be smiling upon you today," he said.

"I've had good news, Father. Please sit down and I'll tell you." The transformation in Maria's appearance was startling. Her eyes were brighter, her posture more erect, her hair shone, and the color was back in her cheeks.

"My father-in-law brought me a letter today – a letter from Marco! He's alive, Father, my husband's alive!"

"Praise be to God," the priest murmured before bowing his head in a short, silent prayer of thanks, once more marveling at the power of hope to lift the human heart.

"Perhaps you were right, Father. Perhaps He does hear our prayers." Maria brought the letter from her pocket. "He says he suffered a leg wound – nothing too serious, thank God – and got separated from his unit. That's when he was reported missing in action. The next day, he was found by some German troops, and eventually they were able to get him back to his unit."

"Does he say when he'll be coming home?" Father Francesco asked.

"He says his leg will need a few weeks to heal, and then he hopes to get a furlough." She returned the letter to her pocket. "Oh, Father, I think my heart will explode with happiness!" Maria's eyes began to well up with tears of joy.

Father Francesco nodded and reached over to pat her hand. "I am so very happy to hear this wonderful news, my child. And your friend, Jay, will be happy to hear it, as well."

"How is Jay, Father?" she asked with a shy smile.

"Jay is well, Maria. And eagerly awaiting the arrival of his fellow American soldiers. He says they should be here soon." They both knew what the arrival of American forces in Rome would mean: Maria's freedom. "Jay inquires about you often, and asks to be remembered to you."

Maria looked wistfully away from the priest as she remembered the happy times she had spent with Jay. "Please tell him I send him my loving friendship. God willing, I'll be seeing him soon."

Father Francesco smiled and nodded, praying with all his heart that she was right.

"And now," she added, "now I have something to live for!"

VILLA RANIERI CELLAR.

"You still haven't given me your opinion, David. What do you think I should do?"

Lawrence looked up from his newspaper. "I don't know, Jay," he answered guardedly. "It's a very difficult situation." He hesitated before speaking again. "Jay, I think – the situation –"

"Come on, Lawrence, spit it out."

"Somehow, you've got to raise the ten thousand dollars. For the sake of Signora Corvo and her family." There was an urgency in his voice that he did not try to hide.

"I know, David, I know." Jay stubbed out his cigarette. "Don't remind me of the obvious – she's a padrone. You said it yourself – torture at Via Tasso followed by the firing squad at Fort Bravetta. Just the thought of it makes me want to puke."

"It's not just Signora Corvo, Jay." The Englishman struggled for his words. "She has connections with, to…"

Jay sat up straight. "Connections to what?" he asked sharply. "Stop messing around, Lawrence!"

"I believe she has connections to the Italian partisans, Jay." Lawrence's voice dropped to a whisper. "Any raid could affect the Romans who are fighting the Nazis with bombs and assassinations. There could be further ramifications."

"Ramifications?" Jay shot up and grabbed Lawrence by the shoulders. "Don't give me some long Limey word. How do you know this stuff?"

"I'm, uh, I'm observant," Lawrence stuttered. "I watch what's going on."

"Don't give me that bullshit, Lawrence!" the American shouted. "I also watch what's going on and I haven't seen anything!"

"Perhaps you're too wrapped up in your POW organization." Lawrence glared defiantly at MacPherson. "If that raid takes place, Signora Corvo will have a lot of company on the lorry to Fort Bravetta." He looked away and lit a cigarette.

"Christ!" He gagged on the smoke. "I'd forgotten about the little Jewish girl!"

"Jewish girl?" MacPherson scowled. "What Jewish girl?"

"Luisa. The little girl Nolan made the doll's house for at Christmas."

"She's Jewish?" Jay's eyes widened in surprise.

"Luisa's a survivor of the Nazi roundup of the Jews."

"You mean the roundup that happened last October, just before we arrived in Rome?"

"Yes. The Corvo family adopted Luisa. Not officially, of course. She was brought here by—" Lawrence stopped abruptly. "That doesn't matter. What does matter is that any Nazi or fascist raid must be avoided at all costs. For this and the other reasons I mentioned."

"If only I could, David." Jay pinched his eyes closed and shook his head. "But how in hell am I going to raise ten thousand American dollars?"

"Surely the POW organization can help. Can't you use some of your maintenance funds towards paying off the blackmailer?"

"A few hundred, at most," Jay answered quickly, having already considered that approach. "I might be able to divert what it costs to run the organization for a week or two. But it wouldn't be in American dollars and it wouldn't be nearly enough."

"Then I suggest you speak to Signora Corvo. She's obviously well-to-do, and she has a great deal at stake."

Jay was stunned by Lawrence's knowledge; he was wary, but realized he had little option.

"And I think it might be better all around, Jay," Lawrence flicked his ash into the ashtray, "if we didn't mention this conversation to anyone."

"Huh?" Jay, confused, screwed up his face. "What do you mean?"

They both turned at the sound of heavy footsteps on the stone steps and the door to the cellar banging open. Nolan stood in the doorway, clearly three sheets to the wind.

"Hi, guys!" He stumbled as he made his way to the small room that held their three cots. "I know it's a bit early, but I think I'll hit the sack." On the second try, Nolan's hand succeeded in grasping the door handle and he lurched through, slamming it behind him.

"That's what I mean, Jay." Lawrence ground out his cigarette.

L'Orso Restaurant.

"I'm sorry," Signora Martucci, the owner of the empty restaurant, hovered over their table wringing a napkin, "but we have not been able to receive our usual...supplies." She hesitated over the word, as though to hide the illegality of her black market acquisitions. "I can offer you only a simple dish of spaghetti. *Alla puttanesca,* perhaps?"

"We would enjoy that very much, signora. And please bring us some red wine, as well." Anton spoke for them both, reaching out for Adriana's hand as the woman headed for the kitchen.

"Anton," her hands locked themselves around his, "you have been so kind to me, so helpful, that I feel guilty asking for anything else."

"You have only to ask, darling. And if it is within my power, you shall have whatever you need."

"I need money – a loan – and I need it rather quickly." She saw his look of surprise. "Yes, I know I'm well off and shouldn't come begging." She paused as Signora Martucci returned with the wine. "But I need ten thousand dollars by tomorrow, and that's not loose change."

He gave a low whistle as he heard the figure. "In American money? That's a rather large amount, enough to buy a small holiday chalet in the mountains."

"Or to buy a senior policeman's secure retirement when the Americans arrive and he throws away his fascist uniform."

"Policeman?"

"The money's not for me, but it's absolutely necessary. I could sell my Bellini Madonna, but the legitimate art market has dried up and the only available buyers now are Nazis."

He could sense the panic in her voice, see the uncharacteristic fear in her eyes. "Please, Adriana," he gently squeezed her hand, "keep calm. Tell me the problem."

She took a deep breath, her free hand pulling a handkerchief from a pocket, and leaned forward, speaking quietly despite the privacy of the empty restaurant. "As I said, the money's not for me."

"Then who is it that needs such a large sum of money?"

"The American leader of the organization looking after the escaped prisoners of war housed all over Rome. He's been paying a certain Police Chief Lippi to provide him with the police orders of the day. They alert him to the next raid on one of his safe houses."

Anton forced himself to look astonished, once again suppressing a smile at the irony: he'd been embezzling Nazi funds to bribe a fascist policeman to save Allied prisoners of war.

"And now I suppose the police chief has upped the ante?" he asked, already knowing the answer. She nodded.

"Is there no chance of trying to call his bluff?"

"I'm sorry, Anton, but I haven't explained myself very well." She swallowed hard, trying to put aside her fear. "The upshot is that unless Lippi gets the money, he'll allow a raid on the billet of the POW leader."

"Which is?"

"My house." She bit her lower lip trying to suppress the tears. "I don't think I can take much more, Anton. If they raid, they won't just take the POWs – they'll take Vittoria and find she works for the Resistance." Her lip began to tremble. "And then there's Luisa, the little Jewish girl. No, Anton, not Vittoria, not Luisa, not after Fabio."

Anton caressed the hand of the strong, courageous woman who had never before shed tears in his presence but was now nearing her breaking point. Ten thousand dollars. He wasn't sure he could do it. His usual filching from the petty cash wouldn't raise anywhere near ten thousand dollars. Surely it was impossible to get such a large amount of money so quickly.

And then the answer came to him. It would be difficult. And dangerous. Perhaps a Fort Bravetta firing squad would be waiting for him, too.

But he would do it for the woman he loved.

VILLA WOLKONSKY.

The young lieutenant leapt up from the desk in the foyer of the consulate, his greeting accompanied with a precise salute. "Nice to see you, sir; we don't often see you on weekends," he added.

Anton put down his briefcase and removed his gloves to sign the register which the lieutenant pushed towards him. "Sometimes, Lieutenant," he brushed aside the observation, "I never know what my job will bring."

But the lieutenant was right. Anton turned, left the foyer of the Villa Wolkonsky, and made his way along the main corridor of the august building which served as the German consulate. His visit on the weekend was unusual. There were fewer prying eyes. And he had to act quickly.

Despite the desperate situation, he could not hide a wry smile over his own scheme to get the money to feed Lippi's greed. As special envoy to the consul, Anton had access to all the key areas of the consulate, including the treasury. His shoes sank into the deep pile of the carpet as he turned off the main corridor to the library: in that room was the treasury's safe.

He looked around him. Minor clerks, two privates, nobody else. He didn't need any bigwigs asking awkward questions. In the safe, which held hundreds of thousands of lire to maintain the consulate, was the answer to his problem. Anton pushed open the door to the library and saw the huge safe standing in an alcove.

The idea had formed slowly in his mind before surprising him with its ease and simplicity. There was other money in the safe. Two hundred thousand in United States dollars. Counterfeited by highly-skilled Jewish engravers in one of the camps. The eventual purpose of this money was to disrupt the whole economy when the Americans arrived in Rome. The plan was to scatter it in small bills throughout Rome in various ways as the German army left, causing rampant inflation and economic chaos in the liberated city.

After Anton turned the dials to the access code, he felt the safe door swing open. On the top shelf lay blank identity cards and ration books to which he had earlier helped himself and provided to Adriana. In the large bottom compartment were the counterfeit dollars: two hundred packages of one thousand dollars, each wrapped in brown paper.

He walked away from the safe, back to the door, checking that there was no one in the corridor. He opened his briefcase and pulled out the packets of bill-sized cut newspaper wrapped in brown paper. He squatted down and pulled out ten packets from the safe, replacing them with the ones he had prepared.

Anton shut the door of the safe and spun the code wheels. At least Adriana would be safe.

Nine days later. April 19, 1944

VILLA RANIERI CELLAR QUARTERS.

"You know what I'm wishing right now, Jay?" Nolan, lying on the sofa, tore his eyes away from *Riders of the Purple Sage* and laid the book down on his chest.

"Huh?" Jay, in the process of dozing off, answered grumpily. At long last the situation with the POWs seemed to be under control and he could relax again. He had not heard from Lippi since he had been paid off and the raids on the safe houses had stopped. Perhaps the questore figured that, given Lippi's success rate, the raids were not worth the gasoline. "Okay, Buck, let's hear it. What are you wishing right now?"

"I'm wishing I could be back in Pop's Place in Milton, Massachusetts. In front of me, on the black marble counter, is a big banana split with three scoops of ice cream, vanilla, strawberry, and chocolate. I pop the maraschino cherry in my mouth and then my spoon sinks into the whipped cream—"

As the door banged open, Nolan craned his neck. "Well, well, look who's here. Our man about town and roving reporter. Hey, English, what's going on in the outside world?"

Lawrence unbuttoned his coat and held up his copy of *L'Osservatore Romano.* "Haven't you seen the paper?"

"Wouldn't matter if I had," drawled Nolan. "Even though I'll admit that my Italian is really coming along." He sat up and swung his legs from the couch. "I've mastered *bierra, vino rosso, vino bianco.* Maybe even *scaloppino di vitello,* except there's no more *vitello* left in Rome nowadays."

Lawrence grinned. "Not surprising when you consider the Germans corner all the supplies."

"Well, that's par for the course. I wouldn't put it past the Krauts to start pulling bottles out of the mouths of babies."

Jay cut in. "So what's all this stuff you're reading in the papers, David? Translate the headline for us."

"It says, 'British bombers attack Vatican convoy.'" He tossed the paper on the table.

"What the hell is the pope doing with a bunch of trucks?" Nolan asked lamely.

"Don't you keep up with any of the news, Nolan?" Lawrence shook his head in mock despair.

"The only news I'm interested in is when Uncle Sam's army is going to get off its butt in Anzio and get to Rome so I can go home. Okay, so tell us about this convoy of the pope you Brit flyboys shot to hell. I'll bet it had been hijacked by the Nazis, right?"

"No, it hadn't. The trucks were full of food the pope was shipping into Rome."

"And you guys shot them up?" Nolan asked incredulously. "The people of Rome are starving to death, and you guys stop the food from coming though?"

Jay intervened. "Wait a minute, Buck; maybe it was an accident. The bombers probably mistook the trucks for a German convoy."

"Oh, it was no mistake," Lawrence said. "The paper says all fifty trucks were clearly marked with the Vatican insignia."

Norton's scowl deepened. "And the sons of bitches in the RAF still bombed them?"

"Doesn't matter who bombed the convoy – the convoy had to be stopped," Lawrence said sharply. "Don't you know anything about military tactics, Nolan? If ignorance is bliss, you must be in seventh heaven."

"What's that supposed to mean?"

"The Germans, as occupiers, are responsible for feeding the population of Rome. To relieve them of that responsibility would be to free up their resources and thereby strengthen them. Every pressure possible has to be brought to bear on the Jerries to leave Rome as soon as possible."

Nolan stood up and faced the Englishman. "And you think taking food out of Roman mouths is the way to achieve that?"

"I have to say, David," Jay rose and stood next to Nolan, "that I think Buck has a point."

"I have more than a point, Jay." Nolan's face was red with anger. "This guy's a goddam monster."

"You'll never understand." Lawrence, still in his coat, re-buttoned it. "You live the life of Riley in this mansion while our soldiers are dying on the Anzio beaches!" He ran his hand across his brow. "I have to get out of here." He turned and bounded up the stone steps.

"That suits me just fine!" Nolan shouted after him. "And why don't you do us a big favor and don't bother to come back!"

L'ORSO RESTAURANT.

A month had passed since Fabio's death, but Anton could see that Adriana was still in the depths of grief, although she always tried to put on a brave smile. Her eyes gave away her barely-hidden sorrow, an unfocused look that somehow drifted away from him and from the moment, as if seeking someone who wasn't there.

"I'm sorry, Anton, but I'm a little tired." She finished off L'Orso's wartime version of *panna cotta* and pushed the dish away.

"I understand, darling." Anton signaled to the proprietress for the check.

He had more bad news for her. Last week she had told him that, just before the Via Rasella attack, Vittoria's friend Lorenzo had gone missing. He had tried to keep aloof from the partisan politics, matters that could threaten him and his relationship with Adriana, but she had pressed upon him the need to find out what had happened to the young man. So he had searched all the records.

"You have some bad news for me, don't you?" Her words surprised him, as if she could read his mind. Perhaps she could.

271

"Why do you say that?"

"Because I can see you brooding about something, and if you had anything good to tell me you would have told me at the start of the meal." She arched her eyebrows and gave a half-shrug of her shoulders. "You've found out something about Lorenzo Rossi, haven't you, and it's not very good. Then there's no doubt?"

He stared down into his ersatz coffee to avoid her eyes. "I'm afraid not. I've seen a copy of the list of those killed in reprisal of the attack in Via Rasella. Lorenzo Rossi's name was on that list." His spoon turned slowly and noiselessly in his cup.

"You're absolutely sure?"

"As sure as I can be. I saw the typed list. It had Kappler's signature on it."

At the sound of the Gestapo man's name, Adriana stiffened, her grief suddenly transformed into violent hatred.

"Is there anything more I can do to help?" he asked.

Her face softened, her eyes falling in resignation. "As ever, you've done so much, Anton. Now what must be done I have to do alone."

As he laid his hand over hers, her eyes rose to meet his. "I have to tell my daughter..." She bit her lip to stop its trembling. "I have to tell her that, so soon after losing her brother, her lover is dead, as well."

EXCELSIOR HOTEL.

There was a larger than usual crowd in the lounge of the Excelsior Hotel.

Heading to his favorite table in the far corner, Kappler eased his way through small gatherings of officers. The Führer's birthday had brought out the upper echelons of the army in force he noted as he took his seat and gave the waiter his order.

The chatter was loud, and an unusual sense of levity pervaded the smoky atmosphere of the lounge. But there was also an undercurrent of anxiety, Kappler felt, as his eyes scanned the room. As if the officers were using the occasion to drown their obvious fears.

The waiter placed his drink in front of him and he lit a cigarette. Absently studying the prisms of light reflecting on the ribs of the cut glass, he thought about a small problem he had. Nothing of any great consequence; rather it was more a political matter, a matter of pacifying Kesselring. He swirled the amber liquid and observed the kaleidoscopic effect as he thought. The matter Kesselring had raised was annoying, a distraction from his real work of routing the Resistance. Still, it had to be dealt with.

He scanned the room again and his eyes fell upon the object of his search. Ganz. He signaled the Hauptsturmführer to join him and the tall, gangly frame of Himmler's aide worked its way through the crowd.

"Obersturmbannführer Kappler!" Ganz gave an informal salute, his wide smile accentuated by the jagged scar rising from his lips. "Nothing like the Führer's birthday to liven things up, eh?"

"Indeed." Kappler again caught the attention of the waiter. "Let us join in the celebration."

Ganz pulled up a chair. "And once again we are enjoying *Führerwetter.*"

Kappler nodded and smiled. The weather was glorious that day, and everyone recalled that the sun always shone on the Führer's birthday.

Ganz took his glass from the waiter's tray. "Prost!" Ganz stood and raised his glass. "To the health of the Führer!" Kappler also rose as they downed the contents of their glasses in single swallows. "Heil Hitler!" The salutation was taken up by the entire gathering.

As the formality receded and conversation resumed, Kappler and Ganz sat down, the latter ordering replenishments for their glasses. "May the Führer enjoy many more birthdays. And may Kesselring give the Führer real cause for celebration by crushing the enemy at Anzio!"

"Let us indeed hope so." Kappler smiled, musing that the secret reports he had received strongly suggested that Kesselring was unlikely to achieve such an objective. Indeed, Kappler had been told to produce provisional plans to remove his units from Rome at twenty-four hours' notice. But of this he said nothing to Ganz; there was no need to dampen his high spirits. More importantly, he wanted to ensure that Ganz was prepared to provide a needed service.

"I hear you've moved on since our last meeting," Kappler said, gingerly opening his gambit. "The Fort Bravetta command, I hear?"

"That is so." Ganz watched the waiter deliver the replenished glasses. "But the position is not completely to my liking." He looked aggrieved. "I would, of course, prefer a command in the field, fighting the enemy."

"Let me assure you, Hauptsturmführer, the command of Fort Bravetta is as important as any on the front line." For Kappler's purposes, it was necessary to massage his companion's ego.

"How so? I just organize SS patrols, round up a few Jews. And command half a dozen firing squads every week to dispatch a few communist scum." Ganz sipped his drink. "Hardly the stuff of heroes of the Reich."

"But the task is just as important. You may not be on the front line, but still you're eliminating the enemies of the Reich." Kappler ground out his cigarette in the ashtray. "You may rest assured that your excellent work is greatly appreciated." Ganz began to swell with pride. "I've seen the reports. As you know, my office prepares the orders for Fort Bravetta executions."

"I must say I do my utmost to fulfill my duty for the Reich." Ganz stiffened his backbone and raised his chin; his pomposity was almost palpable.

"Of course, of course," Kappler continued, "and I don't want to spoil the mood of the evening's celebration, but I know you have a difficult task to perform tomorrow."

"Yes, that's true." Ganz eased back in his chair. "But you're not spoiling the mood of the celebration and my task will not be difficult, I assure you. Some woman found guilty of harboring escaped enemy prisoners. Probably a communist." Ganz chuckled. "Her case must have somehow slipped through the cracks, because she's been locked up at Regina Coeli for over four months but the military tribunal just got around to ordering the sentence of death yesterday."

"Yes, I know; I received my copy." Kappler said. "No problem, I presume?"

Ganz shrugged. "The execution of a woman is sometimes a problem, and I have to give my men an extra slug of schnapps. But otherwise it's pretty much business as usual. The papers signed by the tribunal are all in order. "I ought to know her name, but..." Ganz squinted as he tried to remember.

"Her name," Kappler spoke clearly, "is Maria Silvestri." One of the padrones Kesselring thought he was being soft on.

"Yes, that's it!" Ganz slammed his empty glass down on the table and stood up. "Well, I must be off." He saluted Kappler. "I must be up early tomorrow. Maria Silvestri, yes, that's her name. But I guess the name really doesn't matter, does it?"

FORT BRAVETTA.

"O, Lord, has it come to this?" Father Francesco felt his soul cry into the crisp morning air that hung over the execution square at Fort Bravetta. Maria, her hands tied behind her, was being pushed across the square by German guards. Father Francesco knew that there were no Italians who would perform such a crime.

Maria squinted into the early rising sun, still low in the eastern sky. Lord, please grant her strength, the priest uttered under his breath. She staggered on the uneven ground, but recovered as one of the guards caught her by the armpit. Her head was held high, but her gaunt face spoke of her suffering. The two escorting guards pushed her roughly against a post.

"Wait! Wait!" Father Francesco shouted. He hitched up his cassock as he ran across the rough ground toward her. "You must make your confession, Maria!"

Her eyes sought his for a moment, then fell away, casting about over the grassless earth at her feet. "I don't think a confession will help me now, Father." There was no sharpness in her voice, only resignation to her fate.

"My child, perhaps your words will help you as you enter the next life. I beg you." He fell on his knees in supplication before her. A harsh insistent command came from the tall German officer.

"Please get up, Father," she said, looking down on him with pitying eyes. "It ill behooves a man of the cloth to beg."

But before he could rise, she fell to her knees before him. "I'm not sure whether my confession will ease my path into the next life," her eyes fixed his, "but perhaps it may ease your way through this existence."

He fought to hold back his tears.

"Besides, I shall have an extra minute to hear the early morning birdsong," she said.

He did not hear her words as she spoke her confession. Like all mortals, she had sinned, but he chose not to know her sins. God would hear her words, and surely that was enough. He made the sign of the cross on her forehead with his thumb and murmured the Latin words of Extreme Unction. *"Per istam sanctan unctionem et suam piissimam—"*

"Enough!" the tall officer with the ugly facial scar shouted in German as he pulled Maria to her feet. "Be gone, priest!"

"—misericordiam, indulgeat tibi Dominus." Father Francesco rose and shuffled away from the stake, looking off into the distance as the six soldiers prepared their rifles. He heard commands shouted by the officer and turned to look at Maria. She was now tied to the stake with a blindfold tight across her eyes. Her whole body trembling, she fought against the ropes that bound her.

"Aim!" The officer's command in German screamed pain in the priest's ear. He took one last look at Maria and saw that tears had darkened part of the blindfold. His eyes rebelled at the awful scene.

"Fire!"

Father Francesco's lids closed quickly at the sound of the volley that took Maria's life. *O, God in heaven,* he began to plead. Then he felt the painful stab of doubt. Was there really a God in heaven?

"Forgive me, Father," he whispered as he crossed himself. His faith struggled to crush the seeds of disbelief.

VILLA RANIERI.

Vittoria sat on the sofa in the drawing room looking down at the box on her lap. She forced her eyes away for a moment as she struggled with her grief, but her eyes kept returning to the box, as if drawn by some fateful magnet.

The box was ordinary, like a shoebox, but larger. Her mother had handed it to her after breakfast with a brief comment. Her mother's German friend, Anton, had obtained it. At great risk to his own safety. Vittoria sighed. Everything that Anton did for them was at great risk.

Her hands ran along the lid of the box, which was sealed by tape on all sides. There was a label with some German words Vittoria didn't understand. But in the center of the label was his name. 'Lorenzo Rossi. *Jude.*' As a Jew, Renzo would deny any next of kin in Rome, so there would be no one to whom his possessions could be sent.

Vittoria felt the tears spring to her eyes and fought hard against the pain, but the grief won. She jumped up, clutched the box to her breast, and ran to her bedroom.

VILLA RANIERI CELLAR QUARTERS.

"There's no easy way to say this," Jay said as he closed the door behind him. "It's very bad news." His voice faded to a hesitant whisper. "Maria is dead."

"What?" Lawrence leapt to his feet. "What on earth happened?"

Nolan, lounging on the sofa, swung his feet down and sat up. "Jesus Christ, Jay, how did she die?"

"She was executed by a German firing squad yesterday morning." Jay's fist beat against the back of the sofa in anger. He looked at Lawrence and Nolan in turn, then shook his head. "For harboring enemies of the Third Reich. Prisoners of war. Us."

"But how could the Germans have found out?" Nolan asked. "Didn't we get away before the raid?"

"Remember I told you there was a second raid?" Jay answered. "One that took place after we left? Well, someone – who the hell knows who? – gave the police exact information on the location of the secret closet where our cots were hidden. Incidentally, the police found not only our cots inside, but also a bit of garbage with some English printed on it. That was all it took to get her arrested and convicted."

"Oh, my God, that's awful, Jay. How did you happen to find all this out?" Nolan asked.

"Father Francesco told me – he gave her last rites."

"Who's Father Francesco?" asked Nolan.

"Just a priest." Jay cursed himself for having let drop his contact's name.

Lawrence narrowed his eyes. "I thought you were Protestant, Jay. How—"

"He's just a priest, okay, guys?"

Lawrence ran his hand over his face and sat down slowly. "I can scarcely believe Maria's dead. She was so very alive. It seems only yesterday she and I were discussing Italian art and music. She knew a lot more than one might give her credit for at first glance."

"I didn't realize—" Nolan began, then hesitated.

Jay cocked his head as he waited for Nolan to finish the sentence. "Didn't realize what, Buck?"

"I didn't realize she knew so much, me not being so good with her lingo, and her not speaking English all that well." He ran his fingers through his hair. "But, oh boy, could that lady cook. She could take whatever odds and ends she could find in the black market and throw together a dish fit for the Ritz."

"Yes, you're right." Lawrence's eyes focused on the far wall. "She was also a genuinely kind woman, as well," he added. "When we first arrived, she saw me sitting alone and asked me what I missed the most about home, and I said, 'Classical music.' So she dug out some recordings of Caruso singing Puccini and played them for me on an old gramophone." He sighed. "What a lovely lady she was."

Jay was not thinking about food or music, nor did he even hear much of what they said. Maria had meant more, much more to him. His throat tightened and he felt a raw ache spreading from his gut to his chest. He had been forced to hide the emotions she had evoked, and he knew she had felt the same. Only the thought of her husband on the Russian front had stopped him from taking her in his arms. His chest began to heave as he tried to push the memories from his mind and Lawrence and Nolan were surprised when they saw a tear roll rapidly down his right cheek.

"She gave her life to save us." His quavering voice stuttered through the words. "If I ever find out who ratted on her, I'll—"

Heading into the bedroom, Jay slammed the door behind him. He needed to mourn the death of this beautiful, courageous woman alone and in his own way.

April 23, 1944

Villa Ranieri.

Vittoria could feel tension in the room. Although her mother sat serenely at the other end of the breakfast table sipping her ersatz coffee, somehow Vittoria could sense that she was holding back while Giorgio and Luisa were still present.

"Get a move on, Giorgio – breakfast's over." Adriana's fingers tapped impatiently on the table. "You have to get Luisa to school on time, and you'd better make sure you're not late yourself."

"All right, Mamma," the boy replied, hanging his head and sliding off his chair. He had not yet recovered from the trauma he'd experienced at Via Rasella. He was cowed, unsure of himself, his playful smile gone, his impishness lost. "Come on, Luisa, let's go." He picked up his books and set off, Luisa trailing meekly, mutely behind him.

Adriana waited for the door to close behind the children before speaking. "Vittoria, I know you're involved again with the Resistance, and I don't think that's wise." The voice was without the anger that Vittoria had expected.

"Mother, I don't expect you to understand," Vittoria said, putting down the thick slice of bread she was eating, "but it's the only way I can cling to sanity." She drew a deep breath. "As well as do something to pay back the scum who killed Fabio and Renzo."

"I understand, dear, believe me I do." Concern etched lines on her mother's forehead. "But I hope you know what you mean to me, Vittoria. What it would do to me if anything happened to you."

Vittoria rose and walked around the table to clasp her mother to her. "I do know. And, please believe me, I'll be careful. But there are things I have to do." She kissed her mother's cheek, slipped from her arms, made for the door, then stopped. "By the way, the box your friend delivered…"

"Anton?"

"Yes. He read the German words on the label for me and said it contained the effects of Renzo."

"Yes, I know – he told me. Is anything wrong?"

"The box contained a crucifix and a smelly old pipe. Renzo was a Jew – and he never smoked a pipe."

ON THE LUNGOTEVERE.

"A day like this can help put the zip back in a guy's step," Jay said as he walked with Buck down the street that ran along the eastern bank of the Tiber. The dome of St. Peter's glowed in the morning sun, the boughs of the plane trees were lacy with new leaves, and even the usually-lifeless river sparkled. He glanced at Nolan shuffling along sullenly, his hands stuffed in his pockets. "You know, Buck, you spend way too much time in the cellar at Adriana's place."

"Jay, I need to talk to you." He motioned to a park bench they were passing.

"Sure, Buck, shoot!" Jay took a seat next to Nolan on the bench.

Nolan's eyes flitted left and right. An elderly man arrived and took the seat next to them, unfolding a newspaper. "Maybe it'd be better if we found another bench, Jay."

"Why so cagey, Buck? If it's so private, shouldn't we wait till we get back to our digs at the villa?"

"No, no," Nolan answered quickly. "I don't want *him* around." He got up from the bench and resumed walking.

"Jesus, Buck," Jay said, catching up to him, "you've always got some ax to grind about Lawrence. Can't you ever let up on him?"

"It's serious, Jay." Nolan stopped and reached into his pocket. "You know how Lawrence always keeps his personal stuff locked up in a drawer in his bureau?"

"Can't say I've paid that much attention, Buck. What are you driving at?"

"Well, the lock's none too secure."

"Are you saying that you—" Jay exhaled in exasperation. "For chrissake, Buck, I keep telling you—"

Nolan's hand emerged from his pocket. "I found this."

Jay's eyes darted to the object in Nolan's palm. It was his watch. The watch he had in his pocket when they were on the German train heading north. The watch that was stolen from him when he'd been attacked after they'd made their escape. Along with the piece of paper with Father Francesco's name and the address of his church.

Villa Ranieri.

Vittoria ran the brush vigorously through Luisa's hair, with scarcely a protest from the girl. How lustrous were the black locks, burnished by a dark bronze sheen.

Vittoria had been remiss of late. Before, she had always helped the little girl with her luxuriant hair, brushing it and tying it back with a ribbon they carefully selected to match the little girl's outfit. Before…

Her hands stopped the stroking motion for a moment and, before the memories could emerge to torment her, the iron plate of the defensive apparatus she had built inside her snapped tightly shut.

"We didn't mean to cause any harm." The child softly spoke the words she had uttered so many times before. "Giorgio and me, we—"

"Don't think about it anymore, Luisa." Vittoria sought to cut off thoughts that began again to batter at the iron-plated shield in her mind. "You have to forget it all." Vittoria tried hard to remove any harshness in her voice; she forced a smile that the child returned in the dressing table mirror. The girl needed to build a shield of her own. Vittoria put down the brush and used a comb to curl the child's locks around her finger.

"Where's Uncle Renzo? When is he coming back?"

Her simple innocence hammered once more at Vittoria's shield. She put down her comb, feeling she had no option but to continue the white lies she had been telling the child. "He's gone away. No one knows where. Perhaps he'll be back soon, but maybe he won't be back for awhile."

Luisa looked at her in the mirror as she considered this. "Giorgio said the German soldiers took him away."

Vittoria silently cursed her younger brother as she arranged the ringlets that dropped around the child's temples. "But he may still come back," she said, struggling to reassure her.

"My mamma and papa were taken away by the German soldiers a long time ago but they never came back."

Vittoria winced. She had half-forgotten the Jewish girl's tragedy. She put down the comb and reached for a wide blue satin ribbon. "This will look lovely with your blue-and-white checked dress, don't you think, Luisa?" she said, forcing another smile.

The ribbon was tied into a bow on one side and the girl reached up and patted it. "I've hoped for a long time that Mamma and Papa would come back, but they haven't." Her curls swirled around her face as she shook her head. "But maybe they will one day. Maybe Uncle Renzo will, too." The child jumped down from the chair. "We'll just have to wait and see, Aunt Vittoria."

Vittoria leaned over to kiss her on the forehead. The child had already built her own defensive shield in her mind, much stronger than hers: she had not yet given up hope. She stifled a sob as the girl ran off to find Giorgio.

On the Lungotevere.

"The watch is yours, isn't it?" Nolan asked.

Jay turned the timepiece in his hand and nodded.

"I always told you the Limey was up to no good," Nolan said with agitation. "When I saw the watch in Lawrence's drawer, I remembered what you told me happened back at the railroad track. Didn't you mention something about an escape address, too?"

"Maybe. But if you're right, Buck, isn't taking the watch going to alert his suspicions?"

"What's the Limey going to do?" Nolan guffawed. "Complain someone's stolen the watch he stole from you?" Nolan's face became serious. "And what about all his mysterious comings and goings since we arrived in Rome? What the hell is he up to? Did you ever consider that maybe he's the one who gave the information on the POW safe house addresses to the fascist police chief?"

Jay scowled as he considered this possibility. "But wait a minute, Buck – if Lawrence is in bed with the fascists, why would he always be cheering whenever the Allies have a big breakthrough?"

"Could be just an act, Jay. Could be just something to throw you and me off track." Nolan fixed MacPherson with a stare. "I hate to say this, Jay, but maybe he's the one who betrayed Maria."

MacPherson tensed, fighting the red mist that threatened to come down over his eyes. "I'll deal with Lawrence later. Let's just try to enjoy the rest of our walk."

Villa Ranieri Cellar Quarters.

"Excellent news!" Lawrence tossed the Italian newspaper aside and reached for his pack of cigarettes.

"So what passes for good news these days, David?" Jay asked.

"Another bomb attack by the Resistance. Three Germans killed." He lit the cigarette, leaned back on the sofa, and exhaled smoke at the ceiling. "The Resistance is refusing to be intimidated by that atrocious reprisal massacre."

"Wait a minute, Lawrence," Jay felt his hackles rising, "over three hundred innocent Romans are killed by the Germans in reprisal for a Resistance bombing, and you think that episode can just be ignored? That the partisans can just go on bombing and killing more Germans?"

"Of course the massacre can't be ignored." Lawrence sat up straight and swung his legs from the sofa. "It must be avenged!" he said, spitting out the last word.

"But what if the Germans order more reprisals?" Jay asked, his scowl deepening. "Wouldn't the deaths be on the conscience of the Resistance? Maybe even on your own conscience?"

"Don't you think the deaths should be on the Germans' conscience?" Lawrence asked archly. "Are you really saying that the Resistance shouldn't attack the Germans, who are inflicting abject misery on all of Rome, because the Jerries might kill people? We might as well run up the white flag now."

"I'm just saying that—"

"Listen, Resistance guerilla actions are legitimate acts of war, and in war there are often unfortunate and unintended consequences. Just think of all the innocent people killed by Allied bombs." Lawrence angrily stubbed out his cigarette. "But just as Allied bombing must continue until the war is won, the Resistance strikes must go on until the last German has left Rome." He shot up off the sofa and reached for his jacket. "Because a bloody nose is the only language the Jerries understand. Now I have somewhere to go."

MacPherson positioned himself between the Englishman and the door. "Not so fast, Lawrence."

Lawrence began to walk around MacPherson, but the American grabbed his lapels. "Frankly, I really don't care all that much about your crazy ideas on ignoring reprisals on innocent people. What I do care about, what really burns me up, is the way you go gadding all over Rome at all hours."

Lawrence tried to pull himself free, but Jay tightened his grip. "My, my, Jay – seems you're a bit touchy today." The Englishman's lips began to ease upward in a smile.

Jay shoved him hard against the wall. "I'm entitled to be touchy." He shoved him again, and the Englishman's head cracked against the doorframe. "I've told you to stop time and time again, but you keep ignoring me." Another shove. "The Germans are sure to notice. You're putting my entire POW operation at risk, not to mention the danger to Adriana and her family." He relaxed his grip. "I need a straight answer, Lawrence, and I need it now. What exactly are you up to?"

RESISTANCE BOMB FACTORY.

Vittoria tamped down the explosive in the bomb. She was proud that, despite the horrors of the Nazi reprisals, the Resistance in Rome had refused to be cowed and the bombing campaign continued. The Nazis had to pay in blood for the martyrs who had been mercilessly slain. She adjusted the light above the workbench to help her insert the fuse.

The Nazis had to pay for the deaths of Fabio and Renzo. Her fingers selected a fuse from the shelf above the workbench. Making bombs was an activity she had come to enjoy: the task kept her occupied, keeping thoughts of her brother and Renzo at bay. More than that, it brought the satisfaction of anticipated vengeance for their deaths. She gently eased the fuse down the side of the tube holding the explosives.

Thoughts of Renzo still troubled her: the box supposedly containing his possessions didn't ring true. A pipe? Good God, a crucifix? For a Jew who never smoked a pipe? She forced herself not to clutch at straws. Perhaps the Germans had made a mistake, labeled the wrong box. The pliers in her right hand slowly pushed the fuse into place.

But did Germans ever make mistakes? And what if Renzo had escaped the massacre? He was arrested because he was a Jew, betrayed, she had heard, by the Black Panther, the woman who betrayed her fellow Jews for German money. Vittoria clipped the fuse into place.

Even if Renzo had somehow escaped the massacre at the caves, surely he would have been shipped to the north by now, like all captured Jews. To the camps from which no prisoner ever came out alive.

The reprisal massacre or the camp. Either way, Renzo was dead.

She slowly sealed the lid of the bomb and set it aside. Retribution. Revenge.

OLD SECTION OF ROME.

"Jesus, Lawrence, you're talking too fast! You gotta give me some time for it all to sink in." Jay sat with Lawrence on the same bench he and Nolan had sat just the day before. He leaned forward and planted his elbows on his knees. The Englishman had just told him he wasn't, in fact, an officer of the Royal Air Force but a member of MI6. As a fluent speaker of Italian, he had been recruited by the British secret service and had been landed from a submarine on the coast south of Rome the summer before; his mission was to coordinate the response of the

Roman Resistance to the German occupation to prepare them for the German retreat and the Allied entry into Rome. But during his landing there was some sort of accident and he was captured and interned as a prisoner of war.

"Let me get this straight," Jay said, running his fingers through his hair. "You were arrested as a spy but thrown into a POW camp? I'd say you were one lucky bastard."

The Englishman smiled. "Yes, I'm well aware of that. As an agent of the secret service, I would have been tortured and eventually shot. I won't go into all the details, but suffice it to say that as a result of the mishap I never met my contacts and I also lost my fake identity papers. But fortunately I still had the RAF uniform that had been provided in case of such an event."

"And then, while you were at the camp, Italy signed the armistice and your POW camp guards walked off the job like ours did. And then you escaped and hooked up with Nolan and me. Come on, let's walk some more – maybe it'll stimulate my brain."

They got up from the bench and threaded their way down the narrow streets to the Piazza della Rotunda. "I could see this marvel a million times and always be awed," said Lawrence, gazing up at the Pantheon. "Do you realize its dome is bigger than that of St. Peter's?"

"Keep walking, Lawrence, I got a lot more questions." Jay hardly gave the monument a glance as he headed south down an empty side street. "So what you're saying is," he looked around to make sure there was no one following them, "that it's all your work with the Resistance that keeps the revolving door turning at Adriana's."

"That's correct."

"But who's calling the shots? Don't you have to get your orders from somewhere?"

"That's also correct. I'm in communication with my head-quarters by radio on a frequent basis. Where precisely the radio is hidden I won't say."

"I don't need to know that, David, but for chrissake couldn't you have told me about your work sooner?"

Lawrence scowled and was silent for a minute or so. "Lesson number one at spy school: never reveal your mission to anyone who doesn't have a need to know. Even trusted friends may talk when undue pressure is exerted."

"Oh, Jesus, that's swell! By 'undue pressure' you mean torture! So now you're putting me, Nolan, and the whole POW operation at risk. Why did you even want to hole up with us, anyway? With all your contacts, couldn't you find a place of your own?"

"Lots of them. But, frankly, staying with you and Nolan as an escaped POW is part of my cover."

"Oh, Jesus," Jay muttered under his breath.

They walked down the Via Arenula to the old Jewish ghetto, Jay trying to assimilate all that Lawrence had just told him, angry that his presence at Adriana's was putting them all at even more risk.

Lawrence continued. "I hope you understand that what we've just been discussing is strictly between the two of us. Please don't share this with anyone, not even with Nolan or Adriana." In the Piazza Giudea they stopped and looked up at the shuttered synagogue. "What a sad, sad sight this is," the Englishman said.

Lawrence slowly turned to look at his companion. "Look, Jay, I know you're concerned about my staying with you and Nolan and I know my frequent need to go out is an annoyance and possibly a danger." He paused as they locked eyes. "But please just think about how much is at stake."

Tiber Island.

Jay Mack sat alone on the steps leading down to the river. Lawrence's tale was almost beyond belief, he thought, as he picked up a stone and hurled it into the water.

He stood up and brushed off the seat of his pants. He didn't know what to believe. Lawrence sounded sincere, but his story was so far-fetched. Maybe he was going out to visit the partisan chiefs – but who was to say he wasn't secretly meeting instead with the fascists? After all, someone leaked all that information on the safe houses to Lippi, someone close to the source of the information. Maybe he was even working with the Gestapo. And maybe – Jay's jaw clenched at the thought – maybe Nolan was right, maybe it had been Lawrence who had tipped off the police when Maria was arrested. Maybe he was responsible for her death.

Jay headed down the single street of the small island toward the ancient Roman bridge. If his story was true, why hadn't he told it to him sooner? He said he was under strict orders not to reveal his mission to anyone other than those with a need to know, but the need to know should have included him – as leader of the POW operation, he had a real need to know about any threats to his organization. Besides, it would have been easier for all of them.

He paused on the bridge, running his hand over the top of a stone head as if seeking wisdom from one who had stood watch over Rome for two thousand years. He knew there was no way he could ask Lawrence to confirm his story. The Englishman would say he would have to reveal the partisan leaders he worked with, and Jay knew that was out of the question.

Nolan's instincts about the Englishman had perhaps been better than his; for a long time Buck had been saying there was something fishy about him. Now, Jay had no option but to watch Lawrence like a hawk, try to see if he ever made contact with the enemy. He didn't have to ask Nolan to keep an eye on him; he already was.

And then there was the matter of the stolen watch Nolan had found in Lawrence's drawer. Lawrence's reaction to seeing it would be the clincher.

Jay sighed and shook his head as he crossed back into the city. He had to tread cautiously since a confrontation could easily turn violent, and he didn't know if Lawrence carried a hidden weapon. He shuddered. He had to choose his moment carefully. Very carefully.

EXCELSIOR HOTEL.

"Ha! Kappler! Come, join me in a drink!"

The muscles in Kappler's neck tightened involuntarily as he heard the unmistakable voice. He could do without the distraction of Ganz at that moment, now that the enemy had broken out of Anzio and were closing in on Rome. But Ganz had been useful at the Ardeatine Caves reprisal and with his Fort Bravetta firing squad, and he didn't wish to offend an officer who could continue to be of use, particularly one with links to those close to Himmler.

"But of course, Ganz." Forcing a smile, Kappler removed his cap and made his way to the corner table where the Hauptsturmführer sat. The waiter saw Ganz's signal and a glass of schnapps appeared almost as soon as Kappler sat down at the table.

"Prost!" The Hauptsturmführer's toast was perfunctory. The Gestapo chief raised his glass silently, sensing that Ganz would be looking for information on the developing military situation south of Rome. His suspicions were soon confirmed.

"What's going on?" Ganz twirled his glass nervously. "I hear rumors that the enemy is threatening our last line of defense before Rome."

"If rumors in Rome were tanks, we would have won the war long ago." Kappler laughed, although he realized that Ganz was sensing the truth. For his part, as head of the Gestapo, Kappler was well aware of the overall military situation and had spent most of the day putting the finishing touches on plans for evacuation.

The Gestapo chief cleared his throat. "I understand there may be a problem," he said in a lowered voice, scanning the crowd at the unofficial after-hours watering hole of German officers in Rome.

Ganz blew slowly out of almost-closed lips. "Perhaps, but I'm certain Generalfeldmarschall Kesselring will succeed in containing the enemy."

From his reports, Kappler knew the Caesar Line was about to collapse. Probably within a day or two. "I hope you're right, Ganz, but unfortunately I have to make preparations in case you're wrong."

Ganz looked pensively at Kappler, recalling an earlier conversation they had had. "By 'preparations' you mean your plan to round up the escaped prisoners of war? Send them to head up any withdrawal from Rome?"

Kappler tapped the side of his nose. "I think we need to be a little discreet, Ganz." He leaned forward across the table. "But, in essence, you are correct. I'm expecting my informant to provide the complete list of their hidden locations shortly."

"Perhaps I can help," Ganz enthused. "My unit is expert in roundups, as you'll recall from our success last October in the Jewish ghetto."

"As a matter of fact, that's already occurred to me, and—" Kappler was cut short by an aide appearing alongside the table. The Gestapo chief took the sealed envelope from the silver salver and ran his index finger down its spine to tear it open.

"Bad news?" Ganz asked with concern.

Kappler read the message and smiled. "Not at all. I've received an invitation from Generalfeldmarschall Kesselring," he chuckled, "to attend a gala matinee performance of *Un Ballo in Maschera* at the Rome Opera House."

"What? Is he mad?" Ganz sputtered. "The enemy is on our doorstep and he comes here to put on a production of, of—"

"*A Masked Ball.* I'll keep you informed, Ganz. In the meantime, please excuse me." Kappler quickly finished his drink and rose. He now knew the battle for Rome was lost. Kesselring would be retreating. But he would leave Rome in grand style.

VILLA RANIERI CELLAR QUARTERS.

"Now where the hell are you going, Lawrence?" Jay slammed his book down and jumped up from his seat as the Englishman made for the door. "This makes the third time you've waltzed out of here today, and I'm getting fed up."

"But Jay, didn't I tell you?" Lawrence reached for his jacket and slung it over his shoulder. "The Allies are about to break through Hitler's last line of defense before Rome. In a few days they'll be here." He looked around to make sure Nolan was still out. "I've got things I need to attend to, Jay. You know that."

"We've had this chat before, David." MacPherson strode over, placed himself between the Englishman and the door, and crossed his arms. "And I'm getting tired of it. If I've said it once I've said it a million times: you're putting my POW operation at risk."

"Yes, I know we've had this conversation before. But you ought to be able to figure out for yourself that as the Nazis leave and the fascists scramble, Rome will be a sitting duck for any element that wants to stir up trouble." He tried to get around MacPherson, who continued to block his way. "As I've already explained to you, Jay, I'm working with the Resistance. Don't you understand? I've got to get them ready to step in and maintain order until your people – God bless 'em – the Yanks arrive."

"Somehow your story just doesn't add up, Lawrence," MacPherson shouted. "How am I supposed to know that what you're telling me is true?"

"Because I said so," Lawrence shouted back, pushing the American aside. "And now, if you'll get out of my way, I've got to go!"

"Not so fast, Lawrence!" Jay reached into his pocket. "What do you know about this?" He dangled the watch in front of the Englishman.

Lawrence averted his eyes for a moment, scowled, and shrugged his shoulders. "It's a watch, Jay." He pushed open the door and began to go through, then spun around angrily. "Perhaps it's my turn to ask questions. Exactly what kind of a game are you playing?"

Villa Ranieri Cellar Quarters.

His fingers worked quickly on the loose screws which held the small ventilator grille tight on the wall beneath a table in the POWs' small kitchen. Nobody had ever noticed the ventilator, which suited his purposes well. The last screw came loose, the grille pulled free, and his hand reached in to grab the shoebox hidden inside.

Again he stopped and listened. He wasn't expecting anyone; the other two were out and not expected back until later. He lifted the battered lid of the box to uncover the contents: the watch was no longer inside but, in addition to the sheets of paper on which he was working, there was a wad of huge thousand-lire notes, the money Lippi had paid him, along with two packages of one thousand dollars wrapped in brown paper, the proceeds of his last big deal with the fascist. He pulled out the sheets of paper: they comprised the list of POW safe house addresses he had been compiling. Kappler, who knew nothing about his side deal with Lippi, had at last called for a full and final list.

He'd guessed Kappler's plan: to arrest and use the escaped POWs hiding at these addresses as a shield when the Germans retreated from Rome. Nobody would dare to bomb the retreating column. Up to that day, Kappler hadn't been interested in the list; he said he'd been happy to let the American and British embassies in the Vatican pay for the POWs' room and board. Besides, Kappler had said, he had no need for anything other than the complete and final list.

He replaced the lid on the box, putting it back in its hiding place and securing the screws, and carried the list to the desk in the cellar's living room: there were a few more addresses he had to add by copying from the original.

He sat down and began applying a pencil to a blank piece of paper. As the pencil flew back and forth, the ghostly letters began to emerge: they would form the last additions to his list, gleaned from the indentations made by Jay's pencil on the previous piece of paper on his notepad. He'd always done it this way, tearing off the blank top page from Jay's notepad after Jay returned from visiting his contact. Three new addresses emerged. He added the addresses to complete the master list he'd deliver to Kappler later.

He was startled when he heard footsteps coming down the stone steps, but sighed with relief when the door flew open and he saw it was only Giorgio running across the room.

"One of the doors on Luisa's doll's house just fell off. Can you—say, what are you doing there, Signor Nolan?"

He shoved the papers quickly into a drawer in the desk. "Come on, buddy, let's go find Luisa. It's not nice to make a lady wait." He smiled and ruffled the little boy's hair playfully.

MEETING OF RESISTANCE LEADERS.

"Comrades! Comrades!" Bartoli called for order as he looked around the meeting of district commanders of the Roman Resistance. Everyone was there, and through the smoke-laden room above the bar at Luigi's Restaurant he nodded at an old friend, Manfredo Zeoli, the socialist leader of the Trastevere Resistance. All were seized with excitement and expectation. The Allies, having broken out of the Anzio beachhead, were approaching Rome.

"Order! Order!" Bartoli's hand slapped loudly on the table, the wine sloshing in his glass. The chatter abated as the Resistance chiefs sought their seats.

"Comrades, I have taken the unprecedented step of gathering us all together for an important briefing. Many of you have already met Signor Lawrence." He nodded at the Englishman,

302

who sat to his right. "As you know, Signor Lawrence is our liaison with the headquarters of the Allied armies in Italy. He's responsible for communication and coordination between us and the Allied high command. Today he has a message of great importance for us."

Lawrence rose from his chair and cast his eyes over the hardened faces of the partisan chiefs. "I am happy to report that yesterday I received word that the Allied army has broken through the Caesar Line and Kesselring's rearguards have been overwhelmed. It is now probable that some spearhead units of the American Army will be in Rome by late tomorrow." He paused for what he assumed would be applause and cheers.

"It's about time!" a sarcastic voice called out. "We were beginning to think we'd have to go down and give your men a hand!"

As a gale of laughter coursed through the room, Lawrence realized his task was going to be even harder than he thought.

VILLA RANIERI.

"How did you get these, Giorgio?" The sheets of paper rustled loudly as Adriana waved them in front of her son's face.

"I told you, Mamma – I took them out of the desk drawer in the cellar while Signor Nolan was working on Luisa's doll's house in the playroom."

"And I've told you many times, Giorgio," her eyes glowered in anger, "that you do not go searching into other people's private things!"

"I'm sorry, Mamma," Giorgio hung his head in shame, "but I thought Signor Nolan was doing something funny."

"That's really no concern of yours!"

"But, Mamma, you haven't even looked at what I found." Giorgio pointed to the top piece of paper, torn in haste from a notepad and covered with pencil shading. "I'm sure the pad these came from belongs to Signor Jay – I've seen him with it many times."

"You're talking nonsense again, Giorgio. It's just a sheet of paper on which Signor Nolan was doodling."

"Please take a closer look at it in the light, Mamma."

When Adriana moved over to the window, what Giorgio's sharp eyes had seen became clear. Pencil shading covered most of the sheet – except in the places where the writing on the sheet that had been above it on the pad had indented the paper. The page reminded her of a photographic negative, a dark background with white writing. She squinted: there, in the lines and curves the pencil shading could not penetrate, words and numbers emerged. Three addresses. She realized that she knew two of them.

She flipped quickly through the next pages, which comprised a long list of addresses in Rome. Her finger moved rapidly down the addresses until it came to one that left her stunned. Her own.

"Giorgio, it's time to take Luisa to your Saturday morning art class." She ushered him through the door. She could sense big trouble coming her way.

MEETING OF RESISTANCE LEADERS.

Bartoli rose to call for order. "Please, comrades!" His hands gestured for quiet. "Whatever has happened before, the moment we have all been waiting for is at hand. Let the man speak."

Lawrence resumed as the laughter abated. "I'm not making any apologies." There was anger in his voice. "Our men, the Americans and the British, have gone through hell."

"So have we," Bartoli said in a low voice. "Let's move on."

"Before our armies arrive at the gates of Rome, it is essential that your Resistance forces be prepared."

"We already are," said a voice at the back of the room. "We're ready to hit the German swine with everything we have." There were murmurs of approval.

"There will be no need for that." Lawrence's words brought shouts of disapproval. "Let me explain." Lawrence held up his hands and waited for quiet. "Allied army headquarters have intercepted a message from Kesselring's headquarters to Berlin." He paused. "The Germans will not defend Rome."

There were shouts of disagreement. "How can you be so sure?"

Lawrence waited for the hubbub to die down. "We believe Hitler doesn't want another Stalingrad on his hands. If he decided to defend Rome, you," his finger swung around the room, pointing at each Resistance leader, "you would ensure that Rome would be another Stalingrad."

"You're damn right!" one of the Resistance leaders shouted. "We'd fight the Germans in every street!"

"And I'm sure the actions of your men and women would be valiant and well-meaning. But, as I said, our intercepts show that the Germans are not prepared to defend Rome. We expect them to leave tomorrow." Lawrence punched out his words. "It's now up to you – Rome must be spared the horror of being reduced to rubble."

VILLA RANIERI.

"You need to keep that boy of yours under control!" Nolan shouted to Adriana. "You should teach him to keep his mitts off other people's property."

"By 'other people's property' do you mean these?" Her hand, clutching a wad of loose sheets covered with his writing, came from behind her back.

"Yeah, yeah, the kid stole those from me. Let me have 'em." Nolan made a grab for the sheets, but Adriana pulled her hand away and stepped back quickly.

"I think Giorgio was right to bring these to me." She moved away warily as the American continued to approach. "You got these from the pad that belongs to Jay, didn't you? He often carries it, but you never see any writing on it, do you? But you figured out how to find out what he's been writing – you made images with your pencil. They're addresses, aren't they? What are you up to, Nolan?" She backed away towards the fireplace as the American approached; the morning had been chilly and a small fire burned inside.

Nolan came toward her, his arms outstretched. "You've got no right to keep that stuff – it's mine." He grabbed her, his left hand reaching for the papers she held behind her back.

"Let me alone – get away!" Adriana struggled to escape his grip.

"Just give me those papers – now!" He tightened his grip.

She lifted her leg and brought her high heel down sharply on his foot. His scream of pain screeched in her ear as he let her go. Before he had time to recover, she threw the documents into the fire. The flames that quickly consumed them lit up his horrified face.

VIA TASSO GESTAPO HEADQUARTERS.

"You senseless fool, Nolan!" Kappler thumped his desk. "The list of POW addresses was vital to my plan to protect our retreat from Rome. What am I going to tell Kesselring? You've ruined the whole plan!"

Nolan winced at Kappler's outstretched finger pointing like a gun at his chest. "I don't think there's any need to panic just yet," he said boldly, trying to hide his anxiety. "Give me a few hours, Colonel – I'll get you a replacement list." The American smiled to hide what was little more than a bluff to buy time. He wasn't sure Commassario Lippi had kept the lists of safe houses he had given him, but he was worth a try. Of course, he dared not reveal to Kappler the profitable side deal he had made with the fascist police officer.

Kappler picked up his cigarette pack and tapped it absent-mindedly on the desk. "Preparations to withdraw from Rome are in full swing right now. I'll give you two hours."

"Agreed. And I also need you to arrest Signora Corvo."

"Signora Corvo?" Kappler could barely contain his exasperation. "What use would that be? By your own admission, she knows nothing – the addresses have disappeared in smoke up her chimney!"

"If you want me to report from behind the lines after you leave Rome, you'll have to arrest her."

Kappler glowered. "I'm not sure I understand you, Nolan. You're asking me to arrest a doyenne of Roman society? There would be a huge outcry – and not just from the Romans. I wouldn't be at all surprised if she were on Kesselring's invitation list to the opera this afternoon! I cannot—"

"She knows too much."

"But you said she burned the list. How can she threaten our plan?"

"The woman knows enough to raise doubts after the Allies arrive. She could point a finger at me, and then..." Nolan finished by drawing his finger across his neck, leaving Kappler to arrive at his own conclusions.

The Gestapo boss thought for some time before picking up the phone and barking out some orders. "Very well, Nolan. She'll be arrested within the hour and brought here to my headquarters at Via Tasso. But let me make one thing clear: I can do no more. I cannot possibly contemplate taking her north with us when we leave tomorrow."

Kappler rose and paced the floor nervously, then sat down and lit a cigarette. "When we leave, we do not intend to retreat too far north. You already know how to get your reports to me." He leaned back and exhaled a slow stream of smoke up at the naked light bulb. "But – and I repeat – I cannot take the Corvo woman. She will be left in a cell here at Via Tasso."

His eyes came down from the light and fixed Nolan with a cold stare. "If you think she's a threat to you and our plans, you must deal with the situation yourself. Do I make myself clear?"

Nolan grunted his understanding.

"I take it you're still up for earning the not inconsiderable sum of money promised you for acting as my agent in Rome?" Kappler reached into the lower drawer of his desk.

"Of course."

"This," Kappler said, pulling out a Luger pistol and handing it to Nolan, "this is for you to use as you see fit." He squashed his cigarette in the ashtray. "Now get out of here and get me those addresses. Leave by the back door, if you please."

VILLA RANIERI.

Adriana tried to fight the snake of fear slithering through her body. She gazed at the fireplace where the ashes of the documents lay, her lips sucking hungrily on a cigarette.

She looked at the phone, begging it to ring. As soon as Nolan had left, she called Anton. He was meeting with some dignitaries, his orderly had said; he would ask him to return the call immediately upon his arrival back in his office.

Adriana pushed away a stray lock of hair from her forehead. Nolan had gone into a rage after she had destroyed his papers. He had manhandled her and thrown her into a chair, letting fly a stream of foul invectives. When he stopped, he had stared mournfully again into the fireplace for a few seconds before storming out.

Crushing her cigarette in an ashtray, she thanked heaven that Giorgio and Luisa were still at their art class. But where was everybody else? She was uneasy being alone in the house. Jay and the Englishmen had both been busy ever since hearing the news of the Allied breakout, but surely one of them would be back soon. She glanced again at the small table by the fireside: the phone refused to ring.

She got up abruptly, her decision made. Nolan could come back at any time, so she had to get out. She picked up her hat and gloves from the hall table. A walk to the Largo Argentina would do her good and would be safer, and from there she could take the tram to the Villa Wolkonsky and just wait for Anton to return. The children would be fine for a while at their art class, and after that Vittoria would be picking them up. As she checked her makeup in the mirror, she knew her decision was right.

The doorbell rang. Hesitantly, she reached for the lock.

The man at the door politely doffed his hat. "Signora Corvo?" She nodded, flinching at the German accent.

"We have a warrant for your arrest, Signora Corvo." The Gestapo man's cold eyes peered from beneath the rim of his hat.

"What is the meaning of this?"

"Please just come quietly with us. I assure you it's merely a formality."

"I'll come, but only under protest!" Adriana held her head high. "And you can rest assured that a complaint about your behavior will be received by the German ambassador before the end of the day!"

The Gestapo agent, unfazed by her threat, gently took her by the elbow and began pushing her in the direction of the waiting car.

NEAR THE VILLA RANIERI.

Nolan was angry. Angry with Kappler, angry with the Corvo woman, and, above all, angry with himself. He should have known that any attempt to retrieve the address list from Lippi would be a fool's errand.

He'd gone to the fascist commissario's mansion on the out-skirts of Rome only to find the windows shuttered, the drive-way littered with debris, and the place abandoned. Abandoned apart from an old family retainer who'd told him in faltering English that the commissario's duties had taken him away from Rome.

Had taken him away from Rome as fast as his fat little legs would carry him, Nolan thought. As the Allies were arriving, the police chief was leaving, leaving with all the money, all the treasure, and all the bribes he had amassed. Nolan couldn't blame Lippi – with the Germans leaving Rome, high-ranking fascists had to find a way out – but still he was angry.

Earlier, he'd told Kappler he'd have the list of POW safe house addresses in a couple of hours, and he was out of ideas. On the tram back from Lippi's house, he considered the pos-sibility of trying to get the list from Jay, but there didn't seem to be any point. Jay wouldn't have a complete set of addresses, he thought. Jay had only a few addresses at a time on his pad; it seemed clear that Jay was receiving the addresses on an as-needed basis.

As bad as the present was, the future held another problem. The lucrative deal he'd made with Kappler to stay in Rome and report on Allied army movements would be made even more dangerous if the Corvo woman was around. She knew too much. At any time after the Americans arrived, she could finger him.

He reached the Corvo house. Was it safe to go inside? Probably; the Corvo woman would have been taken away by that time and neither Jay nor the Limey had any reason to be suspicious of him. He opened the back door and listened care-fully: the house was empty. He made his way down the stone steps to get his things together and leave. Where he spent that night didn't matter, but it had to be somewhere else.

As he began to collect his gear, he stopped, his mind racing and his head pounding as he again cycled through his prob-lems. He had to take care of the Corvo woman. But before that he had to face Kappler and break the bad news that there would be no list of POW addresses. He wasn't sure which prospect was worse.

The sound of someone coming in the back door startled him.

GERMAN EMBASSY.

Anton von Breitland hung up his jacket and sank down into his leather desk chair with a sigh. The almost interminable meeting with the Italian diplomatic officials had dragged on and on. He wondered why there was still any need to play diplomatic games with the Italians – they all knew that the games were as good as over, that the German army was about to leave Rome, yet they still continued to act out roles of pretense.

He drummed his fingers on his desk as he absently gazed out the window at the ancient aqueduct that passed through the grounds of the Villa Wolkonsky. He was feeling very keenly the pressure of time on a decision that he – and only he – could make. The army and all the diplomatic staff would leave the next day; he, himself, had been shown a copy of the order by the ambassador. The arrangements for the departure of the diplomatic staff had been von Breitland's responsibility, and he had to finalize the plans that lay before him on his desk. He turned away from the window and began to check off the items with his pen; when the plan was finished, the ambassador had only to give the order and they would all leave.

But would he?

VILLA RANIERI.

Lawrence took the stairs two at a time as he made his way up to the back door of Adriana's house, preoccupied with reviewing the details of the Resistance meeting. The Resistance chiefs had been cynical at first, and that was understandable, given that the Allied troops had been stuck on the Anzio beaches for almost six months. But in the end he had won them over to the plan: as the American army approached, the partisans would take charge of the city and ensure that order was maintained. He fumbled in his pocket for his key. There might be a few minor attacks on the retreating Germans, but there would be no general uprising.

Stepping into the hall, he immediately sensed that none of the family was home: the usual sounds of kids playing or of Adriana on the telephone were missing. The silence struck him as strange, and he checked his watch: one-thirty. Perhaps the signora had gone out with the children. As for Vittoria, she had rarely been around of late.

He hoped the cellar would be empty, as well – he would welcome the solitude. It was never a pleasure to be in Nolan's company, and lately even Jay had become antagonistic. He wasn't sure Jay believed his story about his work, and then there was that curious business with the watch.

He made his way down the stone steps, his heart sinking as he saw Nolan alone with a look on his face that suggested either drunkenness or rage. The last thing he wanted now was another confrontation with Nolan.

"What the hell are you doing here, Lawrence?" Nolan barked. "Shouldn't you be somewhere else, like sneaking around dark alleys with whatever no-good bums you hang out with?"

"I live here too, Nolan."

"Yeah," Nolan said, approaching Lawrence, "and for a guy who's almost never around, you really have a way of dropping in when you're least welcome."

Lawrence sighed. "Let's not get started, Nolan. I'm not in the mood for an argument right now."

"Oh yeah? So when are you in the mood for an argument? Did I ever tell you how much you get my goat, Limey?"

Lawrence turned away, ignoring Nolan's taunt.

"What's the matter, Limey?" Nolan spat out, coming closer. "Cat got your tongue?"

Lawrence knew he had to put the insult aside, avoid conflict; more important things concerned him now. Turning away, he opened a drawer in the bureau.

"Hey, pal!" Nolan gave the Englishman a sharp poke in his arm. "Pay attention! I'm talking to you!"

Lawrence tried to ignore him. In a few minutes, after he had collected what he had come down for, he would leave. It was the best way.

The blow that crashed upon his skull took him unawares. Half-stunned, he stumbled as he turned to see Nolan's face contorted with rage, a wooden stool raised in his hands.

Lawrence reeled and fell as the stool again hit his head. As the blows continued, his consciousness began to slip away and his vision dimmed, but he could still make out Nolan's angry voice. "That's for killing my father during the Troubles! And that's for sending in the Black and Tans! The Black and Tans, you Limey bastard!"

The stool came down once more and splintered into pieces. Nolan tossed the remnant of wood still in his hand on the floor and gave Lawrence's body a kick. "And that's for all the grief you Limeys gave my mother!" But Lawrence no longer heard his words.

GERMAN EMBASSY.

Von Breitland completed checking the departure plans for the diplomatic staff, laid down his pen, and rested his chin in his hands. Soon he would have to make the most important decision of his life.

In one sense, he knew he had already made his choice. The image of Adriana filled his mind and his heart, and the thought of having to continue his life without her was unbearable. But other images came to him, as well. He picked up the framed photograph of his elderly parents. They, like him, detested the Nazis but loved their country. And their only son. It would break their hearts to learn that he had deserted his post.

The buzz of the intercom and the voice of his orderly interrupted his thoughts. "The ambassador wants to see you at two o'clock, sir." Von Breitland glanced at his watch. Fifteen minutes. "He wants to review and sign off on the plans."

"Very well." Anton's finger began to reach for the intercom's off button, but his orderly continued. "And there was a message from Signora Corvo." Anton's brow furrowed. "She asked that you call her at once – she said it was an urgent matter."

Von Breitland snapped off the intercom and reached for his phone, his fingers rapidly spinning the dial. After a few moments, the tone rang in his ear. He let it ring for two minutes, then dialed again. Perhaps he had made a mistake. Still the phone rang again and again. The intercom buzzed. "The ambassador wants to see you now, sir."

Anton continued to let the phone ring as he gathered up his papers with his free hand.

There was no answer.

Villa Ranieri.

Nolan wished the annoying upstairs telephone would stop ringing as he checked that everything was in order. He had gathered up the shards of wood from the shattered stool and placed them at the bottom of the wood pile, where they were not likely to see the light of day anytime soon. And he had positioned Lawrence's body at the bottom of the stairs, one foot on the third stair from the bottom; anybody would believe the Englishman had died by falling and cracking his head on the ancient stone steps. The police would be overwhelmed with the consequences of the arrival of the American army in Rome and their investigation would be superficial, at best.

But Nolan still had two problems: not only could he not deliver the list of POW addresses to Kappler, but, if he was to continue as a spy for the Gestapo in Rome after the Americans arrived, the Corvo woman had to be taken care of. He had expected Kappler to handle the last matter and had been surprised at his squeamishness. The Gestapo man had led the organized massacre of over three hundred Italians. But they had all been men. Perhaps Kappler drew the line at killing women.

Nolan could not afford such moral laxities – the Corvo woman knew too much and would blow his cover when the Americans arrived. From Kappler, he learned that the Americans were about a day away. He looked down at the gun that lay in his palm and realized that within twenty-four hours he would have to use it. Not only because of his role as a Gestapo spy – he was already reconsidering that prospect – but also because his very his presence in Rome, as a former American prisoner of war, would be threatened. The Corvo woman would tell MacPherson of her fears, and he would begin to make all the connections.

He stuffed the pistol in his waistband and went to the kitchen to retrieve the money from his hiding place in the shoebox behind the ventilation grille. When he lifted the last wad of lire, he noticed a slip of paper still nestling at the bottom of the box. His fingers reached for the scrap, and he suddenly remembered he had grabbed it from MacPherson's pocket the night he had stolen the watch.

The note bore an address that he had long since forgotten. "Father Francesco, Santa Maria della Gloria." Father Francesco – where had he heard that name before? Nolan's mind suddenly began putting the pieces together. After the foolish Silvesti woman had been shot, MacPherson slipped and told him and Lawrence that a Father Francesco had given him the news after giving her last rites. But why was MacPherson in contact with this priest? He wasn't religious – he wasn't even Catholic – and he had never mentioned the priest before.

Nolan grasped the answer within moments: the priest was MacPherson's contact, the source of all his POW addresses! The news would be music to Kappler's ears; he would contact the Gestapo chief immediately. Kappler might not be able to kill a woman, but he would have no qualms about torturing a priest.

He pushed the paper in his pocket and replaced the grille, checked again the position of Lawrence's body, and bounded up the stone stairs.

OUTSIDE THE VILLA RANIERI.

Von Breitland realized that people were regarding him oddly as he stood on the corner at the end of the street on which Adriana's house stood. Because of the urgency of the situation, he'd rushed across town immediately after his meeting with the ambassador had finished, and there hadn't been time to change out of his uniform.

The place appeared empty, but he hadn't dared to knock on the door. In his uniform, he might compromise Adriana and put himself in grave danger. She had told him of Bartoli's threat, of how undisciplined members of the Resistance might take independent action against them. He'd thought at the time that Bartoli had been blustering, trying to sabotage their relationship, which the Resistance man said was a danger to his organization. His fears grew as the minutes passed.

He looked at his watch: waiting was sheer torture, but his love and concern for Adriana was overcoming his fear. He boldly strode across the street and began hammering on the door with the knocker. There was no response. He peered through the downstairs front windows but could see nobody. A renewed bout of knocking brought no answer. Nothing. Anton turned to see a few people looking at him curiously from across the street. He went to talk to these neighbors, but all except one quickly disappeared. He addressed the one remaining, an elderly man, in Italian. "Why is the house empty? Where is Signora Corvo?"

The old man looked at him sullenly and answered gruffly. "Taken away. In a car earlier today. About three hours ago."

"Did you see who took her?" Anton grabbed the lapels of the old man's coat.

The man looked at von Breitland and waited for him to release his grip before answering. "It was the Gestapo. I'd recognize them anywhere." His voice was surly. "But you're German. Shouldn't you know?"

VILLA RANIERI.

Jay needed no sixth sense to realize there was something wrong as he pulled his key from the lock. The house was deserted, quiet as a tomb. He glanced at his watch: a little after four. Normally on a Saturday afternoon Giorgio and Luisa would be home running around with squeals of laughter and Adriana would be shouting at them. Where was everybody?

There was a noise. A low moan. He looked around, his ears straining. Again. He rushed across the hall to the door of the cellar. The noise grew louder. His feet clipped on the stairs as he started to go down quickly, then stopped.

At the bottom of the steps, Lawrence lay crumpled on the floor, blood seeping slowly through his hair from a nasty scalp wound. He was alive, his breath rasping in his throat as he strove to speak.

"Wait, David, just wait a second." Jay dashed to the bathroom and returned with a towel, which he used to gently dab the head wound. "You've had a bad fall, David." He wadded up the towel and placed it under Lawrence's head.

"Jay, you have to know..." The words came slowly from Lawrence's lips as he tried to raise his head. "Nolan, he..." His head fell back on the towel.

"Later, buddy." Jay leapt to his feet. "First we gotta get you to a hospital. I'll call an ambulance."

Turning toward the staircase, Jay suddenly stopped and looked up. A pistol was pointing straight at his stomach.

VIA TASSO GESTAPO HEADQUARTERS.

Kappler placed another document on the pile of critical papers he had to carry out of Rome in his briefcase the next day. The pile comprised a relatively short stack next to the tower of documents that had to be destroyed before he left. At the shrill tone of the telephone, he lifted the receiver, his eyes narrowing as he recognized the caller.

"Von Breitland, I would never have expected a call from you today. I thought that like all of us you'd be attending to your departure preparations. How are you?"

Kappler's eyes widened. "Signora Corvo? No, I have no idea where she might be...No, no idea, none. The last I saw of her was at Contessa Morosini's dinner party two weeks ago. She looked radiant. Surely, you were there, as well?"

Pausing as he listened, the Gestapo man suddenly guffawed into the receiver. "Arrested? By the Gestapo? Surely this is some sort of ridiculous joke. Who told you such nonsense?"

After another few moments, Kappler gave a sardonic chuckle. "My dear von Breitland, you really shouldn't believe what you hear on the street from random Italians. However, if the situation is worrying you, I'll have my men make an investigation...Of course...Yes, as quickly as possible, but I'm sure you'll understand that my men have much to do tonight…Yes, yes, of course I'll get back to you. *Auf Wiedersehen.*"

VILLA RANIERI.

Vittoria motioned her pistol toward Lawrence. "What happened to David?"

"It looks like he fell down the stairs," MacPherson said, frowning. "He's in bad shape and I think we'd better call an ambulance." He focused on the gun which was still pointing at him. "Unless you think I'm a German spy."

"No, no, of course not." Vittoria pushed the pistol back into her pocket. "I'm sorry about that – I'm not myself right now. I just heard from neighbors that my mother was arrested a few hours ago."

"Adriana? Arrested?"

"Yes. Or so they think. They saw what looked like Gestapo men come and take her away in a car. When I heard that I didn't know what to do, so I rushed to pick up the children from their art class and take them to a place where they'll be safe. But I still have no idea what's going on, and I'm at my wit's end." She nervously ran her fingers through her long hair. "Where is my mother?"

Jay turned and knelt at Lawrence's side. "Godammit, Vittoria, I don't know what's going on either. All I know is that right now we need to get him to a hospital. Fast."

Lawrence's eyes opened and he tried to lift his head. "Nolan." His voice was no more than a whisper. "Nolan." His eyes closed as his head fell back against the towel.

"Nolan *what*, David?" Jay raised his voice. "Nolan *what?*"

There was no response. "Go call an ambulance, Vittoria. Now!"

As she rushed up the stairs he called after her. "And as soon as we've got Lawrence to the hospital, you and I need to get out of here. I don't know what's going on, but I don't think your mother's house is safe right now!"

"I couldn't agree more," Vittoria called down from the top of the steps. "If my mother is in the hands of the Gestapo, we're all in danger."

As he got up to collect his notepad and belongings, Jay heard Vittoria dialing and speaking rapidly into the hall phone.

"The ambulance will be here within a few minutes," she said, running back down the stairs. "And maybe I can help with a safe house. The Resistance has a number you could use."

"Thanks, but I know a place I can go." Jay squatted back down on the stone steps to check on Lawrence. "There's a steady pulse." He heaved a sigh. "As soon as I know Lawrence is in safe hands, I'll take off and see my friend."

"Are you armed?" Vittoria asked coldly. "Because if the Germans are about to pull out as everyone says they are, it could get quite dicey on the streets. The Germans will be extremely anxious about the approach of your troops, so they could be trigger-happy."

Jay shook his head.

"Let me make a suggestion," she said, "and also ask a favor. Let me—" The knocker on the front door interrupted her. "That'll be the ambulance." She ran up the stairs and returned with the medical crew, who immediately began attending to Lawrence.

"Let me come with you to your friend's house," Vittoria continued. "I can offer you some protection." She patted the pistol in her pocket. "Then, if I can ask a favor in return, I'd like you to come with me to Via Tasso to see if we can get my mother released from the Gestapo headquarters."

"I'd do anything to help, Vittoria, you know that. But why me? What use would I be?"

"When the Germans pull out – and everything points to a withdrawal tonight – then the presence of an American could be important." She watched as the ambulance crew gently lifted

Lawrence onto a stretcher. "My guess is the Germans will leave an Italian staff behind at the Via Tasso headquarters. I think an American would command respect right now, what with liberation by the American army about to occur."

"But I have no uniform."

"I've thought of that. I'm going to tell them you're attached to the American embassy in the Vatican." Her eyes were imploring. "Please, Jay. You could make all the difference."

Jay thought for a few moments before nodding his agreement. "Okay. But first we have to make sure David's all right." They followed the crew with the stretcher up the stone steps.

"By the way, where does your friend live?" she asked.

"At Santa Maria della Gloria. You may know the place – it's a church."

ROME OPERA HOUSE.

"Well, Kappler, what do you think of my farewell to Rome?" Kesselring, in full dress uniform, gave the Gestapo chief an avuncular smile.

Kappler had hoped to avoid the field marshal during the final intermission of the matinee performance. Nearly every officer in Rome was in the Opera House, but Kesselring had managed to find him in the crowd.

"A magnificent occasion, Field Marshal." Kappler clicked his heels in salute. "Perhaps the choice of *A Masked Ball* is a little poignant."

"I'd forgotten that you know your opera, Kappler." He mused for a moment. "But yes, the time for action is upon us. We must leave Rome and prepare better defensive positions farther north. So this gala opera is my farewell to Rome."

Kappler nodded. The decision to make a tactical withdrawal was clear cut, but he had ambivalent feelings about leaving Rome. "I love the city, sir. Part of me would like very much to stay."

"You have done good work here, Kappler, and in very difficult circumstances." Kesselring lowered his voice. "But the city you love will change once General Clark arrives and the Italian hotheads begin to run riot." He gave one of his broad smiles. "Not a time for the likes of us to be around, eh, Kappler?" He raised his field marshal's baton in an informal salute. "Well, I must get back for the last act."

Kappler inclined his head to return the salute and found a secluded area in the vestibule away from the pressing throng. His feelings about leaving Rome were mixed. He had fallen in love with the city long before the war, marveling at its art, overwhelmed by its antiquity, never tiring of its beauty. When he first arrived to take command of the Rome Gestapo – was it only nine months ago? – he thought he'd never want to leave. He remembered how the words of a poem often played out in his mind back then.

> While stands the Colosseum, Rome shall stand
> When falls the Colosseum, Rome shall fall
> And when Rome falls – the World.

Now Rome was about to fall, and with it a good part of his own world. But the last nine months had shown him another, darker side, one of murder and violence.

He finished his wine and placed the glass on a table. Kesselring was right: Rome would not be the same tomorrow. And, despite his passion for their city, Romans would never tolerate his presence back in Rome again. They would not understand that an officer had to obey orders. They would not understand that every single day he relived the twenty-fourth of March: the shots, the cries, the fallen bodies. Every day. He felt no guilt, only a vacuum at the center of his existence. There was no deep recess of his mind into which he could bury the images.

He walked into the concert hall for the last act of *Un Ballo in Maschera*. The twenty-fourth of March would return. Every day. Every single day.

NEAR SANTA MARIA DELLA GLORIA.

Although he still couldn't grasp what was going on, Jay was sure of one thing: to be abroad in Rome at that moment was dangerous. He and Vittoria needed to go somewhere safe, find a place of refuge.

They made their way up Via Arenula, carefully watching out for German soldiers and fascist police. Vittoria nudged him with her elbow as an obvious Gestapo car cruising by slowed down, the leather-coated occupants scouring the sidewalks for prey.

"Ignore them." Vittoria whispered her advice. "Walk slowly, as if we're a couple on an evening stroll." She laced her arm through his; the car sped away.

"I'm sure your friend will be fine," she said, but her words sounded more like a statement of faith. The doctors at the Fatebenefratelli Hospital had a less reassuring opinion: Lawrence's survival, they said, was a matter of touch-and-go. Jay would have hung around the hospital to await developments, but he knew he and Vittoria had to move on.

Over and over again they had tried to fathom the events of the day, but could come up with no rational answers. Why had Adriana been arrested? Had Lawrence really fallen down the stairs? What had happened to Nolan? The three events seemed unconnected, and none of them seemed to have any viable explanation.

Jay had other thoughts on their situation, but he dared not reveal them to Vittoria. If the Gestapo had arrested Adriana and interrogated her – his stomach lurched at the thought – neither of them was safe. As head of the POW organization, he was sure to be at the top of Kappler's list. And Vittoria, as a key member of the Resistance…

But it was no use endlessly pondering questions they could not answer – the important thing at that moment was to get to a place of safety. He still had mixed feelings about his decision to go to Santa Maria della Gloria. Father Francesco would welcome them with open arms, he had no doubt, but he had to be sure he was not leading any enemies to his church.

"There's something really strange about Rome today," Vittoria said. Jay could sense the curious atmosphere, as well, as people giddily bustled along the streets. With the imminent arrival of the Americans, hope was in the air; but with the Germans still encamped in the city, everyone was still apprehensive, afraid that something could wrench the chalice of joy from their lips at the last minute. Would the Germans leave Rome without a fight? Jay shared everyone's apprehension.

His fear surged as they turned into the piazza that fronted the church of Santa Maria della Gloria. Vittoria grabbed his sleeve, pulling him into a doorway. "Gestapo!" she hissed in his ear.

The leather-coated goon guarding the vehicle parked in front of the church confirmed Vittoria's view. Before there was time to consider any action, the door to the church vestry banged open and two Gestapo agents frog-marched Father Francesco down the steps, thrusting him violently into the car.

Vittoria looked at Jay. She spoke no words, but her message was clear: there were too many of them. If she used her pistol, she and Jay would both join the priest on a journey to Gestapo headquarters.

Jay despaired of his impotence as he briefly glimpsed the priest's face in the car speeding from the piazza. Anguish tore at his heart.

They watched helplessly as the Gestapo vehicle disappeared around the corner. The American pinched his eyes closed and hung his head. "I feel as if somehow I've betrayed him," he said.

"You can't blame yourself." Vittoria reached out to lay a comforting hand on his arm. "There was nothing we could do."

"Jesus, Vittoria, I feel so goddam helpless!" He clenched his fists. "I need to do something. Get down to Via Tasso. Try to help Father Francesco. Find out what's going on with your mother."

"Jay, as much as I'd like to agree with you, I'm sure you realize there's nothing we can do right now. The two of us against all the Germans on the street?" As if to emphasize her point, four German motorcyclists sped by. "Besides," she glanced at her watch, "curfew's in twenty minutes – we'd be picked up by the patrol guards as soon as they saw us. And with this in my pocket, they wouldn't waste time shipping us to Via Tasso." She pointed her finger to her temple and brought down her thumb. "The best thing we can do now is get to a safe house."

She bit her lower lip as she thought. "There's one that I know that's not too far away, but we've got to walk fast. Come on, let's get going."

Jay resisted the tug on his arm. "No, there's a better one that's closer by. Father Francesco's monastery. Just behind the church. We'll be okay there, Vittoria."

Via Tasso Gestapo Headquarters.

The soul-shattering screams ripped through her with a force that was almost physical. Adriana shivered as she struggled to raise her aching frame from the blanket lying on the bare floor. Running her fingers through her disheveled hair, she shook her head: less than a day in Gestapo headquarters had transformed her. She searched in her pocket for the comb and mirror she knew were not there; the guards had made her surrender all her personal things, even her wristwatch.

Why didn't Anton arrive to straighten out this terrible mistake? Surely he had received her message? Her hands tapped the empty pockets of her jacket, this time looking for the cigarettes that might have eased her frustration and tension.

A small filthy window showed the last grey light of dusk and a bare light bulb cast a baleful glare around her cell. She scanned her surroundings. On the wall near the door, a previous prisoner had marked the days spent there with scratches. She counted them: five, ten, fifteen, seventeen, and then there were no more.

Another scream rent her soul before ebbing into agonized sobs. Would they torture her, too? But why? She had nothing to tell. The image of Vittoria came to mind: she was well aware that her daughter was working for the Resistance. And if the Gestapo found that out, they had ways of getting other information from her. Were they still seeking those who had masterminded the Via Rasella attack?

Surely she would never betray her daughter, no matter what they did to her. Would she? Anger opposed the element of doubt hovering in her mind. She rushed to the corner of the room, picked up the chair, and smashed it against the light.

At first, the darkness felt welcoming, hiding everything. But renewed screams of agony shattered the false moment of relief. What was the Gestapo doing to that prisoner? And would they do the same to her? Adriana put her hands to her ears and pressed hard.

She could shut out the screams, but she could not shut out the fear.

THE MONASTERY.

Jay smiled at Vittoria across the small wooden table in the kitchen of the monastery where the two of them sat. The monks had offered them sanctuary without hesitation, despite their anxiety over Father Francesco. Although the monks' averted eyes made Vittoria uncomfortable, she knew that, apart from the elderly widow who prepared their meals, no females ever crossed the threshold of the brothers' monastery.

"It feels good to be finally off the streets of Rome tonight." Jay dragged a crust of dark bread around the bottom of his bowl to sop up the last bits of the hearty soup of vegetables, beans, and macaroni. "You know, Vittoria," he broke another hunk of bread off the loaf, "I'll never get over how courageous it was for your mother to take us in. She never seemed to worry about the risks."

"Oh, Mamma was well aware of the dangers," she said softly. "Despite her devil-may-care attitude, she knew the risk she was taking."

"So did Maria." Jay dropped the half-eaten slab of bread into his bowl and leaned back in his chair.

"Maria?"

"She was—" He checked himself. He thought it best not to increase Vittoria's concern for her mother by telling her that Maria was a padrone who had been executed. "She was my friend."

"Where is Maria now?"

"Dead." The word, barely whispered, fell reluctantly from his lips.

Vittoria did not press him for details. "She was something special to you, wasn't she?" She had seen the slight tremble in his lips.

"Yes. Could have been." He sought to hide his emotional confusion by turning the conversation away from Maria. "But you've suffered, too. Your brother, Fabio."

"Yes. Fabio." She gave a sigh as a long-suppressed memory of that hideous day in March was called from its lair. "But he was a member of the Resistance. He knew – we all knew – the risks." She tried to force the memory of that day back into its box, only for another to emerge. "I think the losses that really hurt are the ones you feel that you, personally, could have prevented."

"Yeah, I know what you're saying." Since Maria's arrest, not a day had passed when he hadn't bitterly regretted not having been more cautious while they were in her home. "I keep thinking that somehow, some way, I could have prevented her death. Know what I mean?"

"Yes," Vittoria said as she thought about Renzo. "I had a good friend. All he wanted was a little comfort, a little—," she knew the word but found another, "a little affection, but I—" She stopped. The memory was too painful. For a minute she took deep breaths, fighting to hold back the imminent onslaught of tears. "But 'could haves' and 'should haves' don't help. Renzo is out there, somewhere, in the Ardeatine caves. Dead. And I know he needn't be." Her chest began to heave and she reached into her pocket for a handkerchief.

Jay looked away, allowing a few moments before he spoke. "Perhaps we shouldn't be so hard on ourselves. Maybe it's not entirely our fault. Maybe what's to blame is something much, much bigger that put us in this goddam situation in the first place."

"You mean the war?"

"Sure, the war, but it's much more than the war." He sought to give discipline to the thoughts unfolding in his mind. "The war – it's too remote, too impersonal, too easy to condemn." His words began to come quickly. "It's hard to get angry at 'the war.' It's the people who caused the war – Hitler, Himmler and the other Nazi fiends and their henchmen, like Kappler and his ilk. They're the ones who caused it all. They killed Maria. They killed your brother. They killed your friend. And, damn it all to hell, I intend to fight them. Fight them with my very last breath until they kill me, too." He realized that he was almost shouting.

He lowered his voice. "None of this would have happened if people had just stood up to those creeps in the very beginning. But they didn't, and that's how they got all their evil power." He ran a hand through his hair. "It's too late to change past history. But if we stand up to them now, play our part – no matter how small – to defeat them, then perhaps we can," he paused as he sought a particular word, "can *extirpate* all this guilt that we shouldn't have but do. Guilt that we have because of them, because of these monsters."

Both sat silently, lost in thought. A noise at the door drew their attention. The widow who cooked for the monks said something in rapid Italian to Vittoria.

Vittoria translated for Jay. "She says she'll take me to the annex, where I'm to sleep on a cot. You're to go upstairs and a monk will show you to a cell in their dormitory. We'd better turn in so we can get an early start tomorrow. We've got a lot to do."

Jay rose and prepared to leave. "Yeah, we've got a big day coming up." He looked down at her. "Maybe this time tomorrow your mother will be free." He gently kissed her forehead. "Maybe this time tomorrow all of Rome will be free."

REGINA COELI PRISON.

"Chowtime's over, Del Pietro." The voice came through the grille of the cell. "Pass me your tray." The guard took the mess kit and dropped his voice to a whisper. "Hey, Del Pietro, I just heard that the American army is expected to arrive soon. Maybe tomorrow." The grille was slammed shut and the guard walked away.

Even after a couple of months he still couldn't get used to being called Del Pietro. It wasn't his name, but he didn't deny it anymore. His memory fingered the pages of the past. March. The name belonged to his cellmate at that time, Vito Del Pietro. A petty thief. Del Pietro had wanted to escape.

His mind took him back to that day in March. The guard had told him to gather up his things, that a German soldier would be stopping by for him. But not for Del Pietro, and his cellmate had cursed his luck. In the past, prisoners had been transferred to Germany to work on forced labor gangs there,

Del Pietro had said. If he was put on a train, there was always a chance he could jump and escape.

There was little he could remember about the rest of that day. Presumably, Del Pietro had slugged him from behind. In any event, he'd come to later with a throbbing headache, alone in the cell – Del Pietro had taken the call instead of him.

It turned out to be bad luck for Del Pietro, but he, himself, could scarcely believe his own good fortune. Other inmates later told him that the prisoners taken away on that March day – many of whom had been Jews – had all perished; Rome was still talking about the German reprisal. So Del Pietro, instead of getting a chance to jump from a Germany-bound train, had hit Renzo over the head only to become one of the victims of a brutal massacre.

He had long since stopped mulling over his good luck. Just keep your head down had been his rule. The wardens could call him 'Del Pietro' till the Tiber froze over. What was it to him? Same grey walls, same grub, same stench. And Del Pietro had been a Catholic – a blessing in a regime that killed Jews.

And now the Allied army was approaching Rome. Maybe they would free him. Then he could shout it from the rooftops: *My name is Renzo. Renzo Rossi. And I'm a Jew!*

VIA TASSO GESTAPO HEADQUARTERS.

Kappler gazed through the window of his office at the night sky hovering over a blacked-out city. "Tonight, Nolan, the moon looks down on a Rome under German occupation. One more spin of the earth and she will bestow her light on the Americans."

He turned and spoke sharply to his visitor. "And all my plans to cover our withdrawal with enemy prisoners hiding in Rome are ruined." He sat down at his desk and lit a cigarette. "The priest knows nothing."

"That can't be right!" Nolan leapt from his seat. "I'm sure he's MacPherson's contact! He knows the addresses all right! Your interrogation officer must have got something out of him!"

Kappler's lips spread in a sardonic smile. "Interrogation officer? 'Interrogation' is not the precise word to describe what Father Francesco has undergone." He leaned his head back and blew plumes of smoke toward the ceiling. "True, the man was interrogated, to be sure." He tapped the ash of his cigarette into his ashtray. "By experts skilled in getting answers – if you understand what I mean."

Nolan understood but said nothing.

"The priest offered few words." Kappler shook his head. "Of course, he screamed a lot, but unfortunately not one useful word came from his lips. When he did speak, the idiot had the naivety to say that God provides all answers." Kappler stared absently at his cigarette. "Do you think he was brave, Nolan?"

The question startled Nolan, who could only shrug his shoulders.

"The man was a fool." Kappler pulled over the ashtray and slowly ground out his cigarette. "And now, Nolan," he steepled his fingers, "thanks to your stunning incompetence, instead of a column of hundreds of enemy prisoners, I have only a couple dozen half-dead inmates of the Via Tasso to take along as hostages." He locked eyes with the American, letting his words hang in the air.

"My staff and I will be leaving before dawn." He shuffled the papers on his desk into a neater pile. "We'll be taking all the Via Tasso prisoners, including the priest." He rose and placed the papers in his briefcase. "All the prisoners, Nolan. Except one."

REGINA COELI PRISON.

Renzo couldn't sleep. All day there had been an air of anticipation throughout the prison, but he could also sense a feeling of unease. On his walk in the prison yard that morning, the prisoners were all buoyed up by rumors of the Allied army's advance; but, like him, they also harbored doubts about what could happen in the meantime.

He settled back on his cot, his hands clasped under his head and his thoughts turning to Vittoria. Her image had rarely been far from his mind, sustaining him over the past two months. By now, he thought, she might consider him dead, slain in the massacre or sent to a death camp. He had tried to get a message out to her, but the guards wanted big money for that, and he had only a few lire. One of the prisoners in the block was due for release the day after tomorrow; maybe he could help.

But did Vittoria really care? The last time he had seen her, she had been cold and distant. Perhaps she had moved on, found another. One who came from a better part of town. One who wasn't a Jew.

He had not passed a single day within his cell without such thoughts tormenting him. He pushed them from his mind, but the image of her face remained and fed his desire, his desire to be free of the filthy jail, to run in the open air of Rome, to see Vittoria's warm brown eyes light up with surprise.

Noises outside broke the spell of his reverie; he got up and stood on his bed to peer through his small, barred window down into the dimly-lit prison precincts. He could see some Germans – and an SS officer who was talking to the prison warden.

Would the Allies really arrive tomorrow? Would there be yet another delay? Maybe the Germans were going to defend the city. A thousand rumors echoed from the prison walls and Renzo knew he dared not believe any. He lay back down, his fists clenched in frustration.

The small grille in the door slid open. "Del Pietro," the guard growled, "get your things together. A German truck will collect you and some others in the morning." Then he spoke more softly, and a hint of pity was in his voice. "I'm afraid you're going north, Del Pietro. Slave labor in Germany."

332

VIA TASSO GESTAPO HEADQUARTERS.

Kappler snapped his briefcase shut. "You've said that you'd be unable to spy for me in Rome without the elimination of Signora Corvo." Kappler sat down and lit another cigarette. "I quite agree with you, Nolan – your spying mission would be jeopardized by her presence in Rome."

"She has to be suspicious. She saw that I was collecting the POW addresses." Nolan said, his words coming quickly. "I don't think she figured out the whole plan, but, still, she knows too much."

"Clearly. She's nobody's fool." Kappler paused, choosing his next words deliberately. "But you are aware, Nolan—"

Kappler's eyes turned suddenly to look sternly at the ringing telephone, an unwelcome intrusion. "Yes?" he barked into the receiver. "Ah, von Breitland," he said with a mellowed voice, "I've been meaning to call you. My men have made as thorough an investigation as they could, given the demands of the day, and can determine nothing regarding Signora Corvo. Other than, as you say, she is not at home at present."

Kappler rolled his eyes at Nolan, who was puzzled by a conversation in a language he did not understand. "Yes, of course we'll keep the investigation open until we leave, although there's not much more we can do...Yes, we'll do that...We both must get some rest now, von Breitland – we've got an early start tomorrow. *Gute Nacht.*"

Kappler hung up the telephone. "Where was I, Nolan? Oh, yes: you have to keep in mind that Signora Corvo has great influence among the officer corps in Rome. At the opera this afternoon, Kesselring was searching the crowd for her; he wanted to invite her to the reception he gave after the opera. Despite the circumstances, it was a gay affair—"

"I'd appreciate it if you would come to the point."

"The point is, Nolan, that I cannot take her away from Rome as a hostage. Too many questions would be asked. Neither do I dare—"

"No need to beat about the bush," Nolan said. "I know what has to be done."

Kappler looked him in the eye and slowly nodded his head. "Your opportunity will come soon after first light tomorrow." He rose from his desk chair, buttoning his tunic. "You can stay here at Via Tasso tonight in my private room." He pointed to a door at the back of his office. "During the night, all the other prisoners will be removed. By dawn, the whole building will be cleared. I trust you brought the pistol I gave you?"

Nolan nodded sullenly.

Kappler crossed the room toward a rack, on which hung the keys to the cells. He carefully selected one. "Ah, here it is – the key to Signora Corvo's cell." He pressed it into Nolan's palm. "And now I wish you a good night's sleep." He picked up his briefcase and left.

GERMAN DIPLOMATIC STAFF OFFICERS' QUARTERS.

Anton von Breitland sat on his bed in his officer's quarters trying to fathom what to do next. Adriana dominated his thoughts, eclipsing all else in his mind. His inability to uncover her whereabouts had driven him to distraction.

One thing was certain: wherever she was, she was being held against her will. There were only two possibilities. He quickly discarded the notion that the Resistance had taken action because of her relationship with him. Adriana had told him of Bartoli's warning, but he had viewed it as bluster. Besides, the Resistance would probably have acted against him, not her. There was only one other possibility.

He looked at his watch: just after midnight. An hour since he had spoken to the Gestapo chief. Kappler was lying, he was sure of it. All the evidence pointed to a Gestapo arrest. But why? What could be Kappler's motivation? He was well aware of Adriana's standing with the officer corps.

Anton stood up and paced the floor. He had to stop trying to double-guess Kappler, but he was still unsure what to do. He had to get to Via Tasso, but his quarters were located in the Parioli district, far from the center of Rome, and with preparations for the withdrawal from Rome in full swing it would be impossible to get a staff car. And yet, in a few hours, Kappler and the whole German army would leave Rome.

Except for him. That point stood at the core of his dilemma. He sat back down and picked up the photo of his parents by his bedside. Perhaps they would understand. Perhaps not. He set the snapshot down and reached for the photograph Adriana had given him at Christmas. He would never leave her. He would find her and stay with her in Rome for the rest of his life.

In the morning, somehow he would find a way to get to Via Tasso to look for her. He began to take off his uniform. He would never wear it again.

Via Tasso Gestapo Headquarters.

The noise awoke her from a restless sleep. The noise of doors opening and slamming, of shouts, of feet shuffling along the corridor. Adriana's knuckles rubbed her eyes as the nightmare of where she was reassembled in her mind. A pencil line of light from the crack beneath the door cast a dim ghostly glow that made the contours of her cell barely visible.

The noises from outside grew. They were unlike the usual sounds of Via Tasso – the groans, the screams of pain. She heard the muttering of voices, growled orders from the German guards. Adriana got up from her blanket and moved the few paces to the locked door of her cell, pressing her ear to the wood.

After listening for a few moments, she had no doubt. The Germans were moving out. And, for some reason, they were taking the prisoners with them. But the small window at the top of the far wall was still dark: outside was night, with not even a hint of dawn in the sky.

The noises began to fade away. She heard the clump of feet on the stairs leading down to the way out. Her hand reached for the door handle but found the cell still locked. She was about to shout, but stopped.

They had forgotten her. Why should she draw attention to herself? Before she was arrested, she had heard rumors that the Germans were about to leave. If indeed that was then happening, then the Americans would arrive soon.

Adriana tried to contain the glimmer of hope that entered her heart. Given time, either Anton or Vittoria was sure to find her. Or even some American soldier. She didn't know why, she wasn't sure how, but the Germans had forgotten about her. She lay down on the blanket on the floor and pulled her jacket over her. Surely now a restful sleep would come.

Regina Coeli Prison.

Renzo started as he awoke. Throughout his life, the first light of day had always roused him from his sleep, and the pale light coating the small cell window proved no exception. But that day would be different, Renzo knew. He rose from his cot and pulled on his pants. Before the day was ended, he and many other prisoners would be on a train heading north. To Germany. And to slave labor. And when they discovered he was a Jew...

Every prisoner knew the German plan – the Italian guards had told them the night before. The trucks had arrived the previous night and were parked in the courtyard below his window. Open trucks ready for their human cargo, ready to take them to the train.

Trying to lift his spirits, he remembered the advice of his erstwhile cellmate, Vito Del Pietro, the man who had doomed himself. Perhaps, he thought, he could escape from the train on the journey north. Vito's strategy had seemed more or less sound, even if his timing had been poor.

Renzo brightened; maybe there would be no train journey. The previous evening, the warders had passed on other, better information. The Americans were at the southern outskirts of Rome. Perhaps they would arrive early; perhaps they would thwart the German plans.

Renzo's hopes evaporated at the sound of engines revving in the courtyard below, truck doors slamming, raucous German voices shouting. Italian warders came through the corridor banging on cell doors and calling, "Prisoners get ready! Prepare for transfer!"

Renzo picked up his small bundle of possessions as his cell door swung open. Disconsolate, he joined the other prisoners as they trudged down the stairs and into the courtyard.

In the prison courtyard, the droning of the trucks' engines drowned out all other sound and the heavy smoke of their diesel engines stung Renzo's nostrils. He felt afraid; as he looked around at the crowd of prisoners, he saw fear writ large on their faces, as well. But anxiety also haunted the faces of the German guards, whose fingers ran nervously over the stocks of their rifles. The outer gate of the courtyard opened, preparing for the departure of the trucks.

"*Achtung! Achtung!*" All eyes turned to the German officer who came quickly through the gates. Renzo couldn't understand the rapid German orders.

He was surprised when he saw the German guards climb back into their own trucks. The officer shouted an order as he jumped up on one of the trucks and sat down next to the driver. The engines roared as all three trucks rumbled through the open gate at the end of the courtyard. As the last truck disappeared, two Italian warders heaved the large prison gates shut.

"Everyone back to their cells!" the duty warder shouted. Renzo was confused, but smiled with relief. He was safe for the moment. And maybe the Americans would soon arrive.

ON THE WAY TO VIA TASSO.

When Jay and Vittoria emerged from the monastery, there was just a hint of light in the eastern sky and they could hear a low rumble. As they headed down narrow streets, the noise grew, and when they reached the wide Via del Corso the source of the noise became visible: the German army was leaving Rome.

"Looks like they stole every piece of transport they could lay their hands on," Jay observed, studying the unkempt, sorry troops making their way north in trucks and stolen cars, on bicycles and horse-drawn wagons. "Look at their faces. They all look kind of scared."

"Oh, they're scared all right," Vittoria said. "They're scared of us, of the Resistance. They've seen our power, they know our strength – and they know they'd better behave themselves if they want to make it out alive." An open truck crammed with soldiers rolled by followed by a soldier pushing a wounded comrade in a wheelbarrow. A number of heavily-laden Germans struggled by on foot.

"And look who's tagging along!" Vittoria pointed at an expensive car filled with well-dressed Italians following the soldiers. "Some of the fascist pigs who didn't want to be caught overstaying their welcome."

Jay and Vittoria had to cross in order to get to the Via Tasso, but there was no let-up in the stream of equipment and German soldiers clogging the street. Jay looked on in awe; he knew he was witnessing the sight of a lifetime. "This even beats Macy's Thanksgiving Day Parade," he murmured.

As they waited for an opening in the procession to cross, the sky grew lighter and the city began to awaken. Eventually, they were joined by Italians coming out of their homes to line the street and silently watch along with them. Vittoria looked around. "I'm proud of these people, proud of my fellow Romans," she said. "When the Germans marched in last September, all pride and arrogance, they trained their machine guns on them. Now that the shoe is on the other foot, now that the Germans are marching out, it's a wonder any Roman can just stand there and politely watch them leave in silence."

Jay looked at his watch. "We'd better get going. I think I see a gap in the traffic." After a piece of heavy artillery rattled by, they dashed across the street and continued on their way.

VIA TASSO.

The early morning light from the window slowly prompted his consciousness. His eyes opened slowly, then, startled by the strangeness of his surroundings, Nolan leapt from the cot. His mind needed but a few moments to remember where he was and to reconstruct the past. And to spell out the future and what he had to do within the next few hours.

The thought made his hands shake as he pulled on his shirt and pants. Everything had seemed so logical the night before during his discussion with Kappler; now, with the deed at hand, his resolve wavered.

He walked through Kappler's office, trying to will his heart to slow down, but his hands found the key and pistol in his pocket, reminding him of the inevitability of what he had to do. He opened the door to the hallway. All was quiet. As Kappler had promised, the building was deserted. Except for him. And the Corvo woman in the cell at the far end of the hall.

AN APARTMENT IN ROME.

"I don't think you should play outside today," Signora Samarone said to Giorgio and Luisa as she looked out the window of her second-floor apartment. "There's too much traffic on the streets. These Germans, they cause so much trouble."

"Have you heard anything about our mamma?" Giorgio asked. He hadn't liked staying at Signora Samarone's apartment, but Vittoria had insisted. Their mother was ill, she had said, and had to be taken to the hospital. He loved Vittoria, but sometimes she told him fibs.

"She'll soon be all right. Back home tomorrow, I'm sure."

Giorgio could tell by Signora Samarone's strained smile that she, too, was telling fibs.

"The Germans are leaving! The Germans are leaving!" Luisa jumped up and down at the window overlooking the street, the large bow in her hair flopping with each impact. "Perhaps now my mother and father will come home!"

"Maybe, Luisa, maybe." Signora Samarone was telling another fib, Giorgio knew. When Luisa had first arrived to stay with them, he overhead his sister talking to Renzo. He felt sad, sorry for Luisa. Her mamma and papa would never come back.

"Come see! Come see!" Luisa shouted, beckoning Giorgio to the window. The boy ran to the window and looked down. They weren't real soldiers. Not like the men they'd seen marching along the Via Rasella. Giorgio immediately tried to force the memories from his mind. Fabio. The bomb. He wanted to forget.

"Signora Samarone, can we please watch from the balcony?" Luisa asked. "I want to see the Germans leave."

The woman hesitated for a moment, then opened the French doors and joined the children on the balcony.

"Look, Giorgio!" Luisa pointed down to the street twenty feet below. "Look how sad the Germans seem! I'm glad they feel sad!"

Apart from the roar of the trucks' engines, the streets were quiet. The Romans stood on the sidewalks watching, hiding their emotions, saying nothing.

"Look, Giorgio! There's Father Francesco!" Luisa pointed at the back of a German truck.

"Can't be." Giorgio said, his eyes following her finger. "But you're right!" The boy remembered the kindness of the priest from their time taking tracings in his church.

"Father Francesco! Father Francesco!" Giorgio shouted. He saw the priest look around for the person who was calling his name.

"His spectacles," Luisa shouted, "they're broken!"

As the truck pulled away, the priest lifted his head and saw the children. He raised his hand and made the sign of the cross before the truck turned the corner and was gone.

"He'll come back, too," Luisa said quietly.

"Maybe," Giorgio said without conviction. He wanted so many people to come back. Above all, his mother,

Via Tasso.

Nolan retreated into Kappler's office, sat at the Gestapo man's desk, and lit a cigarette. He didn't want to kill the Corvo woman. Killing Lawrence had been easy. He had hated the Limey bastard. But the woman – there was a difference.

The money was no longer an issue. He'd already made enough in his dealings with Police Chief Lippi to set him up when he got home. The bulging money belt at his waist spoke of a comfortable future once he got back to Boston.

If he got back. He drew heavily on his cigarette. He didn't want to kill her, but he had to. The Corvo woman would talk. If she got out of the prison cell alive, she would blab to everybody, tell Jay about the address list. She didn't have any evidence, but Jay would put two and two together. And...

Nolan sighed, the cigarette smoke cascading over the desk. MacPherson would easily make the connection between him and Maria Silvestri, the padrone who'd been shot by a firing squad. Nolan pinched his eyes closed. Hell, he never thought that would happen. He hadn't meant for her to die...

You have to kill the Corvo woman, his rational mind insisted. You have to kill her. He felt the sweat on his brow as he pulled the pistol from his pocket and placed it on the desk. If only he could arrange for a firing squad to deal with her. So impersonal. So easy.

His mind conjured up images of strolling down Beacon Street after the war. A man of substance. A man to be respected. He reached for the pistol and checked the bullets in the magazine.

Regina Coeli Prison.

Renzo was taut, nervous, as he paced anxiously up and down the confines of his cell. The sun was now shining, but no one had come to release him. He knew others were being freed. Political prisoners and Jews, according to the fast-working prison bush telegraph. Although the Americans had not yet arrived, a prison warder had told him, the leaders of the partisans had seized control of the prison with the chief warder's cooperation.

Renzo rattled his metal mug across the bars set in the small window of his cell door.

"Hey, Del Pietro! Who's rattling your cage?" the warder asked dryly. "I told you, room service will be delayed today."

"And I told you my name is not Vico Del Pietro – it's Renzo Rossi."

The warder rolled his eyes. "Amazing how we called you Vico Del Pietro for all those months and you never complained."

"But I'm a member of the partisans!"

"Sure, Vico, and I'm Joe Stalin." The guard threw his head back and laughed.

Renzo hurled the mug to the floor in exasperation. "But I asked you to tell them that my name was Renzo Rossi. Did you do it?"

"I did. Wish I hadn't." The warder looked disgusted. "They almost came up here to beat you up, Del Pietro. Seems this Renzo Rossi is a great hero of the Resistance. But he's dead, they said – killed by the Germans."

Renzo, deflated, sighed. "I'm begging you to ask them just once more."

"No chance. Why not cut it out, now, Del Pietro? You're just an old con. Nobody's interested in releasing a two-bit thief like you."

VIA TASSO.

As Jay and Vittoria began to approach Via Tasso, they found the streets deserted. Without any German patrols, the sight of the block where Gestapo headquarters had been located seemed unreal.

"Sure looks like they've all flown the coop," Jay said, walking briskly at Vittoria's side as they hurried along.

"Let's not get carried away yet." Vittoria gripped the pistol in her pocket, her eyes darting into every alley and doorway. "There could always be a nasty surprise." She checked behind them as they approached the large yellow building on the corner. The hated Gestapo headquarters.

Jay pushed on the outer door, standing back as the door swung open. "Well, what do you know!"

"Wait, I'll go first!" Vittoria pulled the pistol from her pocket and ran up the four steps to the inner doors, which were also open. Jay was close behind her.

They entered slowly, looking around and listening for any sounds.

"I think they forgot something," Jay whispered, looking up at a life-sized portrait of Hitler that still hung on the wall.

"Shh." Vittoria put a finger to her lips and continued to listen. "I don't like this – there's something fishy here." She slowly moved into the hall beyond the door. Nothing. Nobody. Not a single sound.

"Maybe we're overreacting," Jay said. "Maybe there really is nobody here." He wondered why he was whispering.

"But where are the prisoners? What about my mother?"

"They're either being very quiet, or they're somewhere else. I don't like to say this, Vittoria, but maybe the Germans took them away. As hostages." Or, he thought to himself, they could all be dead in their cells.

"Then we're too late." Vittoria fought to stave off tears. "But we should still check the building. Maybe we can still find her."

Jay thought she was grasping at straws. The place was as silent as a tomb – clearly, there was no one in the building. At least, no one alive. "Okay. I'll check this floor and you can check the one above."

Vittoria nodded her agreement, then watched as Jay disappeared down the corridor. She began to climb the stairs, then stopped. Her hand tightened on the pistol. There was a noise above her.

Nolan knew he had to act quickly, even though his mind was putting forward a myriad of reasons for delay. He reached for the pistol and checked the magazine again before moving into the hall. The locked door to her cell stood at the end of a short corridor next to the stairs that descended to the ground level. The rest of the cell doors hung open, all deserted, everyone gone.

There was not a sound, and he decided to check on her through the guard's peephole. Maybe she was asleep. That would be good; it would make his job easier. His hand on the butt of the pistol was clammy and he felt sweat fall from his brow as his trembling fingers pulled aside the metal flap, revealing the peephole.

Although it was dark inside her cell he could see that she was awake, pacing the small room like a caged beast. Suddenly, she looked directly at the peephole. Damn! She had heard him! He quickly let go of the tiny metal cover, which swung back over the aperture. Too late. Her heels clattered on the cement floor and her fists pounded on the door. His shaking fingers pulled the key from his pocket and plunged it into the lock.

Vittoria trod carefully, pausing on every stair to listen. She looked up: a bare bulb lit the top of the stairs and a door led off the landing to the left, but apart from that she could see nothing. Her fingers clutched the pistol as she took another step.

Suddenly she could hear a new noise, like someone pounding at a door.

The cell door flew open. Adriana was stunned. "Nolan, what on earth are you doing here?" She looked down, her question soon answered by the gun in his hand. For some reason, he hesitated and she threw herself on him, her feet kicking at him and her nails tearing at his face. The crack of the pistol exploded in her ear.

The voice was her mother's! Vittoria abandoned all caution as her feet flew up the final few steps, her whole body jerking when she heard the gunshot. She turned into the doorway at the top of the stairs and saw her mother, apparently unharmed by the shot, wrestling with Nolan. As Vittoria raised her arm to take aim, Nolan saw her, grabbed her mother around the throat, and pointed his pistol at her mother's head.

Jay was sure the place was deserted. All the doors were open, the cells all empty. Sweat and stale urine odors assailed his nose, but he felt he sensed another. The smell of fear. The smell left a memory of those who had been tortured in those rooms, a smell of—

The sound of a gunshot blew away his thoughts and his feet pounded a path to the foot of the stairs.

Nolan knew he had no option. His arm clutched Adriana around the throat, pulling her body across him as protection against the pistol in the girl's hand. There was no other choice. He pushed the gun against the woman's head, but knew he had to kill them both. When the girl's hand wavered as she saw the threat to her mother, Nolan saw his chance. He turned the gun towards Vittoria and pulled the trigger.

Jay reached the top of the stairs and paused for a moment to lean forward and peep through the crack of the doorway. At the sound of the gun, he heard Vittoria's cry of shock and saw her slump to the floor, her pistol spinning from her grip. The scream of anger and rage pulled Jay's eyes to the struggle at the other side of the room. What was Nolan doing here? He had a gun, but Adriana was shouting, kicking him. The nails of one of her hands slashed at his face, the other clutched at the hand holding the pistol. Nolan was struggling desperately to free his gun hand.

"You swine, Nolan!" Adriana dragged her nails across his face as she fought to keep the pistol at bay. "You've killed my daughter!" She kicked backward at his shins, pummeling her high heels into the tops of his shoes. But he was the stronger and slowly, inch by inch, he forced the hand holding the pistol back towards her. She kicked and screamed but knew that within a few moments the muzzle of the gun would be pointed at her head. His arm clutched her throat tighter. In desperation, she dropped to the floor, dragging Nolan with her. He pushed the gun toward her head.

Jay raced across the room toward Nolan, his foot lashing out at the wrist of the hand holding the weapon. As the gun spun from his grasp, Nolan relaxed his grip on Adriana, his face showing shock and fear as he recognized his assailant. Jay swung his foot again, but Nolan grabbed and twisted his ankle. As Jay fell, Nolan scrambled across the floor for the pistol.

Jay recovered, pulled himself to his feet, and moved towards Nolan, but knew he was too late. Nolan reached for the gun and trained it on Jay. Jay felt the clutch of fear, felt the blood draining from his head. Nolan's finger was on the trigger.

Suddenly, the traitor's head snapped back as Adriana's foot slammed into his windpipe. Nolan dropped the gun as he grabbed his throat, wheezing loudly as he struggled for breath, then toppling sideways to the floor as he lost consciousness.

"Vittoria! Oh, my God!" Adriana rushed across the room to her daughter, who was sprawled on the floor with her back to the wall, a trace of blood beginning to appear through the upper sleeve of her jacket. Vittoria winced and moaned as her mother gently edged the sleeve off her shoulder. Just above her left elbow there was a large bloodstain on her white blouse.

"Wait a moment." Adriana reached under her skirt, pausing as she looked squarely at Jay who, after a few moments, understood and averted his eyes. She pulled down her silk halfslip and stepped out of it, then began to tear the garment into strips, each about two feet long.

Adriana knelt by Vittoria's side. "It doesn't look so bad, dear," she said, trying to ignore her daughter's groans as she tightened a strip of silk around her upper arm. "But we can't take any chances." She looked at her daughter and forced a smile. "You're lucky the damned fool couldn't shoot straight."

Jay smiled as he crouched over Nolan's unconscious form. "Maybe you played a part in that. You were very brave, Adriana, tackling an armed assassin."

Adriana raised an eyebrow, dismissing Jay's praise. "If you hadn't come in, he would have shot me, too. Anyway," she tore two more strips from her half-slip, "maybe you can use these to tie him up, in case he comes to. In the meantime, I'll try to call an ambulance." Giving Vittoria a reassuring smile, she rose. "I'm sure somewhere in this wretched place there must be a telephone that still works," she said as she headed down the hall.

Jay was astonished at how cool and practical Adriana was so soon after being in mortal peril. He tied Nolan's wrists behind his back and was beginning on his ankles when he heard Vittoria's moan of pain. Turning his head, he saw her grimace as she reached across the floor for her pistol.

Vittoria picked up the weapon and checked the magazine. "I think I have some unfinished business here," she said.

"No!" Jay shouted, causing her to recoil. "God knows I, myself, have every reason to want to kill this bastard after what I think he may have done to my friend, Maria. But that's—" He paused and took a deep breath, struggling to contain his emotions. "But that's not the way." He gave the silk strip an extra-hard yank as he finished tying Nolan's ankles together.

Jay stood up. "A quick bullet in the head – that's too good for this bastard." He took the pistol from Vittoria's hand. Sensing that Nolan was regaining consciousness, he made his next words slow and deliberate for the traitor to hear. "A long and grueling court martial will expose everything he's done, and he'll have a lot of time to ponder his fate. Then he'll face the firing squad and get a chance to find out how Maria felt."

"I agree." They both looked over to see Adriana's face reappear in the doorway. "That despicable creature should be made to suffer as long as possible." She looked down at her daughter. "Darling, the ambulance will be here in just a few minutes." She turned to Jay. "I took the liberty of calling the police, as well." She took a few steps and scooped up the key which Nolan had dropped on the floor. "In the meantime, I suggest we drag this swine here into my old cell. I shall take great pleasure in turning this key in the lock." A sly smile crossed her face. "If only I could throw it in the Tiber."

REGINA COELI PRISON.

Renzo was in a state of desperation. The Resistance had been organizing the release of political prisoners and Jews all day, but he was being ignored. No one wanted to know him because the prison records showed him to be Vito Del Pietro, a thief and burglar. Everyone in the prison, since that day in March when the real Vito Del Pietro had stolen his identity with fatal consequences, knew him as Vito Del Pietro. He had come to detest the name.

"Hey! Can I have a pencil and paper?" he called through the grille to the warder.

"Haven't you had enough yet, Del Pietro? You've got more horseshit than the Colosseum after a chariot race."

"Just do this one thing for me and I'll stop pestering you."

The guard dug into his pocket for a pencil. "Here. I don't have a pad – you'll have to use toilet paper."

Renzo tore off a sheet and began to write. *Vittoria. Ludovico. Sofia. Fabio. Cesare. Bernardo, no longer living.* The names of the partisans in the Resistance group of which he had been a member. He began to hand it to the guard but pulled it back and wrote one more name. *Bartoli.* The leader of the cell.

"Take this to the people who are vetting the records," he said, handing the sheet to the warder. "And tell them again I'm Renzo Rossi."

"I'll give you full marks for balls, Del Pietro," the guard replied, pocketing the piece of paper. "But you'll still be here when I come up for retirement in 1949," he added, walking away.

Renzo sat on his bed. He had taken his last gamble. If he wasn't out of the jail within the next hour, the warder was probably right.

"Who's the guy who wrote these names?" The voice in the corridor leading to his cell was familiar to Renzo. "The man's a fraud, an imposter. Renzo Rossi has been dead for over two months. The Germans killed him in the reprisal massacre."

The footsteps came nearer to his cell door and Renzo recognized the voice. Ludovico. He remembered how Ludo and his wife, Sofia, had obtained vital documents by assassinating a German officer.

There were mutterings from the guard, but Ludovico was insistent. "Open this cell! Renzo Rossi is a dead hero of the Resistance – we've got to expose this imposter once and for all!"

When the door opened, the astonished face of Ludovico appeared. "Renzo! You're, you're…"

"Hello, Ludo. How's Sofia?"

FATEBENEFRATELLI HOSPITAL.

"I'm afraid you can stay only twenty minutes." The white-coated doctor ushered Jay along the hospital corridor. "Signor Lawrence has suffered serious injuries and, although he's off the danger list, we still have to watch his condition closely. He's in a small room all to himself with around-the-clock care." He pushed open a door off the corridor. "Ah, he's awake. I'll leave you to talk, but remember: twenty minutes." He wagged his finger and closed the door behind him.

"Hello, Jay. Nice to see you." The voice was weak but there was a smile on the face in the bed with blackened eyes; bandages covered most of his head.

"You've no idea how relieved I am to see you, David." Jay reached out and gently squeezed Lawrence's hand. "To be honest, when I found you I thought you were a gone—" He stopped short, worrying that his words might upset the Englishman.

"It's all right, Jay. They say I'm out of the woods, even though it still feels like the worst hangover possible. But please tell me – what's the latest? What's happening right now in the city?"

"All good news, David. The last of the Germans are slinking out with their tails between their legs and – get this! – word has it that our guys are now on the outskirts of Rome!"

Lawrence, charged with emotion, pinched his eyes closed at the news. "I can hardly believe it – we've waited so long."

Jay nodded. "Say, David, can you tell me what happened at Adriana's house yesterday?"

"I'm not really too sure, Jay. I dropped by to pick up some things, but my timing must have been off and I walked into one of Nolan's black moods. Without provocation, he attacked me. What's up with him, Jay?"

Jay heaved a sigh. "Long story, David." He eased himself into a chair by the bedside and began to recount the events of that morning.

NEAR VILLA RANIERI.

Anton was beside himself with worry. He glanced at his watch. Half-past four. He had been unable to find even the slightest trace of Adriana.

He had set out for the Via Tasso early that morning, but his long journey on foot from the Parioli district had been delayed by the German army he was abandoning clogging the streets at every turn. The weary troops leaving the city and the huge crowds of Romans made it impossible for him to reach Gestapo Headquarters much before noon, by which time the place was completely deserted. Anton relived the moment of horror when he realized that Kappler might have done the unthinkable – taken Adriana with him as a hostage.

He had then set out for the Regina Coeli prison in the slim hope that the Gestapo might have taken her there. When he arrived, he realized he had no authority, having discarded his uniform for civilian clothes. In any event he had found the place in the hands of the partisans, who ignored his questions and cared little about his dilemma.

Out of options, Anton returned to the street where Adriana lived. Perhaps there would be someone at home – Vittoria, maybe – who knew what had happened to her or where she was. As he approached the house, his anguish grew. He had deserted his post because he wanted to stay in Rome, to be with his love, but perhaps she was now on her way to Germany. He grimaced at the irony.

He found no neighbors to question as he walked along her street. They too must have gone to watch on the main thoroughfares and witness the departure of their hated occupiers. He arrived at the Villa Ranieri and turned to face it, preparing himself for more disappointment. Reaching for the knocker, he rapped on the door with a sigh of resignation.

The shock on Adriana's face resolved into a warm smile as she welcomed the clasp of his arms.

FATEBENEFRATELLI HOSPITAL.

The Englishman scowled as he tried to digest all that MacPherson had told him. "Jay—" Lawrence paused for a moment. "Jay, how come we didn't twig Nolan? I know there was bad blood between him and me, but I'm angry with myself for not realizing what he was up to."

"I'm angry with myself, too, David." Jay shook his head. "All that time I had no idea he was grabbing my pad and making pencil rubbings of the padrones' addresses."

354

"But his betrayal of Maria? I missed that by a mile."

"We both did. I was so stuck on the notion that Maria's downstairs neighbor had ratted on her that it never occurred to me it might have been an inside job. I wish it had." Jay looked away suddenly, clenching his jaw. "I failed her. Maria's dead because I wasn't smart enough to know what Nolan was up to." He looked back at Lawrence. "And there's someone else he betrayed, as well."

Lawrence frowned and tilted his head questioningly.

"My contact in the POW operation, Father Francesco. A sweeter, gentler, kinder man I've never known. His name and address were on the piece of paper Nolan took when he stole my watch. Vittoria and I saw Father Francesco being arrested. Now I fear he's one of the hostages accompanying the Gestapo back to Germany."

"Don't blame yourself, Jay." Lawrence, with difficulty, leaned forward from his pillow to place his hand on Jay's knee. "Thanks to you, hundreds of our boys remained safe in Rome and can now come out of their hiding places. And thanks to you, Nolan's in the stockade. After his trial, I'm sure he'll pay the ultimate penalty."

"Yeah." Jay took a deep breath as he considered Lawrence's words. "And you know what? I'd like to be a member of the firing squad."

Lawrence fell back on his pillow and turned his head.

"Anything wrong?" Jay asked.

Lawrence looked at him with tired eyes. "No one can forgive what Nolan did, perhaps least of all me. Still, what happened when Nolan was a child in Ireland – during what the Irish call 'The Troubles,' when the Black and Tans went in and killed many like his father – that was a very bad chapter in my country's history."

"It still doesn't begin to forgive what he did."

"True, and I'm not trying to forgive it. I'm simply saying that perhaps Nolan went over to the Nazis not because he thought they were the right side, but because he believed that any side that included England, the country that killed his father, had to be the wrong side." Lawrence closed his eyes, weary from exertion.

"Sorry, David, but I'm still not buying it." Jay could not keep the passion out of his voice. "Nolan may have had a grudge against England, but for him to betray his own country – the country that welcomed him and his mother and gave them freedom from fear – that's worse than unforgiveable."

He sighed and looked at his watch. "I think my twenty minutes are up, buddy." He patted Lawrence's hand. "Adriana's throwing a party tonight to celebrate the liberation of Rome; wish you could be there. I'll stop by in the morning, David. Get some rest – tomorrow's a big day."

VILLA RANIERI.

"Mamma, Mamma!" His face flushed with excitement, Giorgio burst into the party in the drawing room. "Can we please go watch the soldiers parade into Rome tomorrow?"

Jay was relieved to see the boy arrive – Giorgio had broken the awkward silence that had just followed Jay's introduction to Anton. Although aware of how much help the German had been to the POW operation behind the scenes, Jay had never been in the same room with someone from the opposite side of the war, and he didn't know what to say.

Adriana set a tray of canapés down on a coffee table and looked up at Giorgio. "Of course you can go see the parade." All of Rome was abuzz with the well-founded rumor that the Americans were going to make their formal entry into Rome the next day. "We're all going to go watch the parade, and we'll make sure you and Luisa have the best view."

"But I want to ride my bike alongside the American jeeps – I haven't been on it in such a long time, Mamma." Giorgio's bicycle, like those of many others in the city, had been placed in hiding soon after the start of the occupation, when the Germans began helping themselves to Roman bicycles.

"I'm not sure riding your bicycle alongside the troops is a good idea, dear."

"Surely he'll be all right, Adriana," Anton gently pleaded with a raised eyebrow. Giorgio beamed and nodded, glad to have a new ally.

"I'll keep an eye on him, Mamma." Vittoria adjusted the sling that held her left arm across the front of her body.

"And Luisa shall have the best view of all," said Anton. "She can watch the parade from above my shoulders." As he stood and scooped up her small frame, the girl squealed with delight, wrapping her arms around his neck and her legs around his waist. He lowered her to the floor and she ran off giggling.

Adriana passed around the tray. "It's not much, I'm afraid. The pâté is out of a can that predates the war, but the bruschetta is freshly made."

"Personally, Mamma, I find it difficult to celebrate. We've paid heavily for this victory." Vittoria slouched down in her chair.

"Yes," Adriana said softly, lowering her eyes and thinking of Fabio. Anton looked awkwardly off to the side; Jay, not catching the rapidly-spoken Italian, helped himself to the appetizers.

Adriana brightened. "We must always remember the past, dear, but a whole new future lies ahead for all of us." She glanced at Anton, who smiled back at her. "And look – I've decided to celebrate this new beginning with the '24 Chateau Margaux I've been keeping for such an occasion." She poured a little into a glass to taste it. "Superb! But where are your friends, Vittoria? This party is for them, as well."

"Dante Barioli is still out on the streets with Cesare, patrolling for trouble-making stragglers. As a parting gift the Germans blew up the San Lorenzo railway yard and the Fiat plant. I think—"

Her thought was interrupted by a shriek from Luisa at the window. *"I tedeschi sono torni! I tedeschi sono torni!"*

Jay thought he understood. "Is she saying—?"

"Yes, she says the Germans are back," Giorgio replied, running with Jay to join the wide-eyed girl at the window.

Jay's eyes followed Luisa's pointing finger. "They're ours!" he shouted, looking down on the Sherman tanks moving slowly up the street. "An advance patrol!"

Jay felt a catch at the back of his throat, a welling-up in his chest. There were Americans in those tanks and in the jeeps behind them, and the next day there would be more Americans streaming into Rome. He had had three months in a prisoner-of-war camp followed by eight months of hiding out. Eight long months of dodging Nazis and fending off fascists. And losing friends, good friends. Now at last he could step out of the shadows. He desperately wanted to go home, but the Americans who would be arriving in Rome – guys from all over the United States – were the next best thing: home was coming to him.

Crowds began to gather down on the street and applaud the procession. Then a cheer rang out. Adriana, Anton, and Vittoria rushed over to see what was happening.

"Oh, please, Mamma, may I go down to watch?" Giorgio pleaded, his eyes shining with excitement.

"No, Giorgio, not tonight. There will be plenty for you to see tomorrow, when—"

There was a knock on the door.

"I'll go!" Giorgio scurried back across the room and disappeared down the staircase.

"I suppose that must be some of your friends, Vittoria?"

"Probably Ludo and Sofia. They've been at Regina Coeli for most of the day freeing imprisoned partisans, but I imagine—"

"Vittoria! Vittoria! You'll never guess who's here!" The astonished face of Giorgio reappeared at the top of the staircase.

Vittoria turned her head. Behind Giorgio was Ludovico and Sofia. And also—

"It's me, Vittoria."

Her mind struggled with the image of his face. It was so long ago. Could it be?

He rushed across the room and grasped her free hand.

"Is it really you, Renzo? Are you real?"

Renzo took her in his arms and began covering her face and neck with kisses.

"Ouch! You're real, all right!" Vittoria squealed, laughing with joy. "Renzo, you're hurting my arm!"

Via Veneto.

Giorgio's legs pedaled furiously as he maneuvered his bike alongside the column of marching American soldiers, cheering crowds cramming the sidewalks. He had long since become separated from Luisa, Anton, and his mother and he knew she would yell at him again, but this time he didn't care. Because the excitement was like none he had ever seen in Rome, even when the pope came out on his balcony at Easter. The noise of the cheering and the church bells ringing resounded in his ears; people tossed flowers and clapped for joy as the Americans marched by.

The soldiers, a few wearing roses in the camouflage netting of their helmets, smiled and waved back at the people, and Giorgio was thrilled when a passing soldier winked at him and tossed him a package of chewing gum. He stuffed it in his pocket; he would try some later. At that moment, Giorgio was excited by everything about him, the marching soldiers, the roaring crowd, the flags, the church bells, the plane that did a victory roll over their heads, the pretty lady who clambered up onto a tank. And just knowing the Germans had gone.

He turned his bike around, riding against the flow of the marching soldiers. His interest turned to jeeps – those strange cars Americans drove. Ahead of him was a jeep stuck in the road.

Giorgio looked at the officer sitting behind the driver: all the others saluted him – he was obviously important. As the officer looked around, his eyes landed on Giorgio. "Say, son, by any chance do you speak English?" he asked.

The boy got off his bike, pushing it towards the jeep. "Yes, I do, sir, yes."

"What's your name, son?"

"Giorgio, sir." His eyes were drawn to the stars on the officer's shoulders.

"Well, Giorgio, my name's General Clark." He reached out and patted the boy on the head. "Do you know a place called the Capitoline?"

"Yes, yes I do, General." The Capitoline, one of the seven hills, had been the most sacred place in all of ancient Rome.

"Can you lead us there? I'm supposed to be there right now," the general said.

"Yes, I can. I know the way very well, sir."

"That's more than I can say for my officers. Let's go!"

Giorgio got back on his bicycle and pedaled away, looking behind from time to time to make sure the general's jeep was still following.

As the city whizzed by, Giorgio hummed in contentment at the thought that he was leading a victorious general to the Capitoline. Maybe this time his mother wouldn't yell at him. Surely this time she'd be proud.

AUTHOR'S AFTERWORD

* When the German army left Rome, the hostages taken from the Via Tasso prison were loaded into two trucks. Several miles north of Rome, the prisoners in one of the trucks were all shot. The second truck never made it out of Rome: its motor may have been sabotaged by the Resistance.

* As the American army entered Rome, hundreds of former prisoners of war from the Allied nations poured out of their hiding places in the homes of courageous Romans to welcome them.

* Of the 1,026 Jews rounded up on October 16, 1943 and shipped to Auschwitz, only sixteen survived to return to their homes in Rome after the war.

* The agonizing process of exhuming and identifying the victims of the Via Rasella reprisal began shortly after the liberation of Rome. The bodies of the 335 men and boys slaughtered and left inside the Ardeatine Caves were reburied in a mausoleum, its roof a stark slab of concrete suspended over the rows of coffins like the ceilings of the caves that gape nearby. The site is now an Italian national monument and a state commemoration of the massacre is held every year on its anniversary.

* Twenty-six of the victims of Celeste DiPorto – the "Black Panther" who betrayed many of her fellow Jews after the roundup – died in the Ardeatine Caves. DiPorto was arrested after the war, sentenced to twelve years in prison, but released after serving seven.

* In 1948, after a long stretch in Regina Coeli Prison, Herbert Kappler was tried and sentenced to life imprisonment. He escaped to West Germany in 1977 but died six months later of cancer.

19725818R00200

Made in the USA
Charleston, SC
08 June 2013